ONLY THE LUCKY

THE SINFUL STATE SERIES
BOOK 4

ISABEL JOLIE

ISABEL JOLIE

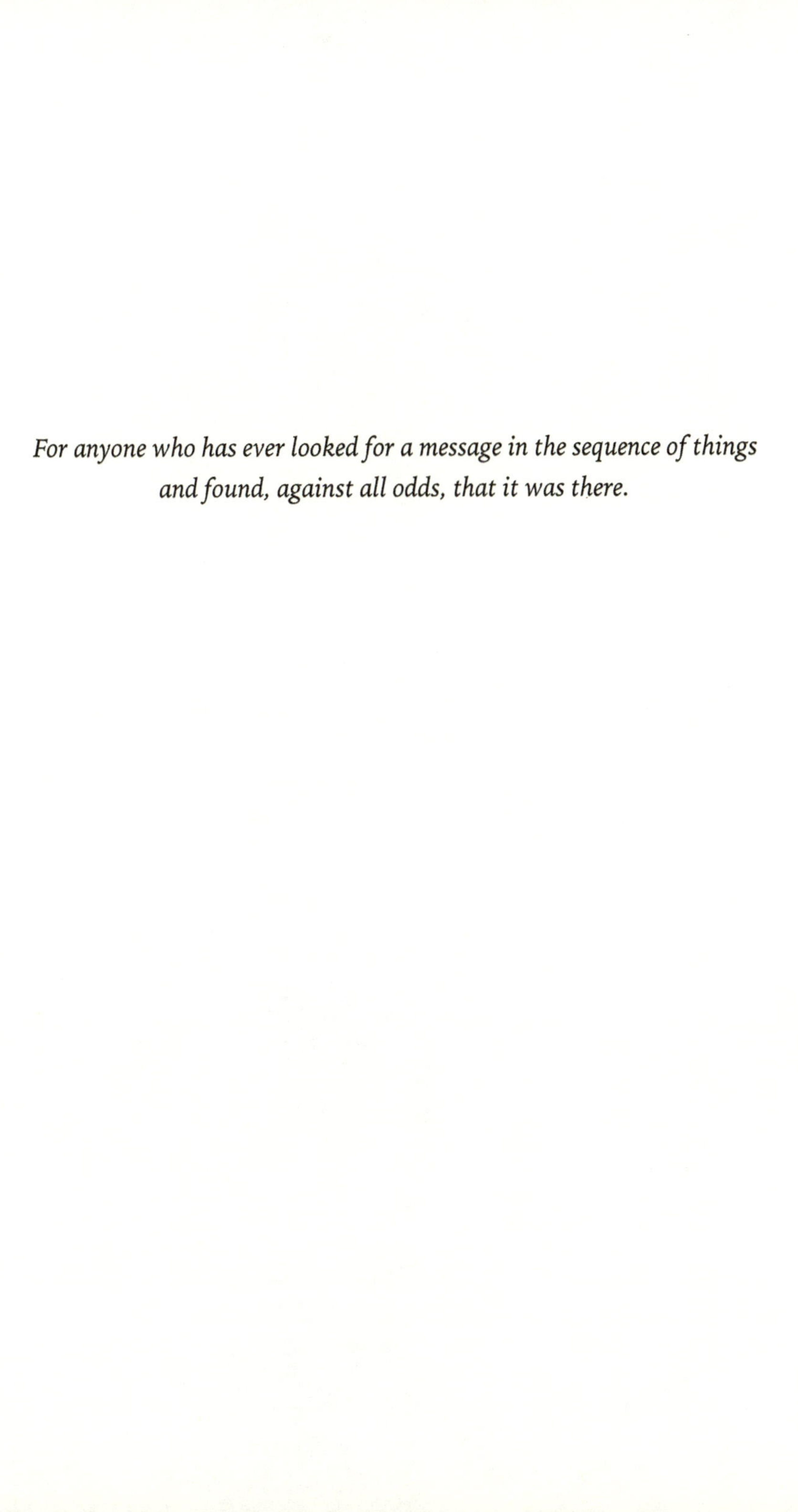

*For anyone who has ever looked for a message in the sequence of things
and found, against all odds, that it was there.*

"If you once realised that envy and ambition are poisonous, vicious, cruel, as deadly as the sting of a cobra, you would awaken to them. But the mind does not want to look at these things too closely; in this area it has vested interests." – Krishnamurti

"Never underestimate the power of jealousy and the power of envy to destroy. Never underestimate that." – Oliver Stone

PROLOGUE

ALICIA

Two weeks earlier

Brie Anderson doesn't sit.

The KOAN operative—the woman who helped put Elena Vasquez in a box—moves in a quick, practiced sweep—windows, desk, the hallway beyond the glass wall—before she turns back to me.

"This won't take long," she says. "But you should hear it."

Behind her, a man I don't recognize steps in without introduction. Navy suit. FBI badge displayed prominently.

"Ms. Morgan," he says. "Special Agent Turner."

Brie closes my office door and I gesture to the chair across from my desk. Neither of them takes it.

Brie sets a small evidence bag on the corner of my desk. Inside is a flash drive. No label. No explanation.

"This is a recording," she says, "from the confrontation with Elena Vasquez."

The name lands with familiar weight. I've managed the fallout from her actions for months. Senator David Crawford's case. The investigation.

"She's dead," I say.

"Yes," Brie replies. "But what she said before she died matters."

Agent Turner adds, "The FBI was monitoring the exchange in real time. The audio is now part of an active federal file."

I fold my hands together, the familiar posture of someone preparing to receive bad information. For a second, I consider refusing. "Play it."

Brie plugs the drive into my laptop. A waveform fills the screen. She lowers the volume before pressing play.

I hold my breath.

At first there's only ambient sound—the distant rush of wind and hollow acoustics. Then Elena Vasquez speaks.

Her voice is controlled, precise, carrying the faint accent of someone who has lived in too many capitals to belong to any of them.

She's confident. Mocking. Explaining, in elegant detail, how she plans to destroy Adrien d'Avricourt—the man whose cooperation unraveled her entire operation—by igniting an investigation she knows will take years to unwind.

I listen, jaw tight, as she describes fabricated records and reputational damage like they're inevitable facts.

Then Brie's voice cuts in on the recording—steady, calm— telling Elena the FBI has surrounded the house.

There's a shift. Subtle, but unmistakable.

Elena stops performing.

"You have no idea what you've done," she says.

Brie presses her. Asks for names.

Elena laughs, brittle now. "You think he was the only one buying? You have no idea how deep this goes."

Defense contractors. Pharmaceutical companies. Foreign intelligence services.

She doesn't name them. She doesn't need to.

Then there's a sound—she's moving.

"Elena," Brie says on the recording. Her voice sharpens. "Don't."

"I won't rot in a cell," Elena replies. Not afraid. Resolute.

There's a pause, and when Elena speaks again, it's with deliberate clarity.

"Tell Alicia Morgan she knows too much."

Blood rushes in my ears, but I don't look away from the laptop.

"Tell her the network remembers its friends—and its enemies."

The recording captures movement now.

"Oh," Elena adds, almost casually. "And your little company. KOAN."

Her tone shifts—almost amused.

"They're being watched. The Moores… Tell them they're making enemies."

Brie's voice cuts in again—firm, urgent—but the moment fractures.

An unmistakable gunshot. Flat. Final.

Brie stops the audio before the chaos that follows spills into my office.

Silence settles, thick and oppressive.

Agent Turner speaks first. "That statement is now evidence. Whether she was exaggerating or not, it exists in the record."

I lean back in my chair, every instinct urging me to compartmentalize. "So I'm…what? A footnote?"

"A person of interest," he corrects. "To people who don't want their names spoken under oath."

Brie meets my eyes. "We didn't bring this to scare you."

"No," I say quietly. "You brought it so I would understand the stakes." Elena Vasquez was the White House Chief of Staff. "I'll likely be called in during any investigation, discovery, or congressional hearing."

She nods once.

Agent Turner's gaze flicks, briefly, to the framed photo on my desk—Stella at the beach, hair tangled by wind, smiling without reserve.

"Right now," he says, "we don't believe anyone will move overtly. That kind of attention draws scrutiny. But caution isn't paranoia. It's preparation."

Brie picks up the evidence bag, returning it to her jacket. "The recording is in federal custody now. But Hudson wanted you to hear it directly. Dorian and Caroline Moore have been informed."

Of course.

I close my laptop, the click decisive. "Thank you for letting me hear it." I keep my voice level, professional.

Brie's expression softens by a degree. "Call me if you need anything."

They leave as efficiently as they arrived.

When the door closes, my office feels too quiet.

I pull up Stella's school schedule on my phone. Play practice until five thirty. Safe. Accounted for. Elena Vasquez is dead.

But her clients aren't.

And the people who benefit from silence rarely gamble with their freedom.

CHAPTER
ONE

ALICIA

My phone lights up with an unrecognized number: three nines in a row.

I force myself to answer.

"This is Alicia Morgan."

"Alicia, good. I got you."

I glance at the screen, switch to speaker, and set the phone on my desk. The afternoon sun slants through the window in my home office, the light too bright. I should close the blinds, but I don't move.

"Dorian? Where are you calling from?"

"Colorado. Caroline was just updating me—"

"The answer is no."

"Alicia…" He blends disappointment, censure, and warmth into one word.

"They won't be in your way," he insists.

"I agreed to security at my office and in select public locations. Not my home."

"I've been to your home. No cameras. A gate that opens onto a public sidewalk. Anyone who wants to watch you walks right past it on their morning run."

"I live in Georgetown, Dorian." I square the corners of the file folders on my desk until they form a perfect ninety-degree angle. "Tell Caroline I said hello."

"She's the reason I'm calling. Correction. Your daughter is the reason. If someone wants to reach you, Stella is the easiest way."

My fingers drift to my grandmother's vintage Cartier watch on my wrist, the metal cool against my skin. "No one is coming after me."

"The woman who claimed they would is dead. Does that not concern you?"

"She killed herself to avoid prison."

"Or she knew what was coming."

I lean back, press my head against the chair, and exhale through clenched teeth. "Dorian, you're one of my best friends—"

"Really? Every time we invite you out to visit us, you decline."

"I have a twelve-year-old. Weekends away aren't an option."

"Because she's your world. Which is why I can't believe you refused security." His tone softens. "I nearly lost Caroline once. Don't make the mistake I did. If something happens to Stella, you won't recover."

Well, now that he's gone and said that...

"Do you even have proof this supposed network exists? Yes, my client was blackmailed. Yes, people paid. But no one has contacted me."

"A congressional hearing is in the works. You'll be called

in. If someone doesn't want their name exposed, they might silence you."

A tension headache stirs behind my eyes. "I manage crises, Dorian. I'm not *the* crisis."

"Then let me help you."

"You mean let Caroline help me."

"She has resources. Use them."

"Your money funds them."

"What's mine is hers."

"That's generous," I mutter.

"Alicia, please. Just a couple of weeks. For Stella."

The doorbell chimes.

I jolt, nudging my mouse to wake the monitor. The grainy feed shows a tall man in dark clothes, collar flipped high against the wind. He scans the street—alert, methodical, controlled.

I've been in enough rooms with KOAN people to recognize him—one of their operatives, peripheral to the Crawford case. "Noah Bennett," I say quietly.

"Yes," Dorian confirms. "He'll cover nights. Your day rotation will remain the same. You'll barely notice his presence."

"You sent him already?"

"Because I knew you'd resist."

"I thought you said security isn't one of KOAN's services."

KOAN wasn't a traditional security firm. They handled high-risk contracts—extractions, intelligence, and discreet problem-solving for clients who didn't want headlines. Bodyguard duty wasn't spelled out in their mission statement.

"Caroline's expanding—blending contracts, rescues, security. It's her first year. The model's evolving."

The bell rings again.

"What exactly do you expect?"

"Noah Bennett is currently assigned night shift. He's there at your door to touch base with you. The night shift—it's just precautionary."

"Unnecessary."

"Yes, it's in an abundance of caution, but please, for me. For Stella."

My gaze lands on the silver frames of Stella, ranging from her as an infant in my arms, to a toddler photo with a wide, chubby-cheeked smile, to last year's school photo in her middle school uniform where she appears to be far too old for her preteen years. She's my life, and if something happened to her...

"You won't even know he's there. He'll stay in the car—"

"You think my neighbors won't notice a man sitting in a car on the street all through the night?"

Even in my driveway, someone would notice. Dorian's being ridiculous. People walk their dogs and push baby carriages up and down the sidewalks constantly, looking in windows, judging everything from flower beds to holiday décor.

"He can work from the guest room in the basement. But he's the only one who has access inside my home. The others...they can meet me out front, at my businesses. I don't want this arrangement to scare Stella. I'll tell Stella that he's..." I struggle for a way to spin it that won't alarm my daughter. "I'll tell her that he's in charge of security for my business and he's ensuring continuity. She knows I've had security during the day. I'll tell her that he's from out of town and so I offered him our guest room while he gets everything set up. She doesn't need to know that he's working nights.

Two weeks. That's all I'm giving you. No more than that. Understood?"

"Two weeks," he agrees quickly.

"Caroline's listening, isn't she?"

Her voice chimes faintly in the background. "Thank you, Alicia. I feel so much better."

"Not a problem," I lie, rising from my desk.

The clock on my monitor shows the time: 3:33 p.m. I do a double-take. Repeating numbers have always snagged my attention—numerology's quiet language, patterns the universe uses to communicate if you're willing to look. Alignment. Protection. A reminder the universe is pervasive, even if I don't want to believe in omens.

CHAPTER
TWO

NOAH

The Federal-style home sits on a corner in Georgetown's East Village; its black door set back behind a stretch of brick sidewalk, still damp from last night's rain. Two slender trees stand behind an iron fence, roots pushing through frost-cracked brick. A side gate opens to a narrow carport. Real estate gold.

From a security standpoint, it's a nightmare.

Too many windows. Too many entry points. The side glass panes beside the door offer a clear view straight through the house. Two more windows sit equidistant to each side of the front door, all four windows at climbable height. On the side street, four more climbable windows face the curb. In back, a low brick wall encloses a yard lined with glass doors that eat half the first floor. Pretty—and easily accessible.

Cold air carries the faint scent of chimney smoke and diesel from the delivery truck idling a block over. November has done its work on the trees—the elms bare, the oaks holding their last brown leaves—but the ivy clings to the brick, thick enough to hide a man standing flush against the wall. The street is quiet—only the soft hiss of passing tires, the distant bark of a dog.

Georgetown's East Village is safe, on paper. But if someone wanted Alicia Morgan or her daughter, this corner makes it easy. A van could pull up, grab the target, and vanish before the alarm thrusts the police department into action.

My gaze scales the three-story brick facade. They said townhome, but this place stands alone, wide and solid. Maybe the term applies because it shares a brick fence with the adjacent home, but by local standards, this is luxury.

I lift my phone and take perimeter shots for the team. If she's a high-value target, she needs to move. No system on earth makes this secure. Corner property. Open sightlines. Six, maybe eight, rooftops with clear sniper angles. All it takes is time.

I ring the bell once. Wait. Ring again.

No answer.

She's supposed to be home. I could circle the block, check the rear approach, but from here I can already monitor both the gate and door. Another vulnerability.

Intersection cams might have visual coverage. I'll ask Quinn to pull the CCTV feed.

Footsteps click beyond the wood. Then the lock turns.

She opens the door dressed for business—silk blouse, tailored slacks, heels that bring her closer to six feet. Dark hair past her shoulders, blue eyes that hold mine for exactly two seconds before she extends her hand. "Noah."

I've seen her in briefings. Watched her manage a room the way other people manage individual conversations—effortlessly, and with complete awareness of everyone in it. Knowing that didn't prepare me for her at close range.

I take her hand. Her grip is firm, professional. She lets go quickly. Everything about her reads controlled. Composed. The gold necklace, the careful makeup, the way she stands in the doorway without stepping back to let me in yet—this is someone used to managing impressions.

The staircase rises behind her, elegant and imposing. I can see through the entire first floor from the front door. Beautiful. Vulnerable.

"Come in. I was on the phone with Dorian." She says the name like it explains everything. It does. "He mentioned you'll be covering night shift. I'll set you up in the basement guest bedroom."

I pause. Hudson's instructions had been clear: nearby surveillance, not on-site. But I'm not about to argue in her foyer.

"That works," I say, following her through the wide hall, toward a kitchen with windows to the back courtyard.

Inside, sunlight spills across dark maple floors, reflecting off stainless steel fixtures and glass walls. The scent of fresh coffee lingers, cut with citrus—some type of cleaner, maybe lemon oil.

The back wall is almost entirely glass, overlooking a patio where ivy shivers in the breeze. To the left, a dining room behind glass doors; the white, modern kitchen gleams beneath pendant lights; down the hall, twin living areas flank the foyer—one formal, one casual.

It's minimalist, curated, and far too open. Too exposed.

"You have a beautiful home," I say.

"Thank you." Her gaze flicks to my boots, then through

the window where I've parked in the short driveway that runs along the side of her home.

"You can't park there overnight. If you're blocking the sidewalk, you'll get ticketed. The carport fits two, but my daughter plays basketball after school. Once she's in bed, I'll move my car so you can park behind me."

I can think of bigger logistical issues than parking, but I nod. Hudson can get the report later.

"I wasn't expecting you today," she says, descending the stairs to the floor below, the faint spice of her perfume trailing behind her. "Forgive the chaos."

"No problem." That's what I say, but I see nothing out of place that would indicate chaos of any kind.

In the basement, the air temperature drops, and instead of lemon, I pick up notes of detergent and fabric softener. Laundry.

"You'll stay here. It's a better place to set up than the street. Besides, street parking can be a challenge."

The guest room is neat, the sheets crisp, pulled back over the comforter in a hotel-worthy turn-down display. Across the hall, a bathroom. To one side, an exercise room; to the other, a den with a heather-gray sectional, oversized TV, and grasscloth walls, their texture catching the recessed light. The thick carpet muffles our steps. A bar gleams under recessed lighting. No chaos in sight.

"That fridge holds wine," she says. "The other's stocked with water and soda. Use the kitchen upstairs if you'd rather. Laundry room's there." She points. "Cleaning service comes Thursdays. They handle laundry, too."

"That won't be necessary." She might think I'm living here, but that's not actually the plan. I have an apartment in

NoMa—North of Massachusetts Avenue, close enough. I'm night shift.

She doesn't respond, simply climbs the stairs ahead of me. I keep my eyes on the hallway.

We continue, past the main floor I entered into, and up an additional flight of stairs.

Up here, the light grows warmer.

She gestures toward an open doorway. "My bedroom." She points in the opposite direction. "When I work from home, I work in there."

She points to a glass-walled home office that mirrors her office in Manhattan.

KOAN has been running daytime protective services for her about a month now. No specific threats identified, but the congressional investigation is gaining traction—and the people it's likely to expose aren't minor players. Elena Vasquez was White House chief of staff. The names connected to her network reach high enough that even the president isn't above scrutiny. Anyone tied to the original case becomes a potential target, and Alicia Morgan is tied directly—she managed the senator's crisis, she knows names, she'll likely be called to testify. Until recently she'd insisted nine to five coverage was sufficient. Hudson disagreed. So did I.

The hallway walls are lined with photos—sun-drenched candids of her and a dark-haired little girl with freckles and a wide smile. Unexpected warmth against all the white.

"My daughter's bedroom is upstairs," she says, pointing to the next flight. "Two rooms and a sitting area. One's her hangout space, one her bedroom. The top floor's hers."

"That's good," I say. "Safest floor."

She tilts her head, either as a question or in annoyance. I'm not sure which.

"And that one?" I gesture to a closed door beside her room.

"My closet." A small, satisfied smile. "Converted bedroom."

Of course. Control, order, design.

She steps into her office, opens a drawer, and hands me a set of keys. "These open all exterior doors."

"You have an alarm."

"Yes." She retrieves a black folder, passes it across the desk. "Instructions, codes, contacts. I only know mine—you can set your own."

Her movements are smooth, efficient, but a slight tightness at the corners of her mouth betrays fatigue.

I clock the framed photos on her desk. Her daughter— blue eyes, freckles, messy pigtails, joy unfiltered. A reminder that somewhere beneath all this polish, warmth exists.

"If you need anything, contact Caroline," she says, then hesitates. "Or Hudson. I mix them up sometimes."

"Hudson's my supervisor." When she mentions Caroline, she must be referring to Caroline Moore, KOAN's founder. Dorian is her husband, a billionaire who has been in the news periodically over the decades thanks to his political family. That must be the Dorian she mentioned earlier.

"Right." She nods. "Let Hudson know."

"I'll do a walk-through," I tell her. "Check sightlines, entries, blind spots."

"Whatever you need." She turns back to her computer, the soft clack of keys filling the silence. "When Stella gets home, I'll introduce you. I plan to tell her you'll be here a couple of weeks to get my business security team in place. Just so she's not spooked."

"Appreciate that."

She smiles without looking up. "Good."

I lift the folder. "Thanks for this."

"Of course."

I head for the stairs. The house is quiet except for the faint hum of the HVAC and the distant trill of a phone upstairs.

At the landing, I pause. Sunlight spills through the glass, white and still. Outside, a siren wails far away, fading fast.

I've assessed hundreds of situations. But as I move downstairs, one thought stays with me—we can secure the perimeter. What I'm not sure of is how to secure *her*.

CHAPTER
THREE

ALICIA

"If I understand you correctly, Robert"—I glance at the timer on my phone: thirty minutes; *Lord, this man can talk*—"You'd like for me to meet with your PR team to coach them on rehabilitating the image of oil and gas."

"Image isn't the word I'd choose. It's the public perception. We've been under fire for decades and our lobbying team has spent so much time focused on legislation we haven't paid enough attention to public perception and that's—"

"I'm going to stop you right there, Robert. I think you've misunderstood what I do."

"You're the fixer."

"Sir, Morgan & Company manages crisis communications and public affairs for politicians, celebrities, and major organizations facing scandal. We develop strategies to protect reputations and navigate crises."

"I know," he drawls. "That's why you're perfect. All I

want is for you to come in and train my people for a day. Talk with us. Consult. I know you usually work with individuals, but we're an organization."

I have absolutely no desire to work with the lobbying arm of oil and gas.

"Name your price."

I close my eyes, exhale slowly. "Tell you what, Robert. Let me give it some thought. I'm not currently accepting new clients—"

"Now we both know that's not true. When a crisis hits, you're there. And this is a crisis."

"Let me think on it. Perhaps I can send someone—"

"No, ma'am. We want you."

Thirty-three minutes. If I end this now, I can still save the hour.

"Thank you for the call, Robert. I don't believe we're the best fit. I wish you well."

With quiet satisfaction, I end the call.

Was that shortsighted of me?

My father's stern voice infiltrates the silence—*Business is business. If you don't do what you need to do to get ahead, someone else will leapfrog right over you.*

"Sorry, Dad," I murmur to the empty room. "I've built this company from the ground up. I've earned the right to say no."

I have more business than I can manage—and what keeps me grounded is that my clients have faces. They may have screwed up, but there's always someone behind the head- lines: children, parents, employees. People who rely on them. Most just want a way through the storm, a chance to do better.

Maybe it's naïve, but it's how I rationalize what I do. And

I have zero interest in crafting smoke and mirrors to cloud the transparency of a lobbying group.

I scan my email, determine nothing requires a response before tomorrow, and push up from my desk, done for the day. I cross the hall, enter my closet, and change into a cashmere lounge set, taking care to box my heels and place my slacks and blouse in the drycleaning pile. I always dress professionally, even when working from home. One never knows when a crisis might arise—or when one might have to face the press.

It's early to be finished, and maybe I'm tempting fate by ending my workday before six, but I promised myself I'd cook dinner for Stella tonight. There's a glass of wine near the stove with my name on it.

It's early evening, but the sun has set and outside a blend of red brake lights and white headlights blurs. The back patio is lit via floodlight, casting a golden glow.

As I pour myself a glass of wine before setting about cooking dinner, I watch Noah Bennett. He appears to be studying the roofline. The collar of his jacket is raised to his angular jaw, his dark hair cropped short with military precision. Even at this distance, the faint scar through one eyebrow gives his face a harder edge. A scarf covers his neck. He was tall and undeniably attractive, warm bronze skin and hard angles softened only by the quiet steadiness of his expression. The kind of man women noticed first and only afterward began to study.

KOAN provided his resume when he worked on Senator Crawford's case. Joined the Army at eighteen, multiple deployments. Speaks conversational Spanish, basic Arabic, and Pashto. Expert marksman, martial arts training, tactical driving, first aid certified.

Thirty-one. Born in 1995.

So many choices still ahead.

I pull ingredients from the refrigerator—salmon, potatoes, herbs for the salad—and my mind drifts to where I was myself at his age. Juggling a newborn, an unraveling marriage, postpartum depression, and a fledgling business I refused to let die. He's out there assessing rooflines. I was trying to keep my life from collapsing. I wonder what it's like —to end a day and *actually* be done.

No responsibilities. No one depending on you.

It's hard not to envy that.

His deep brown eyes meet mine through the glass, pinning me in place. I blink, realizing I've been staring. I nod —unembarrassed. He's on my patio, after all. And a man like him is probably used to catching stares.

His easy view inside to me is a reminder that at dusk, my house turns into a fishbowl. I grab the remote and press a button. The soft whir of descending shades fills the silence. Privacy restored, I cue up an evening playlist and check my phone, tracking Stella's location.

Her father passes her school on the way home, so he'll pick her up after play practice and bring her home. She should be back by now, but sometimes practice runs long. Based on her location, she's still at school. I hope that means play practice is running long, and Richard isn't running late.

A knock at the front door startles me. When I open it, Noah stands there, framed in the street lights.

"You have a key. You can come in."

A slow, subtle smile spreads. "It's still your home. I want to be respectful."

"Well, come on in. Did you decide we're safe for the night?"

"After you lowered the shades—yes. I checked the sight-lines around your house—the shades are effective."

The door clicks closed behind him. "My friend, Dorian, insisted I hire professionals to outfit the place when I purchased this house. Hence, shades."

"Did you move in recently?"

"After my divorce—or, well, separation, really. So…" I run through the years, the separation, moving out of our marital home against my lawyer's advice, buying this place against my friend's recommendations, Stella having to adjust to two homes when she was in first grade… "About six years? Would you like some wine?" I offer, padding silently in my fuzzy socks back to the kitchen. A chill entered the house when I opened the door, so I click a button and the gas fireplace comes to life with golden flames.

"Oh, I don't want to be in your way," he's quick to say.

"Please. Join us. I don't always cook dinner, but I did tonight and there's more than Stella and I can eat. Since you'll be around, it's better that she meets you in a friendly setting in case you cross paths, and besides, I don't like drinking alone."

That last bit isn't exactly true, as a glass of wine at the end of the day is my ritual. If I'm not out for a work event or dinner, I drink that glass alone and find it therapeutic. But tonight, saying it feels welcoming.

He unbuttons his coat and pulls at the scarf looped around his neck.

"Here," I offer, taking both, "I'll put them in the entry closet."

He hands them over and I can't help but notice the pull of the sweater across his chest, his broad shoulders, and the narrow waist. *Definitely fit.*

I return from the closet to find Noah standing by the kitchen island, hands resting lightly on the marble countertop, his gaze tracking the room with quiet assessment. Even relaxed, he's watchful, evidenced by the way his shoulders angle toward the door, the slight tilt of his head as I approach.

"Wine?" I ask again, lifting my glass.

"Water's fine, thanks."

I fill a glass from the filtered tap and slide it across the counter. "You're on duty?"

"Always." He takes a sip, then sets it down carefully. "Did you do the renovation on this place?"

"No. Stella was in first grade when I moved so I searched for something turnkey." I stir the potatoes, adjust the heat. "It was...a difficult time. The divorce, I mean. My lawyer thought I should stay in the marital home until everything was finalized, but I couldn't. And my friend Dorian—" I gesture vaguely, "—he thought this place was too exposed. Corner lot, too many windows. But I liked it. It felt like mine. And it had been gutted. Total redesign. You couldn't get more turnkey."

Noah nods slowly, his expression neutral but his eyes attentive. "It's a good house."

"You're just being polite."

"No," he says, and there's a surprising firmness in his tone. "It's a good house. Just...needs some adjustments. But we'll handle that."

The way he says *we* shouldn't feel as reassuring as it does. It's preferable to believe Dorian's being absurd.

Before I can respond, my phone buzzes on the counter. Stella's location shows her moving—finally. Richard must have picked her up.

"She'll be here in a few minutes," I say, more to myself than to Noah. "My ex-husband drops her off. He's particular about routines."

"Understood."

I pull the salmon from the oven and check the potatoes. The kitchen fills with the scent of herbs and lemon. It's a small domestic ritual, but it grounds me—proof that despite everything, I can still create order, still provide.

"Do you cook?" I ask.

Noah's mouth quirks. "I can manage. My mom made sure I wouldn't starve when I left for basic training. Nothing fancy, but I won't burn the house down."

"That's reassuring, given you're living here."

His laugh is low and genuine. It softens his face, makes him seem less like a security operative and more like...just a man. A man in my kitchen, drinking water while I cook dinner.

The front door opens, closes with a bang, followed by rapid footsteps.

"Mom? I'm home!"

Stella appears, backpack slung over one shoulder, cheeks flushed from the cold. Her dark hair—so much like mine—is pulled into a messy bun, and her school uniform is rumpled, skirt hitched up slightly from the car ride.

Then she sees Noah.

She stops mid-step, eyes widening. "Oh. Hi."

"Stella, sweetheart, this is Noah Bennett. He's part of the security team and is going to be staying with us for a couple of weeks."

Noah steps forward, extending his hand with an easy confidence. "Nice to meet you, Stella."

She shakes his hand, her expression torn between curiosity and caution. "Are you like...a bodyguard?"

"Something like that," Noah says. "I'm helping your mom make sure everything's running smoothly with her business."

Stella's gaze flicks to me, then back to Noah.

"Dad asked me why you have security people around now. He seemed kinda annoyed. And now there's someone *living* here?" She drops her backpack. "Are you gonna tell him?"

I smooth my hands down my lounge set. "I'll address his concerns when we speak. There's nothing for you to worry about, sweetheart—"

"Mom." Stella levels me with a look far too knowing for twelve. "You always say that."

My throat tightens. She's too smart. Too observant. I open my mouth to deflect, but Noah speaks first.

"You play basketball?" he asks, nodding in the direction of the carport where a hoop hangs against the back brick fence wall.

Stella blinks, caught off guard by the shift. "Yeah. I mean, not like on a team or anything. Just for fun."

"What's your range?" Noah asks, leaning one hip against the counter. "You a three-point shooter? Mid-range?"

A small smile tugs at Stella's lips. "I'm working on my free throws. Dad says I shoot too flat." Her father is the one who installed a basketball goal at the end of the carport—with my permission.

"Your dad might be onto something," Noah says easily. "But flat's better than too much arc. You can adjust flat. Too much arc, you're fighting gravity the whole way."

Stella's smile widens. "You play?"

"Used to. Pickup games mostly, back in Chicago, where I

grew up. Haven't had much time lately, but I can still hold my own."

"Maybe we could play sometime?"

"Anytime," Noah says easily. "I'd love to."

Stella glances at me, then back at Noah, her earlier tension easing. "Cool."

I exhale slowly, relieved she let the questions drop. "Dinner's almost ready. Why don't you go wash up?"

"Okay." She grabs her backpack, then pauses in the hall. "Noah?"

He turns. "Yeah?"

"Marvel or DC?"

"Marvel. Captain America."

Stella grins. "Good answer."

She disappears upstairs, her footsteps light and quick.

I turn back to the stove. "Thank you," I say quietly. Talking to my daughter isn't in his job description.

Noah shrugs, picking up his water glass. "She's a good kid. Smart."

"Too smart sometimes."

"That's not a bad thing."

I plate the salmon and arrange the potatoes. "She'll ask more questions later. Especially if her father keeps playing it up."

"Then we answer what we can," Noah says simply. "Kids know when you're lying. Better to give her the truth—just the version she can handle."

I glance at him, surprised by the steadiness in his voice. "You sound like you've got some experience."

"I have a younger sister. Maya. When she was a teen…" He trails off, a faint smile touching his lips. "Let's just say I got good at managing questions I didn't want to answer."

"And how did that work out?"

"She still doesn't trust me when I say everything's fine." His smile widens. "But she knows I'll tell her when it matters."

I set the plates on the island and call Stella back down. As we settle into dinner—awkward at first, then easier as Noah asks Stella about school, about her play rehearsals, about her friends—I realize something.

For the first time in weeks, I'm more relaxed. Less fearful.

And that grates almost as much as the threats Dorian insists exist.

NOAH

Dinner at the kitchen counter is unexpectedly casual. I've spent a month trailing Alicia Morgan—DC office, New York office, always at a distance. Out of sight, out of mind. She's been polite but resistant, clearly unconvinced she needs protection. This—sitting at her kitchen island with a bright, talkative twelve-year-old between us—wasn't part of the plan.

This afternoon I touched base with Gabriel Martin, a recent addition to the KOAN team. He's got a military and intelligence background and comes from a black ops group on the West Coast called Arrow Tactical. Said he wanted to make the move to the East Coast, so they pitched him on KOAN. He's come to the East Coast for personal reasons, so when Hudson brokered the shift change, I took the night shift. It'll free up Gabe's evenings, and having my days open isn't a bad thing. My dad's in Jersey. Easier to get up there when I need to. We're not always on the same page, but I still show up when it counts.

As it is, I'm here—listening to Stella walk us through The Crucible with the kind of intensity that suggests she's not just playing a role, she's inhabiting it. She talks with her hands, her voice rising and falling as she reenacts scenes I barely remember from school.

"I'm the bad guy," Stella says, grinning. Pure joy at getting a part.

"The kind Captain America would go after?" She laughs, and when she does, Alicia lights up. All that time trailing her, and this is different—sparkling eyes, wide smile, relaxed.

"No. It's far more subtle. No guns. I'm Mary Warren—she gets caught up in the witch hysteria and lies." Stella leans forward, animated. "Can you imagine? Someone could just say 'You're a witch' and if enough people agreed, you'd burn."

"About as believable as a red-caped hero flying through the sky," I say.

Stella grins. "Exactly. And you know what? It was all about land. The 'witches' owned property, and back then women could only inherit land if they were widows. Total land grab disguised as hysteria. Not that that's what the play's about. That's more about jealousy. And hysteria. Arthur Miller didn't touch the land aspect. He was more about the emotion."

"Smart kid," I say, glancing at Alicia.

"Too smart sometimes," Alicia murmurs, but her pride shows.

"When is this play?" I ask as Alicia gets up and lifts her plate from the counter. I quickly push my stool back, aiming to help.

"The week before Thanksgiving."

"Nothing like a lighthearted holiday play to kick off the holidays."

"Oh, it's not a holiday play," Stella's quick to correct me.

"I think he knows that, Stella," Alicia says.

"Do you want to shoot hoops?" Stella asks.

"How much homework do you have?" Alicia asks, a hand on her hip.

"None. Got it all done at play practice." She exhales with overplayed exhaustion. "It wasn't even my scene, but I had to sit there the whole time anyway."

"If you're done…go." Alicia catches my eyes, and behind Stella's back, mouths, "Is that okay?"

She's wondering if it's okay for Stella to go out at night. We don't have any reason to believe it's not. Other than one declaration that an unknown group might go after Alicia, and a certainty there are several who won't want her testimony public, we've uncovered no credible threats. She's not on lockdown.

If anyone comes for Alicia, I expect it'll be the same way they targeted her client—through blackmail. Or possibly with a calculated effort to undermine her business, and therefore, her credibility. We're here in an abundance of caution.

As for going out tonight, I run the assessment: locked gate, no sightlines, me positioned between them and any approach. If anyone comes for Alicia or her daughter, it won't be tonight with a street grab in her carport.

I meet her gaze and nod.

"Okay," Alicia says. "But when he's had enough, he's done. Got it?"

Stella charges out as if she didn't hear a word her mom said.

"You really don't have to do this," Alicia says before I slide out the door behind Stella.

"Are you kidding? I love to shoot hoops." And it's true—a few shots at the hoop beats monitoring movement notifications from the basement.

The floodlight casts a golden glow across the carport. Cold air bites my face. Alicia's Rivian is parked at the far end, practically touching the iron gate, leaving the court clear.

Stella's already bouncing the ball by the time I step outside.

She's quick—two dribbles, a pivot, a shot that clangs off the rim.

"Rusty," she says with a grin. "I haven't played much lately. Dad says I should stick with theater, but basketball's more fun."

I catch the rebound and pass it back. "You play with him often?"

"Sometimes." She shrugs, dribbles once. "He's kind of overprotective. Says Mom being on the news makes her a target." She glances up, searching my face. "Now with you here? He's gonna freak out."

Her words flow freely as she dribbles, but if I'm reading her right, she's testing the waters. I keep my reply neutral. "Your dad just wants to make sure you're both safe. That's what dads do."

"Yeah. He's different than Mom." She takes a shot, sinks it clean.

"Nice," I say, catching the ball and passing it to her.

"Mom's great, but she's intense. Everything's gotta be perfect—grades, the play, everything. She wants me to be 'the best version of myself.'" Stella makes air quotes with one hand while dribbling with the other. "Sometimes it just feels like a lot."

She shoots. Another swish. I pass it back, watching her reset for another shot. "Sounds like she believes in you."

"She does." Stella's voice softens. "It's just…a lot."

She shoots again. The ball arcs high, smooth, perfect form. It drops through the net with a whoosh.

"Sweet," I say.

She grins. "Guess I still got it."

She's just a kid—laughing, fearless, free—griping about her parents.

"What's your favorite team?"

"Dad likes the Knicks." She shrugs. "I don't really watch basketball."

"Like your mom."

"Yeah." She grins. "Guess I got that from her."

"Yet you play?"

"Yeah." Her ponytail swings as she circles, getting in line for another shot. "You gonna play, or you gonna just stand there?"

"Smack talk, huh. Let's go."

We keep shooting until the motion of the ball and the sound of her laughter fill the carport, likely carrying over into the neighbors' spaces. Across the street, lights glow warm through the window. Normal life. Family life.

For the first time since joining KOAN—maybe since enlisting—I let myself wonder what that would be like. Then Stella misses a shot, groans dramatically, and the moment passes.

"First to ten?" she asks.

"Let's go."

CHAPTER
FIVE

ALICIA

"Why are you studying in the car?"

Stella's head is bent over her notebook, hair spilling across the page. For someone who claimed she didn't have homework last night, she's unusually focused on the drive to school this morning.

"Meredith said that she thinks we're gonna have a pop quiz today."

"And I bet Meredith studied last night, didn't she?"

"Mom. It's fine. I know the material."

"I hope so." I flick my signal and check the rearview.

The curb is empty. No black SUV. No shadow in my mirror. He actually listened.

A knot between my shoulders loosens—but only a little. I don't like being managed, especially by men. Aside from my personal hangup, a protection detail doesn't eliminate risk. And if it's too visible, it could impact Stella. I don't want her to be scared.

I really need to speak to Dorian again. I understand he has reasons to take concerns seriously, and I appreciate his friendship, but he's projecting his fears onto me.

Stella's school comes into view, and she says, "Stop here, Mom." I'm a block away from the carpool line. "That's Meredith."

She points at a uniformed girl I recognize. She's been a friend of Stella's for years—bright, studious, and gifted. I've been in more than one parent-teacher conference where a teacher mentioned her casually in conversation. I'm grateful she's one of Stella's close friends as she'll help motivate her to push herself.

Given I'm pressed for time and skipping the carpool line will be a blessing, I pull to the curb and Stella hops out.

"Hey," I shout, forcing her to pause before slamming the car door. "I love you."

She rolls her eyes. "Love you, too."

"Have a good—"

Bam. The car door slams, but she waves and blows me a kiss.

I'll take it.

Thirty minutes later I'm pulling up to the valet at the Four Seasons for the Policy and Media Symposium. I check the time as the valet hands me a tag and pause when my gaze catches on Gabriel Martin.

I told Noah I wouldn't need security here. Gabriel was supposed to meet me at my office. So much for listening.

The last thing I want is for people in my industry to pick up that I have a security detail—and this is DC. The attendees are savvy to security.

My heels click on the polished marble as I make my way

to the side of the lobby where Gabriel Martin stands near concierge.

"Gabriel," I say, choosing his first name, because I met him last week.

"Ms. Morgan," he says, voice clipped, gaze slipping past me, on alert.

"I do not want you here."

"No one knows I'm here for you."

I tilt my head, recognizing he has a good point, but that's not the point. I said no, and here he is. I told my daughter to do her homework, and she said she had none. None of this is acceptable.

I pull out my phone and dial Hudson Stone.

He answers with a crisp, "Ms. Morgan."

"I'm safe at the Four Seasons. Tell your employee to wait for me at my office, as planned. If you don't follow my requests, I'll call Dorian and tell him to pull the detail."

"Understood."

He likely continues to speak, but I don't hear it as I disconnect the call and turn to Gabriel. "Call your boss."

With that handled, I proceed through the lobby, following the signs to the symposium and The Corcoran Ballroom. When I arrive at the location overlooking the canal, I pause in the doorway, scanning the scene of attendees. Many wear name tags, and there's a low hum of chatter. The foyer is set with a continental breakfast—white linen tables, silver urns of coffee, and croissants under glass domes. The marble floors reflect the light from the large windows and, with the light at their backs, it's more difficult to discern facial details.

But one man in a pin-striped suit turns, and I recognize him instantly.

Matthew Delacroix.

Heat floods my face, then drains away just as quickly.

His presence is unexpected. He hates these events.

His eyes find mine across the room. That smile. Slow, knowing.

The clink of china and polite laughter grate against my nerves.

A friend approaches, and I welcome her with a smile.

"Christine," I say, greeting her with an air kiss to her cheek. "How are you? Come with me to get coffee?"

"Sure. The banana muffins they set out, let me tell you, they're worth the calories."

"Well, I've already had breakfast." It's a lie, but I don't eat muffins. "But I would like coffee."

"Did you notice that they dropped the women's leadership panel?"

"I actually did not." I participated in it last year, but this year I'm here strictly as an attendee. "Is it a worthwhile agenda?"

"Meh," she says and pauses to wiggle her fingers at someone across the room. "It's fine. Nothing new. Introductory remarks, then we break out. I think I'm going to attend the session on effective press releases."

"These days, it seems most papers print the press release verbatim—might as well write them like you want the article to read."

Out of the corner of my eye, I see Matthew slip away from the assembly, heading in the opposite direction. Away from the crowd.

I force my attention back to Christine. She's dating someone new and I'm cautiously happy for her. The reason for my caution vibrates in my hand.

Christine glimpses the notification on my screen. "Ah,

look who it is. The dick."

With a frown, I swipe to read his entire text.

Dick: Alicia, we need to talk. Can you please call me?

My stomach knots. Of course, he could have left it at that, but that's not Richard's style. A second text follows, and it's written with the formality of someone who has been coached that all texts might one day find themselves before a judge.

Dick: Bill Canon filled me in on the situation. I believe it's in Stella's best interest that she live with me during this time that you require a security detail. Please call me. I'd like to handle this without involving outside counsel.

Who the hell is Bill Canon? Senator Crawford shared details with few people. But given the White House Chief of Staff committed suicide and there's an open investigation, I suppose nothing stays secret on the hill.

"Alicia? Are you okay?"

People are filtering into the Corcoran room for opening remarks. But I need to call Richard. If I don't, he'll assume I'm ignoring him and be on the phone with his lawyer within the hour.

Outside counsel.

Once a prick, always a prick.

"Alicia?" Christine repeats.

"It's fine. It's Richard."

Concern etches her eyes—she's one of the few who stayed close through the divorce. She understands.

"Just more of the same," I say, speaking the truth. He expected that his lawyers would win him full custody, and he's never let it drop. Stella has been choosing to spend more time with me recently, and I swear that's getting under his skin as well.

I meet Christine's worried eyes, and while I'd love to unload on a friend, a public forum isn't the place. "Will you save me a seat? I'm going to call him before he gets his lawyer involved."

Her eyes widen. "That bad?"

Through the open door I can see someone milling around the podium. Most of the seats are filled.

"How many years has it been since your divorce?"

Too many for him to still be threatening lawyers, but I'm too worked up to speak, so I set my coffee cup down on a tray and breathe deeply.

This is my punishment for marrying a narcissistic, egotistical man-child.

"I'm going to go—" I gesture with my head in the opposite direction of the assembly. "Save me a seat?"

"You got it." She pulls out her phone and taps on it, "You know what? Let's do a private lunch. I'm going to get us a table at Bourbon Steak. We don't need to do the group lunch thing." She's talking about lunch at the hotel restaurant, and under normal circumstances, I'd tell her not to bother, that we should network, but I'm not feeling particularly up for sitting at a round twelve-top with polite conversation.

As I exit the conference area I pass a steady stream of professionals gathered off to the side, speaking on phones, often through earbuds. Small high-top tables line the hall-way, and most are claimed by professionals tapping away on laptops. It's difficult to leave the office behind, and little is gained from sitting through opening remarks.

Up ahead, the business center sign catches my eye. Private. Quiet. Perfect. My reputation is critical for my career, and I can't risk losing my calm in public. A private meeting room is exactly what I require to set Richard in his place.

Behind the glass business center door I spot a line in front of the business center reception desk. I expected it to be empty. Since it's not, I change direction, away from the business center, moving further down the hall.

I dial Richard.

As it rings, I spot a door cracked open along a narrow hallway that's to the side of the business center, and I head that way.

The phone is still ringing, and with each unanswered ring, my blood boils. That jerk knew I'd have a busy day, expected that I would drop everything to call him, and now he's not answering. Classic prick.

It's a power play. That's all it is.

I push the door open and realize it's a small meeting room, but there's a door that opens onto the deck.

I close the door behind me, ending the call, eyes on the gray sky and the view over the canal. I'll give him a couple of minutes and call again.

No. I'll message him. Tell him I called him back. That way there will be a record of my attempt.

The air smells faintly of coffee and carpet cleaner. The hum of the lobby fades.

No, I don't need to message him. If he wants to play it this way and bring in lawyers, I'll show them my call record.

If he wants to play hardball, he can explain to the judge why he'd send a text like that and then not answer.

My hand finds the door handle to step outside—and I freeze.

A coffee cup, overturned on the carpet. Dark liquid spreading across beige fibers.

And beside it, a hand.

My breath catches.

Tobacco leather shoe. Gold buckle. Pinstriped cuff. I know that suit.

"Matthew?"

Kneeling beside him, I touch his cheek. It's clammy, chilled. "Matthew!"

I lift a hand. Heavy. I drop it and sit back, taking in the scene.

He's unconscious.

I run my finger beneath his nose—but he's not breathing.

"Help!" I scream. "Someone call 911!"

I recall the CPR training I received years ago—something Richard insisted on for Stella's safety—and pinch his nose and breathe into his mouth. I push down on his chest. It's harder than I expected—resistant beneath my palms.

I'm not doing this right. I know I'm not doing this right. One. Two. Three. I've lost count. Breathe into his mouth. His lips are cold. Push again. Nothing.

I run to the closed door and fling it open, yelling down the hall. "Help! A man's down. We need an ambulance!"

NOAH

"Any press outside Morgan's?"

I step out for a clearer view. No vans. No lenses. Just typical traffic along the street.

"None that I can find. You think she's going to attract media attention from this?"

"I'm skeptical. Our client is concerned." He means Dorian Moore, the founder's husband and Alicia's friend. Moore's lived under a spotlight before; paranoia's a reflex.

"The heart attack victim should be the story—not the woman who found him."

"Lab confirmed toxic digoxin levels an hour ago—well above any therapeutic dose. It's officially a homicide." Hudson lets that sit for a beat.

My gut tightens. "He was murdered. Any evidence that indicates Alicia was the target?"

"Data doesn't point that way," Hudson says. "Yet. We may need to increase coverage."

"Or move her to a temporary location. I told you, this house is…" I checked the listing on Zillow and the estimated value is a cool five mill, but the corner location gives new meaning to the word exposed.

"Right. Moore said the same."

An older woman walking two small dogs smiles as she passes, and I back up from the curb and venture down the side street. Further down, I spot a sedan, a blue four-door Mazda, parked with a driver sitting behind the wheel.

"How's she doing?" Hudson asks.

"Haven't seen her. Martin messaged that she's on the way home. But given she went into the office this afternoon and held client meetings, I'd say she's holding it together." I know firsthand that you can be emotionally shaken and still hold it together, but if anyone won't unravel, from what I've seen, it's Alicia Morgan.

Cars rumble past at a leisurely pace, but I keep an eye on the Mazda. "Did Quinn learn anything about the vic? Any connection to Magpie?"

"Nothing so far beyond what's public. Used to own a public relations firm and now he's a lobbyist. Quinn's doing a deep dive on his clients."

"Bet the cops are too." That's where I'd start. "I know it's risky to buy into coincidences, but the extortionists we're worried about—the Magpie network, the blackmail syndicate that's been trading secrets from Washington's elite —murder isn't their calling card. They're in the business of threats."

"Agreed. But need I remind you that the White House Chief of Staff claimed the people she feared would come after Alicia Morgan?"

He doesn't need to remind me because I heard it on the

comm. She laid that down right before pulling the trigger and ending her life.

"When Alicia gets home, ask her about her movements that morning. If she was supposed to meet him, if they crossed paths, if anyone could have known where she'd be."

"You're thinking the target was Alicia and they got the wrong body."

"I'm thinking we need to rule it out. I agree. It's unlikely. Just figure out what you can. We need to understand what Alicia was doing that morning to confirm she wasn't targeted."

"Copy that."

A woman in a long coat approaches the Mazda and gets in. Passenger side. The car pulls out into traffic, and I clock the plate. Probably nothing, but everything matters now.

"Martin said he hasn't spoken to her. She also sent him home this morning. I understand she's not thrilled with our presence, but is there more going on between her and Martin I should be aware of?"

Gabe mentioned she dismissed him at the conference. He shrugged it off—par for the course with difficult clients.

I don't have any info for the boss. "Not to my knowledge."

"Keep an eye out. If we need to rotate staff, we will."

"I'll keep you updated, but I haven't observed anything to indicate a personal conflict. From what I've seen, she's frustrated with the situation. Doesn't believe we're necessary and she's concerned about her daughter getting spooked."

"I can understand that," Hudson says.

I head back to the intersection. "I'll get a play-by-play of this morning and send it to the team."

"Sounds good," Hudson says and ends the call.

I'm at the street corner when I spot Alicia's Rivian with its turn signal on. The metal gate rumbles as it glides open. She turns the car into the carport without acknowledging my presence.

A Toyota 4Runner parks on the drive before the gate. Martin. He lowers the window, the picture of unbothered confidence.

"She's all yours," he says in greeting.

"Any press show up at her office this afternoon?"

"No." He shakes his head. "When she arrived at the office, she went about her day like nothing happened. If I hadn't received Hudson's update, I would've never known."

"Anyone at the office talk about it?"

"From what I observed, no one was aware. I spent most of the day in the reception area, and the receptionist never mentioned it. There's no television in reception, so…"

"Right. I don't think it's made the news yet." Then again, I haven't been watching either.

"Who died?" Gabe swallows hard. "I mean, what's his story?"

I get what he's asking.

"We're still figuring it out. A lobbyist."

"One of her clients?"

That's an interesting angle I hadn't considered. "I'll ask."

"Good luck with that," he says with a half-smile.

I rap my knuckles against the door. "You have a good one."

He rolls up the window and flips on his blinker, falling in line behind the three cars at the stoplight.

The traffic on these streets is typically light, except around this time of day when folks are coming home. The neighborhood's calm—families walking dogs, someone unloading groceries. One hundred percent normal.

I look at the front door and hesitate. She just found a body this morning. Walking in through the front feels like an intrusion. I head to the side gate instead, entering through the carport. Looking up at the lights, I can tell she's on the second floor.

Under normal circumstances, I'd head downstairs—out of sight, out of mind—but I need to speak to Alicia, so I pull a barstool from the kitchen counter where we ate last night and wait.

A few minutes later, footsteps descend. Alicia's changed into a cream sweater set, hair sleek and pulled back. Everything controlled. Except her eyes. Those give her away—washed out, hollow, like the day scraped something raw.

"Wine?" she asks.

"No, thanks."

"I'm drinking. You can have water, and we can pretend you're joining me."

"That works," I say, fully understanding where she's coming from. "Heard you had a rough day."

"One for the books," she says, the lightness forced.

"I plan to stay out of your way, but before I duck downstairs, I was hoping you'd tell me about this morning."

She opens the fridge and reaches for a wine bottle, eases the stopper out, and pours herself a generous glass.

The bottle clinks on the countertop when she sets it down. She closes her eyes and leans against the counter. "You heard it all, right? And that the lab found digoxin." She opens her eyes, reaches for another wine glass, and turns on the tap. Sliding the water to me, she says, "A police officer called me this afternoon. They'd like to ask more questions.

This morning, it was… I think we all thought he'd had a heart attack or something. I tried CPR." She laughs once— brittle, sharp. "Haven't done that since Stella was a baby. Richard insisted I take a class."

Frustration oozes. If I were to guess, the frustration stems from her perceived failure.

"You tried. That's more than most."

She takes a sip, sets the glass down, stares at the counter.

"When you went back to that room," I ask, "were you supposed to meet him?"

Her eyes snap up. For a fraction of a second, something flickers—then it's gone, replaced by that steady assessment. "No. I was looking for somewhere private to talk. My ex called. I thought we'd argue, so I wanted space." She swallows. "I walked in and he was already down. I don't remember much after that."

"Did you know him?"

"The victim?" Her voice catches slightly. She clears her throat. "Public relations is a small world. I've seen him at events." She picks up her wine glass, takes a deliberate sip.

"That's all?" I ask.

"That's all."

"So you weren't scheduled to meet?"

Her posture stiffens; both hands flatten on the counter. "Dorian thinks the poison was meant for me? Is that what this is?" She looks toward the ceiling, then straight at me. "No. It was a self-serve breakfast bar. Two hundred people were there. I left my coffee cup on a table outside the conference room before Richard messaged."

"Got it."

She's flustered now, her control thinning around the

edges. I push back from the stool. "Think any media will come knocking?"

Her mouth parts, incredulous. "I work behind the scenes." She picks up her wine and starts for the stairs. "I should call Dorian. If he's worried about media, he's panicking."

I watch her climb—shoulders squared, glass trembling slightly before she disappears from view.

Maybe she can hold it together.

Or maybe she's holding on by her fingernails, and I'm the only one present to see it.

CHAPTER
SEVEN

ALICIA

Upstairs, I don't have the energy to call Dorian, so I text.

Me: Know you're worried, but I'm good.

Dorian: Did you know him? Any connection to your business? Or to a client's?

I swirl my wine, watching twilight drain from the sky. The window throws my reflection back—tired eyes, pale skin, the outline of someone barely holding on. Outside, the lone tree in my postage-stamp backyard shivers, leaves curling like paper set too close to flame.

Did I know him?

If I say yes, it will sound like a confession. Dorian may read it as heartbreak.

Stick to what's relevant. No more, no less.

I take another sip—and text again.

Me: You're looking for connections where there are none.

The phone vibrates. *Of course.*

"How are you, really?" Dorian's voice is rough with worry. "And don't give me *fine*. You were with a man who died today."

"I'm still absorbing it."

"Matthew Delacroix. That name rings a bell. Where do I know him from? Did he work with—"

"Mom! I'm home!" Stella's voice cuts through.

Dorian exhales with a loud breath. "Tell her hi. Call me tomorrow. I'm digging into—"

"Don't," I cut in. "It's—"

"Mom, Dad's here! Can you come down?"

I close my eyes. *Perfect.*

"Richard," Dorian mutters.

"You're on speaker," I warn. "I've got to go."

He grumbles and disconnects.

I leave the wine where it sits—caught by the window's fading light—and square my shoulders before heading downstairs.

Stella stands by the door, backpack sliding from one shoulder, as Richard and Jessica wait in the foyer.

My chest tightens. Still, my smile holds. "Hi," I say

evenly. "Jessica. I don't think I've seen you since—when was it? Spring?"

She's impeccable: cream blouse, navy skirt suit, heels that shape her calves, hair blown out, makeup fresh. It's six-thirty on a Monday.

"Things have been busy," she says brightly. "You have a beautiful home. We've dropped Stella off so many times, but this is the first time I've been inside."

Her gaze drifts across the foyer, over the furniture, the light fixtures, resting on the family photos.

"Stella, would you give your mother and me a minute—"

"Sure." She's gone in a flash, footsteps drumming upstairs.

"See you tomorrow," Richard calls.

"Homework," I remind her, calling after her retreating back.

Silence settles, thick, close, and awkward.

I should offer coffee, maybe wine. But hospitality feels like surrender.

"I'm not the bad guy here," Richard says, repeating the same line he's been using for years. "I'm concerned for my daughter."

Of course he is. Always the martyr.

"The security is precautionary," I reply. "For Stella's safety."

Jessica steps forward, expression soft, gaze roaming. "Where is the security, if you don't mind me asking? I didn't notice anyone outside."

"At the moment, downstairs." *Or in the carport. Or anywhere he chooses.* "The night detail stays in the guest suite. The day team checks in with me in my office."

"Smart," she says. Her gaze flicks toward the keypad. "Is that new? It blends right in."

"Yes."

"Good choice." Her tone is soft, benign, but that contradicts my read on her. "I told Richard you were smart to act after what happened at your office."

"It wasn't *my* office."

"Of course." She touches the console table lightly, her manicure catching the light. "Still, it must have been awful. I can't imagine walking into something like that."

I press my palm against my thigh to steady it. "We're fine."

"You founded Morgan & Company, right?"

"Yes."

"Crisis management?"

"Among other things."

"Fascinating," she says, sweet as honey. "You must know every trick for staying calm under pressure."

"I've learned a few."

She steps forward as if it's just the two of us having a friendly conversation and Richard isn't in the room. "Do you ever represent politicians? Or corporate clients?"

"Sometimes."

Where is she going with this?

"Then you're used to complicated situations."

A beat of silence. Her gaze shifts to the staircase.

"Stella must love it here," she says. "It feels safe. Familiar. Warm."

"She does."

"She's lucky." Jessica's smile doesn't quite reach her eyes. "A mother who can handle anything—that's rare."

The compliment has teeth. "Thank you."

Richard clears his throat. "We were hoping you'd consider letting her come with us for fall break. It'd mean a lot—to both of us."

"You're going through a lot right now." Jessica adds softly, "I'd love to help with her. I volunteer with kids; they keep me grounded."

"Let's revisit that closer to break."

Richard shifts his weight. This was the real reason for coming inside—not just to verify security, but to push for this.

"Of course." Her agreement is smooth, instant. "We just want what's best for her."

The security panel beeps twice—the carport entry.

Richard stiffens. Jessica's head tilts.

Noah's voice carries from the hallway. "Evening."

He steps into view—steady, unreadable, his stature and presence emanating a quiet authority.

Jessica's smile sharpens the second she takes him in. "You must be with security."

"That's right," Noah says.

"It's comforting to know Alicia and Stella are in good hands. Richard worries about them."

Warm words. Cold edges.

Richard exhales. With that one subtle, disciplined sound, I know what he's going to say before he says it. "We should go."

Jessica threads her hand through his arm. "Take care of yourself, Alicia. I'm sure things will settle soon."

"Goodnight," I say, holding the door.

They step into the night, and Jessica's perfume lingers—something sweet and youthful.

The latch clicks.

Noah studies the closed door, then me. "Friend of your ex?"

"Girlfriend." Though wife is probably the goal.

"She asked a lot of questions."

I meet his gaze. "That's what she does."

ALICIA

Jessica's perfume hasn't cleared the foyer yet.

"Does Stella like her?"

"She does," I admit, glancing toward the stairs and the wine I left behind. "At least I think she does. Give me a minute."

With that, I climb the stairs, continuing on to the third floor. I give a quick rap against the open door, announcing my presence. Stella's sprawled on her bed, iPad inches from her face.

"That doesn't look like homework."

"Mom—I just got home."

"What's the rule?"

She combines an eye roll with a stare in the way only a preteen can manage. "Fine." She drops her iPad on the bed, face down.

"I'm leaning toward pizza."

"That works," she says with a brighter note in her voice—

my only clue she likes the idea. Not that I need a clue. She's loved pizza since she was three.

"Okay. I'll call you when it's here."

I pause, waiting for her to at least *pretend* to start homework. With a dramatic huff, she opens her laptop.

"My homework's on here," she says.

I give her a thumbs-up. "Just checking."

She rolls her eyes again, but this time there's a grin behind it.

I'm one step into the hall when I pause and ask, "Do you want to go on fall break with your dad?" He didn't mention where they are going, but knowing her father, it'll be fantastic.

She shrugs. "Sure. I don't know. Not really. Is it better for you if I go with him?"

"Not at all. You know I love having you home. But if they're going somewhere fun, I don't want to hold you back."

Richard and I have holiday custody agreed to for the next five years, but we also agreed to be reasonably flexible.

"The Cape," she says, referencing Richard's parents' vacation home. "Although Jessica mentioned going someplace warm, Turks and Caicos maybe? I don't know what they've decided."

I almost tell her it's up to her, but stop myself, not wanting to put the decision on her shoulders. She might act like a teen, but she's still a kid, and Richard and I should talk it through. If she's with him, he'll need to trade a future holiday.

"Alright, well, I'll call you down when dinner's here."

She's already got her headphones on, eyes back on the

screen before I've cleared the doorway. Hopefully schoolwork.

In my office, I place an order for pizza, retrieve my wine, and head downstairs to find Noah at the kitchen island, a phone in hand, scrolling.

"I can go downstairs if you prefer. But you said to give you a second…"

"No, please, stay." I slide onto a stool. "I like the company. I mean, I know that's not what you're paid for—"

"Happy to hang out." His lips twitch. "Does she know what happened today?"

"No." My brow furrows. "Richard wouldn't…" I trail off, second-guessing myself. There's Jessica.

I thumb a message to Richard, just to be sure.

"It's gotta be hard for three adults to parent together," Noah says.

"She doesn't—" I stop. Maybe I've been pretending Jessica's temporary because it's easier.

"I get it," he says. "They're not married. When my dad started dating Linda, it took me a while, too. Can't say I see her as a stepmom even now."

"Are your parents divorced?"

"My mom passed away. Linda was one of my mom's friends." He half-chuckles, then scratches his jaw.

"Was that good or bad?"

He tilts his head, thoughtful. The kitchen light catches the gold in his brown eyes. He's leaning against the island, relaxed—one arm on the counter, hand wrapped loosely around his water glass. The sweater he's wearing fits close enough that I notice the breadth of his shoulders. I look away.

"Weird," he says finally, a half-smile tugging at his mouth. "But I got over it. I wasn't around much anyway."

"Military," I guess.

He nods. "Yeah. I enlisted right after Mom got sick. Thought she'd beat it."

His words swirl emotions that on a normal day I'd redirect, keep things professional. But after today—finding Matthew, the interrogation, Richard—my defenses are down. I want to offer comfort.

"When we're young," I say softly, "it's almost impossible to fathom death. Unless you've lived through it."

He pushes up, refills his glass with water, then lifts the wine bottle without asking, and refreshes mine. The gesture's easy and natural.

"You close with your parents?" he asks.

"My parents both passed away."

He's silent, giving me space. It's strangely easy to keep going. "Car accident. I was fifteen. I don't think I even said goodbye that night."

He exhales, leaning back against the counter. "That's rough. And here I was feeling sorry for myself."

"It wasn't all bad," I admit, and smile faintly. "I mean, losing them was horrible, but my grandmother took me in. She saved me, really. She let me mourn but didn't let me wallow."

"She sounds like a force."

"She was. Harvard was her idea. She passed away five years ago."

He winces in sympathy. "You're three-for-three. That's brutal."

"She lived a full life," I say. "And honestly? I'm glad she didn't have to see my divorce. That would've crushed her."

"How long ago?"

"Finalized two years ago. Separated four years before that. So there was this…window." I gesture vaguely. "When I pretended things were fine for her sake."

He nods, eyes soft. "You were protecting her."

I huff a quiet laugh. "Maybe protecting myself too."

He doesn't rush to reassure me or offer platitudes. Just nods like he understands exactly what I mean.

He comes around the island and joins me. "Linda's…fine. She makes Dad happy. That's enough."

"I haven't thought of Jessica as Stella's stepmom," I say slowly, "but maybe I should. My instinct's to keep her at arm's length."

"Protective instinct," he says. "Nothing wrong with that."

There's a brief silence, the good kind—warm and unforced.

"You and your ex seemed cordial earlier," he says. "That for show?"

"Not a show. Just a rule. We're always civil in front of Stella."

"Smart. She doesn't need the crossfire."

"Exactly. But Richard and I don't always see eye to eye."

He grins. "If you did, you wouldn't be divorced."

"True." I glance at him, noticing how relaxed he looks here—one arm draped over the back of the stool, a faint smile playing at his mouth. "You? Ever married?"

"No. Not even close. I've had serious relationships though." He taps his glass against the counter. "They were good people. I'd like to think I am too. But together? We didn't fit. I've stopped seeing breakups as failures."

Thirty-one and self-aware enough to not force something that doesn't work. I respect that.

"That's an evolved view."

"Or just practiced," he says lightly. I laugh, and it feels good. The first genuine laugh all day.

He studies me for a beat. "You're not judging me for being single. That's what *you're* getting at, right? When you say evolved?"

"No judgment," I echo. "Period."

He glances toward the dark windows and the flickering headlights passing in the street. "You walk around and close these every night, or..."

I reach for the remote beside the fruit bowl. The mechanical hum fills the silence as the blinds descend. Noah watches them lower, one by one, until we're cocooned in soft light.

"That's convenient," he says.

"Dorian insisted."

Just as the blinds click shut, the doorbell rings.

"Pizza," I say, setting down my glass. "Please, stay. Eat with us."

He stands. "Only if it's my treat."

I arch a brow. "I ordered two pizzas. Stella can eat half a pizza on her own."

"Works for me." His smile widens—possibly the first real one of the night.

The doorbell rings again, impatient this time.

Noah opens the door before I can. He exchanges a few words with the delivery guy, tips him, and returns with both boxes balanced on one forearm. Like this is normal. Like he belongs here. The thought catches me off guard.

The smell of melted cheese and garlic fills the kitchen.

"Careful," I warn. "She can smell pizza from a mile away."

"Should I brace for impact?"

"Probably."

Right on cue, Stella's voice calls down the stairs. "Is it here?"

"Yep. Come on down!" I shout.

She appears a moment later, sock-footed, hair back in a messy bun, her face lighting up at the sight of the boxes. She freezes mid-step when she sees Noah at the counter.

"Oh. Hey."

"Hey, Stella." He nods, friendly but not forced.

"I got half pepperoni, half veggie and a cheese. Gave you both options," I say.

Stella eyes the boxes like she's choosing between desserts.

Noah lays both out on the island, tops back to display the contents. "You get first dibs."

She cracks a grin, and something softens in her expression. "Thanks."

We sit around the island—me with my wine, Stella with a soda, Noah with his glass of water—and everything that happened today dissipates—or at least, it doesn't feel as present.

"Do you always eat at the counter?" Noah asks, lifting a slice.

"Depends on the night," I say. "Rarely in the dining room. Sometimes on the couch if we're watching a movie."

"Mostly here," Stella pipes in.

"Good call." Noah asks Stella, "You a movie person?"

"Depends on the movie," she says around a mouthful of cheese. "If Mom picks, it's usually something depressing with subtitles."

I gasp in mock offense. "Excuse me—educational."

"Exactly what I said," she mutters.

Noah chuckles, the sound low and easy. "I'm guessing you prefer something with explosions."

"Or dogs," she says, wiping her mouth. "Explosions *and* dogs would be perfect."

He grins. "You ever seen *John Wick?*"

"Mom won't let me."

"For good reason," I say. "Dogs, yes. Explosions, yes. But also nightmares."

Noah raises his hands in surrender. "Fair. I forgot about the nightmare potential."

Stella giggles. "Mom checks everything with Common Sense Media."

Conversation drifts from movies to food—her school lunch options, the healthy items that I cook that she's not crazy about, Noah admitting he once set off a smoke alarm trying to make pancakes in a hotel room.

By the time the pizza box is empty, the air has loosened. Stella's leaning on her elbows, telling Noah about play practice for *The Crucible*.

"The monologues can get tedious. But the later scenes… you can really get the hysteria—and that's with middle school kids performing."

"I bet," Noah says, genuinely interested. "You like performing?"

She shrugs, but her eyes brighten. "Kinda. It's fun. Even if you don't get a big role."

"She's being modest," I say. "She has perfect timing. Always has."

"Timing's everything," Noah says, smiling. "You know, that's true for the field too."

"What field?" she asks.

"Security," I say quickly. "He used to work in military security."

"Oh." She studies him with sudden curiosity. "Like guarding people?"

"Sometimes," he says lightly. "Sometimes watching out for things they didn't know were there."

Her brow furrows as she thinks that over. "Like spies?"

He chuckles. "Not quite that cool. More like keeping people safe without them noticing."

"Like you're doing now," she says.

There's a short silence—unexpectedly tender—and I see Noah glance at me before answering.

"Exactly like that."

Her grin is bright and unguarded, and I can't help smiling too.

"Can I be excused?" she asks, plate already lifted in the air.

"Homework first," I say automatically.

"Already done."

I raise a brow.

"Mostly done," she amends.

"Go on."

She leans in to hug me—quick but real—then waves to Noah. "Bye. Thanks for the pizza."

"Anytime," he says.

When her footsteps fade upstairs, the house goes still again, but it's a comfortable kind of quiet.

"She's great," he says.

"She is." I watch the spot where she disappeared, a smile still tugging at my mouth. "Most of the time."

"Strong-willed."

"She gets that honestly."

He laughs softly, wiping his hands on a napkin. "I figured."

We sit there for a moment—two adults at a quiet counter, the remains of dinner between us. There's an ease that wasn't there before, something unspoken but likely mutual.

"I should let you get some rest," he says finally, standing.

I want to ask him to stay—just a little longer, just for the company—but I only nod. "Thanks for dinner."

"Anytime," he echoes, with that faint smile that lingers long after he's gone downstairs.

The house feels different with him in it. Less empty.

But it doesn't take long after I've cleaned and headed upstairs for bed, for the full force of the day to return. Matthew lying on the floor, unresponsive. The medics, lifting him onto the gurney. Their unhurried departure—because there was no one to save.

NOAH

The phone drags me from sleep at nine a.m. I check the screen—Hudson—and swipe to answer.

"Morning," I say, voice rough. Night shift means I crashed around six after my perimeter check. Three hours isn't enough, but it'll do.

"You underwater?" Hudson asks.

I sit up, rubbing my face. Through the basement window, rain sheets against the glass. "Raining heavy. No flooding."

The team agreed I'd stay on through the weekend, staying on site at Alicia's, given everything that's happened. Gabe's on standby if I need relief, and Hudson flew in Jake, another teammate, for additional backup. But I've got it covered.

"Any signs of press?"

"Not yet. Alicia says the press doesn't care about the person who found the body. Even if they cared, they aren't standing on the curb in this weather."

"How's she doing?"

"Haven't seen her yet today. But this week, she's been strong. She's got a daughter to put on a front for, though. Stella's with her dad this weekend—but I'm not expecting a change."

"Copy that," Hudson says with a grimness that tells me he didn't just call for a sit-rep.

"What's up?"

"As you know, they determined on day one it's a homicide."

"Right. They found the digoxin residue on the coffee cup he was drinking from. Did they find fingerprints?"

"According to our source, only his." He hesitates for a beat, long enough to put my senses on alert. "Alicia Morgan is now a person of interest in the investigation."

I sit up straighter. "Because she found the body?"

"Possibly. But there's more."

"Gabe said the police spoke to her at her office yesterday."

"They did."

"At this stage, everyone who was around him that day would be a person of interest, right?"

"Has she mentioned that she knew Delacroix?"

"She said it's a specialized industry—she knew of him."

"He was also on her board of directors for Morgan & Company when she started it. Left in 2019."

My gut tightens. Board member. Not just someone she "knew of."

"Six years ago," I say carefully. "That's the kind of detail you offer up when police ask if you knew someone. And that makes her a person of interest?"

"My guess is it's more how she answered the question when the police met with her."

"If Alicia thought it was relevant, she would've

mentioned it." Even as I say it, doubt creeps in. She was evasive when I asked about him. I saw it in her eyes. Not sharing that with Hudson.

"The officer hasn't filed a report yet, but when he does, we'll see if we can figure out what she said that's increased their interest in her."

"That's not public information, is it?"

"No. And I'm not sure how much longer our source is going to bend rules for us. But that PR firm they worked at together? It was small. Less than fifty people."

"That doesn't mean anything."

"If she didn't have any experience with police investigations, I'd be inclined to agree with you. But she's got a history of clients with police run-ins. Admittedly more of the DUI or possession variety, but…"

"Right. She's got experience with guilty parties and police investigations. She's got no experience with an investigation that has no leads."

"Police might bring her in for more questioning. Tell her to be straight with them."

"Should she get a lawyer?"

"I don't think so." He doesn't sound convinced. "If it comes to that, my source should give a heads-up."

"Copy that." There's nothing worse than cops without leads. "How'd the boss take it when you told her there's been no movement on the Magpie case?"

We agreed in our team meeting yesterday that we have zero evidence of threats on Alicia Morgan related to the Magpie case.

"Caroline understands. She wants security in place through the congressional hearings—at least until after Alicia testifies. Once she testifies, Caroline believes she'll be in the clear."

"Got it," I say.

"You good through the weekend?"

"Yes. Alicia canceled her social plans tonight. She's planning to stay in during the deluge."

"Anything changes, reach out."

After the call, I work out, shower, and try to nap, but can't. Person of interest. Board member. The pieces don't fit what she told me.

I wait until lunch before heading upstairs, giving myself time to decide whether to bring it up.

Rain lashes the glass, a steady percussion confirming the storm hasn't let up. All the blinds are still down, so it's dark. The only lights are the motion-activated lights in the kitchen and a lamp beside the sofa. The smell of coffee hits me before I see her. She's curled up on the sofa, a blanket pulled to her waist and a book in both hands. Something about the image is disarmingly unguarded. Not the version of her I've seen all week.

She looks up when I come in, one finger marking her page.

"Morning," she says.

I nod toward the windows. "Rain's not letting up anytime soon."

"I know." She tucks the blanket higher. "Good excuse to do nothing."

When thunder rolls close enough to rattle the glass, she flinches, and for a second, I see the truth she's been holding together all week. She's uneasy.

"Do you need anything downstairs? I didn't check—" Her legs hit the floor like something important has come up.

"Rest. I'm good," I reassure her.

She slowly pulls her legs back beneath the throw, reluctant, like she'd rather not.

"You're not used to staying still, are you?" I ask quietly.

Her smile's faint. "No. Stillness gives you too much time to think."

"You look comfortable," I say.

"I can't get into this book," she admits, smiling faintly. "No meetings. No phone calls. Just rain."

"Mind if I join you?"

"Please do."

I pour my own cup and take the chair beside her. Outside, the rain pounds steadily, muting the world. I can't pinpoint why, but I feel Stella's absence in the house.

"Thanks for joining me," she says softly. "It's nice. Not being alone in a storm."

The lamplight reveals her eyes, steady and searching.

"You're not," I tell her.

She holds my gaze for a moment, then looks away, back to her book. But she's not reading. I can tell by the way her eyes don't move.

I settle into the chair, coffee in hand. The rain is hypnotic—steady white noise that soothes.

"Can I ask you something?" I say after a minute.

Her eyes lift. "Of course."

"Matthew Delacroix. Hudson said he was on your board when you started Morgan & Company."

Her expression doesn't change, but something flickers in her eyes. "He was. Briefly."

"Why'd he leave?"

"Creative differences." She takes a sip of coffee. "He wanted the firm to focus on corporate damage control—oil companies, pharmaceutical litigation, that kind of thing. I wanted to work with individuals."

"So you parted ways."

"Yes."

It sounds plausible. Professional. But there's something she's not saying—I can feel it in the careful way she's choosing her words.

"When's the last time you spoke to him? Before the conference."

"A year, maybe longer." She meets my eyes directly. "We didn't stay in touch after he left the board."

"But you recognized him immediately at the symposium."

"It's a small industry."

I nod slowly, watching her. She's good—answering every question without volunteering extra information. It's exactly what I'd do if I were hiding something.

But I'm not going to push. Not today.

"Fair enough," I say, leaning back.

She relaxes slightly, sinking into the cushions. "Are you asking because the police asked you? Or because you're curious?"

"Both."

"I didn't kill him, Noah."

"I know that." And I do. Whatever secrets she's keeping, murder isn't one of them. "But the police are going to dig into every connection he had. You should be prepared for them to come back with more questions."

"I will be." She sets her mug down. "This is what I do, remember? I prepare people for hostile questions."

"Yeah, but usually you're on the other side of it."

"True." A faint smile. "It's strange being the one who needs the coaching."

"If you want to practice, I'm happy to play interrogator."

She laughs—soft but genuine. "I think I've had enough interrogation for one morning."

"Fair."

The rain intensifies, drumming harder against the windows. She pulls the blanket higher, tucking it under her chin.

"This is the first Saturday in months I haven't had plans," she says, changing the subject. "It feels...odd."

"Good odd or bad odd?"

"I'm not sure yet." She glances toward the window. "Part of me thinks I should be doing something productive. The other part just wants to hide under this blanket until Monday."

"Hiding under a blanket sounds pretty productive to me."

She smiles. "Is that what you do on your days off?"

"I don't get a lot of those."

"When you do, though. What's your version of hiding?"

I consider her question. "Running, usually. Long runs where I don't think about anything except putting one foot in front of the other."

"That sounds awful," she says, but she's grinning.

She's grinning, and I find myself wanting to say something else just to keep it going. "You're not a runner?"

"I was. In college. Now?" She gestures to herself, wrapped in a blanket. "This is more my speed."

"Nothing wrong with that."

"Stella thinks I'm boring," she says lightly. "She's probably right."

"You founded a company, manage high-profile crises, and raise a kid on your own. That's the opposite of boring."

"Tell that to a twelve-year-old who thinks I should let her watch R-rated movies."

I laugh. "Yeah, that tracks. My sister was the same way at that age. Thought our dad was the most uncool person alive. Drove Dad insane."

"Was he?"

"Uncool? Absolutely." I grin. "But Maya got over it eventually. Now she calls him for advice on everything."

"How old is Maya now?"

"Twenty-seven. She's a nurse in Chicago. Stubborn as hell, heart of gold."

"She sounds wonderful."

"She is. Drives me crazy, but she is."

Alicia's expression softens. "It must be hard, being so far away from her."

"Hmm. We talk. And I visit when I can." I pause. "What about you? Any siblings?"

"No. Only child. My parents were older when they had me—I think I was a surprise." She smiles faintly. "A happy one, but still."

"You mentioned they died when you were fifteen."

"Car accident. My grandmother raised me after that." Her fingers trace the rim of her mug. "She was...formidable. Strict, but she loved me fiercely."

"And she's the one who pushed you toward Harvard."

"She didn't push—she expected. There's a difference." Alicia's voice is fond. "She'd already lost her daughter. I think she was terrified of losing me too, in a different way. So she made sure I had every opportunity, every advantage."

"Sounds like she did a good job."

"She did." Alicia's quiet for a moment. "I wish she'd lived long enough for Stella to know her as she got older. She died when Stella was seven. Old enough to remember her, but not old enough to really know her."

"That's hard."

"It is. Stella asks about her sometimes. I tell her stories, show her pictures, but it's not the same."

Thunder rumbles, distant now. The worst of the storm is passing.

"Do you have family photos around?" I ask. "I noticed the ones of Stella, but I haven't seen any of your grandmother."

"Upstairs. In my office." She tilts her head. "Why?"

"Just curious. Trying to picture the woman who raised you."

"She looked like Grace Kelly. That's what everyone said." Alicia smiles. "Very elegant, very composed. She wore pearls every day, even to the grocery store."

"And your Cartier watch is like her pearls."

She glances down at her wrist, surprised I noticed. "This was hers, actually. One of the few things I have left of her."

She's looking at the watch, not at me, and I take the extra second to study her face. I shouldn't. I look away, toward the rain-streaked glass. "It suits you."

"Thank you." She's quiet for a beat. "Can I ask you something?"

"Shoot."

"Why security? I know you said you wanted to stay state-side, but...why this specifically? You could've done anything."

I lean back, thinking. "I like solving problems. And I like helping people who can't help themselves. This job lets me do both." What I don't tell her is that when I was recruited for KOAN, they pitched it as more than security.

"That's noble."

"It's selfish, actually. Makes me feel useful."

She studies me with those sharp blue eyes. "I don't think you're as selfish as you pretend to be."

If she met my dad, he'd set her straight. "Maybe not. But I'm no saint."

"Good. Saints are boring."

That makes me chuckle. "Is that your professional opinion?"

"Personal experience. I've worked with a few. They're exhausting."

"I'll keep that in mind."

We fall into comfortable silence. The rain has softened to a gentle patter. Outside, the sky is still gray, but lighter now.

"This is nice," she says quietly.

"What is?"

"This. Just...talking. Not about cases or police questions." She looks at me. "Just talking like normal people."

"We are normal people."

"Are we?" She smiles, but there's something wistful in it. "Sometimes I forget what that feels like."

I understand exactly what she means. When your job, or your sense of worth, revolves around others—you can lose track of your own life.

"For what it's worth," I say, "I think you're doing pretty well at normal."

"Liar," she says, but she's grinning.

"Okay, maybe you're slightly more put-together than normal. But that blanket is very relatable."

She laughs—real and unguarded. I'll take it.

The storm rolls on outside, but in here, it feels warm. Easygoing.

"Noah?"

"Yeah?"

"I'm glad you're here." She says it simply, without artifice.

The last time it mattered that I was somewhere, I wasn't. I've been trying to square that ever since. I look toward the window. The rain hasn't let up.

"So am I."

She shifts on the couch, and for a moment, I think she's going to say something else. Instead, she just pulls the blanket tighter and picks up her book.

But this time, when she opens it, I notice the faint smile.

I grab my phone and settle in, content to just sit here while the rain falls and the world outside stays quiet.

For the first time in weeks, there's no rush. No immediate worry.

We're just...here.

And that feels like enough.

ALICIA

We've been sitting here for over an hour, just talking about nothing important—his favorite running routes, my disastrous attempts at learning to cook when I first lived alone, the books we've been meaning to read. Easy conversation interspersed with comfortable silence. Then my phone lights up, shattering the quiet. I stare at Dorian's name on the screen, resentful of the interruption.

The temptation to ignore his call is great, but temptation is not the path to greatness.

"Let me get this," I say to Noah, holding up the phone.

He checks his watch. "It's lunchtime anyway. You up for grilled cheese and tomato soup?"

"Where are you ordering that from?"

His grin is slow. "I'll make it. When you're done with the call, join me in the kitchen."

I lift the phone and swipe, but all my attention is on Noah

as he leaves the room. Flannel shirt, corduroys, socks—completely casual, completely comfortable in my space.

"Dorian," I say, forcing my focus back to the call.

"Hi. Checking in."

"You know you don't need to, right?"

"Underestimating your opponent is the best way to let them win."

I laugh softly. "There's no opponent. Just a woman who panicked facing a prison sentence."

His silence is its own response. "You're genuinely concerned about this network she mentioned."

"Caroline is. It's conceivable. A group of powerful, connected individuals who believe they know what's best? Those groups exist. And if they feel endangered…" He trails off. "At any rate, you know I'm right."

I don't want to argue. And honestly, if it means keeping Stella safe, I can live with the security detail. "What are you and Caroline up to this weekend?" The conversation shifts—farmer's market, his father's health, his upcoming London trip to visit a mutual friend, Stella's school year. Normal topics. But I can't shake the feeling he's circling something bigger.

"These shadowy people you're worried about are more likely to be my clients than my enemies."

"Maybe," he says. "But you know how easily powerful people hide their messes. If Caroline's right, you're not out of their orbit yet. At least not until the hearings."

I stare at the dark screen after the call ends, Dorian's words echoing. A secret group. A hidden enemy. I shake it off, set the phone down, and follow my nose to the kitchen.

Two placemats are set on the kitchen island, and two bowls of tomato soup are set out. Noah's at the stove, spatula in hand, watching over two sandwiches sizzling on the grill. Reality smells like butter and basil, not conspiracy.

It's so...domestic. Unexpectedly intimate.

"Just in time," he says, grinning.

"Where'd you get all this?" I ask.

"It's all from my grocery run yesterday. Soup's reheated—but it's freshly made by a brand called Mama Calloway. We'll see if it's good. And the grilled cheese...this is a Bennett family recipe."

"Stella would love this."

"I'll remember that for next time."

Next time. The assumption is casual, unstudied–and I like it. "I'm pretty sure cooking detail isn't on your list of job responsibilities."

"I don't mind. I like cooking. Reminds me of being home."

"You know, you don't need to hang out here all weekend. I'm not planning on going anywhere. This is a safe neighborhood. There have been no threats made. I'm good."

"Where am I going to go in this weather?"

On the back patio, rain pelts the concrete and my covered patio furniture. It's early afternoon and yet the sky is as dark as a typical evening.

"That's a fair point."

"If you want me out of your hair—"

"No," I say quickly. "You're more than welcome. It's nice having you here."

"What have you got planned for the rest of the afternoon?" He plates the grilled cheese with the smoothness of a short-order chef.

"Oh, I have a few work projects I need to tackle."

"Working on the weekend?"

"I gave myself the morning to enjoy the rain."

"Gotcha. And plans for tonight?"

"My friend Christine bailed. She's not one for going out in bad weather."

"Understandable."

"Lazy," I say, grinning. "Or maybe smart. But I don't mind. I'd much rather stay in."

"I'm thinking I might power up your media room that's downstairs. Pop some popcorn. You want to join me?"

"Maybe."

That maybe dangles in the back of my mind all afternoon as I catch up on email correspondence, review the accounting reports for Morgan & Company, and flick through news articles and trade reports.

By seven o'clock, the rain has intensified to a steady roar. I've accomplished more than expected, but my mind keeps drifting to Noah's invitation. The house feels too quiet with just me on the second floor. I close my laptop and head downstairs.

The basement media room glows with soft amber light. Noah's already there—popcorn on the coffee table, two glasses of water, throws pulled from the closet and draped over the sectional. He's set this up. For us. The realization sends warmth through my chest.

"Perfect timing," he says without looking up. "Action, thriller, or comedy?"

"Surprise me." I settle into the opposite corner of the sectional, tucking my feet beneath me. "According to Stella, it's always best if someone else picks."

He scrolls through options, pausing occasionally. He selects something—*The Fall Guy*.

"Ryan Gosling. Can't go wrong."

"Stella made me watch this last month."

"And?"

"And I fell asleep halfway through."

"Want to pick something else?"

"No — I'd actually like to see the ending."

He grins. "I'll try not to take that personally."

The movie plays, but I'm distracted. By the way he laughs. By how relaxed he looks, shoulders loose, defenses down. By the blue light from the screen catching the angles of his face. When our fingers brush reaching for popcorn, neither of us pulls away immediately.

When he laughs at a particularly ridiculous stunt, it's genuine.

"What?" he asks, catching me staring.

"Nothing."

I'm far more aware of the man beside me than of the movie playing out on screen. I'd like to believe that's because I've seen this before—but that's not what this is, and I know it.

Ten years younger. Here for a job. I know exactly what this is, and I know better. I should call Christine and curse her for canceling. If she hadn't, I'd be at a restaurant making small talk, not sitting here hyperaware of every shift in his posture, every casual brush of contact. This is absurd. I'm over forty. I know better.

The movie plays on, but I swear the energy between us is palpable. Of course, it's all in my head—one-sided attraction. At least, that's what I need to believe. I don't have time for a relationship, and I'm a single mom. It wouldn't be remotely responsible.

When the stunt guy saves someone in a thunderstorm,

Noah murmurs, "Unrealistic. But I guess that's the point. You don't do that with a helicopter."

"Speaking from experience?"

"Maybe." His eyes meet mine, and the frisson of energy spreads through my chest. The sensation is ridiculous—more fitting for a teen on a date. "But yeah, I've got my pilot's license. Wish I'd gone Air Force."

"Why didn't you?"

"Wasn't thinking through decisions particularly well at that point in my life." He smiles. "Wrong recruiter caught me first."

When I reach for popcorn again, his hand is already there. Our fingers tangle briefly before I pull back.

"Sorry," I murmur.

"Don't be."

I don't look at him. But I heard him.

The air between us feels electric.

The storm outside rumbles like a restless animal, rain streaking the narrow windows near the ceiling. On-screen, the stuntman dives through fire, but I barely see it. All I can feel is the warmth radiating from the man next to me, the faint scent of cedar and clean soap.

"You always this quiet during movies?" Noah teases, voice low.

"Only when I'm enjoying them."

He goes still. Not for long—just long enough to tell me something registered.

His gaze catches mine—steady, direct. For a heartbeat, I forget how to breathe. He leans slightly closer, like he might whisper something, and my pulse trips over itself. The air feels charged, humming. One more inch and—

What am I doing?

I don't pull away.

Thunder cracks directly overhead. The lights flicker. Once. Twice.

Darkness.

Complete, absolute darkness.

"Stay there," Noah says, his voice clipped. Professional. Alert.

I hear him stand, feel the shift of air as he moves. My heart pounds—not from fear of the dark, but from the sudden shift in his energy.

"Generator should kick in," I say.

"Should have already." His voice comes from near the hallway. "When did you last test it?"

"Is 'never' an acceptable answer?"

I hear him exhale—half amusement, half exasperation. "If it's the truth. Stay here. I'll check the panel."

I reach for my phone and search for electrical outage updates. There's no point in finding my electrical panel if everyone in Georgetown lost power.

"Ah…it's in the closet, down here," I say, getting up while scanning news articles, making my way to show him. Nothing's coming up about an electrical outage, but it just happened. Maybe that's why there's no update.

Using my phone's flashlight, I shine the light along the wall, looking for the narrow closet door.

Thunder shakes the foundation of the house.

"It's in that closet," I say.

Noah opens the door and flips the metal cover open. He uses his phone for a light.

"Hmm," he says. "Okay. Power's out, but on the chance the system's compromised, I want you to come with me while I retrieve something from my room."

A gun. He's talking about a gun. He thinks something other than a storm—someone—could be behind this.

My heart hammers uncontrollably, but it's just the storm. We're all being paranoid.

When I reach out blindly, his hand finds mine. Warm. Steady. My fingers curl around his instinctively. For just a moment, that's all there is.

Then the reality of where we're going settles in. To his room. To get his gun.

Paranoid or not, I'd never admit this to Dorian, but right now I'm grateful he insisted on security. Grateful for Noah's hand in mine, solid and sure. Grateful it's him here in the dark with me. Especially him.

CHAPTER
ELEVEN

NOAH

The lights flicker on, power restored. A moment later, the television hums back to life—the movie resuming mid-scene. I pause in my bedroom doorway, listening. The sound drowns any footsteps.

Chances are the storm caused the outage. Still…

The downstairs bedroom has one entry point—one door. The narrow windows near the ceiling don't qualify as egress, which any fire marshal would flag, but tonight that works in my favor.

"I'm gonna do a loop. Check things out."

I stride to the bedside table and remove my handgun.

"It's just the storm."

"Probably," I say, agreeing with Alicia. "I'm still going to do a loop. Stay here."

Rain lashes at the windows. The shades are drawn and the hall is dark. By the stairs, I flick a switch, blanketing the downstairs in light.

"Widespread outages are being reported," Alicia calls from the bottom of the stairs, holding her phone.

I grit my teeth—she's not doing what I told her.

The security panel glows red down the hall—solid light, system secure.

"Stay down there," I call.

I pull out my phone and check the app I loaded on my phone when Alicia gave me the security company file. We lost electricity, but the app shows the backup kicked in—the system was never down.

Within five minutes, I've cleared the second and third floor. There's no sign of entry. No telltale wetness near an entry point.

Upon returning to the basement, the film is paused but Alicia's already on her feet, the empty popcorn bowl and our glasses in hand like she's been waiting to make her exit.

"I'm going to call it a night. Paused it for you."

"You're not going to stay and finish?" The question comes out before I can stop it—more interested, more disappointed than I should be.

She won't quite meet my eyes. "It's late. I'll see you in the morning."

Something shifted while I was upstairs. Maybe it was sitting here in the dark together, rain outside, movie playing —too much like something real. Too comfortable.

She's already halfway up the stairs before I can respond.

I tell myself it's nothing, but when I finally stretch out by the monitor, the sound of rain isn't what keeps me alert. It's the memory of her laugh during the movie. The way she'd curled her feet under her on the couch. How right it felt before everything shifted. By the time I fall asleep, I still haven't figured out what I did wrong.

Sunday morning, nothing's clearer. The blinds are open to reveal a gray cloudy day. There's no sign of Alicia.

I take out my phone to check in with my dad.

"Hey, Dad," I say.

"Hey there, son," he says, his words warm, his tone less so.

"You heading to church?"

"We are. Linda's finishing getting ready. What about you?"

"Working today," I answer reluctantly. Work isn't a good subject with Dad. "Did that storm hit you guys last night?"

"Hugged the coast. We didn't get more than a couple of inches of rain. Upstate got some sleet. Winter's coming."

"Yeah, it is. What've you guys got planned for the day?"

"Meeting some friends for lunch. I might catch some of the game."

"Who's playing?"

"The Giants. Can't remember who they're playing though. Seahawks, maybe. You got any news?"

"No."

"But you're working on a Sunday—still in DC?"

"Yep. For now."

"Putting in the time, but what kind of advancement is possible?" Same conversation, different week. In Dad's world, if you're not building toward something the world measures—you're wasting your time. After all, he started as a lowly mechanic and became a franchise king.

I hold in the sigh—he'll hear it and it will spark an argument. "That's not what this is about."

"What kind of work are you doing?"

"That's not for me to share."

"Linda saw Sarah Watkins at the market. Her son's a captain now."

I don't have a response to that, so I don't offer one.

"You think you'll be home next weekend?"

Doubtful. "Not sure."

"If you are, plan on joining us for church. We can catch the games after."

"I'll let you know."

"Alright, son. I gotta go."

The call ends with all of the standard unsaid things. He'll never get it. Never understand that some things matter more than a ladder to climb. He'll likely never forgive me for leaving the Army—at least not until I can tell him I've achieved a rank others recognize.

I rinse out my coffee cup and head down to Alicia's home gym. She's got a nice set-up. A top-notch treadmill, rowing machine, stationary bike, a full weight set, and three television monitors on the wall that her cardio machines face.

Thirty minutes into a hard run, testing the limits of Alicia's treadmill, the wall monitors flicker on. I nearly trip, catching myself as I hit the red stop button.

Alicia's in form-fitting leggings, a matching jog bra, and running shoes. Her dark hair is up in a smooth ponytail, and she's intent, pointing the remote like she's wielding a weapon.

Newscasts from three different channels flick on, all set with subtitles. The overhead speakers come alive with The Weeknd.

"Morning," I say.

Her gaze snags on me—sweaty, shirtless, still breathing hard. Her eyes track down, then quickly back up.

Alicia raises a brow, the faintest smirk curving her mouth. "You're giving that treadmill a workout."

"Figured I'd make sure your equipment survived the storm."

"Always thinking of my welfare."

Her tone's teasing, but there's something behind it. I don't trust myself to look too long at her.

"There's no damage from the storm outside," I say, grabbing the towel from the side rail. "Security system never went down. Backup held."

"Guess I should've trusted you," she says lightly, adjusting the volume on one of the TVs.

"Guess you should've stayed where I told you."

That earns me a look over her shoulder.

"I'm not great at following orders."

"Yeah," I say. "I've noticed." Her mouth quirks, and for a second the air shifts. There's nothing playful in her expression now—just awareness, sharp and magnetic.

She breaks the stare first, taking a long drink from her water bottle.

Alicia Morgan doesn't break eye contact—she wins it. Which means something just rattled her.

"You want breakfast?"

"I was gonna make you something," I say. "Figured you earned it after surviving the blackout."

"Coffee and heroism. Hard to beat that combo."

"I do my best work in emergencies."

She laughs, soft and real, and the sound goes straight through me. I should head into my room, grab a shower, reset the morning. Instead, I find myself leaning against the doorframe, unwilling to move.

"You always this put together on a Sunday morning?" I ask.

"You always this sweaty before coffee?"

"That depends. You always watch three news channels at once?"

"Helps me get all sides of the story."

For a moment, neither of us moves. The music overhead fills the space between us.

She tugs one earbud free, her voice quieter now. "Last night… Thanks for hanging out."

"Wasn't a big deal."

"It felt like one," she says. Her gaze lifts to meet mine again. "For a minute there, I thought…" Her lips part, like she has more to say.

I don't move. Don't breathe. If she's going to finish that sentence, I'm not going to be the reason she doesn't.

The silence stretches with a charge, the kind that feels like it could ignite if either of us moved an inch closer.

The left screen flashes red—breaking news. The moment shatters.

Judiciary Committee Schedules Closed-Door Hearing with Senator David Crawford.

Alicia turns back to it, blinking, her expression shuttered again. "Apparently the storm took out power in three counties. Looks like power's restored across the grid," she says, reaching for the remote. "Guess life goes on."

"Yeah," I murmur. "Guess it does."

But when she walks past me, close enough that her shoulder brushes mine, I feel her everywhere. She doesn't apologize. Just gives a small, knowing smile before seating herself at the rower.

I stay where I am, towel still in hand, heart rate climbing

again for reasons that have nothing to do with cardio. She settles at the rower, muscles flexing as the machine whirs to life. The controlled power in every movement, the focused intensity on her face—I'm watching her the way I'd watch a threat. Except everything in me knows she's dangerous for entirely different reasons.

Every flex of muscle, every controlled movement—I should look away. Should head upstairs. Instead I'm memorizing the curve of her shoulder, the line of her thigh, the way she moves like she's in complete control of everything. Including me.

I need to move. Need to get upstairs, get space, get my head back in the job. Instead, I grab my water bottle and head for the weight bench. If she can pretend last night didn't happen, so can I. Even if neither of us believes it.

CHAPTER
TWELVE

ALICIA

I spot Christine at a back corner table in Maman. The cozy café is packed with the Sunday morning brunch crowd, and I weave through patrons lined up for pastries.

"Ordered us our usual," Christine says as I'm unwinding my scarf. She looks past me. "I thought you said you have security."

"I do." I glance over my shoulder. "But I slipped out."

"You gave your bodyguard the slip?" Christine's eyebrows climb. "That's very Jason Bourne of you."

"He couldn't exactly stand in here without looking conspicuous. Besides, what was he going to do—lurk outside in the rain like a stalker?"

"If he's hot, I'd allow it." She raises her champagne glass. "Here's to rainy day brunch and questionable life choices."

We clink glasses, and I let the bubbles settle my nerves. We've been doing this since the first weekend after my divorce—that first Sunday when the house felt too quiet and I'd questioned every decision that led me there.

"How are you holding up?" Christine asks, her voice dropping the playful edge.

"I'm good."

"Alicia." She gives me *the look*—the one that says she's known me too long for bullshit.

"I am," I insist. "Mostly."

"You were close to Matthew."

"Not that close." The words come too quickly, too defensive. "You worked with him too."

Her eyes narrow slightly, noting that deflection. "Elena's taking it hard."

I close my eyes, picturing Elena—his wife. Their kids, who must be in high school now. My heart clenches—that sharp, cold ache you get when you've inhaled winter air too fast.

"Are you in touch with her?"

"No. I haven't seen her since one of those holiday parties years ago." Christine fidgets with her glass. "I bought a condolence card. Can't decide if reaching out would be supportive or weird."

"Let me know what you decide. I'll send flowers."

"Britney Calloway said the kids are worried about her. Seventeen and fifteen."

"God." The word escapes before I can stop it. "Those are brutal ages to lose your father."

I would know.

Christine's hand covers mine briefly. "Hey. Enough heavy stuff. Tell me about the bodyguard situation. Is he hot? Please tell me there's at least one silver lining to this nightmare."

I suppress a laugh. "There are two of them, actually—"

"Two?" Her face lights up. "Even better! Tell me everything. Better yet, show me photos."

"I did not take photos of my security detail."

"Criminal oversight. Are they hot?"

"Actually...yes. Very."

Christine leans forward like I've just revealed state secrets. "Define 'very.'"

"Too young for us."

"Who made you the age police? How young?"

"The one living in my house is thirty-one."

"Thirty-one is not too young. Thirty-one is *perfect*." She waves her mimosa for emphasis. "You're forty-one, not eighty-one."

I cross my arms. "Yes, exactly what every attractive thirty-one-year-old man wants—a relationship with a single mom who has a twelve-year-old daughter."

"That's oddly specific." Christine tilts her head. "And you said, 'the one living in your house' like you've already narrowed it down."

Damn it. "Only one of them is living with me."

"Uh-huh. And?"

"And nothing. He's just...there. Professionally."

"How professionally did you describe him as 'very' hot?"

"I was answering your question."

"Was the question 'describe him in a way that makes me think you've thought about this extensively'?" She grins. "Because that's what I'm hearing."

I pick up my menu like a shield. "What's the special today?"

"You never order anything else." She cackles. "Oh, you've got it bad."

"I do not—"

"What's his name?"

"Noah." Her eyes practically twinkle. I should not have shared that.

"Noah." She says it slowly, testing it. "Okay. So we've established he's thirty-one, hot, lives in your house, and you refer to him by his name. What else?"

"There's nothing else."

"Is he single?"

I nod reluctantly.

"Then what's the problem? You're single. He's single. You're both consenting adults sharing a house."

"He works for me."

"He works for your security company. Not quite the same power dynamic."

"Christine—"

"I'm serious, Alicia. When's the last time you let yourself have something just for you? Not for Stella, not for your career, not for managing Richard's feelings—just for you?"

The waiter arrives with our food, and I've never been more grateful for the interruption.

But as we eat, Christine's question lingers. When *was* the last time I did something just for myself?

"What about your date?" I ask, redirecting.

"Didn't make it past one drink. He spent forty minutes explaining cryptocurrency." She spears a bite of quiche. "I don't want to hear about blockchain. I want to hear about your bodyguard's—" She pauses dramatically. "—skill set."

"Christine!"

"What? I meant his professional qualifications." Her grin is wicked. "Unless you have other data to share?"

My phone rings—Richard's landline, meaning Stella is calling—and I grab it like a lifeline. "Saved by the preteen."

Christine just laughs and reaches for another pastry.

I exit the restaurant so I can speak where it's quieter.

"Hey, honey," I answer. Sometimes when she calls on Sunday things aren't going well and she's looking for an excuse to exit early.

"Hey, Mom," she says. "Where are you?"

"Brunch with Christine."

"Cool."

"What's up?" I left my coat and scarf hanging on my chair. The crisp air cuts through my sweater, nipping at my skin. I'm under an awning, but the air itself feels wet.

"Oh, nothing much. I'm about to head over to Melissa's for a study session."

"That's good."

"Yeah, and then Jessica wants me to join them for dinner tonight, you know, since I'm not spending the whole day with them."

That's not unreasonable, I suppose—but the word *them* lands hard, an unwelcome reminder that I'm no longer the center of her orbit.

"Well, you can just let me know what time to pick you up."

"It's probably going to be a late dinner. The reservation is at eight."

That's very late for a school night, but I'll save that commentary for Richard.

"So, I might just stay with them tonight, then come home after school tomorrow."

"That's fine," I say, scanning the street. Movement from a

man in a black coat beneath an awning across the street catches my attention, but then he steps inside the store.

"Why don't you text me what your snack, lunch, and dinner preferences are for the week. I'll make sure we're stocked up."

"Okay. Sounds good." But the words land flat, missing her usual energy.

"What's wrong?"

"Nothing. I'm just not looking forward to spending my whole day on pre-algebra."

"Oh. Well, time spent doing math problems is never time wasted."

"Mom?"

"Yes."

"You're weird. Later."

The call ends. That's not exactly proper etiquette for ending a phone call, but at least I've nipped her habit of just hanging up without any goodbye at all.

I return to my seat at the table inside. By the time we finish brunch, I've got a mild, happy buzz and a friend who will not let the idea of enjoying my bodyguard go.

"He is your bodyguard," she says, giggling. "And what does that body need?"

I push at her. Together we're sophomoric. Often Angela is with us, but she's recently started dating this guy named Frank, and so we don't see her as often. When she's single again, she'll be a regular once more. It's good she's not here, actually. She'd probably insist on returning home with me to see this specimen for herself.

With a hug and a wave, I step out into the drizzle for a brisk walk home. When I enter the house, it's conspicuously silent. As I'm toeing off my rain boots, the front door opens, and Noah enters. He's in a black coat—a familiar black coat —and my pulse stutters before my brain catches up.

"Did you follow me?"

He's not sheepish at all. "Did you try to give me the slip?"

"It's not necessary for you to follow me to brunch."

"That's not your call."

"I'm fine, Noah. I was having brunch, not walking into a dark alley."

He shrugs, stepping out of his coat. Rain beads along the jacket lining before sliding to the floor.

"Dark alleys are predictable," he says. "Brunch crowds aren't."

I can't tell if he's teasing. His face doesn't give me much to work with, but something about his presence sends my stomach fluttering. I hang my scarf, aware that my fingers are clumsy. The champagne, maybe. Or the way he's watching me.

"I don't need you shadowing me everywhere," I say, though my voice has lost its edge.

"Maybe not. But you do seem to get into trouble when I'm not around."

I open my mouth to argue, but his smile—half-smirk, half-sincere—is incredibly appealing. He crosses the room, placing his keys on the console table. His sleeves are rolled up, revealing the veins and sinew of his forearms, all quiet strength and control, and I have the irrational thought that he could hold me together if I let him.

I should go up to my office. Instead, I say softly, "You're soaked."

"Comes with the job."

I reach for a towel from the hall closet and hand it to him.

His hand closes around the towel, and for a split second, around mine.

It's nothing—and everything.

Christine's voice echoes in my mind: *Who says you can't play?*

Noah watches me, hands idle. "You've had a long week," he says.

"I have."

"Stella's with her dad again tonight?"

"Yes." My throat tightens. "She's…staying over. They're having a late dinner."

Something shifts between us. His gaze flicks to my mouth, then back to my eyes, as if checking whether I'm aware of what's happening. I am. God help me, I am.

"I was going to make tea," I say, stepping past him toward the kitchen. "You want some?"

"Sure." His voice is low, a little rougher.

In the kitchen, I busy myself with the kettle, pretending my pulse isn't thundering—that his presence has no effect and everything is normal. When I turn, he's leaning against the doorframe, watching me again—not protectively this time, but intently.

"You don't always have to be strong, you know," he says.

I swallow hard. "Why do you say that?"

He takes a slow step closer. "Because I sense your daughter isn't the only thespian in the house."

Steam curls from the kettle. I ignore it, because his nearness rattles my thought processes.

"I'm not fine," I admit, defensively. "Not all the time."

"Good," he murmurs. "Then you're human after all. And putting on a show."

His hand lifts toward my face and pauses—just for a second—before he brushes the damp strand from my cheek.

I don't stop him. Although, I should. His touch is careful, reverent. My lips part on an unsteady breath. "This is a terrible idea."

He whispers back, "Maybe. But it feels like a good one."

And then he kisses me—unhurried at first, like he's giving me every chance to pull away. I don't. The past week, the exhaustion, the loneliness—all of it blurs into warmth and want. My hands find his shoulders, his chest, the solid reality of him.

He pulls me closer, the kiss deepening, hungry now, as if we've been slowly approaching an edge and now the restrictions are lifted and we've hit a full run.

He breaks the kiss, but we're still close, no space between us.

His forehead rests against mine, and I can feel his breath —unsteady, matching my own. My hands are still on his chest, and beneath my palms, his heart is racing.

I should step back. I should laugh this off, blame the champagne, blame the stress of the week. But his thumb is tracing small circles on my jaw, and the tenderness of it undoes every careful wall I've built.

"Alicia." Just my name, but the way he says it sends a shiver straight through me.

This is reckless. I don't do reckless. I plan. I strategize. I maintain control. But standing here in Noah's arms, I realize control is the last thing I want. I want to stop thinking. Stop managing. Stop being the woman who has to hold everything together.

His hands frame my face. They're warm, slightly rough from calluses. When his thumb brushes my lower lip, it becomes harder to breathe. The simple gesture feels impossibly intimate.

For a long, suspended moment, we just look at each other. There's the faint tap of rain against the windows, the hush that always follows a violent storm, and the pulse in my throat that feels louder than both.

Christine's teasing still echoes in my head—*Who says you can't play?*—and I realize I've been so careful for so long that I've forgotten what it feels like not to be.

We're not discussing a commitment. This is play. Adult play.

I move first. My fingers graze his hand, testing, and when he doesn't pull away, I link my fingers through his. His eyes darken—just barely—and that's all the encouragement I need.

"Come upstairs," I whisper.

I pull back just enough to meet his eyes and remind him. "Stella won't be home until tomorrow."

He knows what I'm offering. What I'm suggesting.

"Are you sure?" His voice is low. Rough. Strained.

I'm not sure. I'm terrified. But I nod anyway. "I'm sure."

He squeezes my hand gently. Not pushing. Just...present.

That's what gets me. Not the attraction, not the champagne haze—but the simple fact that he's here, and he's letting me choose.

I lead him toward the stairs, my heart pounding as his footsteps follow. Halfway up, I glance back at him, and the look in his eyes—the restraint, the want—makes me ache.

"I've been trying not to want this," he says quietly.

I don't answer. I don't have to.

In the doorway of my bedroom, I pause. The rain has

lifted, the gray light soft through the curtains. "This may be a bad idea, but no regrets," I say, voice barely audible.

He gives a faint, crooked smile. "None whatsoever."

"I need this." What I'm not saying is, I want to stop thinking.

My declaration is all it takes. His fingers thread my hair, and his mouth finds mine—slow at first, then deeper, needier, until thought itself disappears.

When he lifts me, I don't resist. When he lays me down, the outside world fades completely—the storm, the loss, the guardedness. The bedroom is cool, rain-dimmed light filtering through the curtains. I'm aware of everything—the soft cotton of the duvet beneath me, the scent of his cologne mixing with the rain on his skin, the sound of our breathing in the quiet house.

When I reach for the hem of his shirt, his stomach muscles tense beneath my fingers. I feel powerful and terrified all at once. His skin is warm, smooth over hard muscle, and when I press my palm flat against his abdomen, I feel him inhale sharply.

For a second, I freeze. It's been so long. What if I've forgotten how to do this? What if—

"Hey." Noah's voice is soft, his hand finding mine. "We don't have to—"

"I want to," I whisper. And I do. God, I do.

When his hands slide beneath my sweater, I gasp. His palms are warm against my ribs, and every nerve ending ignites. I arch into the touch, surprised by how hungry I am for this—for him—for feeling something other than fear and control.

He undresses me slowly, his hands unhurried, and I do the same for him—fumbling slightly with buttons because my fingers aren't steady, hyperaware of every inch of skin as it's revealed. His shirt drops to the floor and I press my palms flat against his chest, feeling the heat of him, the definition of muscle beneath skin, the way he goes very still when I touch him like he's fighting to let me set the pace.

When there's nothing left between us, he draws back just enough to look at me. I resist the urge to cover myself—the vulnerability of being seen is almost too much, the old familiar inventory of imperfection threatening to crowd out everything else. But the way he's looking at me stops that thought cold. Not assessment. Not performance. Something quieter and more devastating.

"You're beautiful," he says, and the reverence in his voice makes my throat tighten. I don't feel beautiful—I feel exposed, vulnerable, over forty, and imperfect—but the way he's looking at me makes me believe him.

He settles beside me, one hand tracing down my side, learning the curve of my hip, my waist. When his mouth finds mine again, it's slower, deeper, a claiming that makes me forget every reason this isn't recommended.

His lips trace a path down my throat, across my collarbone, lower. When he reaches my breast, I arch into him, my fingers curling into the duvet. His mouth is warm, insistent, and when he draws my nipple between his lips, I cry out—shocked by the intensity of sensation.

"That's new information," he murmurs against my skin, and despite everything, I laugh breathlessly.

His hand slides lower, fingers tracing the inside of my thigh, and I tense for just a second—anticipation mixed with nerves. It's been so long.

"Relax," he whispers. "I've got you."

And when his fingers find me—warm, sure, devastating—I surrender completely.

He takes his time, learning what makes me gasp, what makes me moan, what makes my hips lift helplessly into his touch. When his mouth follows the path his fingers blazed, I forget all thoughts.

I've spent years perfecting the art of restraint, but here, now, with Noah's mouth doing impossibly wicked things and his fingers working magic, control shatters. My hands fist on the comforter. My back arches off the bed. I hear myself making sounds I don't recognize—desperate, needy, honest.

When I shatter, it's with his name on my lips.

He kisses his way back up my body, and I'm still trembling, still catching my breath, when I reach for him. His length is hard against my hip, and I want to give him what he just gave me—want to make him feel what I just felt.

I wrap my hand around him, and the sound he makes—low, strangled—thrills. He's velvet over steel, and when I stroke him slowly, his hips jerk involuntarily.

"Alicia—" A plea? A warning? Both.

He's breathing hard, restraint written in every tense muscle. For a second, I think about what comes next—what I want to come next—and the question tumbles out before I can second-guess it.

"Do you have a condom?"

The words land like cold water. His eyes close briefly, jaw clenching. "Fuck. No."

My stomach drops with disappointment so intense it surprises me. "I don't either."

We're both quiet for a beat, the weight of that settling between us. His hand covers mine where I'm still touching him, stilling my movement.

"We don't have to—" he starts.

"I want to," I interrupt. "I just want more of you."

His gaze locks on mine, darkening with heat and frustration and something tender that makes my chest ache. "There are other ways I can make you feel good."

"Other ways we can make each other feel good," I correct, and I'm rewarded with that crooked smile.

I shift, pressing him onto his back against the pillows. When I lean down and take him in my mouth, his hand flies to the duvet, gripping hard.

I'm unpracticed, tentative at first, but the way he responds—the ragged breathing, the barely restrained sounds, the way his fingers flex against the fabric— emboldens me.

"God," he breathes, one hand gentle in my hair, not pushing, just present. Grounding.

After a moment, he tugs me up carefully, repositioning us with surprising coordination. "Come here," he murmurs, guiding me into a straddling position, facing away from him. "Let me taste you again."

The position registers—intimate, mutual, generous—and heat floods through me. When I feel his breath against my inner thigh, I lean forward, taking him back into my mouth as his hands grip my hips, pulling me down to meet his tongue.

The dual sensation hits immediately and I lose coherent thought. His mouth is warm and deliberate, his tongue finding the exact place that makes my thighs clench, while I take him deeper, learning him by sound—the sharp exhale when I change pressure, the low groan that vibrates against me when I find what he can't control. We move together, finding a rhythm that keeps shifting as we each chase the other's response, and the intimacy of it—giving and receiving at once, each of us trying to take the other apart—is unlike anything I've experienced. I can't perform. Can't manage. Can only feel.

His fingers join his mouth, and I lose the rhythm entirely. I feel myself building again, impossibly fast, and I break first —pulling back, gasping his name, my whole body shuddering through it. The vibration and my response seem to tip him over the edge. His hips jerk upward and I taste him—salt and heat—as he finds his release.

When we finally break apart—both of us wrecked, sated, undone—it's with shaking hands and racing hearts.

He pulls me against him, and I settle into the curve of his body, my head on his chest. His heartbeat is still elevated, matching my own.

"That was…" He exhales, like he's steadying himself. "I've been thinking about that all week." He presses his lips to my hair. "Next time, I want all of you."

"That was…more than I expected," I murmur against his chest.

"In a good way?"

"Oh, yes."

He huffs a quiet laugh, his fingers tracing lazy patterns on my shoulder. "Good. Because I'm not planning to stop there."

His arm tightens around me, and the room goes quiet. For a long moment, we don't speak. Maybe there's nothing to say. Maybe this exists outside of words and plans and careful control. I should feel regret. Guilt. The familiar urge to analyze every decision. Instead, I feel…quiet. Like something wound too tight has finally released.

My phone buzzes on the nightstand—twice, then three times. Work. Always work. I ignore it. Tomorrow I'll worry about what this means. Tonight, I'm letting myself have this rare and terrifying gift of surrender.

CHAPTER
THIRTEEN

NOAH

She's still catching her breath when her phone starts buzzing on the nightstand.

Once. Twice. Three times.

Alicia stiffens slightly against me, and I feel the shift rather than see it—that subtle tensing of muscles, the mental gears starting to turn again.

"You should get that," I say, even though I don't want her to.

"It can wait."

But her eyes are already tracking the screen, reading the preview text even from here. It can't wait. We both know it. She slips from the bed, gathering clothes with practiced efficiency—no self-consciousness, no hesitation. Just movement with purpose. When she steps into the bathroom, I hear the water run briefly, and when she emerges minutes later, she's already transforming. Hair smoothed. Blouse buttoned. Every trace of what just happened carefully tucked away. She moves to her office without looking at me, phone pressed to her ear. Through the open door, I hear her voice—steady, composed, utterly different from the woman who trembled in my arms ten minutes ago.

"This is Alicia Morgan." The response on the other end is frantic, male, panicked. I catch fragments: "…video…everywhere…board sees this…"

"Okay, breathe. You have twenty minutes before the evening cycle picks it up." Her tone is surgical. "I'll text you what to say. And for God's sake, don't delete the post. It looks guilty."

He keeps talking, frantic. She cuts him off—calm, professional, surgical. "No, you don't get to control the story. You respond with transparency and you move forward. You hired me for damage control, not miracles."

There's a silence, then the sound of her keystrokes.

I pull on my jeans, every trace of earlier heat replaced by something else entirely. Admiration, mostly. Maybe a little awe.

When she emerges from her office a few minutes later, she could be anyone's crisis manager—polished, untouchable, the version of herself the rest of the world sees.

I'm leaning against the doorframe when she passes through the bedroom, professional smile in place, like she can compartmentalize everything—including me.

"I need to send a few emails," she says, not quite meeting my eyes. "Rain check on dinner?"

"Sure." I watch her disappear into her office, and the click of the door feels deliberate. I stand there in her bedroom— sheets tangled, the scent of her perfume still on my skin— and realize two things.

One: I want her again. More than I should.

Two: Getting close to Alicia Morgan is going to be a challenge.

I should feel regret. This crossed every professional line Gabriel and I discussed. But regret requires thinking you made the wrong choice, and standing here in her bedroom, I can't bring myself to believe that. What I did feel was the shift—the moment she went from Alicia-the-woman to Alicia-the-crisis-manager. Seamless. Instant. Like she has an internal switch and someone just flipped it.

I've been around controlled people before. Military guys who could compartmentalize anything. But this? This is different. She's not shutting down emotion—she's filing it away, categorizing it, deciding when and how to access it again. It's impressive as hell. It's also unnerving. Because if she can do that with what just happened between us—tuck it away like a completed task—where does that leave me?

An hour later, I'm in the basement, checking the perimeter cameras for the third time when I hear her footsteps on the stairs.

She appears in the doorway—still dressed, still composed, but there's something softer around her eyes now. Tired, maybe. Or just human again.

"Hey," she says.

"Hey."

For a moment, neither of us speaks. The monitors flicker blue light across her face.

"I'm sorry about earlier," she says. "The call. I didn't mean to just—"

"You don't need to apologize." I lean back in the chair. "It's your job."

"Still." She crosses her arms, not quite stepping into the room. "That rain check—I actually mean it."

"Whenever you want."

She nods, then hesitates. Like she wants to say something else but can't quite find the words. "Stella comes home tomorrow after school."

"I know."

"So we should probably…" She trails off, but I understand.

"Keep things professional when she's around," I finish.

"Yeah."

The understanding hangs between us—loaded with everything we're not saying. That this changes things. That we both know it. That neither of us is sure what comes next.

"Alicia." I wait until she meets my eyes. "I don't regret it."

Something flickers across her face—surprise, maybe, or relief. "Good," she says quietly. "Neither do I."

She turns to go, then pauses at the doorway. "Goodnight, Noah."

"Goodnight."

I watch her climb the stairs, and this time, I don't look away.

Later, lying on the bed in the basement, I stare at the ceiling and try to make sense of what happened today.

The job hasn't changed. Alicia still needs protection. We have every reason to believe someone might be willing to harm her to prevent her from testifying. Delacroix's murder is still unsolved. Richard's a variable I don't trust, but I've got nothing other than gut instinct on that one.

But everything else?

Everything else just got a hell of a lot more complicated.

I should call Gabriel. Tell him what happened. Get reassigned before this becomes a bigger problem than it already is. But I won't.

Instead, I close my eyes and see her face—the way she looked up at me, vulnerable and open, before the walls came back up.

Yeah. I'm not going anywhere.

FOURTEEN

ALICIA

On Monday, Stella climbs out of a blue Rivian.

"Larry, I'm going to need to drop off. Jane will wrap up."

It's a client conference call, and I don't wait for a response.

I'm down the stairs and opening the front door before Stella's feet hit the front step.

"There you are. How'd it go?" I'm reaching for her overnight bag. She keeps clothes at both houses, but she spends more time here and often carries a duffel bag with her to her father's.

"Good." She gives me a quick hug and then rushes through the house, headed straight to the stairs. "Bye, Jessica," she calls.

At that, my attention turns to Jessica. She's parked—illegally—on the curb in front of my house.

"Thanks for bringing her home. Did Richard get caught up with work?" He usually texts me when he's running late. I begrudgingly allowed him to be the one to pick Stella up from school—it seemed only fair, given I usually drop her off. But this morning, he dropped her off. But it's not a big deal, and there's no reason to squabble like children.

"Yes, he got hung up, so he called me. I don't mind. With raising kids, it takes a village, right?"

She smiles and inside I cringe, but step outside the front door, pulling it closed to keep the chill out.

She continues, presumably defending Richard. "We all have flexible schedules, but unexpected things come up. Happens to the best of us, right?"

She's stepped closer, onto the bottom step, and I should probably invite her in, but instead I ask, "What is it that you do?"

Richard really hasn't told me much about her, but then again, I haven't asked.

"Oh, I'm in pharmaceutical sales. My territory is the northeast, so I travel quite a bit, but I also have a team under me. That helps—you know, cut down on the travel."

"Right," I nod. "I'm sure."

"You travel to Manhattan quite a bit, don't you?"

I inhale, taking in the woman before me. She's dressed like any of my friends would be, in a professional business suit—but unlike my friends, she's dating my ex—and that really should not be a problem.

"I go into the city quite a bit. The flight to LaGuardia runs more frequently than the train."

"So it's usually a day trip for you then?"

"Well, yeah. I have Stella during the week."

"Right, well you know, Richard and I don't mind keeping her on a weeknight."

"Oh, I know." *It's also not your business—not yet.*

She averts her gaze, looking down the street to her right. "Richard's been really worried."

"About?"

She wraps her arms around her middle, and I mirror her —the wind is brisk and unlike her, I'm not wearing a trench coat.

"Well, you know, the murder investigation. How are you holding up?"

"Me?"

"I mean, you've got security, you must be worried, right?"

"The security has nothing to do with…" I'm not even sure where to go with this because I'm not about to tell Jessica what project I worked on that has my friends worried enough to insist on security.

"Right. Of course. I guess you had them before didn't you? I just get things mixed up sometimes."

She smiles and lightly giggles and it rubs me the wrong way—but in all fairness, everything she does rubs me the wrong way lately, and I probably need to spend some self-reflection time to determine why.

"Richard's just worried that if someone might come after you, they might come after Stella. And I know the custody arrangement is spelled out but it would seem to me that if Stella's safety were in question, you'd overlook that—temporarily at least—and let her stay where it's safest."

"Stella is—"

"I'm not meaning to get involved where I'm not wanted, but sometimes, I mean, you know Richard, he's not always great at representing his interests."

"The Richard I know is excellent at representing his interests. He's a lawyer."

She giggles—again. "If I'm honest, I don't like seeing him worried. He's a good man, you know?"

"Yes." What else am I supposed to say to that? "Thank you for bringing Stella home." Ready to end this conversation, I add a pleasant, "Goodnight." I stay in the doorway—one hand on the frame, Stella already inside.

"Anytime. I just love her."

Jessica smiles and slowly turns down the brick path, her heels clicking with each step. The sound echoes in the evening air—sharp, deliberate, confident. Her car beeps, lights flash, and a second later the Rivian eases away from the curb.

I close the door and lean against it for a second, palms flat against the cool wood. A child can never have too much love, I remind myself. Gratitude, not irritation. That's the mantra. Still, the scent of Jessica's perfume lingers, and it takes a deliberate breath to shake it off.

Upstairs, Stella's sprawled on her bed, half-listening, half-typing, perfectly unbothered. Her world is intact. Mine feels slightly off-kilter.

"Chicken parm for dinner. You good with that?"

"Sure. That's fine." She barely glances up.

"The weekend was good?"

"Yeah."

"And dinner last night?"

She tilts her head back in what's the equivalent of a full-body eyeroll. "Mom…it lasted forever. It should've been a date night for the two of them. I don't know why I had to be there."

"Where'd you go?"

"Some place that takes forever and sets out a dozen silverware options."

"You knew what to do with each of those forks and knives, right?"

"And the spoons, Mom. Doesn't mean I liked it."

"As long as you behaved."

"I'm just glad I don't have to go there this coming weekend. And speaking of, you remember I've got Madeline's birthday sleepover this Friday, right?"

"Of course. I haven't forgotten."

"We need to buy her a birthday gift."

"Right. You don't have play practice Wednesday, right?"

She nods.

"We'll do it then." I slip out my phone and make a notation on my calendar. When I look up, Stella's back to messaging friends on her iPad. "Dinner in twenty."

I don't wait for a response. I'll try and get more out of her later.

When I descend the stairs again, the house smells of simmering tomato sauce and garlic. I focus on the familiar rhythm—chop, stir, taste—grateful for the mundane. It's easier to think about dinner than about the fact that less than twenty-four hours ago, Noah's hands were on my skin, his mouth everywhere, my name on his lips.

Stella's tennis shoe is in the middle of a step, and I nearly go down, catching myself on the banister. Right. Boundaries. Stella's home, and whatever happened yesterday exists in a separate compartment now. I'm excellent at compartmentalizing. Even if my body hasn't quite gotten the memo yet.

Noah approaches from the front hall, shoulders filling the space, and my body registers his presence before my mind catches up—muscle memory from last night making me hyperaware of how close he's standing. I force my voice to be steady.

"Hi," I say. "When did you get back?"

His eyes meet mine briefly, and there's something there—recognition, heat, careful restraint—before he blinks it away.

Noah followed me to the office this morning, met with Gabriel, and then went on his way to meetings.

"About ten minutes ago. Relieved Gabe. Did a loop around the property." He studies me briefly, and I wonder if he's thinking about last night too—wondering how we navigate this now that Stella's home. But there's something else in the way he's hesitating that sets me on edge. "Did you know you left your liftgate open?"

"That's not possible. I didn't get anything out of it." The defensiveness in my voice surprises me. "Was anything taken?"

He shakes his head. "Was anything in there?"

I try to remember. "I don't think so."

"All I saw was an emergency medical kit tucked to the side. And the bag that came with the car for the chargers."

That fits. "Maybe someone was checking for packages." The thought feels flimsy even as I say it. My car's behind the gate; no one should've been close enough to touch it. "You think someone climbed the fence?" I ask quietly.

He lifts a shoulder. "I'll check the perimeter tapes. Are you in for the night?"

I nod. "Dinner with Stella, then emails. The usual."

"Set the alarm," he says, already turning for the stairs.

"Chicken parm if you're hungry."

"Already ate." He glances back once, something unreadable passing across his face. "But thanks."

And then he's gone, disappearing into the lower level where the screens flicker blue and the world outside disappears.

The house feels different once he's out of sight—like the air has thinned. I ladle sauce onto plates, but my thoughts bounce between the car, and Jessica's easy smile, and the way she'd said they don't mind keeping Stella.

It takes me until Stella's in bed, her door cracked open, before I give in and go find Noah.

Downstairs, faint light spills from the security room. Noah's seated in front of the monitors, sleeves rolled to his forearms, focus absolute.

For a moment I just watch him—the steady precision, the way his shoulders fill the chair, the contrast to the chaos always threatening to seep into my world. My fingers remember the feel of those shoulders. My mouth remembers—

Stop.

I clear my throat. "You find anything?"

He swivels slightly, not startled but aware. His gaze travels over me—quick, assessing—and I wonder if he's remembering too. If he's thinking about how different this feels now.

"Not yet. Cameras don't cover where you parked."

"That's…comforting," I murmur.

He exhales through his nose, a sound that's half-sigh, half-quiet laugh. "I'll adjust the angles."

I cross my arms, mostly to keep from fidgeting. We haven't talked about yesterday. Haven't acknowledged it beyond those loaded glances. And with Stella upstairs, this isn't the time.

"Do you think someone was in the carport?"

"Could've been nothing." His tone is steady, but I hear the could more than the nothing. "Could've been curiosity. Or opportunity."

I nod, pulse ticking faster—though whether from the trunk situation or from standing this close to him, I'm not entirely sure.

"Jessica mentioned earlier that Richard's worried someone might come after me. I brushed it off."

Noah looks up then, eyes steady on mine. Something passes between us—concern, yes, but also that same heat from earlier. Banked but present.

"You did the right thing."

"By brushing it off?"

"By not letting her see it rattled you."

The corner of my mouth lifts. "You think it did?"

"I think you wouldn't be down here if it didn't."

He's not wrong. But there's more than one reason I'm down here, and we both know it.

His gaze holds mine a beat longer than necessary, and I feel it everywhere—that pull, that wanting. Then he deliberately turns back to the monitors.

"I'll keep checking the footage," he says. Professional. Careful. "You should get some sleep."

"Yeah." I don't move immediately. "Goodnight, Noah."

"Goodnight, Alicia."

When I climb the stairs, his calm, unflinching presence follows me—along with the memory of how very different he was last night when that control finally broke.

CHAPTER
FIFTEEN

NOAH

Tuesday morning, I'm parked down the street, waiting for Alicia to pull out. It's 7:05 on the dot. Like clockwork. I know other things about her timing now too. How long it takes her breathing to settle after she comes. The exact moment her walls go back up. How she looks in the morning light with her hair still mussed and her defenses down.

Focus, Bennett.

The punctuality—admirable for a CEO. Dangerous for someone with a target on her back. Routine makes you predictable, and predictable makes you vulnerable.

The plan's simple: follow her to the office where Gabe's on duty. I've got a nine a.m. call with Hudson, then a run while the morning's still sharp. I need the run. Need to work off the restless energy that's been building since Sunday night. Since Alicia.

Her Rivian glides from the driveway. I let two cars pass before easing into traffic. As I roll by her corner lot, I glance at the house. With the blinds up, it's a fishbowl—clean lines, big windows, nowhere to hide.

I know which room is hers now. Know the view from her bedroom window, the softness of her sheets, the way afternoon light filters through those curtains. Know things I shouldn't know about a client. Except she's not exactly just a client anymore, is she?

The fishbowl layout bothers me more now. Makes observation too easy. Maybe that doesn't concern her. When working from home, she spends most of her time on the second floor. Still, it makes me uneasy in ways that have nothing to do with the job.

We've had no credible threats. She's agreed to appear before a Senate subcommittee in a closed-door session—untelevised, more about managing political fallout than pursuing justice. If she's called by prosecution into the case against the man who extorted the senator, that'll be public. If there's a televised congressional hearing regarding the deceased chief of staff, that'll be a bigger deal.

My take? Visibility keeps her safe. The guilty prefer shadows, not spotlights. These aren't mobsters; they're polished power brokers with donors and photo ops to protect. They'll bury evidence long before they risk a hit that invites the FBI to dinner.

At least, that's what my gut says—though my gut didn't see the White House Chief of Staff moonlighting as an intel broker either.

Alicia drops Stella at school, right on schedule—7:25—and turns toward her office. Clockwork.

At 7:40 she pulls into the parking lot at Morgan & Company, one of those bland beige blocks that could house anything from accountants to assassins. Gabe's already there.

He gives me a nod; I return it and drive a block up before looping back toward her house. I want to be on a secure line for the call.

That's when a flash of blonde catches my eye outside the corner coffee shop—Novel Grounds.

Jessica.

I slide into a spot across the street. Pharmaceutical sales reps meet clients everywhere, but the coincidence prickles.

Through the windshield, I watch her exit the shop with two coffees. She moves with purpose, heading to a sedan parked four spaces down. The driver lowers his window. She leans in, speaking low. No smile. No small talk.

I lift my phone and zoom. Not Richard. The man's younger—mid-thirties, light brown hair, average build. I snap two photos. Jessica gestures once, quick, precise. Then she straightens and looks across the street.

I freeze, turning my head just enough that she gets a side view, not a face. With the glare on the glass, she probably can't make out detail. This block's busy enough that a parked car shouldn't raise suspicion.

Jessica walks off. A block over, a Rivian that's identical to Alicia's, only a different color, flashes as she unlocks it. That's her destination. I send the photos to Gabe.

The sedan makes a U-turn, heading the opposite direction. I capture a shot of Jessica's license plate and send that too.

My phone rings seconds later.

"What've we got?" Gabe asks.

"Probably nothing," I say. "Richard Whitmore's girlfriend brought coffee to a guy in a sedan—mid-thirties, average build. Thirty-second chat, then gone."

"Copy. I'll keep an eye out."

"Good. You keeping a low profile?"

"If anyone's watching, they'll know we're here," he says. "That's the point."

He's right. Sometimes the visible guard deters more than the hidden one.

"Roger that. You joining the nine o'clock?"

"Negative. Alicia's got a nine-thirty. Wouldn't let me follow her, so driving her was the compromise."

"She still resisting?"

"She's not a fan."

I smile as I end the call. A woman like Alicia Morgan doesn't admit weakness. She draws lines everywhere she can—no follow cars, no sitting in on meetings—then quietly moves the line when something rattles her. That open liftgate rattled her more than she'll say.

Back at the house, I log into the secure portal. Hudson's face fills one square, Jake another, Quinn's bright eyes and glasses a third.

"Aren't you two in the same place?" I ask.

"We are," Quinn says. "But this is faster."

Hudson nods. "Quick update. No movement on the Delacroix investigation. Our source says his wife's now listed as a person of interest."

Jake whistles. "Bet that happened five minutes after they called it a homicide."

"She wasn't at the event, right?" I ask.

"No," Quinn says. "Rock-solid alibi—league tennis match that morning. But that doesn't rule out a hire."

"Wouldn't be the first," Hudson mutters. "Jake?"

Jake leans back, casual as ever. "Been making the rounds—coffee shops, DC watering holes. Talked to a reporter from *The Hill*. Says the congressional inquiry's yesterday's news.

Focus has shifted to Argentina's bailout and that public-land housing bill."

"That makes no sense," Quinn says. "Urban areas need housing, not national forests."

Jake grins. "Since when has logic led the charge?"

They keep talking politics, but my mind drifts back to Jessica—her quick glance across the street, the man's neutral face. Something about it itches.

And if I'm being honest, my mind also drifts to the way Alicia's fingers traced my collarbone Sunday night. The sound she made when I—

"Noah? You still with us?"

Hudson's voice snaps me back. Jake's grinning like he knows exactly where my head went.

"Yeah. Sorry. Thought I heard something."

"All clear on your end?" Hudson asks.

"All clear." Mostly. If you don't count the fact that I can't stop thinking about my principal in ways that would get me fired off any other detail.

"Good. Regroup next week."

Quinn wraps with financial accounts tied to Magpie's network, then we disconnect.

I don't mention Jessica's coffee run. Gabe has the images. If he sees her or the sedan near Alicia's office again, we'll revisit.

The rest of the day slides into rhythm. Seven-mile run—harder than usual, pushing until my lungs burn and my thoughts finally quiet. Kickboxing at the gym, where I can hit something and pretend I'm not thinking about the curve of Alicia's hip or the way she said my name.

It doesn't work. By the time I'm showering off, I've replayed Sunday night three times. The way she looked up at me. The way she tasted. The moment she transformed back into the crisis manager, walls snapping into place like she could compartmentalize anything—including me.

We haven't talked about it. Haven't acknowledged it beyond careful distance yesterday when Stella was home. And I don't know what the hell happens next.

Late lunch with Jake and Daisy helps. Jake talks about sofas—apparently there's a war over what's best—and it's normal enough that I almost convince myself I can handle this.

Back at the house, I review camera angles and add one more unit under the ivy for a clean line on the brick fence that rings the property.

My phone buzzes.

The Queen in transit to the castle.

Gabe's code for Alicia heading home.

I check the time—early. She had meetings until five, Stella's rehearsal until eight.

My pulse spikes before my brain registers why. Stella's still gone. We're alone. And Alicia's coming home early.

Could mean nothing. Could mean she wants to work from home. Or—I tell myself not to read into it, but my body's already responding to the possibility. From the basement feed, I watch the gate swing open, the Rivian glide in. The front door closes. Heels click across hardwood—each step sharp, deliberate. Instead of heading up to her office like she usually does, the sound grows louder. Heading down. Toward me. Every nerve ending goes on alert—and not the professional kind.

I step into the hall as she appears at the bottom of the stairs.

"Light day at the office?"

"Client canceled." Her eyes find mine—that stunning blue, completely unreadable. "I've been thinking about something."

I wait, pulse edging up despite myself. We're alone. She's here. It's highly unlikely she's about to say what I'm hoping.

"About what happened between us."

There it is.

I brace for the regret speech—the one where she explains this was a mistake, we crossed a line, it can't happen again. I've heard versions of it before, though never from someone I wanted this much.

Except—

"I can't stop thinking about it," she says quietly.

The words hit like a gut punch in the best possible way.

She places her handbag down, and there's something deliberate in the movement. Something that makes my mouth go dry.

"I went to the store. Stella's practice runs late tonight."

It takes me a beat too long to process. She bought condoms. She came home early. She's telling me—

"If you don't want—"

"I want." I close the distance between us in two strides, my hand finding her waist. "I've been thinking about you since Sunday. Been trying like hell to focus on anything else."

"And?"

"Failing." I pull her closer, feeling her heartbeat against my chest. "Completely failing."

CHAPTER
SIXTEEN

ALICIA

"Completely failing."

Something in my chest loosens. He's been thinking about me too. Struggling the same way I have. I'm not alone in this.

His hand is still on my waist, solid and sure, and I let myself lean into him for just a second—let myself feel the relief of mutual want before my brain kicks back in with all its careful calculations.

I reach into my bag and pull out the small box. Set it on the console table. The sound of cardboard against wood is absurdly loud in the quiet space—final, irrevocable.

His eyes drop to the box. Back to me.

Something dark and hungry flashes across his face, and I watch his throat work as he swallows. When he speaks, his voice is rougher than before. "You went shopping."

"I did."

"For this?"

"For us." I meet his gaze directly, refusing to be embarrassed. "We have a couple of hours."

For a beat, he doesn't move. Doesn't speak. Just looks at me with an intensity that makes my pulse skip.

I may have miscalculated this. Maybe he's already decided this is a mistake. Maybe the reality of premeditated sex feels different than the spontaneous heat of Sunday night.

"If you don't want—"

"I want." He closes the distance between us in one stride. "God, Alicia, I want."

Relief and desire flood through me in equal measure. Suddenly he's there—close enough that I can feel the heat radiating off him, smell the faint scent of soap.

I reach up, fingers curling into the front of his shirt. "Stop making me wait."

His hands find my waist, but he doesn't pull me closer. Doesn't kiss me. Just looks at me with an intensity I feel everywhere.

"I absolutely want this. But you're sure?"

"I know what I'm doing." I tug him toward the den, toward the sectional sofa bathed in the gray light filtering through the high windows. No one can see in. We're completely alone. "I want this. I need *this*."

What I don't say: *I need to stop obsessing. I need to get this out of my system so I can focus on the hundred other things demanding my attention. And all I've been able to think about in every quiet moment is what he'd feel like inside me, how he'd stretch me.*

His mouth crashes onto mine. His hands tighten on my waist, pulling me flush against him, and all those careful rationalizations of how this is to get it out of my system scatter.

This isn't about putting something behind me. This is about want. Pure and simple.

I break the kiss long enough to pull his shirt over his head, my hands immediately finding the warm, solid planes of his chest. He's beautiful—and I let myself look, because I planned this and I'm not going to be coy about it now. Lean muscle, bronze skin, a body built by discipline rather than vanity. A scar bisects his left ribs—thin, old, faded to silver—and I trace it without thinking, feeling the way his breath catches when my fingers drag lower. He's warm everywhere. Warmer than I expected. I press my palm flat against his sternum and feel his heart hammering.

Good. I'm not alone in this.

"You're overdressed," he murmurs against my mouth, fingers already working the buttons of my blouse.

"Then do something about it."

His laugh is low and sinful, and then my blouse is sliding off my shoulders, pooling at my feet. His hands span my waist, thumbs brushing the underside of my ribs, and I shiver despite the warmth of the room. I stand long enough to step out of my pants, and the way his eyes track down my body is worth every second of lost contact.

"Fuck—when I close my eyes, this is what I see," he says, fingers tracing skin, lips close behind.

I reach for his belt, fingers steady despite the urgent need building. "I'm in charge today."

Not because I want to dominate him—but because I don't want to feel unmoored.

Something flares in his eyes—surprise, maybe, or approval—and he lets me push him back onto the sofa. I follow him down, straddling his lap, and the feel of him hard beneath me sends a jolt of pure want through my system.

"Alicia—" He breathes my name, hands finding my hips, steadying me, pressing me hard against him exactly where I need friction.

I kiss him again, deeper this time, and when I rock against him, the groan he makes is the most satisfying sound I've ever heard.

This. This is what I needed. Not control. Not strategy. Just *feeling*.

His mouth finds the curve of my neck, and I arch into the touch, head falling back as his lips trace a path down my sternum. When his hand slides up my back to unclasp my bra, I don't stop him. When the fabric falls away and his mouth closes over my breast, I cry out—sharp and unrestrained.

"I've been thinking about this," he murmurs against my skin. "About you. Every goddamn minute." His mouth drags along my collarbone. "I kept thinking about what you'd feel like." His voice is rough, almost reluctant. "Whether I could make you lose that control you hold onto so tight."

I should feel powerful, being the object of his desire. Instead, I feel *wanted*—and that's somehow more intoxicating.

I reach between us, freeing him from his jeans, and when I wrap my hand around him, his hips jerk involuntarily. He's hard and hot in my palm, and the sound he makes when I stroke him is pure desperation.

"Condom," I manage, voice ragged. "Now."

He reaches for the box I set down—already here, already within reach because I planned this, engineered this—and tears a condom open with shaking hands. I watch as he rolls it on, and the sight of him—hard, ready, because of me—makes me ache.

His hands find my hips, drawing me over him. I brace

against his shoulders, and for a moment we just stay there—poised, hovering—his eyes on mine in the gray light. His jaw is tight with the effort of waiting. Letting me set the pace. Giving me the control I came down here needing.

I line myself up and hold his gaze as I take him in—slow, deliberate, one inch at a time, because I want to feel every second of this.

The stretch is—God. It's exactly what I imagined and nothing like it. The fullness is almost too much, and I stop halfway, breathing through it, adjusting, while his jaw goes tight and his hands grip my hips hard enough to bruise. He holds perfectly still, giving me the control I said I needed.

I take the rest of him in one slow sink and we both go still.

I've forgotten what this feels like, being joined with some-one, and with Noah it's somehow more intense than I remember.

"Okay?" he asks through gritted teeth, hands gripping my hips like he's fighting for control.

"Perfect," I breathe, and then I move.

The rhythm comes without negotiation—my hips rolling, his hands at my waist tightening, guiding, pressing me down as I rise. I set the pace, and he lets me, and for a while that's enough: the slow drag of him inside me, the friction building with each roll of my hips, the sounds I'm making that I'd be embarrassed about if I had any capacity left for embar-rassment.

He watches me with dark, heated eyes that see too much. That's the part I didn't account for. I planned for the physical. I didn't plan for being *seen* while it was happening.

I kiss him just to have somewhere to put that feeling.

I wanted control. I wanted to dictate the terms, keep this physical, manageable.

But my body doesn't recognize those rules. It only recognizes him.

When his thumb finds the sensitive bundle of nerves between us—when he starts moving in counterpoint to my rhythm—control becomes irrelevant.

"Noah—" His name breaks on my lips, and I'm not in charge anymore. I'm just a woman chasing sensation, chasing release, chasing something I can't name.

"I've got you," he murmurs, one hand sliding up to cup the back of my neck, bringing my forehead to his as his hips thrust upward, hitting a spot that has me gasping.

"There—"

The sofa creaks. My muscles tighten. Even my toes curl so tight pain laces ecstasy.

"That's it. Let go."

The world narrows to friction and breath and the relentless press of him inside me.

When I shatter, there's no graceful way to describe it. My thighs clamp against his hips, my back arches, and the sound I make is nothing I'd ever willingly produce in front of another person—sharp and raw and entirely beyond my control. His name breaks off somewhere in the middle of it. Every muscle in my body seizes and then releases in waves, pleasure so acute it tips briefly into pain before it dissolves into something I have no word for.

He follows moments later, his grip tightening, hips stuttering as he groans my name into my hair—like it's the only word he knows, like he's using it to anchor himself.

Afterward, we stay tangled together—my head on his shoulder, his arms wrapped around me, both of us breathing hard. The basement is cool, but his body is warm and solid. Grounding.

I should move. Should say something light and dismissive, establish boundaries, remind us both that this was just physical release.

Instead, I close my eyes and let myself stay right here.

His fingers trace lazy patterns on my back, and I feel the rumble of his voice when he finally speaks. "You okay?"

"Mmm." It's not an answer, but it's all I can manage.

He shifts slightly, and I feel him slip free. The loss makes me want to protest, but he just reaches for the throw blanket draped over the sofa back and wraps it around my shoulders.

The gesture—so careful, so considerate—tightens my throat in a way sex never does.

"Alicia." He tips my chin up, forcing me to meet his eyes. "That was…"

"Necessary," I finish, cutting him off. Trying to rebuild walls even though we're still pressed together, his heart still racing against mine. The response may have been instinctive, but it felt unnecessarily harsh. "I needed… I couldn't stop thinking about it. About you."

The admission isn't shared easily, and I see him register it —see the way his expression shifts from disappointment to something softer.

"So this was you focusing?" His thumb traces my collarbone, and I shiver.

"This was me giving up on trying to focus." The truth slips out without any editing. "I told myself I could compartmentalize. Apparently I was wrong."

"Right. Of course."

Except it doesn't feel right. It feels like a lie.

But I'm good at lies, at compartmentalizing, at building

walls around the things that scare me. And whatever this is with Noah—whatever's happening between us—unnerves me more than any threat Dorian's conjured.

"Stella will be home in a couple hours," I say, standing on unsteady legs and gathering my scattered clothes. "I should shower. Get dinner started."

"Alicia—"

"Thank you," I interrupt, not looking at him. If I look at him, I'll lose my nerve. "For...this. It helped."

The silence that follows is uncomfortable, weighted with everything I'm not saying.

When I finally glance back, he's watching me with an expression I can't quite read—hurt, maybe, or understanding. Possibly both.

"Anytime," he says quietly, but there's a slowness to the word, like he doesn't mean it.

I gather the rest of my things and head for the stairs, acutely aware of his gaze following me. At the bottom step, I pause.

"Noah?"

"Yeah?"

I should say something meaningful. Something honest. Instead, I chicken out. "Put away the condoms. We don't need Stella finding those."

His laugh is soft, lacking its usual warmth. "Copy that."

I climb the stairs, and with each step, the weight of what just happened settles more heavily on my shoulders.

I told myself this would help me focus. That satisfying this craving would sate the unfinished between us and nip this in the bud.

But as I step into my bedroom and catch sight of my

reflection—flushed cheeks, swollen lips, eyes too bright—I know the truth.

This didn't help at all.

If anything, I'm more distracted than ever.

Because now I know exactly what I'm trying *not* to think about. And Noah Bennett—patient, careful, devastatingly thorough Noah Bennett—is all I can see when I close my eyes.

Worse, he's what I feel when I open them.

I step into the shower and let the hot water wash away the evidence of what we've done.

But it can't wash away the feeling.

I should've known better.

CHAPTER
SEVENTEEN

NOAH

I'm halfway through disposing of the condom and straightening the basement when her words hit me fully.

Thank you. It helped.

My hands still on the throw blanket I'm refolding.

Helped. Like I'm a massage therapist or a stress ball. Something useful. Forgettable.

I've had casual hookups. I've had relationships that didn't work out. Hell, I once had a woman tell me straight up I wasn't enough for her. But this—Alicia's careful categorization of what just happened as necessary rather than wanted —lands differently.

Because for me? That wasn't casual.

That was closer to everything.

I grab the box of condoms from the console table—tuck them in the drawer under the security monitors where Stella won't accidentally find them. Following orders, even when I'm annoyed about it.

I finish straightening up, pull on my clothes with more force than necessary. Grab leftover Thai from the kitchenette fridge. I'm not hungry, but eating gives my hands something to do that isn't texting Hudson to request reassignment.

I pull up security feeds on my tablet, but the words keep replaying. *Thank you. It helped.*

Like I solved a problem for her. A task she completed.

The shower turns on upstairs—faint through the ceiling but audible. I track the sound of her moving through her routine. Door closing. Drawers opening. She's putting herself back together. In every sense.

I don't expect her to come back down. Smart money says she avoids me until Stella gets home and we can pretend this didn't happen.

Which is why, twenty minutes later, when I hear footsteps on the stairs, my head snaps up.

I set the tablet down and stand as she appears—barefoot now, in soft gray lounge pants and an oversized sweater that slides off one shoulder. Her hair is damp, face scrubbed clean. She looks younger without makeup—more vulnerable, more real—and it takes effort not to reach for her.

"Hey," she says, stopping at the bottom step.

"Hey."

She glances at the empty takeout container. "You ate."

"Didn't think you'd be back down." I lean against the counter, arms crossed. "Figured you'd avoid me."

Her mouth twitches. "I have no plans to avoid you."

"Liar."

That gets a small smile.

"It may have crossed my mind but I don't practice avoidance."

The silence stretches, and I let it. I'm not going to make this easy for her.

She steps into the kitchenette, opens the fridge, pulls out a bottle of water. Unscrews the cap. Takes a sip. Classic Alicia—buying time, organizing her thoughts.

Finally, she turns to face me. "About earlier—"

"You needed to get it out of your system," I finish, keeping my voice level. "So you could focus. I remember."

She winces. "Noah—"

"Look, I'm happy to help you meet your needs," I say, and her eyes widen slightly at the edge in my tone. "But if we're doing this again—and I'm assuming that's why you're down here—I'm going to request that dinner date."

"Noah—"

"I'm not asking for a ring, Alicia. Just dinner." Something normal. Something that doesn't disappear the moment it's over. "Maybe some conversation where we're both wearing clothes."

She sets the water bottle down with more force than necessary. "We've shared plenty of conversations."

"About Stella. About your work. Surface-level shit." I push off the counter. "I don't even know your middle name."

"It's Marie."

"See? Progress." I take a step closer. "What's your favorite movie?"

She blinks. "What?"

"Favorite movie. It's a simple question."

"I don't...I don't watch a lot of movies."

"Favorite book, then."

"Why does this matter?"

"Because I know how you sound when you come, and I don't know your favorite book."

Her cheeks flush, and I see her debate retreat—shoulders tensing, walls going up.

"There's a ten-year age difference," she says quietly. "You're thirty-one. I'm forty-one. That matters."

"To whom?"

"To everyone. To you, eventually."

I shake my head. "You planning to stay single for the next six years? Waiting until Stella's grown before you let yourself have something?"

"That's not—"

"Because that's a lonely road, Alicia." I don't raise my voice—but I don't soften it either. "And for what? To avoid some imaginary judgment?"

"It's not imaginary." Her voice hardens. "People will talk. They'll assume things about you—about me. That I'm desperate, that you're using me for—"

"For what? Your money? Your connections?" I step closer, close enough to sense her tension. "I stopped caring what people think a long time ago. Turned out to be the best decision I ever made. Now, I don't give a damn what others think. And frankly, I'm surprised you do."

She takes a half-step back—instinctive—then stops herself. Forces her ground.

"I have to care. I have a daughter. A business. A reputation—"

"Built on fixing other people's scandals." I reach out, tuck a damp strand of hair behind her ear. "Maybe it's time to stop worrying about optics and start worrying about what you actually want."

She closes her eyes. "You don't understand."

"Then help me understand."

When she opens her eyes, there's something raw in them

—fear, maybe. "I can't afford distractions right now. My business, the investigation, Stella, Richard trying to use all this against me—"

"And you think I'm a distraction."

"I *know* you are." She laughs, but there's no humor in it. "I can't stop thinking about you. I thought if we just... If I could just get this out of my system—"

"It didn't work," I finish softly.

"No." The word is barely a whisper. "It didn't."

I cup her face, thumb brushing her cheekbone. "Good."

"That's not good, Noah. It's a problem."

"Why? Because you don't want to feel something for the guy who's supposedly beneath you?"

She flinches. "I never said—"

"You didn't have to." I drop my hand. "But here's the thing, Alicia. I'm already breaking the professional code of conduct by getting involved with a client. If I'm going to risk my career—my reputation—I need to know it's for someone who sees me as more than a convenient lay."

Hurt flashes across her face. "That's not fair."

"You came down here with condoms and a plan. You took what you wanted. And the second it was over, you couldn't get away fast enough."

"That's not—" She stops, jaw tight. "You're oversimplifying."

"Am I? Because from where I'm standing, you got what you needed and bolted."

"I had to shower. Make dinner. Stella was coming home—"

"Alicia." I wait until she meets my eyes. "If you want this to be just sex, tell me now. I can handle that. What I can't handle is you treating me like some dirty secret you need to wash off." She flinches like I've struck her. For a long moment, she just stares at me, and I watch the careful walls crack. "It scares me," she finally whispers. "This—you—all of it."

The admission vibrates in the air, and I see her immediately regret it. But she doesn't take it back.

"Why?" I ask quietly.

She wraps her arms around herself. "Because I don't do this. I don't sleep with men I barely know—"

"You know me."

"Do I?" She looks up, eyes searching mine. "What do you want, Noah? Long-term. What are you building toward?"

The question catches me off guard—because I don't expect it from her. "What do you mean?"

"You're thirty-one. You're smart, driven, good at what you do. KOAN can't be the endgame."

"You're right," I finally say. "It's not."

"So what is?" The question surprises me—that she's asking, that she's thought about it. Most people see the job and assume that's all there is. I lean back against the counter, choosing my words carefully. "You know why I left the Army?"

Her eyes narrow slightly. "I assumed standard end of enlistment."

"My mom died when I was in basic training. Cancer— fast, brutal, over before I could get home." The words still taste bitter. "I've spent years blaming myself for that. For choosing the Army over being there when she needed me."

Alicia's expression softens. "Noah—"

"When I got out, I told myself I'd choose a path that gives me more control."

"A private outfit?"

"KOAN. Yes, I'm learning the ropes. Hudson is good people. The owner, Caroline, I believe she is too. They're building something real—investigating when the government won't, protection for people who need it." I meet her eyes. "In the military, you get a window. You see your piece of the mission. The guys above you have a bigger window, bigger scope. They see more, so you learn to trust them. But I'm not a particularly patient guy. I wanted to see the full picture."

"So you left."

"So I left," I confirm. "And I came to KOAN because it's small enough that I can learn every aspect. See how it all fits together. Eventually, I'll either partner with them or start something of my own."

She's watching me with new intensity, like she's recalibrating everything she thought she knew.

"You're not just a guy doing a job," she says slowly.

"No. I'm not." I push off the counter. "I'm a guy who knows what he wants and goes after it. Who doesn't waste time on things that don't matter. And who's currently standing in a basement, breaking every professional rule he has, because the woman upstairs is the most fascinating person he's ever met."

Those stunning blue eyes flicker. "Noah—"

"You think I'm young and naive. That I don't know what I'm getting into." I step closer. "But I know exactly what I'm doing. I want this. Not because it's easy—but because it feels honest. Because I don't want to walk away wondering. I'm not afraid of taking chances. Of seeing where this goes. The question is, how brave are you?"

For a long moment, she just looks at me. Quietly, voice so low I can barely hear her, she says, "A dinner date."

"What was that?"

"You wanted a dinner date." Her mouth curves slightly. "I think I can manage that."

Something loosens in my chest. "Yeah?"

"Yeah." She steps into my space, fingers finding the hem of my shirt. "I want to know you better. The real you. Not just the night shift bodyguard. The man who—"

The front door opens upstairs.

"Mom? I'm home!"

Alicia freezes.

"Stella," she whispers, then louder: "Hey sweetheart! I'll be right up!"

She looks at me, panic and regret and something like apology all mixed together.

"Go," I say quietly.

"I'm sorry—"

"Don't be. Just go."

She hesitates, then stands on her toes and presses a quick kiss to my cheek. "Tomorrow. We'll figure it out tomorrow."

Then she's gone, footsteps light and quick on the stairs.

I hear her voice bright and easy as she greets Stella: "Hey honey! How was rehearsal? You're home early."

"Director had a migraine. We only ran through Act Two."

Their voices fade as they move deeper into the house.

I stand in the empty basement, fingers touching the spot where her lips brushed my skin, and I can't help but smile.

She said yes to dinner.

She said she wants to know me.

It's a start.

And for a man who's spent his entire life learning patience in the field but struggling with it everywhere else, I'll take it.

Upstairs, I hear Stella laugh at something Alicia said. The

sound is warm, unguarded—the sound of a mother and daughter who genuinely like each other. Who feel safe together.

And I realize that's what I want.

Not just Alicia in my bed, though God knows I want that too.

But this. The laughter. The easy domesticity. The family.

The thought should have me requesting a different assignment.

I grab my tablet and settle back onto the sofa, pulling up security feeds. Work. Something I can control while my heart figures out what the hell it's doing.

But even as I scan the cameras, check the perimeter, note the quiet street outside, I'm smiling.

Because soon, I'll take Alicia Morgan to dinner.

And maybe—just maybe—she'll stop running long enough to see what I'm starting to see.

ALICIA

Christine answers on the third ring. "Morning, lady!"

She's chipper and happy, and the flutters in my stomach won't quit. Hyperawareness, energy, joy—my body doing its best to override reason.

"Are you available for drinks after work?"

"What's wrong?"

"Why would you assume—"

"You never call in the morning. You're a morning news person. So spill."

I catch a glimpse of the black Chevy SUV three cars back, and heat flushes my skin.

"I may have hooked up with someone."

A pause. "Ho-hum or hall-of-fame?"

Despite everything, I smile. "Definitely not ho-hum."

"Age?"

"Thirty-one."

"The bodyguard!" Her delight is audible. "I don't see the problem."

"Ten years, Christine. He's barely—"

"Are you looking for a husband?"

"No."

"Then have fun! When can I meet him?"

"Saturday brunch? Stella has a sleepover Friday."

"Perfect. And Alicia? Breathe. You deserve this."

The call ends as I pull into the office parking lot. Will I introduce Noah to Christine? Maybe. It's a big step—introducing him to friends. And what if this becomes something that isn't temporary? What would Christine think then?

I glance in the rearview, spotting Noah's car, and despite the anxiety coiled in my chest, I'm smiling.

Until I see Gabriel waiting outside like a sentinel, and the smile dies.

I check the ground, looking for cigarette butts to see if he's been outside smoking, but no, it appears he's outside awaiting the official handoff.

I'm a baton. And I'm developing a teen-like crush on one of the runners, evident by the fluttering in my belly as I watch Noah's SUV pull into traffic after dutifully following me to the office.

Thankfully, once I'm through the door, my client problems take over my own. Their mistakes become my coaching opportunities. Denial, sometimes a powerful resource, is often my clients' worst enemy. It makes for an interesting day, and one that makes me feel more like a therapist than a crisis management expert.

My two o'clock meeting runs fifteen minutes over, and as soon as the call ends, I'm up and gathering my work to head to the school to pick up Stella. There's a rap on the door, and I call, "Come in."

Robert, my assistant, appears in the doorway. Something's off—his shoulders are too rigid, his usual easy smile replaced with careful neutrality. "I know, I'm running late," I say, already gathering my things.

"There's a detective here to see you." His voice is quieter than usual. "I told him you need to pick up Stella, but he said it's important."

A detective? I peer past Robert and spot the detective waiting a couple of feet away, standing near, likely so he can hear what Robert says to me.

"It's okay, Robert. I'm sure this has to do with the incident at the conference."

Robert nods and backs away, returning to his desk in the lobby.

"Detective," I say, hand outstretched. I squint to read the name that's pinned to his shirt. He's a Black man, about Noah's height, but broader in both his shoulders and midsection.

"Ms. Morgan. Thank you for seeing me. I'm Detective Lassiter."

"We didn't meet before."

"No, I'm in the homicide unit," he says, his tone deliberately friendly. "I was hoping you could come down to the precinct to answer some questions."

"I…" I swivel, looking at my desk and my tote resting in my chair. "I need to pick up my daughter. Perhaps I could schedule a time—"

"We'd appreciate your cooperation. As you can imagine, this is a high-profile case and we'd like to wrap it up as quickly as possible."

"Right." I nod, thinking through my options. They did say they might have more questions. I've coached plenty of clients that it's best to avoid the appearance of guilt. And, as inconvenient as this is, I have nothing to hide. "Well, let me see if I can make arrangements."

I pick up my cell and call Trish, one of Stella's friends' moms, and a friend. She quickly agrees to pick up Stella from school.

"This shouldn't take long. Tell Stella I'll be there soon. I haven't forgotten that we're going shopping."

My gaze connects with Detective Lassiter's and he offers a slight smile. At least, I interpret it as a smile.

Gabriel appears by the reception desk, expression tight. "I'll call Noah. Want me to—"

"I'll be fine. It's just questions."

The detective's voice drifts through my office. "An incident. Is that what you call murder?"

I inhale deeply, aware of the slight tremor running through my arms and of my chilled fingers. "That's probably not the best description," I admit.

"Shall we?"

I get my tote bag and I'm about to ask if I need a lawyer, but then I remember the advice I tell my clients, and shelve the idea. I have nothing to hide.

"I'm not sure what I can say that I haven't already shared, but I'm happy to answer your questions."

He offers to drive but I insist on driving myself. If he'd insisted on driving me, I would have called a lawyer.

At the station, he directs me through a waiting room filled with citizens and police officers, up to a second floor, then down a hall.

The precinct's second floor smells like burnt coffee and bad decisions. Detective Lassiter leads me past a bullpen of cluttered desks, each one a monument to unsolved cases and overtime hours. Officers glance up as we pass—some with curiosity, others with the blank stare of those who've seen too many "persons of interest" to care.

Room 204. He holds the door, gesturing me inside with practiced courtesy that doesn't reach his eyes.

The interrogation room is exactly what Hollywood gets wrong: no dramatic spotlight, no good-cop-bad-cop theater. Just a beige box with a scarred metal table, three chairs that have seen better decades, and a two-way mirror that reflects my pale face back at me. The fluorescent light above flickers every seventeen seconds. I count to keep my mind occupied, to stop myself from filling the silence with nervous words— the first mistake I counsel my clients not to make.

"Can I get you anything? Water? Coffee?" Lassiter asks, settling into his chair with the ease of someone who's spent thousands of hours in this exact position. His notepad lies closed between us. No pen yet. That's intentional.

"No, thank you. I really need to pick up my daughter soon."

"Right, right. Stella, isn't it? Twelve years old?" He knows her name. Of course he does. "Must be tough, juggling single motherhood with running Morgan & Company. High-profile clients, crisis management—that's pressure."

Baseline questions. He's establishing rapport while cataloging my normal behavioral patterns—how I sit when relaxed, my natural speech cadence, where my eyes go when I'm thinking versus lying. I've coached clients through this.

"It has its moments," I say, keeping my tone neutral.

"I'll try to keep this brief." He stands, and I think he's leaving already, but no—he's adjusting the wall vent to direct the air flow. The room was already cold. Now it's arctic. Another tactic: physical discomfort breaks down resistance.

He sits back down, finally pulling out a pen. It's a cheap Bic, the kind that clicks. He clicks it once. Twice. Three times. The sound drills into my temple where a headache threatens to form.

He settles back, clicking his pen. "You understand this is being recorded?" He gestures to the camera. "You're free to leave. Free to have an attorney. Want one?"

Here's the trap. Say yes, and I look guilty. Say no, and I'm vulnerable. I think of Noah getting the call from Gabriel, realizing he's probably worried. I think of Stella at school, expecting me to pick her up for shopping. I think of Matthew Delacroix, unconscious on that conference room floor.

"Not at this time."

Click. Click. Click goes his pen.

"Good. That's good, Ms. Morgan. Shows you want to help." He opens his notepad finally, makes a show of writing something down. "Let's start with something easy. How long have you been in the PR business?"

"Twenty years, give or take."

"And you worked at Bright Communications before starting your own firm?"

My spine stiffens slightly. He's done his homework. "Yes. About thirteen years ago."

"That's where you met Matthew Delacroix."

Not a question. A statement. The air in the room shifts.

"We worked there at the same time, yes."

"Same time." He tastes the words like wine. "Same accounts?"

"Occasionally."

He taps a stapled packet—news clippings highlighted in neon.

"The Henderson merger. The Trawley scandal. The—what was it—oh yes, the Fairmont Hotels crisis." He lists them while barely glancing at the pages. He's memorized this. "Pretty intense situations. Must have spent a lot of late nights at the office."

The metallic taste of anxiety floods my mouth. He knows. Or he's fishing. I can't tell which is worse.

"It's a demanding industry."

"Is that why Mr. Delacroix joined your board of advisors when you started Morgan & Company? Because of those...demanding times you shared?"

I force my hands to stay flat on my thighs, not to fidget, not to touch my watch—my tell, Richard always called it. "He had valuable experience. Several former colleagues served as advisors."

"Several." Click. Click. Click. "But Matthew Delacroix was special, wasn't he? He stayed on for—what—five years?"

"Three."

"Three." He makes a note, but I catch his slight smile. He knew the real answer. Testing me. "And when did you last speak to Mr. Delacroix?"

This is where it gets treacherous. Lie, and they probably have phone records, emails, something. Tell the truth, and—

"I hadn't spoken to him in approximately six years."

"Approximately." The word hangs between us like a blade. "So you're saying that when you walked into that conference, you hadn't seen or spoken to Delacroix in six years?"

"We hadn't spoken on the phone in six years. Our paths

had crossed at industry events but we hadn't spoken—that I recall."

He stands abruptly, the chair scraping against the linoleum with the effect of fingernails on a chalkboard. "I'll be right back."

The door closes with a soft click that sounds like a gunshot in the silence.

Ten minutes pass. Nothing.

While Richard is the last person I'd want to bring into this, if this goes long I may need him to pick up Stella. Trish mentioned that Jane, her daughter, has piano lessons at five.

Me to Dick: Are you busy?

The phone rings.

Me to Dick: I can't talk. I'm at the police station. Answering questions. But they've left me in a room. Stella is at Jane's house. I need to pick her up no later than 4:45. If this runs long, can you pick her up?

Dick: I'll get her. Send me the address. I vaguely remember the house.

Me to Dick: Thank you.

. . .

While Richard and I haven't always seen eye to eye—obviously—I have to give credit where it's due. He's a good father and while he has an important job as a partner at a corporate law firm, he always prioritizes our daughter.

Of course, I hate to turn to him for help.

After sending Richard the address, I catch my reflection in the two-way mirror and run my fingers through my hair.

It's obvious, the detective is playing a game. Attempting to frazzle me. But I have nothing consequential to the case to hide.

Of course, I was the one to find Matthew. They may not believe me when I say that I wasn't drinking coffee with him. Maybe I should get a lawyer. If they don't have a suspect, the last person to see him alive could very well be a prime suspect.

I sit in the chair and wait.

No, I'll give them thirty minutes. At that point if he hasn't returned, it's rude and since they haven't pressed charges, I'm free to leave.

Twenty-five minutes pass. Footsteps pass in the hallway outside in a regular pat-a-pat-pat. None slow near my door. I check my wrist, pointedly noting the time, just in case someone is on the other side of that mirror.

My mouth is dry and I wish I'd asked for water.

Five more minutes and I'm walking out.

Footsteps sound outside, then slow.

Finally.

Thirty-seven minutes.

He left me in here for thirty-seven minutes.

Thirty-seven minutes of fluorescent flicker, of my own breathing, of the faint murmur of voices beyond the mirror. My phone sits face-down on the table.

Three missed calls from Christine. One from Robert. None from Noah—but he won't call. He'll wait. He'll be ready if I need him.

When the door finally opens, it's not Lassiter who enters first.

It's Richard.

My ex-husband stands in the doorway like an avenging angel in a Tom Ford suit, his face carved from granite. Behind him, Lassiter looks almost amused.

"Detective, I'd like a word with my client."

"Your client?" Lassiter's eyebrow arches. "Interesting choice of words, Mr. Whitmore."

"Richard…" My gaze cuts to the detective and I push up from the chair. "I needed you to pick up Stella, not come here."

"Jessica is picking her up. I needed to be here."

"But you're not my lawyer."

Detective Lassiter looks to Richard. "Is that true?"

"She's my ex-wife, if you prefer accuracy. Either way, this interview is over unless you're charging her with something."

The testosterone in the room is suffocating. These two men, circling each other with me here like a prize neither actually wants.

"Richard," I start, but he cuts me off with a look I remember from our marriage—the one that says *let me handle this*.

"Actually," Lassiter says, settling back into a chair as if Richard's presence changes nothing, "Mr. Whitmore's arrival is fortuitous. You're an attorney, aren't you, sir? Corporate law, if I'm not mistaken?"

"Your point?"

"My point is that your ex-wife has been less than forth-coming about her relationship with the victim, and I'm wondering if that's something you were aware of. During your marriage, for instance."

The room crystallizes into perfect, terrible silence.

Richard's jaw ticks once. His tell. He looks at me, and in that look is a question I can't answer here, can't answer now, maybe can't answer ever.

"My ex-wife's past professional relationships are not rele-vant to—"

"Professional." Lassiter tastes that word too. He's collecting them like evidence. "Is that what we're calling it?"

My phone buzzes on the table. All three of us look at it.

"Go ahead," Lassiter says. "Could be important."

I flip it over. A text from Jessica, with a photo attached. Stella in the back seat of a car, but something's wrong with the picture. The angle, maybe. Or maybe it's the perfect cut of Jessica's face, like she's holding a selfie stick and using a filter.

Jessica, Richard's girlfriend: Picked up Stella as Richard requested! Taking the scenic route home. She asked for ice cream. Smart girl. ☺

My blood turns to ice water in my veins.

"Problem?" Lassiter asks.

"I need to go." I stand, and the room tilts slightly. When did I last eat? When did I last breathe properly? "My daughter—"

"We're not quite finished here, Ms. Morgan."

"Are you charging her?" Richard's voice cuts through the fog of my panic.

Lassiter's pen clicks once. "Not yet."

The word "yet" follows us out of the room, down the hallway, past the cluttered desks and curious stares, out into the afternoon light that feels too bright, too brisk, too normal for what's just happened.

In the parking lot, Richard grabs my arm. "How long?"

"Richard—"

"How long were you sleeping with Matthew Delacroix?" His voice is low, controlled, deadly. "During our marriage. How. Long." It's not a question. It's a confirmation.

"I need to get Stella—"

"Jessica has her. She's safe." His grip tightens slightly. "Answer the question, Alicia."

My phone buzzes again.

Noah Bennett: On my way. Are you okay?

I look at Richard's face—the anger, the betrayal, the protective instinct still fighting through all of it.

Then I look at the precinct behind me, where Lassiter is probably already building his case.

And finally at my phone, where Noah's message waits for an answer.

I don't know how to respond to any of them.

My watch catches the light. 4:44.

Angel numbers. Protection. Guidance. A sign that you're exactly where you're supposed to be.

But standing outside a police precinct with my ex-husband's hand on my arm and a detective's *yet* still echoing in my ears, "exactly where I'm supposed to be" feels less like reassurance and more like a reckoning.

Everything is about to come out.

I'm not sure I'm ready.

CHAPTER
NINETEEN

NOAH

Leaving now. Talk later.

I'm about five minutes away from the precinct when the text comes through.

Short. Clipped. Guarded.

A world away from how she was yesterday evening—and last night.

I dial Gabriel.

"Hey. We're pulling into traffic now. She should be home in twenty-five minutes, barring gridlock."

"What happened there?"

"No one would tell me anything. Tight-lipped. But Richard, her ex-husband, showed. Flashed his business card, seemed to know someone, and they escorted him up. Less than twenty minutes later they both came down."

"Must've said he's her lawyer."

Which means she called him. Asked him to come down.

Makes sense, I suppose. They share a daughter.

Can't say it gives me the warm and fuzzies—which is probably a warning sign, or as my sister might call it, a flashing red light.

"That's my take," Gabriel agrees. "They had a noticeable disagreement in the parking lot though."

"Shouting?"

"Angry words. I was standing off to the side, couldn't catch all of it, but I'd say something happened in interrogation that didn't sit well with her ex."

"That's hardly her fault."

"Oh, he'd argue otherwise. At least, that's the gist of it. She brushed him off though. Told him it was nothing, he was reading into it, which is what the detective likely wants when they're on a wild goose chase. She told Richard she'd talk to him later when she didn't have a splitting headache."

"Seems you heard a lot."

"Well, that part. She spoke clearly. He got up right on her —talking into her ear. For a split second, I thought he might hurt her, but he backed off quickly. When she spoke, I was a lot closer."

Based on his description, I can envision the scene. From what I've observed, there's controlled tension between Alicia and her ex. They'd both be aware they were in public.

"If the cops had anything, they'd press charges. It's got to be a fishing expedition."

I say it like a fact.

Doesn't mean I believe it.

"Maybe," Gabriel says.

"You don't agree?"

"Based on what I observed today, I don't think we're working with the whole picture."

"What did you say you did before this?"

"Military intelligence."

"Ah, that's right." I knew he was military. It was his whole picture gambit that had me asking. "Why'd you leave?"

"Same as you. Family matters."

His clipped tone tells me that's as far as we're touching the topic.

"Alright. I've turned around, heading back to Alicia's."

"Copy that. FYI, it appears her ex is following her home. But he lives nearby. I'll text if he pulls up. I won't leave until you arrive."

"It was that tense?"

"Tense enough."

"Copy that," I answer, and press down harder on the accelerator.

Minutes after the call ends, my father's name flashes.

I answer with, "Hey Dad."

"What are you up to?"

"Driving."

"I won't keep you long. Wanted to see if you might be home this weekend. Roger's son is in town. He's hiring, and he likes vets. His company is doing well. An IPO within the next three to five years is reasonable. Would be a good time to join."

"I don't think I'll be headed home this weekend, Dad."

"Working seven days a week in a job with no future?"

"The project's intensifying."

"You're going to get burnt out making someone else rich."

"It's not all work. I've got a date Friday night."

"Really?"

"Don't sound so surprised."

"What's she like?"

"I tell you what," I adjust the rearview after catching sight of a green SUV that turned off the exit when I did. "I'll tell you all about it if the date goes well."

"That's fair. Surprised you mentioned it at all. I guess I'll talk to you on Sunday."

He ends the call without waiting for a response, as is his way.

The green SUV turns left, and I stay focused on getting back to Alicia's. But when I arrive, she's not in the house.

I call Gabriel.

"I'm back. Alicia's not here."

"I'm aware. She picked up her daughter and she's headed to M Street."

"You staying with her?"

"I'm on her tail. Her ex headed home. Plan to stay back with her car."

"Logic?"

"She's safe in the crowds. But if someone's targeting her, her car might not be."

"Have you been tailed?"

"Not that I've picked up on. But in this district, this time of day, there are no guarantees."

"Copy that."

After the car incident the other day, his logic is solid.

Ninety minutes later, headlights sweep the carport. I'm at the window before I register movement.

Through the glass, I watch her kill the engine. She doesn't move.

Just sits there, hands locked on the wheel, her silhouette cut sharp against the streetlight.

Stella's already out, backpack bouncing. But Alicia stays frozen.

I count to ten.

Then twenty.

Finally, she moves.

The gate rumbles shut. I force myself downstairs, giving her space.

"Homework," I hear her say upstairs, voice steady. Controlled.

The mask's back on.

I return to the main floor, close the blinds, arm the system. Her office door clicks shut.

Every instinct I have is screaming at me to go up there.

But those are the instincts of someone who cares. Not someone who's paid to guard a door.

She went upstairs without a word. Message received.

It's after eleven and I'm sitting in the basement den watching ESPN recaps when I hear footsteps on the stairs. Stella's light went off an hour ago—I checked the monitors. Alicia hesitates in the doorway. Tension permeates her being. She's pulled her dark hair back into a low, loose bun, and in her loungewear, she's casual, but her eyes, dark in this light, read as worried.

I pat the cushion beside me, gesturing for her to join me.

"You've had a day," I say, brokering the silence.

She grimaces, nods and with slow steps, moves forward.

"Tell me about it," I say, hoping she'll share.

"About the precinct?" She sinks into the sofa and pulls a knee up to her chest, looping her arms around it.

"What'd they want?"

Hudson and I exchanged messages earlier this evening. He's working on his end for information, but the investigative team is being tightlipped.

"The detective may have uncovered something from my past—" She stops and shakes her head, then palms her forehead. "No, he didn't. It's..."

"What might he have uncovered?" I ask, genuinely intrigued. It's hard to imagine this woman having anything shady in her past.

"No," she shakes her head again, chewing on her lip. "It's nothing."

"Tell me," I prod. "I'll tell you if it's nothing."

"No." Her lips turn up slightly on the ends, almost wistful. "I've cultivated the ability to keep secrets and I'm not going to let a desperate detective with no leads dig up something long buried."

"That's...intriguing."

She blinks like she's snapping out of a fog.

"Sorry. I shouldn't have said anything. Two glasses of wine and I'm..." she lets the words trail.

"You know, I'm not a lawyer, but it's my understanding that in a criminal investigation it's best to be upfront about everything."

She cocks her head, studying me. "Maybe one day I'll tell you everything, but for today, all you need to know is that I didn't have anything to do with Matthew Delacroix's death."

"I know that."

Her eyes snap to mine—searching, almost desperate. "Do you?"

"Yeah." I hold her gaze. "I do."

Something in her shoulders gives. Not much. Just enough.

"The detective…" She stops, starts again. "He implied he knew things. Personal things. But he was fishing. He had to be."

"What kind of things?"

She shakes her head, jaw tight. "Things I've worked very hard to keep buried. Things that have nothing to do with murder but everything to do with…" Her voice cracks. Just barely. "Everything to do with who I was a long time ago."

That's a significant statement.

"You don't owe me your past," I say quietly. "But for what it's worth? I've seen who you are now. That's what matters."

Her exhale shakes. "I keep telling myself that."

"Then maybe start believing it."

She stares at the silent TV, where a car commercial plays in muted colors.

"When my parents died, when I was fifteen," she says, voice hollow. "I didn't get to say goodbye. The car accident—so unexpected. And today, after sitting in that interrogation room, all I've been able to think is—if they charge me, if I lose Stella, if everything I've earned disappears—" Her breath hitches. "I'd be that girl again. Alone. Shattered."

I shift closer. Close enough that our shoulders touch.

"You're not alone," I tell her.

She turns then, and her eyes are wet. The armor's gone.

"Noah—" Her voice breaks. "I can't fall apart. Not now. Not when Stella might—"

"You don't have to be strong right now."

"Yes, I do."

"Not with me." I mean it. "Not here."

For a long moment, she just looks at me. Then, so quietly I almost miss it:

"Hold me?"

I open my arms, and she comes to me—not gracefully, but like someone who's been holding herself together too long and finally has permission to stop.

She tucks against my chest, and I feel the moment she breaks—silent tears soaking through my shirt, her fingers gripping my sides like I'm the only solid thing in her world.

I don't say anything. Don't tell her it'll be okay or that she's safe. She's too smart for platitudes.

Instead, I hold her. One hand on her back, the other cradling her head. And I let her shake apart.

Minutes pass. Maybe longer. The TV cycles through commercials. Rain patters against the windows.

Eventually, her breathing evens out. The trembling stops.

"I'm sorry—"

"Don't."

Her gaze drops to my mouth. Hesitates. Then lifts back to my eyes.

The air shifts.

"Noah…" It's not a question. Not quite.

I know what I should do. Stand up. Keep boundaries. Remember she's a client, she's vulnerable, she's miles out of my league in every way that matters.

She pulls back just enough to look at me.

Eyes red. Clear.

I should stop this.

She's vulnerable. I know it. She knows it.

I don't move.

She does.

When she leans in—slow enough that I could stop this, that we both could—I don't.

The kiss is soft. Careful.

Her hand comes up to cup my jaw, and careful becomes something else entirely.

I pull her closer, and she comes willingly—shifting until she's straddling my lap, her fingers exploring my shoulders, my neck, my scalp, her mouth opening under mine.

It's not about comfort anymore.

"We should—" I start, but she shakes her head.

"Don't think. Please. Just…"

"Alicia—"

She kisses me again, and this time there's no hesitation. No testing. Just need—raw and honest and impossible to ignore.

When she takes my hand and stands, pulling me toward the basement guest room, I follow.

Because sometimes the right thing and the smart thing aren't the same.

Tonight, I choose her.

CHAPTER
TWENTY

ALICIA

"Alright. I want all the details."

Christine's light blue eyes are lit with an enthusiasm that comes from what she calls booty chatter. We ended up meeting up for brunch in her home, as she lives close to Stella's school and Stella has Saturday play practice for two hours.

There's not much to tell is on the tip of my tongue, but that won't fly, and it's not true.

"Oh come on. Tell me something," she says, sipping her coffee.

Behind her, bright sunlight streams in through the window and a bluebird lands on a skeleton limb of the maple that shades the kitchen in summer.

"Like, you have a whole security detail, and he personally walked you to my door." She sets her coffee down with a pointed look. "That's not security. That's courtship."

"He's thorough," I say, keeping my voice neutral.

"Mm-hmm." She draws it out in a way that means she believes none of it. "And is he thorough in other areas?"

"Christine."

"I'm just asking." She grins, entirely unrepentant. "Okay. Fine. Tell me what's actually going on—the non-fun parts."

"I don't really need this level of security," I begin, stirring the stick of celery in my Bloody Mary. This morning Christine went all out with the Bloody Mary bar, and picked up bagels, cream cheese, and smoked lox for breakfast. "This is all for Dorian. He's being cautious because of a case I worked on recently."

"The one involving the White House?"

"That's the one, and no, I don't want to talk about it."

"Neither do I," she's quick to agree. She knows everything anyway. "How is Dorian?"

"He's good."

"I always thought you would end up with him."

I roll my eyes. "It was never like that with us."

"If you say so," she says, voice lilting in that way that lets me know she disagrees. "How's that wife of his?"

"She's doing well," I say.

"And she's okay with her husband insisting on another woman having a security detail?"

It's her company is on the tip of my tongue, but I bite it back because Dorian and his wife are private people, and one of the reasons my friendship with Dorian has survived the years is he trusts me.

"Wait. Didn't they get divorced? Is this wife number two?"

"Same wife," I say. The world believes they divorced, but in actuality, they separated for years—neither of them signed the papers, which says everything. But talking about this at all makes me feel like I'm gossiping about Dorian.

"Oh, but I remember." She snaps her fingers. "They split and got back together. Divorce must've been prohibitively expensive. And you'd think of all people Dorian Moore could afford a divorce—I guess you just never know."

"Would you quit it?" I admonish. "Dorian can afford a divorce. He never wanted one."

"But you're not close to his wife, right?"

"Dorian met her after we'd lost touch. She came along after college, after our crowd had scattered. But remember when Nick and Dorian spent that weekend with us in the city?"

"How could I forget."

"He was with her then. I think she had exams or something. And that's kind of the norm. I see Dorian when she's unavailable and he's filling time."

"How is Nick?"

"I'm honestly not sure. Nick hasn't come up in conversation—" There's something in Christine's posture that reminds me— "You and Nick hooked up that weekend."

Now I'm grinning, and she's struggling not to.

"It was a fun weekend. Let's leave it at that."

She sips her coffee, holding the mug with both hands, clearly covering her smile. But when she sets it down on the table, she says, "And now you're with the hot bodyguard that Dorian has insisted stay in your home. Funny how we come full circle."

"He's hot. I'm not going to deny that. But just like you and Nick had fun...that's all this is."

Guilt stabs at me, slicing through my integrity. But it's easiest to downplay it, and I'm not ready to dissect what's going on.

"Because he's younger?" She's probing, as I guess any good friend would.

"He's young. Just out of the military. His whole life is still ahead of him—he's figuring out what comes next." *I'm not a next. I'm a now.* "It's fun. Like you and Nick."

Fun. The word feels too light for what's happening between Noah and me. There's heat, yes—but also comfort. Safety. And that's the part that's unnerving.

"Yeah, that was one weekend. Nick made it clear up front it was only a thing. Has this guy—"

"Noah."

"Yeah, Noah, has he made the same thing clear?"

"Yes, we've had the discussion."

She eyes me with her you-are-full-of-it expression.

"We have." I say it firmly, selling the position. "And come on. He's got his life in front of him. He's not thinking forever with a single mom."

She still stares.

"What?"

"I am so jealous. My date last night?"

"I thought it was work."

"Date," she says. "Fifty-five. Nice enough. What you would call appropriate, right?"

"I think given you don't want kids it makes a lot of sense to date older—"

"Right. So, Mr. Appropriate assumed we'd have sex. Like —just assumed it."

I'm full of questions but I don't need to ask them as Christine will tell all, so I sip my Bloody Mary.

"When I said I didn't want to go back to his place, he'd gotten annoyed. Like rude. Like 'I bought you dinner,' and he wasn't looking for a relationship—mind you. Oh no, he was basically just under the assumption that sex is what happened after dinner."

"Who was this date with?"

"Harold Thompson."

"That name is familiar."

"Divorced two years ago."

I snap my fingers. "I remember. His kids are older than Stella. Yeah, I've heard rumors that he does the escort thing from time to time." Christine's eyes bulge. "I don't know if they're true. I can't even remember who said it. How did you end up on a date with him?"

She waves a hand. "It's not important. The point is, he was an ass. Dating is hard. And I'd be willing to bet if I had sex with Harold, it would suck, and here you are with a younger man who is model-fucking gorgeous and he walked you to my door, and is concerned about you, and I want some of that!"

Yes, I'm laughing.

"Seriously. Tell Dorian I'm in mortal danger and need security," she whines.

And then a flash of last night hits, of the orgasm that rocked through me, and I have to pluck at my sweater to wave it like a fan to cool me down.

"I don't know why you're holding back." Her statement is half-whine and half-serious, and I settle in to have the conversation she's been pushing.

"Richard went through a succession of girlfriends. Stella lived through them all."

"But he's serious with this one, right?"

"Jessica. Yes, he's serious with her—I think. But there's a reason not to do what he does. I need to model good behavior."

"I agree!" Christine jumps in. "Let her see you date. Let your daughter see that dating isn't always unicorns shooting fireworks out the anus."

"So you're saying that you think Richard is in the right?"

"You know I think that guy's an ass," Christine says, waving her celery stick. "But at least he's living. You, my dear, are over here editing your life like it's a press release. And all the while you're having this hot sex—"

"I haven't told you—"

"You don't need to! You know how I know? Because if sex sucked, you'd talk about it. It would've been listed as a reason to not go there again. But the only roadblock I've heard mentioned is age and Stella—neither of which are valid roadblocks."

I open my mouth to disagree.

"Come on," Christine shouts. "If I can date a guy almost fifteen years older why can't you date a guy ten years younger? Who says only men are allowed to date younger? That's bullshit."

I rub my forehead and pluck a pickle from my drink. "He needs someone younger," I counter.

"For what? Sex?" She arches a brow. "When he's with you, does he act like he needs someone younger?"

The memory hits fast—his mouth, his breath, his weight pressing me into the mattress—and I have to reach for my drink just to ground myself.

"Yeah, I'm taking that as a no."

"I mean long term. And he's still figuring things out."

"Okay. Let me go over this with you. Nick being from

across the pond—as in the Atlantic Ocean—that's a distance that warrants fling status. This man is DC-based. The only ocean between you is the one you're manufacturing. He travels for work? So do you. You say you don't even want a husband. You, my friend, are still figuring things out. What's wrong with enjoying what you have in the moment? I would kill to be you."

"Yes, my life is so glam."

"I'm serious," she screeches. "You're always put together. You have a closet to die for. You have an ex-husband who comes running when you call and wants what's best for you and the two of you co-parent like pros. Your reputation in DC practically glows neon."

I wave a hand, waving her off.

"Look, I know you work for it. I'm your bestie. I see how hard you work for it, but the fact it looks so easy is very annoying. But, as your bestie, I'm here to tell you that one thing that's hard is dating." She slams her Bloody Mary down on the table hard enough some of the tomato juice splashes over the side. "If you don't take advantage of what fell in your lap, I'm going to grow livid. Or…no…I'm not. Dump him and I'll come over at night to console him." She snaps her fingers. "That's what we should do." She clucks her tongue. "Give him my number."

"No," I snap back.

"That's right. And if you did end it, he's already in my no-date zone. Because you, my friend, are not one who plays around lightly. You're just in denial—and here's the reality: You're into him, and these little excuses you're making are just that—pointless excuses."

Over the course of the next hour, Christine somehow pulls out most of what's gone on with me and Noah. I admit that I have enjoyed having him close—and that it's hands down the best sex I've had in my life. Christine's response to that last part is entirely unprintable. We never mention my police interrogation—and I'm grateful. I needed this—just time with a friend and focusing on the lighter side of life.

Later on, when Stella and I are back home and Noah has gone out for what he calls his Saturday long run, my brunch conversation runs through my mind on repeat.

"What do you think of Noah?" I ask.

Stella is sitting on the sofa in the living room, watching a TV show on her iPad. For years, I tried to force her to watch television shows on the television screen, but I've about decided the fight is futile.

"He's nice." She tugs at the blanket that's over her legs. "He's cool."

"We had dinner last night. I think he's a nice guy."

She lowers the iPad. "Like a date?"

"I mean…" I toy with my grandmother's watch, silently cursing Christine for egging me into this position.

"Mom." Stella's no-nonsense tone captures my full attention. "It's not like I'm harboring any hope of you and Dad getting back together. I don't care if you date. And I like him. He's helping me improve my game."

"Basketball?"

"Yeah."

"Well, he won't be here much longer."

"Well," she says, playing my word right back at me, "If he is, I like him. He gets my thumbs up." I smile, but something twists low in my chest. Stella's easy acceptance feels like permission—and that, somehow, makes me more uneasy than judgment would have.

She goes back to her TV show and on the way out I

pause, leaning against the doorway, watching her, comforted by the normalcy of it. The smell of coffee still lingers in the air, sunlight pooling across the rug. For the first time in weeks, everything feels ordinary again. Which, of course, is exactly when things usually fall apart.

TWENTY-ONE

NOAH

My work cell rings as I grab it off the charger. Fresh shower, post-workout high—I was just heading out for lunch.

"Noah Bennett."

"Hey Noah, it's Quinn. Do you have a minute?"

"Fire away."

"Hudson asked me to call." There's something in her tone that doesn't sit right. "A background check on you just hit the system."

"Is that right?"

"Can you think of any reason? I mean, are you applying for other jobs or—"

My half-chuckle cuts her off. "No, Quinn." I'm smiling, not that she can see. "I've been with KOAN for a hot minute. I'll give it at least a year."

"Well, we're looking into it."

I rub the back of my head, thinking through the ramifications. "Anything pulled on Gabriel?"

"No. Just you. We tracked the request to a private investigator."

"What's this PI's specialty?" I pose the question but I'm pretty sure I know the answer—local PIs are mostly hired by spouses who suspect cheating, but a paranoid spouse worried about a man living in his ex-wife's home with their daughter might do the same.

"He's been in business for fifteen years. Doubles as a bounty hunter."

"What're you thinking?"

"We're looking into it. We don't think it's anyone fearing Alicia—mainly because we don't think anyone of that caliber would hire this guy—but if this is just intel gathering, they might."

"But they didn't look into Gabriel."

"Exactly. And he's been at her office every day. That's why Hudson wanted me to call you—get your thoughts."

"My gut says it might be her ex-husband."

"Huh. Because you're living in the house?"

"It's a theory."

"Is he the jealous type?"

I think back to my one interaction with Richard. He didn't look pleased to see me, but I read it as concern that Alicia had gotten herself into a situation that might endanger their daughter.

"I don't have a reliable read on that."

"Understood. Well, we'll get the information on who hired him soon enough." I don't ask how she plans on doing that as I imagine her methods might not be entirely legal. "Eyes open."

"Copy that."

The call continues with polite small talk—me asking if

everything's okay down there and her confirming I'm still doing alright up here. When the call ends, I text Gabriel.

Me: You want lunch?

He spends a lot of his time in the lobby of Alicia's offices. Sure, some days he's following her all over DC and even Manhattan, but for the most part, he's stuck on a dull routine.

He responds in the affirmative and I get his order.

Forty-five minutes later, I'm in the parking lot of Alicia's DC office, sitting on a bench that faces the office building's entrance, eating a burger.

"You really think her ex hired a PI?" Gabriel wipes ketchup from the corner of his mouth and angles himself on the bench like he's studying me to see what he can read in my reaction.

"It's possible."

"You, but not me. Because you're in the house?" Gabriel leans back on the bench, sunglasses reflecting the street. Always scanning. The man doesn't stop gathering intel, even over a burger.

"Well, has he seen you?"

"That day at the station," he says. "They were both running hot—shock, guilt, protective instinct. Hard to see past that." What he's saying is Richard didn't seem to notice him.

"You think he's jealous?" Now that Quinn's put the idea in my head, I can't shake the question.

"I'd say he still cares. Enough to hire a PI..." He pauses

and swipes his lips again with a balled-up napkin. "Something going on with you two?"

I sniff and scratch at my jaw.

"I mean…if there is, would he know?" Gabe clarifies.

"No." What's happened between Alicia and me has been on the down low. But… "We went out to dinner last Friday."

"Dinner like a date?"

"Her daughter was at a sleepover. I'll have to ask Quinn when the report was pulled. If it hit after Friday, that narrows it."

I rub the back of my neck. KOAN isn't military, but they still expect discipline—and this crosses some invisible line. We're informal and don't push employee manuals, but there is a code of conduct and expectations. My choices are looking unwise.

"It's worth asking Quinn," Gabe says nonchalantly. "You'll know if someone read into the dinner and you sparked something—I mean, it could just be…" He reaches for a fry and I can tell he's thinking. "Nah. If it was just concern for his daughter, he'd ask Alicia for backgrounds on the men in her detail. He wouldn't go behind her back."

"Might not be him," I say. "Remember the back of her Rivian. It was ajar."

We both look at Alicia's car, parked in her reserved spot.

"You know, I've thought about that, and it's possible she accidentally pushed a button on the key fob to open the rear and didn't realize it."

"No." I point to the back. "See how it's split. The key fob can automatically pop the top window, but the bottom gate requires a manual open."

"It was ajar too?"

"Slightly. Like maybe someone closed it quickly and didn't stick around to double-check it closed."

I ball up my burger wrapper and throw it in the bag, then stroll over to Alicia's vehicle, rubbing a hand over the body. It's all locked up, but I'm remembering how I found the back before. No, someone opened it. If Alicia tried to drive with it ajar, she would've seen the red light on the dashboard.

Now if she did get out, open it, fail to close it properly, and just didn't remember accessing the rear… But this is Alicia we're talking about, and that's unlikely.

On a whim, I squat and peer at the undercarriage. It's dark and I can see through to the curb.

"It's a nice car," Gabriel says, joining me. He studies it with me, pulling out his phone and flicking on the light feature. "Crazy to think it runs on a computer. No engine."

"Right?"

"That tire looks like it's low on air." Gabe pushes up and goes around to the passenger side rear wheel and pushes against the tire. "Treads low too."

I study the four tires noticing how the one tire does look like it's showing more wear.

"Wait. Come here."

I join Gabe by the tire and kneel. Following the stream of light from his phone I see a black plastic box attached to the metal frame.

Gabe reaches for it and I stop him. "We touch it and someone's going to know we're onto them."

"It's a GPS tracker," he says, stating the obvious.

"Which means someone is definitely monitoring Alicia." There have been times I've thought protective detail was overkill, but now… "Someone's studying her schedule."

I pull out my phone and dial Quinn, setting the phone

to speaker. She answers on the first ring. "Quinn. I'm with Gabriel. We located a GPS tracker on Alicia's vehicle."

"And we found the invoice and payment to the PI. Paid in Bitcoin."

"So someone doesn't want to be found."

"Yep. They also gave a fake name, but that's not surprising. The Bitcoin—someone's definitely taking precautions to not be found."

"And it's a fake name because you couldn't find it in the system?"

"Ryan Reynolds," she says.

"Guess he moonlights between Marvel gigs," I mutter, stepping back and away from the car. From this angle, the GPS tracker isn't visible. "Any chance you can trace ownership of the tracker that's on her car?"

"I'd likely need to loop in law enforcement. We could determine the carrier, but then we'd need access to cell records. Is there any defining information on it?"

Gabriel crouches, studies it without touching. "It's attached by a magnet. You see the scrape on the mount? Whoever placed it wasn't new at this—he checked the magnetic hold after attaching. But it's consumer-grade hardware. Someone who knows enough to hide a tracker, not enough to spoof the signal."

Gabriel snaps a pic, and rises.

"We're going to leave it on," I say since Quinn can't see what Gabriel's doing.

Gabriel meets my gaze—silent agreement. Sometimes bait's useful.

"Copy," Quinn says. "Let me check and see what resources we have. Maybe I can find a way to trace the source of the tracker. I'll update Hudson, but I expect he'll want to assign extra resources."

Richard hiring a PI is one thing. A GPS tracker and Bitcoin payments is something else entirely.

I pocket the phone. The afternoon passes humming with traffic, but every sound feels sharper now.

Someone's been watching her. Studying her patterns, her routines, her car.

While I've been focused on keeping her close, someone else has been doing the same thing.

CHAPTER
TWENTY-TWO

ALICIA

There's a sharp rap at the door—three quick knocks that jar my focus and my pulse. I grind my teeth, irritation fizzing in my blood. I have one blessed hour between client meetings. One hour where I told everyone to hold calls. My phone's tucked away inside my handbag. A futile attempt at boundaries, but the gesture matters. This right here is why I prefer to work from home—no interruptions, no eyes watching me hold it together.

"Yes," I bite out, voice clipped.

The door opens and Petra pokes her head in, guilt flickering across her features. "Dorian Moore is on the line. I told him you can't be disturbed, but he said it's urgent."

Of course he did.

Once, Dorian was charming chaos contained in a Savile Row suit. Now he's arrogance wrapped in urgency—too used to people jumping when he calls.

I have half a mind to make her tell him I'll call back, but

I've been staring at the same press release for twenty minutes, the words blurring into static.

"Thank you, Petra. I'll take it."

When the door clicks shut, I lean back, spine brushing cool leather, the faint aroma of coffee rising from the cup I haven't touched. I reach for the desk phone and press the blinking light.

"Dorian," I say, not bothering to hide the annoyance roughening my tone. Then, softening slightly, "Everything okay?"

"The team found a tracker on your vehicle."

I flinch, twisting the chair toward the window. Outside, a skeletal tree claws at a washed-out sky, its branches reflected ghostlike in the glass.

"When?"

"Within the last hour. We're going to increase security."

"That's not—"

"Don't say it's not necessary," he cuts in. "Not when they're tracking you."

I inhale deeply, forcing oxygen into my lungs, forcing logic to override panic. "Who would do this? Can you trace it?"

"They're working on it. As for who—like I've been telling you since charges were filed against Pierce—" Pierce, the defense contractor whose company had been accused of leveraging stolen intelligence and risqué videos to pressure lawmakers into approving Pentagon contracts. "Pierce won't want anything you know—anything you've stumbled onto through your other clients—surfacing in the investigation. If you possess information someone doesn't want exposed in discovery, you're at risk."

My fingertips press against the windowpane, cold seeping into my skin. "What does tracking me get them?"

"In the worst-case scenario? Your schedule. Your patterns. They're patient, Alicia. They find ways to make things look like accidents."

A chill crawls over my arms. "You really believe that? This isn't just your crime-fetish paranoia talking?"

"Unfortunately, no. The investigation into Pierce is widening. And when the circle expands, the expendable targets multiply."

"And you think some of my clients are getting swept up in it?"

"I'd say at the very least, Pierce—who's both wealthy and ruthless—is worried. And maybe others exposed with the Pierce investigation."

"Senator Crawford has access to the same intelligence I do, through his own channels," I counter. "I'm not the only pathway to exposure."

"And for the most part, that would be hearsay. You, on the other hand—clients confide in you directly. Sometimes they hand you the evidence."

I exhale slowly, the sound trembling through the silence. "I don't have anything on Pierce that Crawford doesn't."

"But does he know that? And what about Senator Lopez? Your other client from the Magpie situation—she was working with the same extortionist, different leverage." Dorian's tone lowers, softer now. "Don't forget, Vasquez sent emails before her death that said you possess information."

"This is…absurd." My gaze lifts to the ceiling tiles, willing them not to shift, not to close in. "But why would someone plant a tracker?"

"The tracker's not the problem. It's what they plan to do with what they learn."

A slow throb starts at my temples. "Do you think they'd hurt Stella?"

"If it were me, no. I'd make something look like an accident."

My throat tightens. "Is he really that—"

"It might not be just him. He's connected, Alicia. And we don't know who might think they could get caught up in the investigation. This is bigger than Pierce."

I rub my arms, grounding myself in the texture of wool and the faint hum of the building's HVAC. "You know, before, I didn't understand how much can surface during discovery. Now I'm getting a crash course."

"You mean your police interrogation?"

"You heard about that?"

"I'm kept updated," he says, and I picture the network of quiet watchers KOAN deploys.

"What did they want to know that you haven't already told them?"

"He's out of leads," I say. "He's digging deep, looking for cracks."

"You worked with Delacroix years ago."

"Ten," I reply automatically. The number feels weighted. "Though he stayed on my board for three years after that."

"So the police, they're grasping at straws?"

"Maybe."

"What aren't you telling me?"

"If I tell you—" I stop, pulse hammering. "Never mind. I can't."

"Alicia." The line goes quiet—a silence weighted with

suspicion. "What has the detective uncovered that you don't want public?"

Shit. Too much.

"You and Delacroix. You had an affair."

I close my eyes, shame and memory tangling in my chest—the scent of aftershave and hotel linen, the way guilt tastes like metal on the tongue.

"Nick was right," Dorian murmurs.

"Nick?" The name lands like a stone dropped into still water. Nick. That weekend in the city. The accidental run-in. All these years. "What—"

"That weekend in the city with you and Christine. Nick suspected something was going on with you two when we ran into him in the hotel lobby. I'd forgotten about that—but that's why his name was familiar. How'd the detective find out?"

"I don't know," I whisper. "But he suspects. No one knows. No one."

"If Nick picked up on it after one weekend..." He doesn't need to finish. I know what he's implying.

"We were careful," I say quietly. "Both married. It was stupid. And it ended long before his death. Even before he dropped off my board of advisors."

"Does Richard know?"

"No." The response is whip fast—too quick—but it's true.

"You sure?"

A humorless smile curves my lips. "He didn't then, but he suspects now. If he knew back then, he'd have weaponized it to void the prenup."

"Good point. What made him suspect now after all these years?"

"He came to the station. The detective asked pointed

questions—right in front of him. He confronted me. I denied it."

"Well, having an affair doesn't make you a murderer. But was there someone else? A recent affair? Did Delacroix's wife know?"

"She didn't know about me." I pause. "But maybe someone. He stepped off the board to 'work on his marriage,' but who knows. That's for the detective to solve."

Dorian exhales, low and weighted. "So now you're a person of interest. Do you need a lawyer?"

"No," I say, though I'm not sure I believe it. "At least not for Delacroix's murder case. The affair happened too long ago. Now, as for Pierce. I've already agreed to the closed-door congressional hearing in relation to my client Senator Crawford. With Pierce's criminal case underway…do you think I'll be subpoenaed? What are you hearing?"

"I'd say it's likely."

"You know anything I have on Pierce would surface through the senator's channels too."

"Honestly, I don't think it's Pierce watching you—it's possible, but it's not what I'd bet on. My guess? A peripheral client. Someone with more to lose. Pierce is already exposed."

That tracks. My job isn't always about saving reputation. It's about triage after detonation. I manage the aftermath when the truth's already escaped. But sometimes, the crisis starts before exposure, when someone's desperate enough to hide it.

"Maybe I'll go through my files," I murmur. "See who else worked with Vasquez. Or Magpie."

"You think there's overlap? Something with Pierce you haven't considered?"

"There's always overlap," I say. "In politics, in secrets, in sin."

He's quiet.

"I'm calling in favors to get a read on where Pierce's investigation's headed," he finally says. "But they're keeping it tight."

"Good. Leaks would only scatter them." My tone softens, professional instinct kicking in. "When someone comes to me with a self-inflicted disaster, I conduct my own version of discovery. It's the only way to be ready."

"Because everyone lies."

"Everyone lies," I echo, staring at my reflection in the glass—eyes weary, mouth a practiced line. "But especially the ones closest to implosion."

CHAPTER
TWENTY-THREE

NOAH

"Temperature's dropping," I say to Jake as we finish tightening the final screw on the motion-activated camera, hidden high in the spindly branches of the tree across from Alicia's house. This isn't her property, but we want more angles.

The cold has crept in with that bone-deep stillness unique to DC in late fall—not yet winter but threatening it. My breath fogs faintly in the air as I climb down and check the view on my phone.

It's just one more layer of protection—a discreet vantage point that won't trip alerts with every passing squirrel, but might catch something we'd otherwise miss. Anyone casing the perimeter will be looking closer to the house, not skyward.

"You think this is chilly, you should visit Chicago," Jake says, rubbing his gloved hands together. He spent the weekend back in Chicago with his girlfriend. "The highs were below freezing."

"Seriously?"

He nods, the corner of his mouth twitching.

Jake flew in earlier this afternoon—straight from the airport to the field. He's staying at a hotel nearby.

As the last light fades and the shadows deepen along the sidewalk, the street feels quieter than usual—like it's listening.

"You gonna move to Chicago?" I ask.

"Nah. Still got my place in the Highlands. Daisy and I plan to bounce between our places."

"It's nice you can do that. Long distance isn't easy."

"Yeah." He smirks, pushing his sunglasses up onto his head. "Her gig's flexible. We're lucky. She's flying in tomorrow."

"Is that right?"

"Yep. Hudson's cool with it. His idea, actually. Said he wanted to make sure we get the work-life balance thing right."

"That's good of him." I close the toolkit, the sound of metal clicking oddly loud in the still air. My car's parked under the carport, waiting for me to move it before Alicia gets home. "Glad Daisy was there when you got out of the hospital. You needed someone in your corner."

Jake grins. "I got a bump on the head and some chest pain."

"Didn't you need stitches?" I arch a brow. "The answer is yes. I was there—at the hospital. That guy hit you hard."

He rubs the back of his neck, sheepish. "A few stitches. Nothing major."

"Well, you've got a thick head of hair—hides the

damage." I let the heart condition slide—he wants to downplay it, I can roll with that.

He chuckles, the sound easy and unguarded. "Daisy says a hard head goes with it. But yeah, she's been good for me. We're figuring it out. I upgraded her sofa for better TV viewing, she got me throw pillows for mine. One day we'll consolidate, but this works for now."

"Good for you, man," I say, crossing my arms. I mean it. Jake's a solid guy. The kind who's seen too much but somehow still manages to smile.

He studies me for a second. "You seeing anyone?"

I pause. The question lands in murkier territory than he's aiming to navigate. We're standing between the sidewalk and Alicia's brown grass lawn, the sky a flat gray, the air edged with frost. It's small talk, but it cuts too close.

"Hey—just a question." He lifts a hand, palms up, grinning. "Not digging."

I give him a nod, wordless. Some things are better left unspoken. Especially the kind of thing that's still figuring itself out. Alicia's not someone you talk about—she's someone you protect.

Jake lets it go. "I'll head out. Got to check in with Hudson." He clicks the key fob and the RAV-4 rental chirps in reply.

"Run and breakfast in the morning?"

"Sure thing."

"I'll swing by after the handoff to Gabriel."

"Sounds good."

He climbs in, and I stay there a moment longer, watching the taillights fade down the block. Then I turn back toward the house, scanning the tree—small, leafless, skeletal. It's a backup, but sometimes the backups save lives.

Up the street, headlights in the dusk catch my attention. A familiar Rivian rolls into view, followed closely by a Toyota 4Runner. Alicia and Gabriel. I step forward, instinct tightening my chest.

She turns into the short drive, slowing beside my car. I wave, gesturing that I'll move. She rolls down the window, the glass humming as it slides.

"I'll move to make room," I say.

"It's fine," she answers, voice soft but weary. "We can shuffle later."

Gabriel's SUV idles at the curb. He catches my eye, gives a quick salute—the silent, precise exchange of two men on duty—and then pulls away, his taillights vanishing around the corner.

Alicia shuts her car door and steps forward, shoulders drawn in like the day's weight is pressing down on her. There's a sadness to her tonight—quiet, bone-deep, and impossible to ignore.

"You heard?" she asks.

"I found it," I tell her.

The corners of her lips tilt down, and in the next heartbeat she's against me. Her head rests against my chest, the faint scent of her shampoo threading through the cold air. I wrap my arms around her and hold her there, letting her lean into the steadiness I can offer.

"It's going to be okay," I murmur, meaning every word. "I won't let anything happen to you."

"This is surreal," she says against my jacket. "I just want it all to go away. I feel beaten down and exhausted."

I rub slow circles over her back, feeling the tension in her muscles, the exhaustion radiating off her. My lips brush the top of her head, just once—a quiet promise.

I don't say anything else. Sometimes holding someone is the whole conversation.

Then, a car door slams. Alicia flinches, instinctive, stepping back.

"Mom, I'm home!" Stella's voice rings bright and oblivious, a child's music in a too-tense evening. She runs up, her backpack bouncing, hair flying. "Is everything okay?"

Alicia smooths her daughter's arm, the tenderness in her eyes doing something to my chest I don't have words for. "Yeah, of course it is," she says gently, stooping to grab the pack.

"Alicia, do you have a minute?" Jessica's voice floats from the passenger seat of the SUV still idling by the curb. Richard's behind the wheel, hands braced on the steering wheel, jaw tight.

"Why don't you head inside and grab a snack," Alicia says to Stella.

"Cool! Can we order in tonight?"

"You got it."

We both watch her bound up the stairs. Alicia exhales, straightens, and walks toward the car like a woman going into battle. I fall into step behind her, just close enough to be a presence.

Richard's eyes flick to me—sharp, assessing, maybe hostile. The look of a man doing math he doesn't like.

"Hey, you two," Jessica chirps, too bright and eager to be genuine. "How are you doing?"

"Good," Alicia says, her tone clipped and polite. "Thanks for bringing Stella home."

"Oh, you know we love to." Jessica leans forward, smile wide. "I was thinking, maybe we could all go to dinner sometime. The four of us." She glances at Richard, realizing a beat too late that he's not on board. "Unless that's awkward—"

"Maybe sometime," Alicia says smoothly. "My schedule's a nightmare lately."

Richard scans the street ahead, then the rearview mirror. Everything about him screams *get me out of here.*

"Well, you know, the holidays are coming up. It'd be great to—"

"We'll talk about it later," Richard mutters, cutting her off.

"Oh. Okay." Jessica waves with too much enthusiasm as Richard pulls away, leaving a trail of tension in their wake.

Alicia and I walk back toward the house. Though the air between us hums with unspoken things, I keep my hands to myself.

"I can move the cars—"

"Wait until after seven," she says, pushing the door open. "There'll be more street parking. Or after Stella's in bed, we can pull them both inside the gate."

The carport can hold two—she just leaves space for Stella's basketball hoop. She's a good mom.

Inside, the warmth of the house wraps around us, carrying the faint scent of cedar and something floral— Alicia's perfume, clinging to the air.

"What is that?" she asks suddenly.

Stella's at the counter, refrigerator door open, a soda can in hand.

"It's the only thing—"

"You're not drinking caffeine this late."

"It doesn't affect me the way it does you."

"Stella."

The girl hesitates, reads her mother's fatigue, then swaps the soda for sparkling water.

"What did Jessica want?" she asks.

"Nothing."

Stella tilts her head.

"Dinner," Alicia admits.

"She's so weird." Stella grabs her drink and backpack. "She loves going out to dinner."

"Some people do, hon."

Stella's halfway up the stairs when she says, "She wants us to be a version of *Modern Family*."

Alicia freezes. "Why do you say that?"

"Well, not the gay family part," Stella says matter-of-factly, "but the tight-knit second marriage thing. She asks about you all the time. It's like she wants to be your bestie."

Alicia stares at the stairwell long after her daughter disappears, then exhales. "Text me what you want for dinner," she calls up.

She retrieves a bottle of wine from the fridge and sets it on the counter with a soft clink. Leaning against the island, she closes her eyes for a moment, like she's finally allowing herself to feel the weight of everything.

"Would you like a glass?" she asks quietly.

"No, thank you." I step forward, taking the bottle and the corkscrew from her hand. "Let me. Sit. You've had a day."

Her shoulders drop, some of the tension leaking away. "Yes," she says, voice barely above a whisper. "Yes, I have."

She sits, wraps both hands around the empty glass, and watches me work the cork. I don't mention the tracker, or Richard, or any of it. She knows I'm here. That's enough for tonight.

CHAPTER
TWENTY-FOUR

ALICIA

My phone buzzes against the marble counter, the vibration faint but sharp in the hush of the kitchen. I pad over in socked feet, the floor cool beneath me, wine-soft fatigue in my limbs. Dinner's over. The dishwasher loaded.

Noah and Stella finished their post-dinner basketball ritual in the driveway before he locked up for the night. She's upstairs now, getting ready for bed, and he's downstairs reviewing footage—ever vigilant, always one step ahead of threat.

For the first time all week, my muscles have finally unclenched. My shoulders no longer ache. The wine's warmth hums low and steady through me. I'm ready to close out this day—hell, this entire month—and pretend peace isn't borrowed time.

The phone lights again, and dread coils through me.

Dick: *Call me when you get a chance.*

Of course. The timing is perfect, as always. I should've

known he'd reach out after seeing me in Noah's arms. I stare at the message for a beat, considering ignoring it, but I've never been one to procrastinate on unpleasant tasks.

So I tap *Call.*

"Richard," I say when he picks up on the third ring.

There's the faint click of a door closing on his end.

"Are you dating him?" His voice is sharp, laced with disdain.

My stomach tightens. "That's not your business."

"Oh? Last I checked, we share a daughter who happens to be living in your house."

A car horn bleats in the background.

"Are you outside?"

"I'm going for an after-dinner walk."

"After ten?" I ask, catching the lie. "You mean you don't want your girlfriend to overhear you interrogating me. You're transparent, Richard. Always have been."

He exhales, the sound harsh over the line. "Where's Stella?"

"Upstairs. Getting ready for bed." I roll my eyes at the ceiling, the same way she does when she's frustrated.

"And Noah?"

"Ah, so you do know his name."

"We were introduced," he bites out. "You said he was security—which I'm not happy about."

"I'm aware."

Silence stretches between us. I can picture him pacing his manicured street, checking who might be watching. Always performing, even when no one's around.

Noah rounds the corner into the room, his expression questioning, alert.

"I don't like it," Richard says finally. "How much time is he spending with my daughter?"

I meet Noah's gaze head-on. "He's a good person, Richard. And might I remind you, you've introduced Stella to plenty of women without consulting me first."

"We'll talk later."

The call ends. No goodbye, just static and then quiet. I stare at the phone for a moment before setting it facedown.

"He's unbelievable," I mutter.

"Everything okay?" Noah asks, leaning against the doorway, all controlled strength and quiet watchfulness.

"Yes," I sigh, rubbing my temple. "Just Richard living up to his nickname."

A corner of his mouth twitches. "All secure."

"Locked up?"

"Locked up, lights out, alarms active. Nothing moving but the trees."

Something in the way he says it—so calm, so certain— steadies me. I stand, smoothing my hands over my jeans, trying to shake off the call's residue. "Let me go up and say goodnight to Stella. Then I'll come down."

He nods. "Take your time."

Upstairs, the soft glow from the hallway spills under Stella's door. I knock lightly.

"'Night, baby," I whisper when she murmurs her reply. She's already in bed, half-asleep, her silky strands spread over the pillow. I tuck the blanket around her shoulders, a small ritual that still feels necessary, even as she edges closer to independence.

Downstairs, the house feels different. The air carries that deep late-night quiet—a hush that comes when everything dangerous is kept at bay, if only for now. The scent of him—clean soap, cedar, mint—threads the air.

Noah's on the couch, laptop closed, shoulders relaxed. When he looks up, his expression softens in a way that undoes something inside me.

"All quiet?" I ask.

"For now." He gestures toward the space beside him. "You okay?"

"I will be."

I cross the room and sink onto the couch, my body angling toward his. For a long beat, neither of us speaks. The silence hums, thick and charged, filled with all the things we shouldn't want.

"I hate how easily he gets under my skin," I admit finally.

"That's what he's counting on." His voice is low, worn velvet.

"He still thinks he has a right to weigh in. About everything."

"He doesn't."

I turn toward him. "You sound so sure."

"I am." His gaze holds mine. "You've done enough fighting for other people, Alicia. You don't need to justify what brings you peace."

Peace. The concept fits somewhere between comfort and ache. I glance away, blinking against the sudden heat in my throat. "You make it sound so simple."

He leans closer, the air between us thinning. "Doesn't mean it's easy."

For a second, I forget to breathe. His proximity is its own gravity—steady, inevitable.

"I told myself this shouldn't happen," I whisper.

"Yeah," he says quietly. "Me too. But I'm damn glad it did."

I don't know who moves first—maybe it's mutual—but then his hand brushes my jaw, calloused fingers tracing the line of my throat. My pulse jumps, unbidden.

The kiss is slow, deliberate. Not the hungry kind, not yet —this one is about exhaling and surrendering. About exhaustion finding solace in touch.

When his mouth deepens the kiss, my hand slides up his chest, feeling the steady thrum beneath the cotton of his shirt. I taste warmth and want, mixed with the faint echo of wine.

He pulls back just enough to murmur, "You sure?"

My answer is a whisper against his skin. "Yes."

He rises, taking my hand, and the world narrows to the soft glide of fingers and breath and heartbeats. Upstairs, the house is silent. The street outside, still.

And for once—despite everything closing in—there's no fear, no defense. Just this.

The week finally closes with all the grace of a preteen cleaning her room. Richard picked up Stella from school on Friday, leaving the weekend to Noah and me. Saturday dawns quiet—with Noah in my bed for the first time.

With Stella at Richard's, last night Noah spent the night in my bed instead of me retreating to the guest room and tiptoeing upstairs before she woke. We have nothing planned today. I'd had to agree to that in advance—otherwise, a different team member would've been scheduled as backup.

The surreal quality of it—of him in my bed, of an ordinary Saturday morning—feels especially sharp in the early quiet. The November sun slants through the window, gold and deceptive. From here, it could be summer—if not for the chill beyond the glass.

"Morning." His voice is a rough rasp, sleep-heavy. Then his body jolts. "What time is it?"

"Almost ten."

He's out of bed in seconds, bare feet thudding on carpet.

"I'm late. I never oversleep."

I smile into the pillow. "Late for what?"

"Meeting Jake."

So much for a slow morning. I watch him dress—efficient, focused, tucking in the lethal calm that lives just under his surface.

"You're staying in, right?"

"Yes, sir."

That earns me a grin. He starts for the door, then doubles back, catching me by the waist and kissing me hard enough that my knees weaken. When he pulls away, he glances down at his shorts, mutters, "Damn. Every time," and leaves shaking his head.

"You'll be back for lunch?" I call.

"By one!"

The door shuts and silence returns.

Hours later, I'm cocooned on the couch, blanket wrapped around me, a novel open on my lap and the late-autumn light gilding the hardwood floors. The house feels alive but safe— each creak familiar, each breath of wind harmless.

I rise to make lunch, padding into the kitchen, when I notice my phone lit on the counter. The stillness cracks.

Missed calls. Richard.

Texts stacked beneath his name.

Is Stella with you?
Answer the phone.
Where are you?
Call me.

I frown, irritation flashing first—he always expects instant access—but it drains away as my eyes return to the first message. *Is Stella with you?*

My pulse stutters. I hit call.

He answers on the first ring.

"Where have you been?" His voice is tight, frantic.

"Home. My phone was in the kitchen."

"You didn't see my messages?"

"I was reading a physical book, Richard. Not everything I do requires my phone in my hand. What's going on? Why are you asking if Stella's with me?"

He exhales—long, uneven. Not irritation. Something closer to fear. "We had brunch, came home—"

"And?" My throat dries.

"I can't find her. I've looked everywhere. You think she'd walk to your place?"

Five miles. She wouldn't. "Did you fight?"

"No!" His shout crackles over the line, more fear than anger.

"When did you last see her?"

"Eleven-thirty. She went to her room."

The house flashes in my mind—twelve thousand square feet. It's old. Creaky doors. Hardwood floors. My heartbeat spikes. "Did you stay downstairs?"

"No," he says, voice lowering. "Jessica and I…took a nap. After brunch."

A nap. Of course.

My stomach drops, the air around me thinning. What if she heard them? Went for a walk? "Richard, listen to me. Call her friends. Every one of them that's within walking distance of your house. I'll start checking this end. Do you have her iPad?"

"It's on her bed."

She didn't plan to leave for long then.

The front door opens; I spin—relief, hope—then Noah's silhouette fills the doorway. His gaze locks on my face, reading the panic.

I press the phone to my chest for a second and whisper, "Stella's missing."

The words are simultaneously terrifying, electric, and surreal. His posture shifts—lover to operative in a breath.

"What happened?"

I put the phone back to my ear. "When was the last time—"

"About eleven-thirty," Richard repeats.

Noah's already moving—retrieving his phone, touching the screen, eyes flicking to every window.

And that's when the thought strikes like a blade: *What if this isn't about Richard? What if Dorian was right?*

A rush of cold sweeps through me. "Christ," I whisper. "What if they took her to get to me?"

Noah's gaze snaps to mine—steady, calm, lethal focus. "We'll find her."

The quiet house hums with the weight of that promise.

CHAPTER
TWENTY-FIVE

ALICIA

The sound that wakes Richard's quiet neighborhood isn't a scream or a siren.

It's the slam of his front door as he rushes outside when I pull up.

Noah's out of the car before I am—steady, commanding, impossible to ignore.

"Richard, where was she last seen?"

Cold November air claws through my clothes. My hands shake as I shove my arms into my coat, barely feeling the zipper catch my chin. The wind carries the scent of wood smoke and damp leaves, the world suddenly sharper, meaner.

Jessica stumbles out behind him, in slippers, phone clutched white-knuckled in her hand. "No one knows anything," she says, voice high with panic. "We've called every friend."

I cross the lawn, my pulse pounding so hard my vision pulses with it. "She wouldn't just vanish. She'd text me."

"Then where is she?" Richard snaps, fear and fury indistinguishable in his voice.

Noah steps between us, a wall of calm in the chaos. "We'll find her," he says. "There's a tracker in her backpack. She's close—signal's weak, but I've got a ping."

"Do it faster," Richard growls.

"At first I thought it was your house," Noah says, thumb gliding over his phone, "but it's just off the property. Not exact."

While he studies the screen, I ask, "Are you sure she wasn't angry? Have you checked the treehouse?"

"Of course I've fucking checked the treehouse."

My chest tightens. I can't seem to pull in a full breath. Noah's brow furrows, jaw tightening by degrees. Then his gaze lifts, sharp and certain. "Signal's weak but moving—east, within a mile."

He turns to me. "Keys."

I toss them before he finishes the word. He catches them one-handed, already heading for the car. I'm right behind him.

The drive blurs.

Every street looks the same—brick Colonials, leafless trees, people walking dogs who have no idea my world is splitting apart. The heater blasts, but my fingers stay ice-cold.

"She's smart," Noah says, eyes scanning the sidewalks and mirrors. "She knows how to stay visible. We'll find her."

I nod, though my throat's too tight for words. *Find her.* The phrase repeats like a heartbeat. Images flash—headlines, police tape, Dorian's warning looping like a curse. *They'll find another way to reach you.*

A buzz breaks the silence. Richard, still on speaker through Noah's phone. "We're circling the park. Anything?"

"Not yet," Noah says evenly. "We're headed toward the shopping strip."

"Jesus, Alicia, if something's happened—"

"Don't," I whisper, interrupting Richard, eyes on the windshield. "Don't say it."

"When do we call the cops? The FBI?"

"Hudson's already in touch," Noah says. "They're aware. Letting us take the first pass."

He's trying to sound confident, but I can hear the tension beneath it. He knows this isn't normal.

And Dorian was right. I'd dismissed his warnings, told myself I was being paranoid—until now.

Then, faintly—over the hum of wheels over pavement—laughter.

Noah brakes hard, and my seatbelt locks as I jolt forward. Across the street, two girls sit on a low brick wall outside a clothes boutique, legs swinging, a contraband energy drink between them.

One of them—my daughter.

"Stella!"

Her head jerks up. "Mom?"

Relief hits like a tidal surge, so fierce my knees nearly buckle. I'm out of the car before it stops moving, half-running, half-sobbing. I reach her, grip her shoulders, pull her against me so fast she squeaks. I breathe her in—shampoo, sugar, cold air, the unmistakable scent of her shampoo. *Alive.*

"Do you have any idea—" My voice breaks. "We've been looking everywhere."

"I was just at Amber's," she mumbles into my coat. "We were watching a movie."

"What movie?"

She hesitates. "One you probably haven't heard of."

Noah's beside us now, his hand light on my back, steadying me, grounding me. My heart's still racing, but the world starts to refocus around his calm.

Richard's SUV screeches up the street and stops at the curb. He's out before the engine cuts, fear and fury twisted together. "Where the hell have you been?"

"Dad, I—"

"Do you have any idea—"

"Richard," I cut in, turning toward him. "She's safe. That's what matters."

He looks at me, then at Noah, suspicion flaring. "Safe? You call this safe? You've got whatever circus you're running, and now my daughter disappears for hours—"

"She wasn't taken," Noah says evenly. "She made a bad call, that's all."

Richard steps closer. "And who the hell are you to decide what's safe for my kid?"

Noah doesn't flinch, but I feel the sting in my bones.

"I'm the one keeping your family safe," he says quietly.

Richard blinks, thrown by the calm authority in Noah's voice.

I tighten my grip on Stella's hand, keeping her close.

Amber, Stella's friend, approaches, her small shoulders hunching under the weight of so many adult eyes. Richard recognizes her immediately. "She was with you?"

"I called," Jessica says from behind him, her tone brittle. "Your mom didn't answer."

Amber bites her lip. "She's getting her hair done. Dad's golfing. There's a path in the woods behind my house—it cuts through here. My parents know I take it all the time."

Richard inhales sharply, the flush rising in his neck. "Get in the car, Stella, you're coming with me. Amber, we'll give you a ride home."

Stella's arms loosen around me, guilt overtaking relief. She knows she's in for it. I want to tell Richard no—that she's coming with me—but he'd never allow it. Not on his weekend, and not after this.

He looks at me then, eyes hard, voice pitched low so only I hear. "You need to fix whatever mess you've dragged into our lives, Alicia. Because next time, she might not come back."

That's not fair, and it's not true—but he's already turning away.

"Mom?" Stella's voice is small.

"In the car," Richard barks. His patience—what little he had—is gone.

"It's okay, hon," I say softly. "Go on. I'll see you tomorrow when you get home."

"What's he talking about?" she asks.

"A case," I lie. "Nothing for you to worry about."

"Stella!" Richard's sharp tone makes her flinch.

Jessica hurries around to the passenger side, her usual cheerful energy replaced by nerves. She climbs in like she's the one being punished.

"Go on," I tell Stella again. "I'll see you tomorrow."

Her eyes dart from me to Noah, understanding flickering there—our panic, our closeness, the unspoken truth of us.

"Stella, so help me God—"

"I'm coming," she says quickly, stepping forward. Amber's already waiting at the car door.

Noah's hand finds the small of my back, solid and warm. Relief trickles through my body like water through a cracked dam—slow, uneven, but real. My knees shake, my arms ache from holding tension so long.

I lean into him, just enough to steady myself, keeping my expression neutral so Stella won't see me break. She's watching, wide-eyed, taking in everything.

When the car pulls away, the cold rushes in, empty and merciless. The street falls silent again, but nothing about the quiet feels peaceful.

TWENTY-SIX

NOAH

The house is silent, but it's a heavy silence.

The kind that settles low in your bones and hums there, a warning more than a quiet.

Alicia stands at the window, arms folded tight, watching headlights and taillights mingle on the street. Streetlight gold slides across her reflection: pale skin, tired eyes, the tremor of nerves she's still trying to suppress.

I stand in the doorway, earbuds in place, speaking to Hudson, but watching her. Hudson's voice fills one ear, but every other sense is tuned to Alicia—each small breath, each motionless second.

"Should we place security outside Richard Whitmore's home?"

It's a fair question. Alicia didn't feel it was necessary—and I don't think she wanted to open herself up to her ex's fifty questions. But she might feel differently now.

"If he's open to it, we can place Jake on the street," Hudson says, expanding on his question.

"It's an upscale neighborhood. A man sitting in a car—someone will call in suspicious activity. If we add security, it needs to be on-site." I picture Jake idling at the curb, a stranger in suburbia—exactly the kind of thing that makes neighbors call 911. I'm right on this one.

"Get Alicia's take."

"Will do," I say. "I'll touch base in the morning."

The call ends and I pocket my phone and earbuds. Today ended up being nothing, but it doesn't feel like it. The weight pressing on Alicia proves that.

"She's home safe," I tell her, needing to hear it aloud.

"I know." The confirmation rings thin. "But that doesn't make it stop."

"You did everything right," I say, even knowing logic rarely gets a foothold in fear.

"I didn't protect her."

She's not looking at me, but I shake my head. "You reacted. Fast. You found her. That's protection."

I could remind her that she was at her father's house, that if anyone's at fault, it's him, but today's event isn't what has her shaken. It's what today might have been. It's where the fault might have fallen. It's about everything her mind can do with that kind of opening once fear gets inside.

Her gaze stays on the dark street. "You didn't see Richard's face. He thinks I'm endangering our daughter."

His name rubs like grit. I want to tell her Richard's fear isn't protective—it's possessive, controlling, the kind that wears concern as a respectable mask. But she isn't in a place to hear that. Not tonight.

So I don't say it.

I've spent hours trying to find the thing that will ease this for her, and I'm running out of words. Some things have to burn through on their own.

She finally turns away from the window, her eyes shining but steady. "You ever feel fear in your throat?" she asks, voice rough. "Like it gets stuck there and won't let you breathe?"

"First time in the field—we lost comms for three hours. Static and silence. Every minute sounded like blood in my ears. I thought we'd lost a man. That kind of helplessness"— I exhale slowly—"it'll eat you alive."

"That's what it feels like," she whispers. "Helplessness. Like something's waiting to attack and there's nothing you can do."

I reach for her hands and cover them with mine, trying to bring warmth back into her frozen fingers. "You can't live in that moment forever. You learn from it, and then you move."

"Is that what you do?"

"Trying."

For a long moment, we stand there together, reflected dimly in the darkened glass. Two people held in the same uneasy stillness. Outside, the wind kicks up and sends brittle leaves skittering over the sidewalk.

"Get some rest," I say, knowing she needs to put the scare behind her. "I'll close everything up."

"I can't sleep."

"You will."

I brush a strand of hair behind her ear and cup her face. She's beautiful like this, even wrung out and shaken. Maybe especially like this. All that strength she wears so cleanly through the day is still there, but softer now. More human. More exposed.

"You're allowed to exhale, Alicia."

She nods, but her eyes drift back toward the street.

It'd be easier if Stella were here. If Alicia could hear her moving around upstairs, could put eyes on her whenever she wanted, could sit beside her on the couch and watch something mindless until this sharp edge dulled. Something ordinary. Something that would let her body believe what her mind can't yet accept—that her daughter is safe, that today was only a scare.

The sound cuts through the moment like a crack in glass. I step back and pull it from my pocket. KOAN portal notification.

"Problem?" Alicia asks.

"Maybe. I'll deal with it."

I head downstairs to the guest room to grab my laptop. A few minutes later I confirm it's nothing urgent—just team confirmations for next week's rotations.

Alicia appears in the doorway. I hadn't heard her approach.

"Is there anything I can do? To make this go away? To make these people not want to target me? My family?"

That's the kicker. We still don't know exactly who these people are.

We've got theories. Possibilities. Last week I could've convinced myself this was all precaution, that maybe she wasn't being targeted at all. But someone breached her vehicle. Someone's tracking her. And the best working theory we've got is that somebody doesn't want Alicia's documents making it into discovery.

I hesitate, already hating what I'm about to say.

"You could make everything public."

"I can't do that to my clients," she says. "Besides, we don't know enough."

Her steel-blue eyes go wild for a second—not with panic exactly, but with the desperate need to be understood. Her shoulders draw back. Her chin lifts. Defiance and fear, side by side.

"I hear you," I say, because I do.

Then I pull her into me and hold her.

It isn't much. It isn't a solution. But it's what I can give her, so it's what I do.

By Sunday morning, the house feels hollow, like the echo of last night never really cleared.

Alicia is up before I am. I'm not sure she slept much at all. Last night was the first time we shared a bed without making love, and somehow that felt more intimate than the nights we did. Like we crossed into something quieter and deeper. Less about wanting and more about staying. About being there when there was nothing to offer but your presence.

After coffee, she heads down to her home gym, and I decide to give her some space.

Truth is, I need a little myself.

I step outside to check the carport and call Maya while I walk. It's been a few weeks since we talked. She's busy. I get it.

"Hey you," she says, answering on the second ring.

I huff out a laugh. "Can't believe I caught you."

I was half expecting voicemail. Maya's a pediatric nurse, and keeping up with her schedule is like trying to grab smoke with your hands. If she's on shift, she doesn't answer.

"I'm on break. Good timing. Are you home this weekend?"

Ah. She's assuming that's why I'm calling.

"You know, New Jersey isn't my home base anymore, right? I've got an apartment outside of DC."

"I actually didn't realize that. So when Dad complains you haven't come home, he means to his place."

His place. Him and Linda.

"You don't get the same treatment?"

"Well, I mean, I live in Chicago. A flight is required. It's different."

"Maybe." I'd say it's more that Maya is his baby girl and can do no wrong, and I'm the son that can do no right, but that's not a Maya issue. And I didn't call her to check in on Dad. "What's up with you? How're things?"

"Good. No complaints. Phoenix started her last rotation before she's done with residency. She likes the doctors. And so far it hasn't been as demanding, so we get to see each other more."

"What's this rotation?"

"Dermatology."

"Nice."

"Yeah. It is." She and Phoenix have been together for years now. Phoenix is part of the reason Maya ended up back in Chicago, back in the city where we grew up. "What about you? Dad says you're working constantly. Any truth in that or are you avoiding him?"

"I call him every Sunday."

I don't owe him my weekends. Never have.

"Right." She breathes out, and I can't tell if it's a sigh or a huff. "So what are you working on these days? Dad said it's protection, but I thought you were doing investigative work."

"Yeah, the team I told you I joined—"

"Hunting the bad guys, that's what you said. The ones above the law."

"Yeah, well, still on that team, but this has turned into more of a protective detail."

"For anyone I'd know?"

"Doubtful."

"So you're bored out of your mind."

"Not even close. It's been intense. The twelve-year-old daughter went missing yesterday."

"Whoa. She okay?"

"Yeah. She was actually staying at her dad's. She went out with a friend—didn't tell him."

"Oh, so this detail—it's a divorced woman?"

"Yeah," I say, wondering why her tone shifted with the question.

"Single?"

I glance toward the house. "Yeah."

"Your boss going to have a problem when he learns you're seeing the client?"

My mouth opens, ready to deny, but I don't lie to Maya. Not anymore. Not after telling her that Mom would get better. Not after telling her that nothing was going on with Dad and Linda.

"What makes you think—"

"Dad told me."

I told Dad about dinner. That was it. But he drew his own conclusion. He assumed the worst and I proved him right.

"Well, tell me about her," Maya says. "I've got five more minutes."

I lean against the brick fence and look out over the courtyard.

How do I explain Alicia?

"She runs a crisis management firm. She's on the ball. Sophisticated. Wicked smart." I rub my thumb along the phone's edge, searching for the right words. "She's the kind of woman who always walks into the fire first."

"One kid?"

"Yeah, a daughter who loves playing hoops. A little headstrong, like her mom."

If Mom were alive, she'd like them both. That thought hits out of nowhere and lodges in my chest.

"So," Maya says, amusement creeping into her voice, "a hot single mom has taken my big bro' off the market. That tracks."

I can't help the grin—it's ridiculous and dead-on.

"What tracks?"

"She's not just some hookup."

No. She isn't.

Not by a long shot.

"Tell me more," Maya says, sounding entirely too interested.

Morning light glints off the windows, and I catch a warped reflection of myself. I'm smiling like an idiot.

"What's she look like?"

"Black hair, shoulder length, dark blue eyes... It's a color you don't see often. Heart-shaped face." I pause, searching for something that gets close. "You know Courteney Cox?"

"The *Friends* actress?"

"Yeah. Not exactly, but there's something there. And in the way she carries herself? Dresses? She's got this Olivia Pope thing. You remember Scandal?"

Maya and I have burned through enough television over the years that she definitely remembers.

"So she's white."

She says it casually, but not carelessly.

We're a mixed-up blend by most people's standards. Dad's Mexican American. Mom was white, though her family came out of Alaska and there was Native heritage in her line. Most of my life, people have looked at me and decided what I am before I ever opened my mouth.

"She is." I keep my tone easy. "And?"

"Has she told anyone yet?"

"We're keeping it quiet." I push off the fence and start walking again. "For a lot of reasons. Her daughter. My job."

Maya goes silent.

"You've got an opinion," I say. "Say it."

My tone comes out sharper than I intended, but Maya has dated pretty much every race and background under the sun. Dad married two white women. If she's got an issue, I want to hear it straight.

"It's nothing."

I look up at the hazy morning sky. That's one of Maya's favorite lies.

"Look," she says, "I believe in judging people by who they are. You know that. But there are still assholes out there. That's all I'm saying. If you end up needing somebody to vent to, I'm here."

If Alicia runs into problems because of us, I'd bet the bigger issue is the age difference, not race. But I haven't brought age up to Maya, and I'm not about to start now.

"So far, no issues," I tell her. "It's new. Don't go borrowing trouble. I'm good."

"Mm-hm."

"You go save those kids."

"Yeah, yeah. I do actually need to go. But before I hang up —has Dad said anything about high cholesterol?"

I frown. "No. Why?"

"I don't know. Linda messaged me asking about some results Dad got on a physical. I'm probably going to call her."

Alicia comes into view through the kitchen windows.

She's got a bottle of water in one hand, and from the look of her, she gave herself a brutal workout. Her hair is pulled back in a high ponytail. Lycra skims every long, toned line of her body. She raises the bottle in a silent hello as she passes, and light catches on the sheen of sweat at her throat.

Then she turns toward the stairs, her hips moving with easy, unthinking rhythm.

My body reacts before my brain gets involved.

"I've got nothing for you on Dad. Keep in touch. And tell Phoenix I said hi."

I end the call with every intention of following Alicia upstairs and putting that shower to much better use. But before I even make it off the patio, my phone vibrates again.

Hudson.

With a quiet curse, I drop back into the chair and answer.

"Morning," I say in greeting.

"We received an update on the police investigation."

It takes me a second to switch gears. "The Delacroix murder investigation?"

"Yes. One of the reasons Alicia's a person of interest—"

"You mean other than her being the one who was with him when he died? Who found him?"

"Right. There's a witness who claims she was seen talking to him earlier—drinking coffee—and she followed him to the back."

I sit straighter.

That doesn't match what Alicia told me. Then again, witness accounts get messy all the time. People misremember. Fill in blanks. See what they expect to see.

"Okay," I say slowly, dragging a hand over my face while I absorb it.

Hudson doesn't pause long.

"The witness is missing."

The words hit like ice water down my spine. "What?"

"That's what our source says. There's information in the portal. Can you take some time tomorrow—see what you can find? I'm sure the police are searching—but I don't know how much they care at this juncture as they've got the witness statement on record. I'd love to find this witness though and learn if someone put them up to it."

"You think it ties back to the Crawford case."

"Worth checking."

"I'm on it," I say.

The call ends, but I stay where I am, phone still in my hand.

If this witness was paid to make a false statement—if somebody saw an opportunity to smear Alicia and took it— then disappearing makes perfect sense. They'd have every reason to stay hidden. They took money. They lied to police. They crossed a line that gets a hell of a lot harder to explain once somebody starts asking the right questions.

And if our hunch is right, even if I find them, getting anything useful out of them won't be easy.

TWENTY-SEVEN

ALICIA

I've spent the day combing through every piece of information tied to the Crawford case, along with files on another client—Howard Wells—who faced extortion built on information purchased from the same source.

By late afternoon, my eyes burn from the blue-light glare. The cursor blinks on the screen, patient and relentless, as I sift through every scrap. Nothing stands out as worth risking prison over—just the usual mix of salacious dirt and power games, lies dressed in bespoke suits.

One name appears twice in the payment records—Kwame Asante-Bridges, listed under a media holding—but the transaction is categorized as market intelligence, the kind of purchase any competitive media company would make without a second thought. I file it under unremarkable and move on.

There are a few threads that could unravel into something criminal if pushed hard enough—bribes, financial dealings that could be interpreted the wrong way—but I can't be the only one holding this information.

Of course—what happened with Stella wasn't actually connected to the case. That was my worst-case scenario, spun too fast and too far. And it was wrong.

My phone buzzes.

Dick: OTW with Stella. Are you home?

Me: Y

He doesn't always check. Stella's twelve. She can be home alone for short stretches without issue. But after yesterday, I suppose we're both recalibrating.

I set the phone down and exit my home office, descending the steps. I presume Noah's in the basement, but instead of finding him, I head for the front door and step outside, waiting on the stoop.

The air bites through my blouse, carrying the faint scent of smoke from a neighbor's chimney. I should grab a coat, but I don't move. I need to see that car turn the corner. I need to put my hands on her.

The urge sharpens, impossible to ignore. It's irrational—I know that. Nothing actually happened yesterday. But logic doesn't quiet it. This is something deeper, something instinctive, and I don't have the will to fight it.

Noah has done everything he can to steady me. To be present. To give me something solid to lean on.

And I'm grateful—more than I've let myself say out loud.

Because without him, I would have broken. I would have shown up at Richard's door, asking to sit at their table, pretending I just didn't feel like being alone.

Richard's BMW appears at the end of the block.

Instead of pulling to the curb, he turns into the drive, stopping in the narrow stretch between the closed gate and the street.

Relief hits first. Then dread, close behind it—one feeding the other.

The passenger door swings open, and Stella climbs out, already smiling.

That smile is sunlight.

And behind it—Richard, like a storm rolling in.

She runs straight into me, and I gather her close, my hands moving instinctively—into her hair, over her cheeks, tracing the familiar scatter of freckles like I need the confirmation that she's real, that she's here.

Richard steps out more slowly. He reaches into the car, past the back passenger door Stella left open, and pulls out her overnight bag and backpack. The door slams shut behind him, the sound like a shotgun in the suburban hum.

The front door opens.

Noah steps outside.

"Hey, Noah," Stella says, bright and easy.

I don't let her go right away. My hands stay in her hair, smoothing it back, grounding myself in the feel of her.

Richard and Noah exchange a nod—controlled, measured. It lands less like acknowledgment and more like a line being drawn.

"Alicia," he says quietly, voice tight. "We need to talk. Alone."

"Dad, I told you I'm not—"

"It's not about that sugar bug."

She shifts, reaching for her things. "'Kay. Love you, Dad."

My gaze flicks to the car. Jessica sits in the front passenger seat, watching—likely aware of Richard's request for a private talk.

"Can we speak in your office?" The request for a seemingly official location sets me on edge.

"Sure."

Noah holds the door as we pass, and I catch his gaze, offering a small smile meant to reassure him.

Everything's fine.

Or it will be.

Richard doesn't wait—he leads the charge up the stairs. Of course, Richard knows the layout of my home, and acts like he owns it.

Stella veers toward the kitchen, already at the refrigerator by the time I follow him. As I climb the stairs, Noah heads down the hallway to join her.

When I reach my office, Richard is standing in the room, flustered, jaw tight.

"Close the door."

By common accord, when we argue, we don't do so within earshot of Stella. That's the only reason I do as he requests.

He paces once, the soles of his shoes whispering against the rug, then gestures toward my desk. There are some files on it, but it's neatly organized. Nothing to indicate the chaos I've been combing through today.

"I want to know what you've gotten yourself involved in."

I bite back the instinctive response—that my clients' business isn't his to question.

"There's an upcoming court case," I say evenly. "It's possible I could be subpoenaed. It's exactly what I told you."

"This is related to the Vasquez scandal." It doesn't sound like a question, but I take it as one.

I step past my desk, wanting it between me and Richard, but I don't sit, as I sense he has no plans to take a more congenial posture. "Yes. Tangentially."

Richard lives in DC. He doesn't need details to assemble the broader picture.

"Stella should come live with me."

My stomach drops, and my fingers curl into my palms.

"Think about it."

"Richard. Yesterday had nothing to do with that."

"No. It didn't. But you thought it could have."

I hold his gaze.

I don't want this fight. Not in court. Not dragged out and dissected. But if it comes to that, I won't hesitate.

"If I believe she's in danger—if the security I have in place isn't enough—I'll consider it. But if it comes to that, you'll need to have security too."

"She's safer at my house. And you wouldn't even give me fall break."

Of course he's still sore about fall break, but I don't take the bait. "Is she safer at your house?" My voice softens, but there's no give in it. "Tell me, Richard—how long are your naps these days?"

The question lands exactly the way I want it to—yes, if he brings this into court, I'll find a way to mention yesterday's events.

His mouth tightens, his gaze shifting toward the window. When he turns, there's an anger simmering that I haven't sensed in years. "Let's talk about your *naps*. I don't want the details on Delacroix. I suspected—"

"At the time you didn't care," I say, filling in the blank for him. After I had Stella, he began working round the clock—and we both know it wasn't all office-related.

He presses his lips together, shoving his hands into his pockets. "It's in the past."

Of course it is.

"But now—you're living with a man? What is he? Black? Hispanic? In the same house as my daughter?"

The air punches out of me. For a second, all I hear is the hum of the HVAC, the dull thud of my heartbeat.

"Since when are you racist?" I ask, each word precise.

"I'm not racist," he snaps. "I'm concerned for our daughter. What will her friends say?"

I stare at him.

"Listen to yourself, Richard."

The argument isn't worth dignifying. We live in a part of DC where no one blinks at a multiracial couple. This isn't about Stella. It's about him.

And if I'm being honest—it wouldn't matter who I was seeing. He'd find a problem with it.

Still…something in the way he said Delacroix twists at the edge of my thoughts. I would have sworn he had no idea back then.

He exhales sharply, tipping his head back.

"Damn it, Alicia." With that, he steps to the door, but stops, with his hand on the knob. "And for the record, I didn't know about Delacroix. Even when the detective insinuated, I didn't believe it—but you just confirmed it." Under his breath, he adds, "I should've fought harder for her. Maybe then she wouldn't be growing up in your mess."

He's out of the room before I can snap that he would've been welcome to try, but I would've fought back tooth and nail.

I exit the office and stand at the top of the stairs, one hand on the banister, pulse thrumming in my throat, listening to the echo of the slammed front door fading into silence.

Noah appears at the bottom of the stairs, tension etched across his face.

"You okay?" he asks.

"I will be." My voice sounds foreign—steady when I feel anything but.

He starts up toward me, slow, deliberate steps. "What happened?"

"Richard," I manage. "He thinks he's protecting Stella."

His jaw flexes, eyes dark with understanding. "And you?"

I let out a breath that feels like it's been trapped in my chest all day.

"He's an asshole."

The space between us crackles, heavy with all the things I can't fix tonight—ex-husbands, past mistakes, the creeping shadow of an investigation that's starting to feel way too personal.

Noah reaches the top step, close enough that I can see the light catch in his dark eyes.

"I'll head downstairs," he says quietly. "You and Stella—figure out dinner. I'll go pick something up when you're ready."

I nod, forcing a breath past the knot in my chest. "Thank you."

He lingers a second, like he wants to say more, then turns and disappears down the hall, back toward the basement and the security monitors.

I stand there for a moment longer, then turn back toward my office.

The files sit on my desk like loaded weapons.

Tomorrow.

I'll deal with them tomorrow.

For now, my daughter is home.

Later, after she's in bed, I can run down the miles on a treadmill. Punch a boxing bag if needed. For now, I need to fight the urge to shatter something—and remember that fear and fury aren't the same thing as weakness.

TWENTY-EIGHT

NOAH

The upscale apartment building has the usual amenities—parking, a pool, and a steady stream of twenty- and thirty-somethings rushing through the lobby on their way to work.

I'm here early, positioned near the entrance, hoping to catch Jeri Masters—the witness who's stopped answering calls and opening her door. I'm not ready to call her missing. Not answering during random visits doesn't qualify. Neither does ignoring an unknown number.

Still… it's enough to raise a flag.

And if Alicia had hired an attorney, I'd expect them to be doing exactly what I'm doing—knocking on the witness's door, trying to understand her version of events. More than that, trying to gauge what she actually remembers.

Because there's something that doesn't sit right.

To notice Alicia and the victim in a conference room with over a hundred people, Jeri would've had to know who she was looking at—or have a reason to pay attention. If that's the case, how does she know them?

The apartment isn't a doorman building, but there is a lobby with a front desk. From what I can tell, visitors can access the elevators to the apartments from the lobby, the parking garage, or from a side door. The person behind the front desk looks like she's barely out of college, hair in a ponytail, wearing a rumpled white button-down shirt and a crooked name tag. She's busy scanning packages—which is probably a big part of her job.

On a whim, I head her way instead of toward the elevators.

"Hi," I say.

She looks up from the package she's holding and gives me a warm, friendly smile. "Hi. If you're here for your package, we're getting through them as fast as we can. The person yesterday went home sick. If you want to give me your name—"

"That's okay," I say quickly. "I don't live here."

"Oh." She straightens, and glances down. My gaze follows her to a stack of boxes and envelopes. "Ah, the rental office opens at nine."

"I'm actually looking for a Jeri Masters. She's an old friend, and I was in the neighborhood."

"Oh. She moved." She looks at a bin with mail and a small cardboard box. "I only know because I've had to start collecting her mail to return to sender."

"That's harsh," I say with a casual grin. "You don't forward it?"

"She didn't leave a forwarding address. We would forward it if she had. You should tell her to call with the address..."

She glances back at the basket. "But honestly, it looks like mostly junk mail."

"I could give it to her—"

"No, I can't do that. Federal law." She winces a little, like she wishes she could bend the rule, but not enough to risk it.

Still, she's already given me what I came for.

Jeri Masters moved. Recently.

I tap my fingers lightly on the counter. "I'll let her know she needs to update her address." I pause, letting my gaze drift back to the bin. "Any chance I can take a quick look? Just so I can tell her what she's missing."

She hesitates, then lifts the basket and sets it in front of me.

I flip through the contents.

Her assessment matches mine—junk mail. A local coupon booklet, clothing catalog, bank logos on two return addresses, but they don't look like bills. Then a small cardboard box catches my attention. Handwritten return address.

I pull out my phone and snap a quick photo.

The sender's name reads Josephine Masters.

Family, most likely.

"I'll let her know her grandmother sent something," I say, by way of explanation.

"Yeah," she says. "And tell her to get her mail forwarded. Otherwise, it all goes back."

I nod, thank her, and step out into the November cold.

The air hits sharp, wind cutting between buildings. I forward the photo to Quinn, then dictate a message as I walk: "Jeri Masters moved. No forwarding address. Might be worth checking if her lease was up or if she broke it early."

I reread it once, then send.

With one last assessing view of the apartment building, I

take in the bikes on the balconies and the college flags and decide this isn't the kind of place residents stay forever. A move doesn't necessarily mean anything. But the timing? That's what's interesting.

By the time I'm back in my car, the wind's sharp enough to whistle over the windshield. A message flashes across my phone.

Alicia: Lunch?

Me: Name the time and place.

Alicia: Montrose Café. 12:15?

Me: I'll pick you up.

Alicia: No. I'll meet you. I have a meeting across the street.

Me: Gabriel with you?

Alicia: Nearby. I'll walk over when I'm done.

After checking in with Jake, Quinn, and lastly, Gabriel, I head over to the café.

Quinn confirms Jeri paid a penalty to break her lease early. Official reason: family emergency. That's all there is on record.

How she got it—system access or charm—I don't ask.

Either way, it adds another layer.

And none of it feels like coincidence.

Montrose is one of Alicia's regular spots—brick front, quiet enough for real conversation, tucked just far enough off the main drag to avoid the worst of the noise. We've been here a few times before.

Back when things felt easier.

Before every conversation carried weight.

I park on a side street and step inside. The smell hits first —espresso, butter, the faint sweetness of cinnamon sugar.

Alicia's already there, seated by the window. Her hair is down, her jacket draped over the back of the chair. She looks tired—but not from lack of sleep. This is the kind of tired that comes from thinking too much, carrying too much.

"Hey," she says.

Just like that, something in my chest loosens.

"Hey yourself." I slide into the chair across from her. "Running away from your empire?"

"Just regrouping." She wraps her hands around her coffee cup. "You ever notice people think crisis management means I enjoy chaos?"

I grin. "Occupational hazard."

She laughs—soft, unguarded. For a moment, the tension lifts, like she's letting herself come up for air.

We talk about nothing for a while.

Stella's upcoming play. Jake and Daisy looking for a new place. The heater in Alicia's office clicking in a way that might be a problem—or might be something that's always been there and she's only noticing now. It's easy.

Too easy, maybe, because I don't notice them until Alicia's gaze shifts past my shoulder and her smile falters.

"Noah," she murmurs, voice flattening. "Behind you."

I turn—and find Richard. And Jessica.

They've just walked in. Richard spots us immediately. The flicker in his eyes is small but unmistakable. Possession. Jealousy. Disapproval.

He recovers fast, polite smile in place as he approaches. "Alicia."

"Richard." Her tone is cool, neutral.

Jessica beams. "Oh! Hi, Alicia! And Noah. You helped with—" she lowers her voice like it's a secret, "—that scare with Stella. We're still so grateful and we never really thanked you."

I nod once. "Just glad it worked out."

Richard frowns. "Seems like you're always around to help these days."

"Part of the job," I say easily.

"I'd think your job would involve some distance."

Alicia's hand curls around her cup. "Richard."

He raises both hands slightly. "I'm just saying—it's unusual, isn't it? Security sticking this close?"

Jessica lets out a laugh a beat too loud, glancing around like she's aware of the audience. "You two must be starving. We can find another table—"

"No need," Alicia says smoothly. "We were just finishing."

The steel in her tone is unmistakable.

I reach for the check, but Richard beats me to it, sliding his card toward the waiter as if he's reclaiming territory. "I'll get this."

"Not necessary," I tell him.

"I insist. To thank you for your service."

It's not about gratitude.

It's about control.

About reminding me where I stand.

Alicia opens her mouth, then stops. The tension thickens, stretching tight between all of us.

"Thank you," she says finally.

But her eyes are anything but grateful.

Richard nods, satisfied, and Jessica's expression softens, as if she's relieved the conversation survived without voices rising and heads turning.

Outside, the wind has picked up, carrying the edge of rain.

Alicia slips her arm through mine as we walk toward the corner. Her hand is steady, but I can feel the faint tremor beneath it. Adrenaline. Residual tension.

"He's jealous," I say.

"No. Not jealous. He's just an asshole."

"That too."

She glances up at me, eyes still stormy. "You handled that well."

"Years of practice staying calm under fire."

"I noticed."

We stop beside her car. The sunlight glimmers in her hair, and for a heartbeat, the world goes still again.

"I hate that he still gets to me," she admits quietly.

"He doesn't get to you. He just tries."

Her lips curve faintly. "You're good at this."

"It's my job," I say. "And maybe something more."

She exhales, the tension from the confrontation leaving her shoulders. "You're not supposed to say things like that."

"Why not?"

"Because I might believe you."

"Good."

She shakes her head but doesn't look away. "Dinner with Stella and I tonight?"

"Wouldn't miss it."

After dinner, the house feels warm again—music low, a candle burning on the kitchen island, the scent of pumpkin filling the space. For a moment, it almost feels normal.

Safe.

Then my phone buzzes.

A message from KOAN flashes across the screen.

Warrant filed: Morgan, Alicia. Contact pending.

The illusion fractures.

I stare at the words a second too long before locking the screen.

Upstairs, Stella laughs at something with Alicia— unaware that everything is about to change.

CHAPTER
TWENTY-NINE

ALICIA

The landing creaks, and I know before I look up. Something in the sound of it—too deliberate, too careful—tells me this isn't nothing.

Stella doesn't notice. She's laughing at a video on her screen, her feet tucked under her on the armchair in my office. I set my hand on her shoulder.

"Hey. Go start getting ready for bed."

She looks up, reads my face the way she's always been able to, and doesn't argue. Just unfolds herself and heads up to the third floor without being told twice.

When the sound of her footsteps fades, I face Noah on the landing and gesture to the stairs—we can talk in the kitchen—but he steps past me and enters my office.

With an inhale, I follow.

He closes the door with a click that seems to echo like a gavel.

"What is it?"

"A warrant has been filed."

"What does that mean?"

"They're charging you with the murder of Matthew Delacroix." He says it quietly, as if that softens the blow.

The room swims.

He catches my arm before I fold, his grip steady, grounding.

"How? Why?"

"I'm not sure, but Hudson notified Dorian Moore. He's already contacted a law firm he has on retainer. If they show up tonight, which they might—"

"It's after eight."

"True. But if they want to rattle you and keep you longer, it could be a good ploy. Late arrests control optics—less press, more pressure. If they're looking to make a scene, to ensure word gets out, they may plan on taking you at your office or somewhere more public tomorrow."

"On what grounds?"

"They aren't sharing everything but the prosecutor wouldn't agree with the arrest if they didn't feel they had a case."

I sit down on the edge of my desk, feeling like my world is collapsing. My tongue tastes metallic.

It's an inside view of my client's world that I never wanted to experience. For years I've been the one who strategized calm for others; now I'm the crisis, and there's no statement to spin this away.

"Okay. Well, my first priority is Stella. The thought of Stella waking to flashing lights and the sound of handcuffs—no." She'll never see that. "Should I turn myself in?" Control the scene. No cuffs in my doorway.

Control the story before it controls you. I've said it to

clients a hundred times. Maybe it's time to take my own advice.

"Dorian looped in a defense firm; they've been trying to reach you."

He gestures to my desk where my phone sits. I'd left it there when Stella came in—she'd been in a mood to talk, recounting play practice in a running bloopers reel that had us both laughing. I try not to check work when I'm with her.

My eyes burn. I know why the detective thinks he has a case. Somehow he found out about an affair that occurred ten years ago, and because I didn't admit to it, he thinks I'm guilty. But who would admit to a long-dormant affair?

"Alicia—are you okay?"

It's Noah's warm touch that brings me back to the present—and it's his dark concerned eyes that tell me I owe him the truth. It's going to come out anyway.

"We're investigating connections to Pierce Industries. It's possible this is how they are targeting you."

"What?" I ask, not sure I'm following the line of reasoning.

"You're a murder suspect. If Pierce, or anyone else involved in the Vasquez scandal, was worried about your testimony or contributions to the discovery process—they just removed you from the board. Discredit the witness."

"Wait—" I hold up my hand, trying to understand what he's saying. "You think Pierce, or some unnamed entity, is so afraid of my testimony that they murdered a man and framed me, to discredit my testimony?"

That's insane.

"Alicia, someone has been tracking your whereabouts. Someone did a background check on me—and has been doing research."

"You didn't tell me—"

"Well, we've been investigating. They haven't investigated anyone else on your security detail, which made me think Richard might have hired the PI and it wasn't related to this situation."

"Richard wouldn't hire a PI. You should've talked to me. I could've saved you steps."

"He's not happy I exist in your house, in your life."

"No, he's not, but you're the first person I've dated since we split—at least, that he's known about." I push up and return to my desk chair. "So Richard didn't hire someone to look into you, but who would?"

Speaking of Richard, I should probably call him. He could come over tonight and get Stella to avoid a run-in with police in the morning.

What evidence could they have? My affair with Matthew ten years ago? That I found him? It's not evidence, none of it is evidence. I'm innocent—am I being framed or is this just shoddy police work?

"All of the information we've gathered over the last few weeks will be shared with your legal counsel—it can be used in your arraignment and increase the possibility of pretrial release—but we need for you to select your legal counsel."

Right. I know plenty of lawyers but from working with them on behalf of my clients. I don't have a law firm on retainer.

I glance at the phone screen and the stack of notifications.

Perhaps I should call Richard, but he's not a defense attorney. I pick up the phone, finger hovering over the phone icon.

Noah stands across my desk, a loyal sentry, a silhouette

against the window, all quiet threat and steadiness. Will he want anything to do with me after he learns the truth?

There's no doubt in my mind the affair is what led the police investigator to point the finger at me. It's coming up—possibly in the arraignment hearing.

"What is it?" Noah asks.

It's not like me to move slowly when faced with crisis, to hesitate, or to be torn over priorities. I should tell Noah later, but I can't risk not being the one to tell him.

"I'm going to call Dorian, but once I do, everything has the potential to move fast. I need you to know something—the reason the police suspect me."

He crosses his arms. "Okay."

"I had an affair with Matthew Delacroix. It happened ten years ago. Matt and I…crossed a line. Briefly. For a couple of months. I buried it, locked it away. I didn't think anyone knew." I think back to Dorian's reaction—maybe Matt and I fooled ourselves. "I'm not a cheater. It was… It was after Stella had been born. My marriage was in a bad place. Richard was never home."

"You don't need to explain it to me."

Noah's firm. There's no anger. No, he's calm under fire. And what he's not saying is absolutely correct. I need to focus.

"We can talk about it later. For now, call Dorian. I'm going to tell the team—"

I open my mouth to protest—the idea of my affair being shared with people I don't even know—absolutely not.

"We need all the information." There's so much going on in his expression—maybe he's thinking it, maybe I'm feeling it—but the most significant one is that I should've shared this information with him and the team on day one. "No surprises, Alicia. It's the one rule in defense."

"Right." It's reluctant agreement. As a crisis manager, I always tell my clients I need to know everything to formulate the best plan, and yet I didn't share everything with my team.

He exits, closing the door behind him, and I stay very still for a moment. I've built a career on the principle that secrets unmanaged become crises. I knew about the affair. I knew it was relevant. And I said nothing—told myself it was ancient history, that it wouldn't surface, that I could manage the exposure if it did. I was wrong on all three counts.

I lift the phone and press Dorian's name.

"Dorian," I say, and the shaken uncertainty in the way that one word sounds has me blinking back tears.

"No word yet on which judge you'll be assigned. Once we know, we'll have more information."

"What do you mean?"

"If it's a judge with close ties to Pierce, then someone's pulling strings."

I exhale, knowing his thought process. His father—and I guess Dorian too—work like that. Judge shopping. But this… "I think…" I stop myself. Restart. "There's a strong possibility the police didn't have a good suspect. There's pressure on them to close out the case. This could be nothing more than rushed police work. Because of the affair that I didn't admit to—"

"Maybe. We're looking into that angle too. Are you good with my legal recommendation or are you acquiring your own?"

I close my eyes and rest my head on the back of my office

chair. "I haven't read any of your texts. Noah came to get me. I've been upstairs with Stella."

"I strongly recommend Shelly Madison and Luca Corzone. They're a high-profile defense team for Barclay Law. They're based in DC and are prepped and ready."

"Locked and loaded," I say, pushing aside the swirling nausea. "Should I call Richard?"

"For legal counsel? Hell no."

Dorian and Richard never hit it off. "Why?" He dropped everything to help me when I was called in for questioning.

"His intentions can't be trusted. What if he sees this as an opportunity to gain custody of Stella?"

"He would never." I twist in my seat, uncertain, but then, no: "He'll never want this going public. He'll see it as an embarrassment to him and his family name. He'd never in a million years want to see Stella's mother in prison. He'd find me the best legal resources available."

"Well, so will I—and you can be absolutely certain of my intentions."

"I know. You've been a good friend, Dorian. Thank you. I'll go with your recommendation on the condition the bills get sent to me."

"I have them on retainer."

"Dorian."

"Fine. We'll figure something out."

"But I feel like I need to give Richard a heads up."

"That's your call."

I hear the unspoken disagreement, but Dorian doesn't comprehend how angry Richard can be if he feels slighted. And plus, it feels like responsible co-parenting.

"What are next steps? Do I need to call Shelly or Luca?"

"I'll send them a message. They'll call you. They're officially on your case so from this moment on you'll be protected by client attorney privilege."

"Okay. Have you heard anything on when?"

"They'll come tonight or first thing in the morning. Either way, be ready."

I watch the time count on the top right of my monitor. 8:47…8:48.

The sense of dread threatens to suffocate me, but I call on every cell within my being, and dial Richard. I get voicemail.

"Richard, this is…" I stutter, hit with the realization I sound like I'm calling a client. "Ah, this is Alicia. Call me. It's urgent. Stella's fine. But call me."

I end the call and wonder if he'll ever hear the message. Chances are he'll see I called and call back without ever listening.

There's a light tap on the door and Noah enters. I gesture to the guest chair across the desk.

"I've lawyered up," I say, forcing a smile I don't at all feel, trying to make light of an unfathomable situation.

I'm innocent. I shouldn't be so nervous, but I'd be a fool to not perceive the danger. Our legal system is far from perfect. Innocent people get convicted.

"They could come tonight." My heart hammers in my chest. Outside, the sky is dark, my view of the naked maple partially lit by light from my window and from the street light.

I look to Noah. "No cuffs in front of Stella. No cameras if I can help it. Can we arrange that?"

"The police don't take requests."

Of course, he's right. I know it.

He comes around the desk and pulls me into his arms. I

let myself fall into his strength. The rhythm of his steady heartbeat calls me—grounds me.

It's so late. Well past the end of the workday. Surely they won't come tonight. They'll arrive in the morning.

While I might dread it, they are coming, so I need to prepare.

I pull away from Noah. "I'm going to go prepare. Outfit for the arraignment. A bag, just in case."

He lifts my chin, presses his lips to mine for a soft, comforting touch, then says, "You go do what you need to do. I'll stay downstairs. If they come now, I'll be sure they don't ring the doorbell."

I nod.

Before I go to prepare, I slip upstairs and tuck Stella into bed. It's all I can do to maintain normalcy and calm as I brush my lips over her forehead and say, "Goodnight. I love you."

In the closet, below the fractured light from the chandelier, I marvel at the order and beauty of this room I took such pride in. When I first moved in, I converted this bedroom into a floor to ceiling dream closet—an entire floor in the house dedicated to me. My bedroom, bathroom suite, multiple closets, my home office…a dream. Only somehow my missteps have shattered the dream and locked me in a nightmare. The house is silent except for the hum of the heat and the faint creak of wood as it settles.

Dorian's words echo: *Be ready. They'll come tonight or in the morning.*

Back in my closet, I gather my purse, remove the jewelry from my wrists, slip my phone and charger inside. Little rituals of control. I line up the lipstick, the watch, the ring dish on the dresser—order I can still make. My body moves automatically, my mind drifts somewhere distant.

As if confirming all of my fears, red washes the ceiling. Then blue. Like sirens inside my body—red and blue pulsing through my veins..

Tremors strike.

But I pull it together.

Stella's sleeping. They can't wake her.

I grab the cosmetics bag, hang the suit for the arraignment on the rod where I always hang tomorrow's outfit, setting the heels out too—and rush to the stairs.

Downstairs, Noah's waiting—jacket on, phone in hand, eyes darker than I've ever seen them. Noah has the front door open—true to his word, they won't need to ring the doorbell or knock loudly. Stella is asleep—tucked away on the third floor.

"They're here," he says quietly.

The muffled sound of voices. Footfalls on the path.

The detective who interrogated me—Detective Lassiter—smiles. The smile is slick and sure and the way his gaze travels judgmentally through my foyer makes it clear he believes he's found a murderer—he believes he's caught the bad guy and the streets are safer.

"Ms. Morgan, I see someone gave you a heads up."

"Were you hoping to wake my daughter?"

He has the decency to drop his gaze. There's no justice in involving the children.

"Alicia Morgan, you have the right to remain silent."

As he reads me my Miranda rights, my throat constricts, as do my lungs, and I fight back a dizzy wave.

As one officer reads the warrant, the other asks for my hands.

The metal bites cold around my wrists. The hallway feels too bright. Stella doesn't descend the stairs. *Thank god.*

"Don't worry about the morning," Noah says—his voice even, controlled. "She'll think you're at work."

I meet his eyes, and something inside me steadies. "Take care of her."

The detectives guide me out the door. The night air hits like ice. A car passing slows, watching the scene unfold. Someone's always watching.

They lead me into the police car, the door shuts, and the sound echoes like the end of a chapter I never meant to write.

The ventilation system hums, a low metallic throb that vibrates through concrete walls. Each pulse feels like it's syncing with my heartbeat—mechanical, relentless.

No windows. No clocks. Just the sterile smell of bleach and burnt coffee.

I'm sitting in a chair that's too hard and too cold, spine straight, like posture delivers dignity. The detective who escorted me here has been gone for—ten minutes? Twenty? Time doesn't move in real minutes down here; it stretches and folds until it becomes thought itself.

When they booked me, I counted each step like it was evidence.

Shoes off. Belt removed. Watch unclasped and dropped in a tray. Smile, Ms. Morgan.

The camera flash had felt obscene, a burst of light that stole something private. The after image still burns behind my eyelids.

Now I wait, fingers curled tight around the armrest, fighting the urge to pace.

Footsteps approach. A man in a tailored suit appears— Luca Corzone. The only congenial face in this fluorescent purgatory.

He sets a paper cup on the table and crouches beside me. "Coffee. I asked for real cream; this was the best they could do."

"Thanks." My voice scrapes against my throat. "How bad?"

He exhales, rubbing the back of his neck. "They've charged you with second-degree murder." The words feel like the cold metal chair. "You'll see a judge within the hour. I've already spoken with the DA's office. They're not opposing bail, which means you'll be home soon."

Home. The word feels foreign. Like a place I might not be able to return to without the proper documents.

"Evidence?" I ask.

"They're relying on timeline inconsistencies and witness testimony. We'll dismantle both. But for now—don't speak to anyone. No press, no detectives, no fellow inmates. Understood?"

I nod, but my thoughts are somewhere else—on Stella, who will wake to discover I'm gone, on Noah, who promised to tell her a version of the truth that hurts the least.

After spending a sleepless night in a holding cell, an officer arrives. This time, Luca Corzone is joined by a woman I'm introduced to as Shelly Madison. Both are in crisp suits that speak to their success in court. I'm allowed to change into the suit they brought me, although I have to do so behind open bars where others can see. The fabric clings cold against my skin; dignity, here, comes with a draft.

After what feels like an eternity, a uniformed officer gestures. "Time to go."

My attorney straightens. "We'll be right beside you."

The hallway smells like disinfectants and metal. Every sound ricochets—doors shutting, pens clicking, someone shouting two rooms away. My heels echo like guilt.

We pass a glass window where a reporter waits with a camera. Luca shields me with his body from a lens I hadn't noticed. The flash detonates again, and I flinch. Luca blocks half the view with his body, steering me toward the courtroom.

Inside, it's bright and airless. The judge reads the charges in a measured voice that could belong to anyone's nightmare. Her tone is patient, practiced—like this is paperwork. My name sounds detached, like a brand that no longer fits.

Luca Corzone speaks for me—firm, composed, the way I used to sound when defending someone else's ruin. "Not guilty, Your Honor."

The words echo slightly, fragile as spun glass.

When the gavel drops, the sound is final, brutal, real.

They release me just past noon.

Outside, daylight feels punishing after the artificial glow. A breeze carries the city's pulse—traffic, sirens, snippets of conversation.

Noah waits by the curb, arms folded, sunglasses hiding his eyes.

The moment he sees me, he steps forward, opens the passenger door, and my knees nearly fold.

"Are you okay?" he asks softly.

I manage a nod. My voice won't work yet.

As the car merges into traffic, I glance at the side mirror.

Behind us, the courthouse looms—stone and steel and judgment.

Ahead, the sky stretches wide and indifferent.

For the first time since last night, I let myself breathe. But the air tastes like fear, and something else—resolve.

Because this isn't the end of my story. It's the beginning of my defense.

If this is about Vasquez, about Magpie, about an investigation, then whoever wanted me silenced just made their first mistake. If someone is counting on me breaking, they're going to be disappointed.

NOAH

The woman beside me reminds me of an ambushed warrior —bloodied but unbroken. Watching her pull herself back together rubs a raw spot in my chest. She's regrouping, and surrender isn't remotely an option.

DC hums around us in indifferent rhythm—horns, coffee carts, commuters—an entire city moving on while her world burns behind tinted glass.

"How did things go with Stella this morning?" Five minutes of silence, and this is her first question. "Went well." My throat's dry. I can feel her eyes on me, weighing whether I softened the truth too much. "I was light on the details. Told her that you had to be in court unexpectedly."

"You didn't tell her I've been charged?"

"No. She came down the stairs panicked about being late. Didn't feel like the time."

Her lips purse, and I can't tell if she's annoyed or if she's already moved on in her mind to the next hurdle.

"Do you have my phone?"

I point to the glove box and she opens it, removing it. She left it at the house as the police would have confiscated it.

She flinches.

"Everything okay?"

"Richard." Her lip catches between her teeth. "Wonder when he learned."

"Is he offering support?"

She scoffs. "No. But I am surprised he didn't appear at the hearing. The timing on these messages… He knew before the hearing."

"What's he saying?"

She's scrolling. I can't tell if she's reading his texts or if she's moved on.

"He doesn't want me coming anywhere near the school."

"He can't stop you."

"He's worried about media attention."

"Are you expecting they'll follow you?"

"No." She's circumspect. "But he's right. For today. He'll bring her home after school. Stella doesn't know, and a news reporter following me on campus isn't the way for her to find out."

I sense she's unhappy I didn't give Stella the lowdown, but there really wasn't the time, and she didn't ask.

As I cut through traffic, she's on her phone. Tapping away responses to whoever is out there.

I spent the morning going over everything with the KOAN team. It blurred into intel briefings and half-cold coffee. Gabriel's coordinating with her defense team, tracking Delacroix's widow. Jake's chasing ghosts—namely, the missing witness. Quinn is looking into the judge assigned to this morning's hearing—confirming standard process was followed. She's also doing background on the prosecutor and the detectives. But, given how smoothly the arraignment went, I'm not sensing the judge was shopped. Now, the detectives and the prosecutor… There's nothing worse than a rotten judicial system.

"I'm surprised you're still here." Alicia's soft words bring me back to the vehicle. Her phone rests on her thigh.

"Wouldn't be anywhere else," I say, passing a slower car.

"You mean that, don't you?" Her voice is soft, disbelieving, like she's testing the ground before she steps on it.

I side-eye her, wondering where this is coming from.

"I admitted to you that I cheated on my husband, and you're still by my side."

"Ten years ago, Alicia. If you think I was a saint ten years ago, think again." Hell, at twenty-one, I'd been the furthest thing from a saint. "I don't need to know the details to know that you weren't in a good place. That's not who you are now."

"Oh? I'd say I'm not in a good place at all right now." Her laugh is dry, like she's testing if humor still exists.

I half-chuckle, then reach for her, squeezing her knee. "You know what I mean."

She exhales, the sound half sigh, half surrender, and turns toward the window. Her fingers slide through mine, a quiet declaration: not done, not broken. "I'm still… I'm grateful you're here. Many men wouldn't be."

"Maybe that's true. But I doubt it." My words are the absolute truth. "You didn't kill anyone, Alicia. And even if the world doubts you, I don't. I know, beyond a shadow of a doubt, you're innocent. And if someone is framing you—if this isn't just half-assed police work—then they just slipped. Because you've got an all-star defense team, and they're going to track down the source. By all accounts, the prosecution has a weak case. This is a bump in the road."

She mouths the words: *bump in the road.*

She's still dazed. Likely exhausted. I doubt she slept at all last night.

When I pull into her drive, the gate grinds open, metal on metal. Cold drizzle slicks the windshield. I pull in, and the gate creaks closed behind us.

It's a cloudy day, brisk, and rain is forecast for the afternoon. A woman pushes a baby stroller while walking her dog. Cars pass back and forth on the front street.

No one's lurking.

Satisfied, I enter the house, lock the door behind me, and reach for the remote that closes the shades. Sure, she normally keeps them open during the day, but she's due some privacy.

"Can I get you something? You hungry?"

She braces against the island, palms flat on the marble, eyes unfocused—as if the weight of the world is pressing through her arms.

"I'm not hungry at all," she says, voice airy, like she's speaking to herself and she's all alone. "I want a shower," she says, a hint of finality to her tone.

"Understandable." I want to follow, to guard, to hold. Instead, I stay rooted. "I'll be here when you get out."

She pauses at the stairwell. "Join me?"

She doesn't wait for an answer, just begins the climb. The soft thud of her bare feet on the stairs feels like an invitation and a test.

I fall in behind her.

In the bathroom, I reach past her, turning on the shower.

She undresses slowly, methodically, as if neatness might

rewrite the last twenty-four hours. Each piece folded with the discipline of someone desperate to reclaim control. I undress too, my eyes moving over her with a hunger I don't try to hide. She's stunning—all elegant curves and creamy skin, the kind of woman who stands before a judge without flinching—and still trembles in my arms. The kind that undoes me without trying.

I reach for thick, white towels and set them on the counter near the shower for easy access.

She steps into the shower, tilting her head back, letting the water flow from her crown down. A cleansing.

I step in beside her and reach for the sponge hanging on the hook. I drip soap onto it and drag it over her shoulders, slow and deliberate, the slick trail of lather chasing my touch down the curve of her spine. Her skin is warm silk beneath my hands. She shivers despite the heat.

"Cold?" I ask, my mouth close to her ear.

"No." Her voice is barely a word. "The opposite."

Reaching around her, I wash her curves with unhurried care—the flare of her hips, the soft roundness of her belly, the long lines of her thighs. She leans back into me, her head tipping to my shoulder, mouth slightly open, lashes lowered.

I bend to kiss her. Light. Loving. No expectation other than I am going to take care of her.

I brush my lips over her cheek, then reach for the shampoo.

My fingers work the lather into her scalp, slow and reverent. She makes a sound low in her throat—not quite a moan, but close. Surrender in miniature. A memory forms unbidden—the way my father once washed my mother's hair after her cancer diagnosis. Back then, I'd looked away. Now, I can't look anywhere else.

I follow the shampoo with conditioner, marveling at the silky weight of her strands as they glide through my fingers.

She's facing me now, the water at her back. I cup her face, tilting it up, and kiss her properly—deep and slow, the kind of kiss that says everything I'm not ready to put into words. Her hands spread flat against my chest, then slide up to my shoulders, and I feel the shift in her—the woman who walked out of that courtroom starting to come back online.

Then she presses into me fully, rising on her toes so our bodies align. My erection is trapped between us, hard and undeniable, and when her fingers wrap around me, a rough sound escapes the back of my throat that I don't try to contain.

Steam clouds the glass. The steady thrum of water on tile is the only sound.

She strokes me slowly, grip firm, devastating, watching my face with dark, knowing eyes, and I let her—let her take some of the control back, let her feel what she does to me. My jaw tightens. My hand slides into her wet hair.

"You have no idea," I manage.

"I think I do." Her mouth curves—knowing.

My fingers ghost between her thighs, finding her heat. She's warm and slick, and when I stroke her, her breath stutters on an exhale, her forehead dropping to my chest.

"Noah—"

"I've got you." I work her slowly, reading every catch of her breath, every roll of her hips against my hand, until she's trembling and her fingers are digging into my arms. She's close—I can feel it in the way she goes taut, the way she whispers my name like a question.

I don't let her get there. Not yet.

I spin her gently, pressing her palms to the tile. She

spreads her legs, welcoming me without hesitation, her back arching to invite me in. I grip her hip, positioning myself, and pause.

"I don't have anything with me."

She turns her head just enough to meet my eyes over her shoulder. "IUD. And I'm clean."

I press my mouth to the back of her neck. "Same."

Then I take her in one slow, certain stroke.

Her sharp inhale bounces off the tile.

Mine isn't much quieter.

God, she's—I don't have words for it.

"Fuuuck." The strained expletive is all I get out.

I stay still, jaw tight, one hand flat against the tile beside hers. Steam. The sound of water. Her breathing. That's everything there is for a moment.

Then I move.

One hand curves around to her center, fingers working in rhythm with my hips. The other slides up her ribcage to cup her breast, thumb tracing her nipple until it peaks and she makes a sound that goes straight through me.

"Yes," she breathes. "Just like that—"

I find our rhythm and hold it—steady, deep, angled so every stroke draws a sound from her. Her palms slide on the wet tile. The water's going lukewarm but I don't stop. I learn what makes her breath break and give her more of it, again and again, until she's saying my name in fragments.

Water rains down over both of us. She pushes her hips back to meet me. I feel it in the way she tightens around me —sharp, electric. I nearly lose the rhythm, nearly drive too hard, too fast. Instead, I slow by a fraction, shift the angle just enough to make her gasp, and hold her there—right on the edge.

When she comes, it rolls through her like a wave—her whole body tightening around me, a low, broken cry muffled against her forearm. I follow seconds later, burying myself deep, my forehead bowing to the back of her neck, her name the only thing I manage, my whole body going to static.

For a long moment, neither of us moves.

Then we're sliding down together, a graceless, boneless descent onto the shower floor, tangled and breathless. Her back to my chest, both of us half-laughing at the undignified landing. Water spills over our legs—mine brown with dark hair, hers creamy smooth—and neither of us makes any move to get up.

When she lifts her pruned fingers to show me, something about the gesture cracks me open a little. Proof that time still moves. That we're still here.

"We should probably get out," she says, but doesn't move.

"Probably," I agree, and pull her a little tighter.

Eventually, I help her up, wrap her in a towel, and take my time with her—pressing lotion into her skin with slow, warm hands, kissing the long lines of her throat, the curve of her shoulder, the soft swell of her chest. Not with urgency now. With adoration.

I settle her beneath the sheets, her lashes damp, her breath already softening into the rhythm of sleep. The world outside can spin and burn.

For now, she's safe.

And I'll make damn sure she stays that way.

CHAPTER
THIRTY-ONE

ALICIA

There's an uneasy quiet to the house, the kind that hums under your skin. The dull thud in my head and the queasy roll of my stomach feel like the morning after too much wine—only I didn't drink last night. I just didn't sleep. After waking in the afternoon, I'd been disoriented—and lacked the willpower to shower again and blow out my hair. So I pulled it back into a chignon, applied makeup, and chose a simple business casual outfit of loose jeans, a cashmere cream turtleneck, and a navy blazer. It's not my best outfit, but it'll do to face Richard.

So far he's refused my calls—sending only clipped texts that say we need to speak in person. Given he's a lawyer, it always makes me uneasy when he refuses to put anything more than sterile, professional phrases in writing. That's when I know he's angry, or afraid, or both.

The traffic outside passes like any other weekday. Upstairs, I have a million emails waiting. I've put clients on hold today, giving myself a chance to fortify myself before I address questions and concerns. Some clients may choose to select a crisis management firm led by a woman who isn't herself in crisis, and I can't blame them. I've made my list of clients to call, and tomorrow morning, I'll arrive at the office, hold a staff meeting to explain the situation, then begin making calls.

The irony isn't lost on me. I've spent years talking frantic people off ledges, drafting talking points and timelines. Now I'm the one plotting my own damage control, waiting until I'm emotionally steady enough to listen without breaking. So many times, my clients are the cause of the pain, and I'm the one counseling that an apology with a "but" isn't an apology.

If I were to speak to my clients—or my staff—my apology would most certainly include an *"I'm sorry for this inconvenience, but this is not my fault."*

I didn't kill Matt. I had no part in his murder. But I did sleep with him and bury the truth for ten years. I'm not guilty of what they've charged me with, but I'm hardly innocent.

Another reason I'm holding off on calling clients is I haven't decided how much I'll share. If I were to take my own advice, I'd come clean about the affair. Someone out there clearly knows—it's not like the detective uncovered DNA evidence from ten years ago. He didn't even acquire CCTV or hotel footage from ten years ago. He spoke to someone—which means it could come out in the press with coverage of the trial. It's better to tell the whole story when I have my first call. There's a selfish part of me that still hopes it will stay hidden—that no one else ever has to know what I did.

Noah's reflection appears in the front window panes a

beat before his arms come around me, solid and sure, pulling me back against his chest. I sink into his warmth, my palms sliding over the corded strength of his forearms. At a time like this, it would be so easy to fall in love with him.

Of course, who am I kidding? I've been falling in love with him for weeks—a quiet look, an after-work drink, one steady heartbeat at a time. I'm not sure how I'd get through this without him. Will falling for him make his inevitable departure more painful? Yes, it will. But there's no doubt I need him now.

Christine's coming over later . She doesn't know exactly what happened—I don't think. She's likely heard rumors. Her most recent message said simply: **I'm coming over this evening with vino. After dinner. See you at 8.**

I gave the message a thumbs up. If there's one sign of a true friend, it's when you're charged with murder and she arrives with wine. If I had killed someone, she'd help me hide the body. Not that I would ever resort to murder. Even on my worst days with Richard, I might have joked about unaliving him, might have even fantasized about an untimely demise, but I would never kill. It's disturbing to think others think I would—and it's also disturbing that someone out there did kill and may be trying to pin the murder on me.

The car pulls into my drive, stopping right at the gate, and my grip on Noah's arms tightens. There's pressure on the side of my head as he presses his lips to my hair. I tap his arm and say, "Let me go greet them."

"I'll wait inside," he says.

I don't bother with a coat. I'm too numb to worry about chilly air or the drizzle.

Richard exits his BMW first. I catch sight of Stella holding an iPhone, her shoulders hunched around the glow. She's rooted to the seat, hypnotized by the screen. For a second, I assume it's Richard's. Then I see the case—a sparkly blue thing she'd pick herself.

He closes his car door, and the slam of metal somehow ricochets through me. His eyes are cold, possibly bloodshot, the fine lines around them deeper. Like me, he hasn't slept. Who told him? When did he find out?

I peer past him. "Is she getting out of the car?"

"She got a new phone," he says, as if that explains every-thing. "She's…enthused."

"We agreed—no phone until she's fifteen."

"It's better that she has it," he says flatly. "I can track her if I need to. And you can call her."

I reel back—but the car door opens and Stella's excited voice intervenes.

"Mom—I got a phone! Dad took me to the Apple Store!" She bubbles out of the car, practically bouncing, but halfway to me she slows, eyes flicking between our faces. She's too perceptive to barrel through tension like it isn't there. "Mom? Are you mad about it?"

Richard's glare is threatening. I swallow—this isn't the time to fight this battle.

"No, hon. Surprised, but not angry."

"Stella, go inside and pack your bag. I need to talk with your mother."

"Pack your bag?" My voice sharpens. I want him to hear exactly how little sense that makes.

"I explained you have a lot going on this week," Richard says, voice clipped, the strength of his tone brooking no room for argument. "She'll stay with me. Until you've got more bandwidth."

His plan is to lie to her? And to hope she doesn't find out

from someone else? I open my mouth—breathe. "Stella, why don't you head in. I'll come talk to you upstairs."

"You didn't know," Stella says, looking at her dad with eyes that question—because whether he wants to admit it or not, she's not the little kid who accepts everything he says without question. His plan isn't going to work. "What's going on? I knew it was weird that you'd be too busy for me."

"I'm never too busy for you." I pin Richard with a look sharp enough to stab. If he's going to lie to her, he needs to learn how to do it better. "But I do need to speak with you— and it may be best if you go to your father's for a few days."

This isn't how I would handle it, but I will grant Richard that I don't know how my next few days will go, and along with my workload for my company, I also need to manage working with my defense team. Hopefully I'll stay out of the press's eye—I'm not a public figure. I just often work with public figures—but I work with them enough that it won't be shocking if a reporter recognizes my name and wants to explore a story.

Stella surprises me by wrapping her arms around me and looking up, concerned. "You're not sick or anything, are you?"

Jesus, Richard. My heart punches my ribs. That's where her mind goes first—illness, not headlines.

"No honey," I say, rubbing the side of her face, then bending to kiss her head. I pop her on her butt. "Head on inside. I'll be there in a minute, and I promise you I'll explain everything."

She's slower, but she's got her phone in her hand, and by the time she's at the front door, she's looking at the screen.

She steps into the house, leaving the door cracked open,

and I start to yell after her to close it, but don't. Richard's scowl rakes over me and I can't tell if he's royally pissed or if there's a degree of concern.

"I didn't do it," I say—half wondering if his anger stems from a belief I would do something like that and put our daughter's life in a vise from the repercussions.

"I know," he says after a beat, jaw tight. "But you did have an affair."

We stand there, a wall of cold silent accusations between us. I don't need to ask when he learned about the murder charge, or even what he knows. He's a lawyer—he has friends. It's the same way I had a heads up about a warrant for my arrest being issued. It's the same way I have an idea about what evidence they believe they have—the detectives aren't tight-lipped. Or hell, maybe it's someone on the prosecutor's team.

"I had an affair too," he says, and there it is—the card he's been holding. For a moment I just stare at him, then the truth slips out, simple and bare.

"I know." We never weaponized it in therapy. Maybe because I was guilty too.

His gaze lifts to the sky, then back at me. "I always loved you."

The words knock the breath out of me—that's the last thing I expected from Richard today. We agreed once that we'd always care, that we weren't in love. Now, with murder charges hanging over my head, he chooses "always loved."

I look up at him—really look at him. Does he want to go into this right now? We said as much in painful couples therapy sessions. Of course, as painful as those sessions may have been, neither of us told the whole truth.

A Rivian pulls up to the curb and parks. Jessica hops out, but pauses, her gaze flitting between Richard and me.

"What are you doing here?" Richard asks, sounding almost as angry at her as he is at me.

"I thought I might be able to help," she says, heels ticking over the walk. When she reaches him, her hand glides over his arm. "I wanted to be here for you, baby."

I step back, giving them their moment.

"I also wanted to let you know I spoke to Jamison about expedited custody procedures—"

"What?" The word whips out of me, sharp enough that even I flinch.

Yes, I flinch, but I won't back down. Not on this.

Jessica shrinks, seeming to press herself into Richard, but he can't protect her.

"Jesus," Richard says, stepping away from Jessica. "I'm not—" He looks to me and says, "I'm exploring options in case. You know as well as I do there's no way to know how the court case will play out."

Noah appears at the door—and it's clear from his expression, he's there to protect me.

Noah's presence infuses me with strength—even from the doorway. "You're not taking her away from me, Richard."

"The courts might see it differently," Jessica adds, voice small but annoyingly sure of itself.

Richard's jaw flexes, and he points at her car. "Jessica—go. You aren't helping."

He's firm. Cold. It's like he's talking to a teenager who's overstepped, not the woman he shares a bed with. Some petty part of me enjoys watching her wilt.

She turns her back on me and I get a view of her bright blonde hair and the skirt that hugs every curve of her backside and the thin black hosiery line that travels along the back of her legs.

"Okay, baby," she says. "Remember, I'm here for you. I'll get dinner together, for all of us. You'll probably want to eat at home, right?"

My gaze cuts to Noah, and he descends the two steps to join me on the lawn. I miss whatever exchange occurs between Richard and Jessica, but the result is she gets in her car. We stand awkwardly, on the narrow front strip of grass, in silence until her car door closes and her engine rumbles.

With that out of the way, I focus on what matters. "I need to tell Stella." It's a statement, and I do my best to ensure he reads me correctly—I'm not backing down on this. "I want her to hear it from me."

"She's only twelve."

"And she needs to hear it from me—not a classmate. Christine is coming over tonight. I didn't tell her. Word's out."

"I thought you specialized in keeping things under wraps." His expression is lighter, a hint of bitter humor, but then his gaze flits to Noah and he's heated ice once more.

"I'm a crisis management expert," I say. "And this is how you manage a crisis."

"Fine. But she's coming to stay with me this week."

"That could be for the best," I agree. "But only because I will have some busy days. You're not taking her from me, Richard."

"Well, you better win your case." I'd like to think he's joking, but he's not. He'll absolutely move for full custody if I'm found guilty of murder, but I can't think about that.

"Come on. You can wait inside while I go up and talk to Stella."

As I climb the stairs, I hear Noah ask if Richard's thirsty. That's good—Richard can see for himself that Noah is a decent, respectable person. I continue climbing, reaching the third floor and Stella's open bedroom door. She's got an overnight bag open. She keeps things in both our houses, but she inevitably always has a favorite sweater or jeans that she carries back and forth. Her phone lies on the bed, screen lit—as she likely just laid it down. The screensaver isn't on and I pick it up—spotting the Snapchat icon.

"Snapchat?"

She freezes, then lifts her chin. "Dad said it was okay."

I close my eyes and sink onto her bed. "He probably doesn't know what it is."

"What's wrong with it? All my friends have it."

First, all her friends don't have it because all her friends don't have phones, but I swallow that back. "It deletes messages. Kids use it like it's a magic eraser and forget anyone can screenshot whatever they send." I don't see anything else worrisome on her phone, and we have a big conversation in front of us, so I set the device on the bed. "It can be addictive."

"Mom." She rolls her eyes. "I won't get addicted."

A sharp pain pierces my temple and I breathe in deeply. "We'll talk about it," I say. She opens her mouth, likely to argue, but I stop her with, "I have other things to talk to you about right now."

She sits on the bed, crossing her legs, quiet. My perceptive girl understands whatever I'm about to tell her is of a serious nature.

"Are you and Noah getting married?"

My brain stutters. "What?"

"Jessica said the two of you look serious."

I squeeze my eyes shut, shaking my head—what the hell? Where would she get that idea? And why would she talk to my daughter about it?

"It's okay if you are. I like Noah."

"Okay," I say, opening my eyes and deciding to broach the subject I hadn't planned on tackling at all today—if ever—first. "Noah and I are seeing each other. And I do care about him. But there are stages in relationships and we aren't anywhere close to the marriage stage."

"Do you think you might marry him? Eventually?"

"Honey." How do I explain this? "Honestly, I… We're good for each other right now. But if you haven't noticed, he's younger than me. He's got a lot of living in front of him. Kids of his own. That kind of thing. No, I don't see us getting married. We're just… Sometimes adults have relationships that don't end in marriage. And that's okay. We're supportive of each other and we make each other happy." Her lips turn up into a slight smile. "Not every relationship needs to end in marriage."

"You could have a baby with him."

My stomach drops. "Stella, I'm forty-one."

"So, Maggie's mom had her baby sister when she was forty-four. And besides, I like Noah. Jessica gets on my nerves, but Noah…he's cool."

"I'm not having another child," I say, trying to get back onto the planned topics. "And I'm glad you like Noah. And I probably should have told you earlier that we're seeing each other but I wasn't quite ready."

"That's fine, Mom. Jessica told me."

"Yeah," I say. "And I'm not necessarily okay with that but…look," I shift, searching for the right segue—

"I think Jessica just talks about you two because she's pushing Dad for a ring, and if you're close to getting a ring then she probably thinks she'll get one or something. I think she assumed I knew, so don't get mad at her or anything."

"Stella," I breathe out loudly. "I need to talk to you about what happened earlier this morning."

That gets her attention—at least, she stops talking.

"This morning I was arrested and charged with a crime I did not commit," I say quietly. "That's where I was—at the police station, then the courthouse. Not at work. But I have a very good law firm that will clear my name."

"Why were you charged?"

"I'm not sure, honey." Those blue eyes of hers question me. "Well, that's not true. About a month ago I found a man right before he died. I entered the room—I was actually calling your father and saw him on the ground. It turns out he was murdered—poisoned." The word sticks in my throat. Saying it to my twelve-year-old feels obscene. "And because I found him, well, I was a person of interest, but they also learned I knew him years ago. And I don't think they have much evidence and there was pressure to charge someone—"

"But you didn't do it." Outrage flares in her voice, protective and fierce. Gratitude hits me so hard my eyes sting. My daughter believes in me.

"No. I absolutely did not do it. They don't have any evidence and we'll aim to get the ridiculous charge thrown out."

"Do you have to go to jail? Is that why Dad—"

"No, hon. The judge let me go home while we sort this out. I had to pay bail, but I'm not going to jail right now.

I'm here. I'm with you. And, honestly, I'm hoping we can kick this before I ever see the inside of a courtroom again. It's a big misunderstanding, but I wanted you to hear it from me."

"You think my classmates will know?"

"I don't know, hon. It's possible." My heart aches—the thought of kids ridiculing her.

"Well, you didn't do it."

"No, I didn't."

"You would never."

"No, I would not."

She crawls to me on the bed and gives me a tight hug. I hold onto her until I hear footsteps in the hallway. I expect Noah, but I'm surprised when it's Richard.

"Everything okay?" he asks.

"Yes," Stella says. She sits back on her heels. "You're going to make sure Mom gets the charges dismissed, right, Dad?"

She looks up at him with the kind of faith only a twelve-year-old can have—that her father can fix anything, even this.

"I'll do everything I can, sweet pea." Then he looks at me. "When's your next meeting with your legal team?"

"Tomorrow afternoon."

"Send me the details," he says. "I want to be there."

I don't necessarily want Richard in the room, but it's smarter to have him on my team—and after Stella's request, I'll go along with it. So I give a brief nod.

"Where's Noah?"

"I suggested he give us some time." He spots Stella's overnight bag and bends to pick it up. "You ready, kiddo?"

"Yep. When will I see you?" she asks me, picking her phone up off the bed.

"Well, first, you're going to send me your phone number, right?" She grins. "And, I don't know, let's see today's…"

The calendar blurs in my head, and a weight of dread clouds my thoughts.

"Tomorrow your mother will probably have a late night," he says. "But Thursday? You and I can cook dinner for her. Just us. Family meal."

"Just the three of us? No Jessica?" Stella squints like that's unbelievable and it makes me realize Jessica must be there every single night.

"Are you up for that? It will give us a chance to talk?" His question is to me, but Stella stares up at him, and he adds, "And review your case. Privately."

"Sounds like a plan," I say, even though the word family feels like a language I no longer speak where he is concerned.

Richard waits at Stella's bedroom door, stepping aside for Stella, and then me, to pass. When we reach the downstairs, Noah is nowhere to be found. I assume he's down in the basement, and this time, I hold the front door for Stella and her father to pass.

Richard still isn't happy—his anger fogs the air like humidity, stifling breath. But for now, we have what feels like a truce. A fragile, temporary ceasefire.

All the same, when I talk to Luca and Shelly next, I'll ask about preparing for the worst. Because if this turns into a custody battle, I can't afford to be ambushed.

CHAPTER
THIRTY-TWO

NOAH

The streetlights glow weakly in the early morning dark, and my breath ghosts the chilled air as Jake and I finish the last of our calisthenics. Sweat slicks down my spine. The sun is just beginning to drag light through the trees, gold streaking the bare branches.

We slow automatically—five minutes from the lot, five minutes from getting back to Alicia.

"Great trails. Easier on the joints," Jake says.

"Yeah. The C&O towpath never disappoints." Gravel crunches under our shoes, breath going white in the cold. Five minutes to cool down; fifteen minutes until I need to be back with her.

We're alone, but Jake still lowers his voice. "Am I alone in thinking this isn't feeling like a standard detail?"

"Because the hits don't look like hits," I answer. "They're coming sideways."

"You buying Pierce's involvement?"

"Not yet. If it's Vasquez-adjacent, it's an out-of-the-box way to sideline a witness." I shift pace. "Feels more like a tired detective rushing a bow on a messy file."

"Right." Jake stares ahead to where the towpath spills into daylight. "She tell you about the affair before the arrest?"

"No."

Jake angles me a look. "Bother you?"

"She's paid to keep secrets," I say. "Reflex is survival."

"But…you two…" He gestures vaguely. "There's stuff going on with you two, right? So, you're there comforting her on the day she found him, and she still doesn't tell you?"

"We were early stages." And Alicia carries deep shame over the infidelity—shame I recognize. If my dad gets wind of it, I can already hear him: *You sure that's who you want to latch onto? A cheater?*

When I step through the side door, Alicia's sipping coffee, crisp navy suit immaculate, looking like a woman about to run the world.

"Give me five—I'll drive you in."

She nods, composed, coffee steady.

"Good run?"

"Yeah. Cold does the lungs good." I'm already moving—basement, shower, gear. Momentum is its own comfort.

Alicia's focused on her phone, voice-dictating email as I drive her Rivian to the office. Her request to drive her car has me wondering if something's wrong with my SUV, and since she's clearly working, the question sits in my head the whole ride.

At least until we pull in.

A cruiser idles by the building entrance, exhaust ghosting into the cold.

Alicia's sigh is barely there. "What now." Not a question —just fatigue with a period.

I pull into the spot next to it. No running from whatever this is.

Gabriel comes around the corner. "Break-in."

"When?"

"Window between midnight and four. Another tenant called it in—exterior cams were smashed. Your assistant's with MPD. Looks like your suite was hit."

Alicia takes off to join her assistant and the cops. I hang back with Gabriel.

"Doesn't this push it closer to Vasquez?" I murmur.

"Maybe. Let's see what they took. Feels sloppy."

"In what way?"

"Bashing cams is amateur hour," he mutters. "Pros blind them upstream."

The cops fence us out—standard. Photos, gloves, slow questions. A sharp smell rides the air—ozone and cheap cleaner.

"Somebody hurried their exit," I say. "Should've aired it out."

Hours pass. It's unclear what was taken. Files untouched. Computers untouched. No obvious breach of servers.

Alicia's defense team arrives. Smart. If there's any way to flip this into a procedural concern for the court, they'll use it.

Since everyone's present, the defense meeting gets moved up. Hudson arrives. Richard too. When I step into the conference room, he looks like he wants to argue but decides he doesn't want to do it in front of a table full of attorneys.

We take our seats. Everyone gets the same folder—the compiled timeline, Alicia's verified whereabouts, defense witness statements, prosecution's witness list, autopsy summaries, poison notes.

I flip pages as Luca talks through it.

Delacroix's ex-wife: listed for prosecution. We're trying to reach her, but she's unresponsive. Someone from the firm is being sent today.

Another page. Richard's name—expected. He's willing to testify as a character witness.

Then Jessica's name.

Richard catches it first. "Why is Jessica in here?"

Luca's smooth. "She lives with you, right?"

"No." His gaze darts to Alicia. "She's my girlfriend. She doesn't live with me."

"Prosecution will still meet with her. We want to talk to her first."

Richard nods tightly.

My gaze drops to Jessica's title.

Pharmaceutical Sales Representative – Cardiology Portfolio.

Interesting. Out of everyone in this folder, she's the only one with legitimate access to medication channels. But that doesn't mean she'd plant a tracker, or bash cameras like a drunk burglar. Doesn't fit. It's too soon to chase shadows.

Meeting recesses for ten minutes so people can order lunch and hit the restroom. I join Richard in the hallway.

"How was Stella last night?" I ask, because it's a decent question.

"Fine."

"It's a good thing Jessica was around."

He bristles. "You asking if she stayed over?"

"I'm asking if your kid had a soft landing."

"She did," he snaps. "Jessica's family." He waits a beat. "She isn't...whatever this is with you."

"What's that mean?"

"It means commitment, Bennett." His jaw ticks. "Does your boss even know?"

He's not wrong to ask. That's the part that stings.

Before I answer, Gabe rounds the corner. Richard stiffens, gives us both a sour look, and ducks back into the conference room.

Gabe lifts a brow. "What'd I walk into?"

"Just sunshine," I mutter.

As the meeting reconvenes, something in the earlier report hooks back in my mind—one more detail Gabe mentioned when we arrived:

Building keycard log showed no entries for the overnight window.

No one used the doors.

Which means whoever came in—didn't enter.

They bypassed.

As I take my seat again, the folder open in front of me, the pieces float but won't land. Smashed cameras. No keycard entries. Nothing missing we can identify—yet.

Everyone thinks the vandalism was the point.

But I'm starting to think the point was something else entirely.

Not the cameras.

Not the damage.

What walked out in a pocket.

CHAPTER
THIRTY-THREE

ALICIA

"This is crazy," my assistant says, hovering in the doorway on her way out. The sun has dropped behind the buildings, taking whatever warmth existed with it. "If there's anything I can do…"

"You've been a wonder," I tell her. And it's true—having my small staff and my friends stand by me feels like a lifeline. "Thank you."

"Of course. You'd do the same for me."

Petra hesitates, then adds, "I hope it's over by Thanksgiving. Did you remember to order a turkey?"

Thanksgiving. My mind blanks. Whatever flickers over my face makes her laugh.

"Don't worry. When I order mine, I'll order yours."

"When is—"

"Two weeks," she says gently.

Two weeks. Which means Stella's school play is next week. I need to get my head back in the game.

My phone lights up with a video request. Stella.

"I'll let you get that," my assistant says, waving as she leaves.

I smooth a hand over my hair before I answer. "Mom. Are you still at the office?" Stella's face fills the screen.

"Yes, hon. Are you home?"

"I'm at Dad's," she corrects automatically—home to her is still my place, and the small, greedy part of me clings to that.

She babbles about picking dinner, choosing Indian, then pivots to tomorrow night's cooking plans. Her enthusiasm is my undoing.

"Either one works," I say, fighting a sudden ache.

Richard appears behind her, suit jacket off, tie loosened. He asks to switch to voice, then calls me back without video.

"How did things go?" he asks.

"Good," I say, because Stella is too close to the phone for anything else.

"It's just me," he says after a beat. "How'd it really go?"

I exhale. "Clients were supportive. Better than I expected."

"That's good. Are you working late?"

"No. I owe Dorian a call."

"Dorian Moore?" A beat. "So you and Dorian are still close?"

"I'm too tired for this," I murmur.

"It was a question."

I pinch the bridge of my nose. "Richard, please."

There's a sigh, the kind that comes from the bottom of a long, sleepless night.

"You know you can count on me, right?"

"Can I?" The words slip. "Jessica was looking into custody—"

"She shouldn't have said anything," he mutters.

Of course. Always Jessica's fault.

But then his voice softens. "Our daughter comes first. You know that."

"I won't let you take her from me," I say quietly. "But… thank you. For caring."

A beat of silence passes. I brace for an argumentative response, but instead get, "We'll see you tomorrow."

The line goes dead.

I scroll through Christine's texts—supportive, fiery, threatening to "pay the Dick a visit." I snort. Thank God for her.

I'm finishing email triage when knuckles rap lightly on my doorframe. Noah stands there and warmth rolls through me like a wave.

"Hey," I breathe.

"Work as long as you need," he says. "Just wanted you to know I'm here. Gabriel's off the clock. When you're ready, I'll drive you home."

Something inside settles. "You know what? I'm done."

He helps me with my coat, brushes a soft kiss over my mouth, and ushers me out. Under the streetlights, with his arm around me, it hits me how natural this feels. How safe.

How much I'll miss him when he's gone.

I shove that thought away.

In the car, his hand finds mine.

"Tomorrow the legal team and KOAN are splitting up the witness list—running down anyone who can undercut the prosecution's case." he says. "We'll track down that missing woman."

"Has she resurfaced?"

"No. But we'll find her."

I don't know how he does it—how he makes impossible things sound solvable.

I tell him about dinner at Richard's tomorrow. He doesn't like it—I see it—but he nods. "I'll drive you. And pick you up."

There's something possessive in that. Something steady.

Something I want too much.

By silent agreement, conversation fades as he turns onto my street.

"I think I'm in the mood for another shower," I say softly.

A slow smile curves his mouth. "Is that right?"

But when we step inside, the house is dark, hushed, empty.

And suddenly the shower feels too far away.

Inside, Noah closes the door behind us, then reaches for the keypad and lowers every blind with a quiet mechanical hum. The house pulls inward, private, cocooned.

"We don't have to talk anymore tonight," he murmurs. "You've carried enough on your shoulders today."

Emotion hits me like a tidal pull.

"I can't believe you're still here," I whisper.

He pulls me in, holding me with a strength I sense—and crave.

"Alicia," he says, thumb brushing my jaw, voice low and certain, "I'm right where I want to be. I'm not going anywhere."

He's saying all the right things. Now isn't the time to read into anything—one way or another. But his statement lands with the weight of truth, sliding under every defense I've been pretending still exists.

My breath trembles. "Good," I say, because the alternative is admitting how deep I've fallen and it's not a good time for that confession.

His mouth meets mine, slow, claiming, almost reverent. The kind of kiss that says he's not taking tonight from me—he's giving it. Giving me back to myself.

His hands skim down my waist, guiding me backward until the back of my calves meet the sofa. I sink onto the cushions, and he follows, bracing a knee between mine, his palms framing my face.

"Tell me what you need," he murmurs.

"I want you," I breathe. "Just…you."

He kisses me deeply, and I tug him down with me, our bodies molding into the warm sinking sofa cushions. Clothes come away slowly—his hands at the hem of my shirt, mine at his buttons—and there's none of the urgency of before, none of the desperation. Just his palms sliding up my sides as he lifts the fabric over my head, the press of his mouth to my shoulder, my collarbone, the curve of my throat. Each point of contact feels deliberate. Chosen. Like he's learning me again from the beginning, taking his time because he has it and he knows I need him to use it.

When there's nothing left between us, he pulls back just enough to look at me. Not the dark, hungry assessment of before. Something quieter. Like he's making sure I'm still here.

I am. More than I've been in weeks.

When he moves over me, I reach for his hips and draw him in—and the difference from the first time hits me immediately. Not the shock of it, not the adjustment. Just—recognition. My body knows him now. Knows the weight of him, the warmth, the specific way he fills me. I exhale slowly as he seats himself fully, his eyes locked on mine, both of us still for a moment in the gray quiet of the room.

It's nothing like before. Before was want. This is something I don't have a clean word for.

He moves with a tenderness that unravels everything I've kept locked tight.

Not rushed. Not frantic. Just…present. With me. For me.

The rhythm he sets is unhurried, deep, each movement pulling sensation through me in long slow waves rather than the sharp building friction of before. I feel him everywhere—his chest against mine, his hand cradling the back of my neck, the steady press and drag of him inside me that keeps finding the same place, keeps making my breath catch in the same way.

Each slow thrust feels like an answer to a question I wasn't brave enough to ask.

His forehead drops to mine. "Alicia…"

I clutch his shoulders, my voice breaking on a gasp. "I know."

When I come, it doesn't shatter me the way the first time did. It opens me. A long, rolling wave that starts deep and moves outward, my whole body going soft and loose even as I grip him tighter, his name breaking quietly on my lips. I feel him follow—the stutter of his hips, the low groan muffled against my hair, his arms locking around me—and I hold on, and he holds on, and for a moment we're just two people who've stopped pretending.

When breath finally returns, he eases beside me, gathering me into his arms. My cheek rests against his chest, and his fingers trace lazy circles along my spine.

It feels unwise. Like I'm skating toward a treacherous cliff.

And also completely right.

"You with me?" he whispers into my hair.

I close my eyes, unable to speak the truth—that I'm already in too deep, that I'm already his in ways I shouldn't be.

Instead, I curl closer. "Yeah," I whisper. "I'm with you."

His arm tightens, steady as a promise.

And in the quiet of the shuttered house, I know: It's already too late to fight this.

I've fallen.

NOAH

Elizabeth Delacroix spots me from the tennis court.

Her match has just ended and she's surrounded by three women in white skirts and pastel layers, all of them sheathing their rackets and reaching for water bottles. It takes about three seconds for all four of their gazes to swing my way.

Could be because she mentioned my name.

Could be because I clearly don't belong to this particular country club.

I stay where I am, leaning against the hood of Alicia's Rivian, arms relaxed, posture easy. Neutral. Not a threat, not a supplicant—just a man waiting.

From a distance, the resemblance between Elizabeth and Alicia hits hard. Both are lean, fit women with dark, glossy hair—Elizabeth's pulled back for practicality. Elizabeth is in her fifties, but if I didn't know that from Quinn's file, I'd shave at least a decade off. Solitaire diamonds wink from her ears. A white visor and sunglasses shadow the finer details of her face, but the overall impression is polished, composed—exactly what I'd expect from a country club wife.

Her pleated skirt flares around still-toned legs, the whole look eerily close to a cheerleader uniform—if cheerleaders wore Cartier.

The women's voices rise as they exit the court. From here it sounds like laughing goodbyes. One of them pulls Elizabeth into a hug. She stiffens, pats the woman's back like it's an obligation instead of instinct, and the message is clear: she's not a hugger. Not unless she chooses to be.

When her friends peel away toward the clubhouse, Elizabeth heads for me. I push off the car, straightening.

"Noah Bennett?" she asks, voice crisp. No greeting, no small talk. Just confirmation.

"That's me."

She scans the lot, taking in cars, possibly scanning for anyone who might listen. Then she points toward a covered gazebo just off the courts. "Let's talk over there. I only have fifteen minutes."

"Thank you for agreeing to meet me," I say.

"I appreciate you staying away from my home," she counters.

There's a blade hidden in that line. She's used to wielding it.

"The police aren't as considerate," she adds, without prompting. "It's not that I mind the questions, Mr. Bennett. I want to assist the investigation. But I have children. Neighbors. I don't want them seeing the police on my front steps."

Her voice wavers on the last words, just enough to betray what the sunglasses hide.

"I understand," I say. "As I mentioned on the phone, I'm working on the case."

Inside the octagonal gazebo, she settles on one of the benches, crossing her legs. I take the one directly opposite, giving her space and a clear line of sight to the parking lot.

"But you're not with the police," she says. "You're contacting the witness list and reviewing the persons of interest list." Her tone is matter-of-fact, not impressed. "Are you working for Alicia Morgan?"

Whatever crack I heard a moment ago is gone. Her posture goes erect, shoulders squared, chin lifted. The temperature drops ten degrees.

"I'm supporting her defense team," I say. "You could call it that."

"You don't believe she's guilty."

It isn't a question. Still, I answer.

"No. I don't."

"Is that because she hired you," she asks, "or because you have specific reasons?"

"Both." I let the word sit between us, then add, "It doesn't fit. She had no motive. She hadn't seen him in years. I'm doing due diligence. I think the detective rushed this case—if I can find who actually murdered your husband, I help her and I help you."

"Do you have proof she hadn't seen him in years?"

Silence stretches for a beat. Some things can't be proven—it comes down to pattern, instinct, belief.

"Do you not believe that to be true?" I ask.

"I take it you know Matt and Alicia had an affair," she says.

"Yes," I answer. "A long time ago."

She nods once, sharply. "It was…a painful time. We spent

years in therapy. Forgiveness wasn't easy. I want to believe he didn't see her again. I want to believe I wasn't blind a second time." Her hands twist around her water bottle, the plastic rattling. "But I agreed to speak with you because while I don't like Alicia Morgan, I also don't want her to go to prison for a crime she didn't commit."

She takes a breath that sounds like it hurts. "And I'll admit this, Mr. Bennett—if my alibi hadn't been ironclad, I suspect I would've been on his list. A jilted wife?" Her fingers tap the face of her Apple watch. "I really do have ten minutes now. So. What can I tell you that's useful?"

"How did you find out about the affair?" I ask. "I'm trying to understand how many people might have known."

She slips off her sunglasses and lets them dangle loosely from one hand. Her eyes are red-rimmed but steady.

"Matt told me after it was over. Came up in therapy." A bitter smile twists her mouth. "I'd suspected. You know when you know. I felt…completely gaslit. He agreed to step off her board. Did you know that? He helped her start her company. Recruited her board of advisors. I hosted her in my home."

"You have every right to be angry," I say quietly.

Her lips press together. She drags a fingertip under one eye, like she's removing a stray lash, fighting the sting.

"I was furious," she admits. "I went to group therapy. It helped more than one-on-one. Listening to other women rationalize men who didn't deserve it…" She shakes her head. "Honestly, I would've left Matt, but we had three kids. Raising them alone felt harder than trying to fix us. And the last couple of years…" Her voice thins. "They were good. Or I thought they were good. I thought we'd done the work."

She jams the sunglasses back on like armor. "If I find out

I've been mourning—my children have been mourning—a man who cheated again…"

The anger humming in her tone is the kind that could burn a house down. But it doesn't feel like the kind that poisoned a husband.

"Alicia maintains she hadn't seen him in years," I say. "I believe her."

"I know," Elizabeth answers. "The detective told me she says that—but she also didn't tell him about the affair. Even so, I tend to believe her—I want to believe in him. I tracked his phone for a long time after the affair. At first because I didn't trust him. Then because habit is easier to maintain than dismantle." She gives a tiny shrug. "His office wasn't near hers. A friend of mine was his assistant for years—she managed his schedule. I don't see where they would have… fit it in. But now…"

Her voice fractures. She digs a tissue pack out of her tennis bag.

"I'm sorry," she murmurs, blotting at her eyes. "I keep ping-ponging between missing him and wanting to resurrect him so I can strangle him. That detective kept asking if there was anyone else he could have had an affair with, and now that's all I can think about."

I file that away. "If it helps," I say, "I've been digging into this case for weeks. I haven't seen a whisper of another affair. Not with Alicia, not with anyone else." Although, truthfully, an affair with a woman other than Alicia isn't an angle I've fully vetted.

"Then who?" she asks, voice raw. "Why?"

"Do you know much about his workload lately?" I ask. "What he was dealing with?"

"He's in corporate PR," she says. "His biggest clients are

food manufacturers. He moved away from scandals years ago. Even when he and Alicia worked together, she took the crisis cases. He preferred long-term retainers and predictable contracts." Her gaze meets mine. "He was boring, Mr. Bennett. That's what we wanted. Boring and safe."

"Your group therapy sessions," I say gently. "How many people were in those?"

Suspicion flickers, but she doesn't shut down. "Why?"

"I'm trying to trace the leak," I say. "Someone told that detective about the affair. Alicia believed no one knew. I'm trying to figure out who did."

"'No one knew,'" Elizabeth scoffs softly. "That sounds like her." She exhales. "Ms. Perfect would believe that. For the record, I didn't owe Matt silence. I told a couple of close friends. And the group therapist ran a program with women in difficult relationships. We used first names only, but when you sit in a circle every week, you recognize faces. People came and went. So did I. Three kids, school schedules, carpools." She lifts a shoulder. "I don't have a list. I'm not even sure I'd recognize most of them now."

So much for shrinking the suspect pool.

"I understand," I say. "I just needed to know if we were dealing with one confidante or a wider circle. Sounds like the latter."

She checks her watch and rises. "I really have to go."

"Thank you for your time, Mrs. Delacroix," I say, standing. "For what it's worth, I don't think you missed anything this time. And I don't think your husband's death has anything to do with Alicia reliving old sins."

"I hope you're right," she says quietly. "The police said they have conclusive evidence. I hope they're wrong. I don't want to have to explain Matt's affair to our children. Right now, he's their hero."

She walks toward the lot with a measured stride. A black Mercedes SUV flashes its tail lights as it unlocks. She loads her tennis bag into the backseat, and I take a discreet shot of the license plate as she pulls away—not because she feels like a suspect, but because it never hurts to have data.

On my phone, I tap out a quick update to the team:

Met with ex-wife. Alibi: tennis match. Doesn't feel suspicious. Shared that she told close friends and group therapy about affair.

The last line tastes like ash. If there was any hope of narrowing our focus by limiting who knew about the affair, it's gone.

I shift my weight, and my boot nudges something on the ground. A cluster of plastic disks lies half-hidden in the gravel. I bend and pick them up.

Tournament tags—club name, dates, winners. They're clipped together, and the back piece is engraved *Elizabeth Delacroix*.

Must've fallen out of her bag.

I glance back at the club. I could drop them at the front desk, but this is better—a neutral excuse to cross her threshold if I ever need context again. If she's not home, I'll leave them in her mailbox. No pressure, just consideration. Favor banked.

Thanks to Quinn's dossier, I have her address.

She asked me to stay away, but this is a favor.

The Delacroix house sits in a well-heeled neighborhood— nothing like the distinguished wealth on Richard Whitmore's street, but close enough that the same landscapers probably do both. Two-story colonials line the road, smaller lots, smaller houses, still plenty of money.

I pull into her drive and knock. A dog barks, big and deep, from somewhere inside. No footsteps follow.

Her car's not in the drive, so I head back down to the curbside mailbox. The habit is ingrained: eyes up, scan the street, check for watchers.

That's when I see him.

Four houses down, in a sedan that absolutely does not belong to this ZIP Code, a man sits behind the wheel. He's the same guy I saw arguing with Jessica outside a café near Alicia's office. He's parked in a way that gives him a view of both the Delacroix place and anyone circling the block. It's not the worst surveillance spot, but it's not the best either. Feels like someone who knows just enough to be dangerous.

I open the mailbox, slide the tournament disks on top of the waiting mail, and close it again.

With one eye on the sedan, I type out a quick text to Elizabeth:

Found your tournament tags near the court. Dropped them in your mailbox. Thought you might want them back.

She lives close to the club. With any luck, she'll chalk it up to thoroughness, not intrusion.

I get back into the Rivian, idle forward, and as I pass the sedan, snap a photo of the driver. I don't bother being subtle. He makes a show of looking down at something in his lap. Could be his phone. Could be an act.

I roll another fifty yards, then stop at the corner, lean out the window, and take a second shot—this time of his license plate.

That one he definitely notices.

Good.

Because my gut says he's not tailing me. He's tailing Alicia's car. Checking where she goes. Who she meets. Maybe he's been tracking her longer than we realized, and this is just the first time I've caught him in the act.

I send the tag photo to Quinn with a request to run it, then point the Rivian toward the shabbier side of town.

The PI who ran a background check on me works out of a strip of aging offices that rent by the month—massage, sketchy tax prep, fax-and-print shops clinging to relevance. His door's open. He's at his computer when I step in, shoulders hunched, light from the monitor washing his face in blue.

"What're you doing here?" he asks, fingers twitching on the mouse. I'd bet good money he just closed whatever screen he didn't want me to see. "I told you—I'm not telling you who hired me."

I hold my phone out, the picture of the sedan driver filling the screen. "You don't have to. This guy hired you."

His eyes flick to the image. His jaw works. "If you already know, what're you doing here?"

If I were wrong, he'd gloat. This is the type who loves to tell you you're barking up the wrong tree. Instead, he takes a long pull from his soda through a straw and swivels back to the monitor.

"You here to harass me?" he asks, feigning boredom.

"Nope."

I walk out, satisfied I've got confirmation.

On the sidewalk outside, my phone vibrates.

"Found the guy," Quinn says when I answer.

"And?" I ask, already sliding behind the wheel.

"Name's Danny Frazier."

"Don't know him," I say. "But I saw him arguing with Jessica outside a café near Alicia's office."

"I'm looking at his record," she says, voice tightening. "He's got a rap sheet. Three separate possession charges. One for prescription fraud. Avoided jail on the last one by agreeing to rehab."

"Type of drugs?" I ask.

"Five years ago—heroin. More recently—opioid prescriptions. Oxy, mostly."

I stare through the windshield, processing. Addict. Access issues. Desperation. And Jessica's a pharmaceutical rep. That's one hell of a Venn diagram.

"And he's sitting outside the Delacroix house watching Alicia's car," I say. "He wasn't there by chance. The PI confirmed he's the one who hired him—shoved a photo in his face."

"I'll dig for a connection to Jessica," Quinn says. "Employment overlaps, prescriptions, social links. Anything."

"Do that," I say. The pieces are starting to form the outline of something ugly. "We're onto something here, Quinn. This isn't coincidence."

I end the call, pulse thrumming with something that feels a lot like hope—and a darker, sharper edge that feels like we've finally brushed fingers against whoever decided Alicia Morgan was expendable—and right now, that person is looking a lot like someone with a personal vendetta. The obvious question circles my mind—Is Richard involved? Is Jessica doing him favors?

CHAPTER
THIRTY-FIVE

ALICIA

Melissa enters my office holding an opened brown envelope as if it might bite. "This came for you. Hand delivered to the office down the hall—they brought it here because it was delivered to the wrong suite."

Something prickles at the nape of my neck. "What is it?"

"It's…odd." She crosses the room slowly. "Just a page ripped from a calendar. From 2010. Someone circled October tenth in red ink."

October tenth.

1010.

A faint shiver sweeps through me, subtle but undeniable.

"It doesn't say anything else?" I ask.

"A fortune cookie slip." She hands me the tiny slip of paper. "Stay on your path; cosmic alignment; if you falter, consequences follow."

My stomach tightens.

I tell myself it's a coincidence, but the logic doesn't settle.

1010 is a number that finds me when I'm on the cusp of something—transition, risk, choice.

For someone else, it's just digits. For me, it's a message.

And someone knew to send it.

A cold echo stirs—Crawford's blackmail, the way the first envelope was vague, symbolic.

Could it be them? Could Pierce's people be circling back, even with an active investigation?

No. It's irrational. Even paranoid.

But the pressure beneath my ribs doesn't ease.

"Thanks, Melissa," I say, already rising.

"It's probably nothing, right?" she calls after me.

Probably.

Possibly.

But I'm already in the hall, scanning for Gabriel.

I find him outside the building, eyes narrowing when he spots me. "Is something wrong?"

"A hand-delivered envelope ended up next door."

His gaze drops to the papers. I start to hand them over, but he shakes his head. "Don't touch anything else. I'll get gloves."

The next fifteen minutes unfold in a blur: Gabriel's call to KOAN, building security rewinding footage, a startled junior assistant from the marketing firm next door being questioned.

On the grainy video, a man in a UPS uniform keeps his head down as he hands over a stack of envelopes. Fake uniform. Fake delivery.

Quinn confirms the fraud within minutes.

Nothing identifiable. No face, no distinguishing detail. Whoever sent it knew exactly what they were doing.

When Noah arrives, he moves with a sharp, urgent purpose—*like he feared the worst had already happened.*

"I'm fine," I say before he even reaches me.

He rests his hand on my shoulder, warm and steadying. His gaze sweeps me—a full-body assessment that is entirely professional yet not impersonal.

"Really, I'm fine. It's just…unnerving."

"Does the threat mean something to you?" he asks, voice low.

"'Stay on your path.'" I exhale slowly. "Not much on its face. But the numbers…they carry meaning in numerology. I just don't know why someone would use that, or what 'consequences' I'm supposed to avoid. If it's connected to Pierce, maybe this is their first vague warning. Crawford's blackmail started that way."

"You think it's them?" he asks.

"Maybe. But if they wanted me to stay quiet, why not say it? And with Crawford, the escalation to a threat didn't occur until the second package. I mean, I guess there's no law that says it has to be one hundred percent consistent for it to be the same person, or group of people."

He takes my hand, his grip gentle but certain, and guides me toward the sofa. Gabriel settles into the chair across from us—close enough to be present, professional enough not to intrude.

"I have other updates," Noah says. "I don't know if they connect. We might be dealing with two different parties."

A hint of nausea swirls. His updates aren't positive—I can tell. "What is it?"

"I met with Elizabeth Delacroix today."

My breath stills. "And?"

"A man followed me. The same man who hired the PI.

This time I got his plate. His name is Danny. We've been doing background, learning what we can about him." He pauses, like I'm not going to like what he's about to say.

"Just say it."

"He's Jessica's cousin."

The floor seems to tilt. "Jessica? But…why?"

"I don't know. Could be harmless. Maybe Richard confided something and she took it on herself to look into it—maybe she's doing him a favor, asked her cousin to hire a PI to check me out, make sure Stella's safe with me in the house."

I shake my head. "Richard wouldn't hire a PI to investigate you. I told you. He's controlling but not unhinged."

"Then why follow me? Why track you?" Noah asks. "My guess is that today he was following your car. The tracker is still active. He might've been trying to confirm what you were doing near Elizabeth Delacroix's house."

A hollow chill rolls through me. "That would mean… they're involved in Matthew's case."

"Maybe not the murder," Noah says. "But the framing? Possibly."

"That's insane."

He lifts one brow. "Is it? Richard pushed custody fast. Anything financial coming up?"

"No," I whisper. "Nothing like that. And regardless of anything between us, he'd never want to hurt me. He'd never risk hurting Stella."

Noah's phone buzzes. He glances at the screen—and all the color drains from his face.

"My dad's in an ambulance," he says, voice roughening. "They're taking him to the hospital."

I don't think. I reach for him. "Come on. Let's go."

"He's in New Jersey," he murmurs, still staring at the message as if willing it to change.

"He texted? Can you call?"

"Linda texted. She said she'll call from the hospital."

"Let's go." I tighten my grip on his arm. "Train or plane— what's fastest? Flights to Manhattan run every hour. Where in New Jersey?"

He finally looks at me—and in that moment, everything shifts.

The hospital waiting room reminds me of the packed area in an airport before a flight begins boarding, only instead of anxious fliers, the people here are anxiously awaiting news of a loved one. The seats are equally uncomfortable, and some have opted to sit on the floor, leaning against a wall to stretch their legs or watch a show on a phone in privacy. The scent blends human stress with cleaning products, and the air is cold.

Noah's father is out of surgery, and Linda has been allowed to join him. The initial news is good—he had emergency bypass surgery and the doctor predicts a full recovery. Ever since receiving the news, Noah's been quiet and withdrawn.

He argued at first—told me to stay, that I had other issues to attend to. That I needed to be here for the dinner with my daughter, that I needed to be here to deal with the case. He even debated whether or not he and I should both stay back given everything going on—but I insisted, quietly and firmly, that his father needed him, and that's where we'd be.

I called Stella—catching her during her lunch period—and

explained. Being my little empath, she immediately assured me she'd be okay at her dad's and that of course I should go with Noah. After handling travel plans, I called Richard. He was far less amenable—but I cut the conversation short as we were entering the airport and I had Noah at my side.

The doors open and Linda exits. Her color has drained, likely from a mixture of exhaustion and harsh fluorescent overhead lighting, but her eyes sparkle with renewed life. Noah and I both stand as she approaches.

"Noah, he wants to see you. They've got him in a room. He's awake now but I don't know for how long."

"How is he?" Noah asks.

We received the doctor's update earlier, but he's looking for more.

"He's tired. He's not in any pain—they've taken care of that. Get on back there and see him for yourself before he falls asleep again."

Noah hesitates, looking at me.

"Don't worry about Alicia," Linda says. "I'll bring her down to the cafeteria for coffee—I'll take good care of her. We'll be up soon."

"Do you want anything?" I ask Noah, but he shakes his head, takes a step, then returns. His lips brush my cheek— soft, fleeting, but full of everything he's not saying. Warmth blooms deep in my chest, steadying me in a way nothing else has all day.

"I'll be here when you're done," I assure him.

We both watch him leave, then exit the waiting room, and head to the elevator bank. The cafeteria is on the first floor.

"How are you doing?" I ask.

"Better now." There's a slight tremble in her fingers as

she reaches to push the elevator button. "That was scary," she says, almost to herself.

There's something fragile in her tone, something that tugs at a deep place inside me. She loves him. They all do. And for the first time in a long time, I feel the edges of what it means to step into someone else's family—into their fears, their history, their hopes.

"But he's going to be okay."

"Yes. The doctor says yes. If they'd been slower getting to the house…" she presses her lips together and her eyes grow glassy. "Could have been a very different day."

I squeeze her arm in support as the doors slide open and we step in.

We're quiet moving through the elevator and the cafeteria line. After I've purchased hot tea and she's ordered decaf coffee and a muffin, she gestures to an open table. "Let's sit. Give them some time."

I slide into the booth opposite her, and she cups her coffee with both hands.

"You remind me of her, you know?" she says with a soft smile.

"Who?"

"Sarah. His mom."

"Oh," I say, twirling my tea bag in the hot water. "How so?"

"Well, your dark hair, your poise." Her gaze falls to her mug. Linda has golden brown eyes and gray hair, and she's petite with rounded curves. If she colored her hair, she'd look younger than her sixty-something years. "There's a resemblance, but I think it's more how you handle yourself. Calm, focused. An inner strength. Oh… You know? I have pictures." She fumbles through her handbag and pulls out her phone. She presses against the screen, then hands it to me.

On the screen there's a photo of Linda years ago, with brown hair with blonde highlights, and a woman with dark brown hair and brown eyes. Their arms are around each other and smiling into the screen.

"Sarah and I were childhood best friends. I was the maid of honor in their wedding."

I smile.

"I got married about a year after they did. My husband died unexpectedly when we'd only been married for six years." Her fingers rub the sides of the ceramic cup. "Pulmonary embolism. Art and Sarah were life savers. I had a young child; I hadn't been working. They helped me get on my feet. When Sarah died, it was a dozen years later, but stepping in and helping was natural." Her chest sinks on her exhale. "When I thought I'd lost him too…"

Her voice fractures, and instinct overrides everything else. I reach across the table, covering her hand with mine. A small gesture, but she clings to it as if it anchors her. "But you didn't. He's going to be okay."

She swallows and nods, finally lifting her gaze. "It's good that Noah has you."

The certainty in her voice startles me. I'm not sure what I expected—skepticism, maybe. Distance. But her acceptance slips under my defenses like light.

I blow on my tea and sip. She most certainly doesn't know anything about the current murder charges.

"You know, that kid, he's his father's pride. He's such a good person. Fair. Driven." There's a soft smile. The way she's talking so softly almost to herself makes me think exhaustion is winning and she's weaving through her thoughts. "Could have played college ball. But he chose the Army. Art wanted him to go to college, to take over his business. You know, Art started as a mechanic. Bought the shop from his boss and grew it. Wanted his son to grow it into a franchise."

"That wasn't what Noah wanted?"

She shakes her head with an undeniable note of sadness. "He still got his college degree you know, while on active duty. When he became an Army Ranger—Art was proud. I wish Sarah could have seen it. I think Art started to get behind the idea of his son excelling in the military, but when he didn't reenlist, Art struggled with it." She exhales. "I know Art can come across like he's being harsh. It's just he's worked so hard and he wants his son to do the same."

"Noah loves his father."

She smiles in acknowledgement. "Arturo is proud of his son. Noah may not realize it, but he is. He brags whenever he gets the chance. He's a Bronze star recipient. Did you know that?" Pride softens her features.

I shake my head. Noah hadn't mentioned it.

It hits me then—how little he shares about himself. How much he carries alone. How much I want him to trust me with everything he hides.

"Noah was a leader over there—squad leader, I think? Art would know the exact title. He had men under him. Multiple deployments. Still figuring out what he wants to do next. He's going to do well. He's already doing well. Art just needs to say it out loud more often."

I nod, because he is doing well and he's got plenty of time to figure out his next steps.

"He was considered to be exceptionally advanced in the army…or that's what I'm told. He's a good person."

When I lift my gaze from my tea, I find her studying me.

"He says you have a daughter."

"I do. She's twelve." I pull out my phone and show her a photo.

"She's beautiful," she says. "Just like her momma." She hands me back my phone. "I bet Noah's good with her."

"He is," I say, thinking of them playing basketball. "She's a fan."

"That's good," she says. "It helps when the kids are supportive."

The way she says that makes me wonder how supportive Noah was when his father told him he was dating his mother's best friend.

"You know, Art knew he was serious about you after his first conversation with him."

That comment takes me aback.

"I could see it when I first saw you two together. Isn't it funny like that? How two people find each other—and others just know?"

"He's been good for me," I admit. Saying it aloud feels like stepping over a threshold. A truth I can no longer retreat from—not that I have any desire to retreat.

"Thanksgiving is around the corner," she says. "Do you know what your plans are?"

"Um," I blink, processing the change in conversation. "Other than ordering a turkey, I haven't thought about it."

I've spent Thanksgiving with Richard's family for years, but last year was the last time that will happen. He brought Jessica—and I've never felt more out of place. According to the custody agreement, I get Stella this Thanksgiving—we'll alternate from here on out.

"We'd love to have you," she says. "If you've got family, we could even have a Friday or Saturday meal."

"Oh," I blink, processing. Will Noah and I share the holidays together? I mean, I suppose we will.

"What are your family traditions?"

Her questions draw me back to the conversation and I brace myself for her reaction—but there's no way around it. "My parents passed away. It's just me and Stella." That's not entirely true—I have distant relatives, but distant is the operative word.

"Well you let me know what works for you."

"You're very kind," I say, meaning every word. "And, I want to be clear, I do care for Noah. Greatly. But I'm aware of the age difference. I don't want you to be concerned. I'm not looking to—"

"Age difference? Goodness gracious. Who cares about that?"

"I'm ten years older," I say slowly—although it's possible she doesn't realize.

She waves a hand dismissively. "Age is in the head. As are differences." She breaks a piece off her muffin. "People can miss out on so much if they get too in their head."

Her words resonate. I've spent so long calculating consequences that I've forgotten how to simply choose what feels right—or what I want.

"Look at Art and me. We almost didn't get together because we thought everyone would judge us. That Noah and Maya wouldn't accept us. And you know, we built this mountain up in our heads and at the end of the day, no one batted an eye. We almost missed out on so much happiness…and for what?" She looks at her wrist. "I think they've had enough time. You want to head up now? We'll relieve Noah and you two can head back to the house and get some rest."

11:11 glows on my screen—clean, precise, a quiet omen I can't ignore.

An omen of new beginnings.

And for the first time in forever, I let myself believe that maybe—just maybe—that's exactly what this is.

CHAPTER
THIRTY-SIX

NOAH

Dad's eyes open—slow, like he's surfacing from deep water. Machines beep a steady rhythm around him, oxygen hissing softly through the nasal cannula. His hands feel cold when I take them, but his smile is warm, even if it's on the weak side.

"There he is," he says.

"You know, if you wanted to see me, all you had to do is say so. This right here is a bit extreme."

Dad chuckles—briefly—before his hand covers his chest.

"Hurts, huh?" I ask.

"Meh. I've had better days. Expect tomorrow will be worse."

"Clogged arteries, huh? And all those years of eating healthy."

He grimaces. "I might've strayed a little every now and then."

Growing up, Dad was always about healthy eating.

Admittedly, our interpretation of healthy evolved over the years, but he and Mom were the parents who monitored sugar intake, who went so far as to question Gatorade, forcing me to drink water at sports practices.

"Dad, it happens. You're still pretty fit." I mean, he's got a blanket over him, but judging by the outline of his body and his relatively flat midriff, for a sixty-five-year-old man, he'd pass most people's fit test.

"Yeah, well, something tells me I'm gonna need you to run interference with Linda on that one. Cause we both know Maya will be worse."

We both grin—me more than him—and silence falls.

"You scared me, dad."

It's true. All I could think of was all the canceled plans and unfulfilled promises. The weekends I didn't visit. The stilted, tense conversations.

"Hey. Look at me, son."

I force my gaze up from the thin hospital blanket, from the IV port taped to the back of his hand.

"I understand you've got a life. Your mom understood too."

Emotions detonate in my chest—sudden, brutal. My eyes burn. I search the room for something to focus on: the monitor showing his vitals, the window with its view of the parking garage, anything but the understanding in his eyes. Anything but the unearned forgiveness.

"Maybe it's good this happened." Dad's voice is softer now, fading at the edges.

"What?" I lean forward; certain I misheard. "Dad, you're out of your mind."

"Gives me a chance to tell you what I should've told you back when your mom died. Back then, I was too heartbroken. Self-absorbed. Maybe a little angry. But she understood why you were absent. You didn't have a choice. It's part of life. Commitments. She wouldn't have stood for you walking away from responsibility to sit in a room like this one."

"I thought she had more time." If I'd known it could happen fast…

"Don't. She had complications the docs didn't anticipate. No one could have. It's not your fault—any more than it's mine."

I cover my dad's hand with mine. It's not lost on me that he seems smaller in the bed, older, more frail than the man I know him to be. His eyes close slowly, like his lids are heavy.

"I love you, Dad." His eyes flicker open wide. "I don't tell you that enough." Yes, we have our differences, but none of that matters.

"But I know it," he says. "And I love you too. I'm proud of you."

My eyes sting immediately.

"I shouldn't have pushed you to take over Manny's auto." He taps my hand. "That's something I needed to say. No matter what you do, I'm proud." Then, gaze to the ceiling, he adds, "Thank you for letting me get that in."

Dad's eyelids close and I relax in my chair, watching him. He's got a lot of drugs in his system, so I expect he'll sleep. It's late and while there isn't a time we have to be out of his room by, I expect we should let him rest.

A soft knock breaks the quiet. The door—left ajar by the last nurse—swings wider, and Linda slips in, Alicia just behind her.

I push up, vacating the chair for Linda, should she wish to sit.

Linda moves past me to the bed, touching Dad's cheek. "You've got visitors," she murmurs.

Dad's eyes crack open again—heavy, fluttering—until they focus on Alicia.

And even doped up, as weak as he is, the man smiles.

"Well now," he rasps, the corner of his mouth tugging higher, "so this is the woman who's captured my son's heart."

Heat sweeps beneath my skin. "Dad—"

Alicia laughs softly, the sound small and gentle in the sterile room. "Sir, it's very nice to meet you. I just wish it were under better circumstances."

"Same here," he says. "But if this is what it takes to get you two in the same room with me, maybe it's worth the drama." His gaze slides to me. "She's special, son. Get your act together. Don't be stupid."

"Alright," I mutter. "He's definitely high."

Linda chuckles, smoothing a hand over his blanket. "He's drifting again. Let's let him rest. Why don't you two head back to the house?"

"You're staying here?" I ask, although I suspected she might.

"I'll stay. The bench seat folds out to a small bed. When you come back in the morning, I'll head home for a shower and change. Do you still have your key?"

"Yeah. I do."

I squeeze Dad's hand once more before hugging Linda and following Alicia into the hallway. The door closes with a soft click behind us, sealing the quiet.

Alicia stands beside me, arms wrapped lightly around herself. The fluorescent lighting softens against her hair, turning the dark strands warm.

I take her hand—her fingers are cold from the hospital's low temperature—and lead her toward the elevators. The antiseptic smell finally fades as we move away from the cardiac wing. I blow out a breath I didn't know I was holding.

"Sorry about that."

"Why?" she asks. "He adores you. That was obvious."

"What he said to you—"

"That I've captured your heart?" she finishes, voice soft but steady.

I rub a hand over my jaw. "I just don't want you to feel pressured. He's doped up. Sentimental."

Her eyes lift to mine. Clear. Direct. No flinch. "There's no place I'd rather be tonight. When the text came in, I didn't even think. I just…went with you." She swallows. "Which makes me wonder what we're doing."

I tighten my hold on her hand but slow our pace. "Alicia."

"This is real, isn't it?" Her voice drops to barely above a whisper, like she's afraid to say it too loud.

There it is. The question I've been carrying in my chest, the one I've buried under duty and timing and the certainty that she could do better. That someone like her—fierce, accomplished, untouchable in so many ways—wouldn't choose someone like me unless it was circumstance. Unless it was just proximity and adrenaline.

But the tremor in her voice tells me she's as uncertain as I am. And somehow that makes it more real.

I look at her for a long moment—this woman who walked into a hospital in another state without hesitating, who held my father's hand like she'd known him for years.

"It is from my side," I say quietly.

Her gaze flickers down the hall, toward the life waiting back home, toward the storm she's standing in the center of.

To some, she might be simply looking down the long hospital hall, but I sense she's seeing beyond the moment.

"Noah…maybe you should wait until the murder charges are dropped before you jump all in."

That's her hesitation? She's not pulling back—she wants to protect me from the fallout. Something in my chest shifts. Of all the reasons I expected her to give, this wasn't one of them.

I pull her closer, close enough that I can see the exhaustion shadowing her eyes, the tension she's been holding in her jaw.

"I'm in. No matter what." My thumb brushes across her knuckles. "And the case is weak. Whoever's framing you—whoever's behind this—they made mistakes. Jessica's connection is huge. Our team will tear the rest apart. I'd bet everything the prosecution drops the charges before this sees the inside of a courtroom."

Her eyes trace my face, something fragile and fierce merging there. "You're not afraid?"

"Hell yeah, I'm scared." I tighten my grip on her hand. "But not of the outcome of your case."

She doesn't move away. She doesn't retreat. She just stands there, breathing the same thin hospital air I'm breathing, and it feels like something seismic is shifting beneath us.

A nurse walks by, smiling politely, and the spell softens but doesn't break.

Alicia exhales—slow, deliberate, the way she does when she's made a decision she's not going to second-guess.

"So we'll go back tonight," she says finally. "Come back in the morning to relieve Linda?"

"I'll come back and relieve Linda. You should head back in

the morning. Stella needs you. And you've got enough on your plate."

"Since everything's okay, maybe so." Her voice is quiet, but steady.

We enter the elevator in silence. The doors slide shut, sealing us in that small, fluorescent box. I keep hold of her hand, my thumb tracing absent circles on her palm. The numbers descend: 4...3...2... Each floor a reminder that we're leaving the crisis behind, returning to the world where she's facing charges and I'm her protection detail.

But in this moment, in this elevator, we're just two people holding on.

The doors chime open to the lobby, and she speaks again.

"How long do you plan to stay?"

"I'll stay long enough to make sure he's settled. Until Maya makes it in. Maya has one more day on this shift then she's off for four and flying in. Then I'll meet you in DC." I take a breath. "I'll be there before Stella's play. Even if I'm walking in at the last minute."

Her lips part. A soft, surprised inhale. "Stella will love that."

I nod once. "Will you?"

Alicia doesn't answer right away. She just steps closer, laying her palm against my chest—over my heart—like she's memorizing the beat.

"I will," she says finally. "Let's get out of here so you can get some sleep. Your father needs you sharp tomorrow."

"And you too," I return. "You must be exhausted."

It's not until later—much later—when we're curled together in Dad's guest bed, her back pressed against my chest, my arm wrapped around her waist, that the adrenaline finally drains away. The ghost of fluorescent light fades from behind my eyelids. The antiseptic smell is replaced by her shampoo, something floral and clean.

The echo of her words—*this is real*—settles into my bones with a weight that feels like purpose.

Like home.

Dad was right.

I'd be an idiot to let her go.

CHAPTER
THIRTY-SEVEN

ALICIA

We dropped Stella at the school two hours ago—the drama instructor does the kids' hair and makeup at the auditorium. In past years, I volunteered to help, but this year the decision was easy—being charged with murder isn't something you want to walk into a school volunteer situation carrying. The risk of another parent saying something in front of Stella, or worse, in front of her friends, isn't one I'm willing to take. And with Gabriel shadowing me this week, raising eyebrows felt like a secondary concern I didn't need either. This year, I'm simply an attending parent.

My phone buzzes against the marble countertop.

Noah: *Wish I could be there. Take photos.*
Me: *You're where you need to be. I'll buy the school's video.*

. . .

As I finish tapping out my message to Noah, Gabriel steps into the kitchen, dressed in tan trousers and a sport coat over a black crewneck. He's been staying in the guest room since I returned from New Jersey. His presence feels different than Noah's, more formal, less woven into the fabric of our days. But tonight, as I prepare to leave for the play, I'm grateful not to be alone.

While Noah is highly suspicious of Richard and Jessica, I struggle to believe it. Richard and I have had our differences, but he'd never hurt me, and by extension, Stella. I can almost imagine him asking Jessica to run a background check, and her looping in a cousin for help, but anything beyond that feels like too much of a stretch. It's easier to believe in over-protectiveness than malice.

"I've got my car out front. I can drive," Gabriel says.

"No, I should drive."

I slip my phone into my handbag. Gabriel is watching me, composed as ever. He could step into any private school func-tion and blend seamlessly.

"Wait," I say slowly. "Are you planning on attending with me?"

"If it's a problem, you could introduce me as your brother. Or a family friend."

"I just don't think it's—"

"Necessary," he finishes. "I know. But Noah would never forgive me if I weren't with you tonight. Especially given the attendees."

He means Richard and Jessica.

We still haven't found anything concrete tying Richard to Danny, but Noah's instincts about Jessica have only grown stronger. Richard wouldn't pay Jessica for her help, and he'd never put anything in writing. My legal team wants to approach Danny, Jessica, and Richard when the timing's right —but not yet. They're leaning toward Danny, believing he'll crack first.

But not yet. Not before we meet with prosecutors.

And then there's Elizabeth Delacroix—another theory Luca insists on keeping warm, despite my objections. I've told them to leave her alone, but it hasn't stopped talk. Murder-for-hire. Jealousy. A woman scorned wanting a clean alibi and someone else taking the fall. Luca is clinical, cold, terrifying in his detachment.

And Dorian still believes Pierce's people might be involved.

Too many angles. Too many motives. And none of them clear.

So I've decided to focus on what I can control: my daughter, my business, and keeping my life as normal as possible while my attorneys and KOAN hunt for answers. Every night, I've spoken to Noah. He hoped his father would be discharged today, but it looks like tomorrow is more realistic.

I pause, studying Gabriel—Gabe, as he prefers. Even in business-casual clothing, with his military bearing and watchful eyes, he looks unmistakably like security. He does not look remotely related to me.

Will the other parents assume we're dating? Or that I'm under some kind of surveillance?

It's ironic. My entire career is built on sculpting public perception, and here I am ignoring my own. What would I advise a client in my situation?

Attend with your ex-husband and his girlfriend. Present unity. Signal stability. Let the crowd see you're confident, not hiding.

I would absolutely advise against showing up with a man who looks like federal law enforcement.

And yet, here I am.

"Is something wrong?" Gabriel asks.

I inhale, shaking off the tightening in my chest, and pick up my handbag. "Nothing's wrong. Just thinking."

He lifts his arm toward the front door, jacket riding up enough for me to glimpse his waistband.

"You're not carrying?" I ask, double-checking. Guns are forbidden on school grounds.

"No," he says, amused. "But I'll drive. I don't anticipate needing firepower at a school function, but if I did, it's in my glove box."

"You're not going to need a gun," I say, half-laughing, half-drowning in the surrealism of my reality.

"And I don't plan on carrying one." He opens the front door with an almost old-world gallantry. "After you."

I stride past him. He closes the door behind us, and I lock the deadbolt.

"Prepared for all scenarios," he says after crossing the short stretch to the curb. "That's what they taught us."

"Sounds like advice I'd give my clients."

He opens the passenger door for me, and I slide in, feeling oddly…escorted.

"When you've spoken to Noah, how does he sound?" I ask once he's behind the wheel.

"Strained," he says, adjusting the rearview. "But he's holding steady. His father's getting stronger."

That's my assessment too. But hearing it confirmed helps.

Gabriel drives without GPS. I watch him navigate the back streets toward the school with unsettling ease.

"Are you from DC?" I ask.

"I've spent time here."

"Noah mentioned you're new at KOAN."

"That I am."

"Why'd you leave the military?"

"It was time," he says, glancing over with a grin. "Is that answer a cop-out?"

I smile. Because we're not close, his answer doesn't feel like a deflection—just privacy.

But he must feel like he should expand. "Going private gives you more flexibility."

We approach the school as traffic thickens. I point to the church lot. "Park there. Easier walk."

We pull in. As we exit, I ask, "Family brings you back to DC?"

"Someone I care about. Not romantic." He falls into step beside me. "Actually, it's a case involving some key DC players. You might have a unique perspective."

"Oh?" A parent waves from across the lot, and I wave back. In my role, I'm familiar with many of the players in the area. I'm happy to answer questions, but not where we might be overheard. "Talk to me back at the house."

He nods.

We merge into the stream of parents entering the school. Ahead, about ten rows from the stage, I spot Richard. He sees me and lifts his hand.

There are several empty seats between the aisle and where Jessica sits.

I start toward him, but Gabriel's hand taps my shoulder.

"Can you step back out for a moment?"

I gesture to Richard that I'll be there shortly. He frowns and turns away.

I follow Gabriel out into the wide school hallway—and

stop breathing. Noah stands there. Tall. Exhausted. Unbearably present. My heart lifts so hard I feel it in my throat.

"You made it," I breathe, and I'm moving before I mean to.

"Told you I would." He catches me, and for just a moment, the world narrows to the warmth of his hands at my waist, the solid reality of him here.

"Thanks, man," he says to Gabriel. "I was aiming to meet her at the house. Delayed flight."

Gabriel grins. "Hand-off complete. I'll see you both in the morning."

It's Thursday evening—the first of three performances.

"I can't believe you surprised me," I say, my hand tucked in his. "Stella's going to be thrilled."

Richard glances over his shoulder when we enter. The moment he sees Noah, his jaw tightens, and he turns back to face forward so rigidly I can feel his anger from three rows back. Seats have been taken now, and the one seat he saved is clearly for me alone. But two seats sit open directly behind them, and Noah steers me toward those.

Jessica turns, smiling sweetly. Something in her eyes contradicts the smile entirely. Richard stares forward, refusing to look at us. Fortunately, the hum of activity around us cuts what might be particularly awkward thanks to Richard.

The lights dim. The curtain rises.

As the play unfolds, I'm struck by how easily truth twists in the wrong hands. *The Crucible* isn't about witchcraft—it's about jealousy, ignorance, a community hungry for moral superiority. A willingness to condemn without evidence.

A willingness to destroy.

Stella plays her role perfectly. She told me she was the

villain—but she's not. More of an accomplice. And I like that she knows that. I like that she already understands the danger of following others blindly.

When the final curtain rises, the auditorium erupts in applause. Families spill into the hall.

Noah, Richard, Jessica, and I drift toward the school entrance to wait for the cast.

"She did good," Noah says.

"She did," I agree.

"So, Alicia," Jessica says, linking her arm through Richard's. He keeps his hands in his pockets, gaze distant, bored. "It's good you could be here. I know it means the world to Stella."

I smile politely. Noah's hand presses at the small of my back—a quiet claim that Jessica clocks immediately.

"Do you have a court date yet?" Jessica asks.

I glance at Richard—he knows. He's been updated.

"It's scheduled," I say. "But we're hoping for a dismissal."

"Oh?" she asks, wide-eyed, glancing at Richard as though she's waiting for him to feed her information.

"The evidence we've gathered is strong," Noah says lightly. "I expect prosecutors will drop the case at Monday's meeting. If they do, then no need for the judge to dismiss."

Jessica's lips tighten—a near-flinch.

"Wow. Did you know this?" she asks Richard, sounding affronted.

"Of course," he says flatly.

"Well, I never thought you did it," Jessica adds, aiming it at me like absolution I didn't ask for.

Noah looks at me for permission.

This isn't the approach my legal team cautioned against.

This is just a name, dropped in a crowd. And I want to see her face.

I nod.

"We've located a man named Daniel Frazier," he says. "Does that name mean anything to you?"

Jessica goes still. Not frozen—that would be too obvious. But still, the way a deer goes still when it first hears the snap of a branch.

"We've placed him at the hotel the day of the murder. At Alicia's home. And he hired a PI to investigate me," Noah adds.

"We're still developing the full picture," I say evenly. "But we expect everything to be tied up by Monday."

Jessica's throat bobs. Her fingers tighten on Richard's arm.

And in that moment, whatever doubt I had evaporates. She's involved.

Maybe not alone. Maybe not in the way we first theorized. But involved—without question.

"Noah!" Stella bursts through the crowd. "You made it!"

She darts past me to high-five him. He hands her the flowers he brought, and I kiss her temple. "You were wonderful."

"I messed up two lines," she says. "But Jimmy forgot an entire section!"

"You couldn't tell," I assure her.

Richard bends to hug Stella. When he straightens, he looks around. "Where did Jessica go? We brought you flowers too."

I scan the crowd filtering toward the exits. She's gone. No goodbye. No excuse. Just—gone. Noah's hand finds mine, a brief squeeze.

Richard's frown deepens. "That's...odd."

"Maybe she had a call," I offer, though Noah and I both know better.

Stella chatters about her performance, oblivious to the tension crackling between the adults. And I let her. Because for tonight, she deserves to bask in her success.

As the crowd thins, the certainty settles.

Jessica's absence vibrates through me like a struck wire—sharp, undeniable, truth confirming.

NOAH

Richard stands near the school entrance, phone pressed to his ear, scanning the parking lot for Jessica. I don't wait to hear what excuse she'll give him. When Alicia and Stella are buckled in, I step aside to make my own call, pacing toward the shadows at the lot's edge.

Hudson answers on the first ring.

"Jessica's tipped off," I say, skipping the greeting. "She heard Danny's name, realized we're connecting dots, and bolted. Didn't even say goodbye to Richard. He's looking for her now."

Hudson exhales sharply. "So Richard's not involved." It's not quite a question.

"Yeah." I grind my teeth. "Danny's name meant nothing to him. He wasn't even listening—too busy glaring at me for existing near his ex-wife."

"Our plan was to loop in the detectives in the morning," Hudson says. "But let me get ahead of this. I'll send Jake to

Jessica's—keep eyes on her movements." A pause. "And I'll call Luca."

"Good." I glance toward the car where Alicia's silhouette moves in the soft glow of the dashboard as she and Stella settle in. "I'm going to drive Alicia and Stella home."

"I'll keep you posted."

Later, when Alicia and Stella are upstairs—laughing at play photos making their way through group chats—my phone buzzes.

Jake.

I step into the foyer and answer. "Talk to me."

"No lights on," he says. "No car in the drive. No sign she's home. Back door's ajar."

"You in her yard?" My hand tightens on the phone.

"Townhouse. Tall hedges. If someone spots me, I'll play lost visitor."

"Must be nice," I mutter. "I try that, cops get called before I reach the door."

Jake snorts. "Daisy cut my hair. If I had my long hair, they'd call the cops on me too. Trust."

A faint creak comes through the line.

"Okay," he whispers. "Switching to earbud. Going in."

"Wait," I snap. "You're supposed to be observing, not going full breach. Wait for me."

"Nah. Just stay on the line." His voice drops low. "You gotta stay there, man. We don't know where this chick went."

He's right. And that's the problem.

"Downstairs is pretty sparse," he narrates. "Lots of journals. Books. She's got a medical fetish."

"She's in pharmaceutical sales," I say. "Did you turn on the light?"

"Nope. Using my phone."

Pages rustle. His breath shifts.

"Fridge is barren."

"Fits," I say. "Stella said she practically lives at Richard's."

"I'm going up the stairs."

I start pacing the length of the foyer, the dread settling slow and heavy. This is wrong. He needs backup. I should be there. Every instinct I have is screaming that this is a trap waiting to spring.

I flip open my laptop on the hallway console.

"I'm letting the team know where you are."

"Copy. Tell them I'm solo."

That's the part I hate.

I type fast:

Jake at Jessica's townhome. Back door open. No sign of her. He's inside—no backup.

Quinn's reply is instant.

Quinn: Where are you?
Me: Alicia's. Jessica's whereabouts unknown.

I grit my teeth. I hate being benched. Hate that Jake might be walking into something we haven't mapped.

Quinn: Gabe's on his way.

Me: Jake's using his phone as a light.

"Her room now," Jake says, his voice tight through the earbud connection. "Looks like she left in a hurry. Drawers open. Toiletries missing."

A cold certainty settles in my gut.

Me to team: Drawers open. Toiletries gone. She's running.

"Gabriel's on his way," I tell Jake.

"I'm backing out," he says. "No one's here. She's gone."

Me to team: Jake's backing out. Place empty.

My phone buzzes again.

Quinn: Alicia's security cameras just went offline.

My blood goes cold.

My fingers fly across the laptop keyboard, pulling up the security feed.

Every angle.

Every camera.

Black.

Like someone flipped a switch. Or cut the power from the inside.

"Jake," I say, voice tight. "How fast can you get here?"

"Ten minutes."

"Make it five."

I'm already moving toward the stairs, reaching for my weapon, every nerve on high alert.

ALICIA

A sharp clang slices through the house.

Stella's in her pajamas, curled on her bed, scrolling through posts from the play on her phone—the one her father bought her. The blue glow lights her cheeks, carefree and warm.

But the sound downstairs is wrong.

Too loud.

Too deliberate.

Not a settling pipe or shifting wood.

Something else. Someone else.

Is Noah on the second floor?

Why would he be?

He doesn't come up here when Stella's home—we agreed to that. I go to him in the basement for privacy.

Suddenly, I can't sit still.

If Noah's downstairs, something happened.

With the case.

With Jessica.

With all of it.

A tremor crawls along my spine.

I tap Stella's leg. "Give me the phone. Lights out."

She gives me a tired smile and slides beneath the comforter. I take the phone gently from her hands and set it on the charger at her desk.

"Did I tell you the spring play is going to be *The Secret Garden*?" she asks, voice soft with the wind down.

"Yes," I whisper. "You mentioned it."

"Tryouts are in two weeks."

Another sound cuts upward from below.

A creak.

Then a footstep.

Or the echo of one.

My hand lingers on the light switch.

"How about we get through *this* play before we worry about the next one?"

She smiles, unaware of my pulse climbing. I turn off the light. Her shadow stretches once, then disappears.

"Night, Mom."

"Night. Love you."

The latch clicks softly when I pull her door closed.

And then I move—fast.

Down the stairs.

Rapid. Quiet.

Hand on the banister.

The hallway is dark. Too dark.

My office door is shut.

My bedroom door open—wide open.

I stop at the landing, breath tight.

Noah?

The word is silent in my mind; I don't dare speak it.

Stella would hear.

Within seconds, my palm closes over my office doorknob.

I twist.

A crash explodes inside the room.

Jessica spins toward me.

Her eyes are wild. Her hair is damp—night air or sweat, I couldn't say—and in her shaking hand, she holds a small black handgun. The muzzle wobbles, trembling like her wrist can't bear its weight.

"Close the door," she says.

Her voice is soft.

Too soft.

A dead calm wearing hysteria underneath.

I swallow hard. Then close the door.

Noah's somewhere nearby—I can feel it in my bones—but he isn't here now. Not between me and the trembling gun.

"What's going on, Jessica?"

"Lock it."

My fingers fumble at the bolt. It slides into place with a quiet click.

The corner floor lamp casts a warm golden haze behind her, turning the edges of her hair into a halo, a cruel contrast to the shadow across her face.

"How did you get in?" I whisper.

She mutters something—fragmented, slurred. Incoherent.

Her gaze jerks toward my open drawer.

USB drives. Four of them.

She scoops them up with frantic, jerking motions and shoves them into her coat pocket.

"Jessica—"

Her name barely leaves my mouth before she flinches,

eyes darting to the windows. Mud smears the sill. The latch hangs crooked.

She climbed in.

"Can I help you with something?" I ask, trying to keep my voice soothing and low, mindful of Stella upstairs.

Jessica's laugh is a sharp exhale. "Yeah, I'm sure you want to help. So damn perfect. Always so perfect. He still loves you, you know?"

"Richard?" I ask carefully.

Her arm shoots out—gun thrust forward.

"Don't play dumb." Her voice breaks. "You string him along. Keep him close. He can't move on if there's even a chance you'll come running back. You cheated on him—you fucked around—and he *still* loves you."

She is unraveling.

Unspooling right in front of me.

"That's what this is about?" I breathe. "Jessica…"

I soften my tone. The way I would with a panicked client on the brink of destroying everything. "This is a misunderstanding."

"Oh, is it?" She sneers. "You greedy little whore. You want it all. He only gets her on weekends. Has to beg for holidays. And you—you're so fucking judgey. So high and mighty. Planning your perfect little trips while he just wants a normal family."

"He loves you, Jessica."

"No," she whispers. Her lips twist. "He loves *you*. Still."

Her breathing fractures. The gun trembles, not quite aimed at me—more toward the corner, like she can't hold it steady.

Her gaze flicks again to the window.

"Everything's ruined," she murmurs. "You ruined it."

She starts backing toward the sill.

For a moment, I consider letting her go. Let her climb out and vanish. Let this be over.

But Stella is upstairs.

Stella is awake.

If Jessica circles back—

If she tries the third floor—

If that gun goes off—

No.

A heavy thud shakes below.

Then another.

Faster.

Harder.

Footfalls pounding up the stairs.

The breath I've been holding tears loose.

Jessica's head snaps toward the sound.

Her pupils blow wide with recognition.

And fury.

When she speaks, her voice is a jagged whisper, slicing through the room: "You."

A hiss.

A warning.

Pure, unadulterated hate.

"You."

CHAPTER
FORTY

NOAH

A thin ray of light glows beneath the door.

"You."

The shriek is sharp, warped—nothing like Alicia.

Cold shoots through my veins. She's not alone. Alicia's not alone.

Every muscle goes tight.

My fingers curl in.

My vision tunnels.

The hallway narrows to the one door.

I twist the knob.

Locked.

"Alicia?"

I lean back.

Jam my shoulder.

Once.

The door quakes.

Lean back.

Kick.
Bam.
The wood splinters.
The door swings.
Slams against the wall.
Jessica's cornered.
Half-lit.
My gaze locks on the revolver.
Alicia's five feet back.
The desk between her and a gun.
Pointed at her. Not precisely.
A tremor.
Too damn close.
A flash of terror steals my wits.
For one slashing second, every nightmare I've had about losing someone detonates behind my ribs. Then training shoves terror aside.
"Jessica. Put it down."
Her arm jerks—pointing the gun at me.
That's better.
My weight falls over the balls of my feet.
Shoulders forward.
Hands slightly open.
Ready to strike.
I inch forward.
Slow.
Imperceptible.
The gun trembles.
She's panicked.
Or high. Or gone.
"Lower it."
The whites of her eyes flash.

"What're we doing here, Jess?"
"Jessica's going to leave." Alicia breathes out, voice soft.
Scared.
"We're going to—"
"Shut up!" Jessica shrieks.
The finger around the trigger curls.
Alicia inhales sharply.
Jessica swings the barrel.
I lunge.
Diagonal.
Arms out.
Low.
I torque her wrist outward, pivoting on my hips, forcing her arm away from Alicia and toward the floor.
The gun clicks.
Jessica stiffens against me.
She struggles—but I've got a tight hold.
A scream pierces the air.
High. Sharp. Feral.
Rage. Pain. No fear.
An elbow digs into my ribs.
But my hand's on the muzzle.
The metal slips from my fingers.
She kicks back.
Getting air.
The back of her head slams against my sternum.
My grip tightens.
She twists.
Nails dig into my skin, down my jaw.
With a grip on her bicep, I spin her.
She slams against the wall.
Her head hits.

The crazed eyes calm. Stunned.
The gun drops.
A metallic clang on the hardwood.
I step forward. Kick it away.
Eyes locked on Jessica.
Arms out—ready to grab should she make a break.
She lunges.
A mountain lion.
Claws out.
She swings.
Scratches.
Grabs my collar.
Spits.
Mascara streaks down her face.
Her punches are untrained.
Wild, glancing blows.
The one thing I register—she's no longer a danger.
But she is a train wreck.
I catch her wrists.
Corner her against the wall.
Neutralizing the threat.
Her body twists—with less heart.
"Stop. It's over."
"Noooo."
It's half wail, half trapped animal.
She crumples, knees giving way.
With her full weight hanging from her wrists, I let her fall to the floor.
Alicia steps forward, picks up the gun, and passes it to me.
I spin the chamber. Empty.
She brought an unloaded gun.

"He was supposed to choose me."

Tears and sweat mar her face.

"He said—he *said*—he loved me! We were supposed to be a family."

Alicia's dark blue eyes lock on the quivering wreck on the floor.

Stoic. Horrified.

Jessica lifts her chin and glares past me—directly at Alicia.

She looks at Alicia like she's something beneath contempt, and I might as well not be in the room.

"You ruin everything. You always have." Her tear-blurred eyes lock on Alicia. "People see you and they just—choose you. You ruin lives."

Her voice cracks. Visible tears cascade. "All perfect. So untouchable. He loved me. *Me!*"

The cadence is manic.

Almost childlike.

Mentally unstable.

"He wouldn't move forward while you were still in the picture. He said once you were gone, everything would fall into place."

Once she was gone?

Fury detonates in my chest. Gone? She believed that— actually believed removing Alicia would fix her life.

I shift back, taking her in.

"Stella is happy with us. I'm good for her. She's good with me. But you…you wouldn't stay out of the way. A miserable, fucking gatekeeper."

What's terrifying is that this woman seriously believes every word she's spewing.

Her eyes snap wide.

She pushes up.

I react. Arm over her shoulders.

"Richard was supposed to be mine!"

Hair sticks to the side of her face.

Alicia's frozen, one hand pressed to her chest. Shocked.

Jessica struggles—but it's half-hearted.

Fast, heavy steps grow louder.

Gabriel bursts in.

Gun drawn.

"Don't move." His voice is ice.

I'm still.

But that icy voice is what Jessica needs.

She stills too.

Gabriel steps forward. Cuffs her.

She slumps onto the ground.

In a low, cracked voice, her dark eyes trained on Alicia: "You don't deserve him. You don't deserve any of this. And it's not just me." Her gaze sharpens, glassy and hateful. "You have no idea how many people hate you. Want you gone."

Alicia's frozen. Gabriel's at my side, scanning the room.

"Jake send you?" I ask.

"He's outside. Circling the perimeter. There's a ladder against the side of the house."

"Unloaded gun," I say, gesturing with my head to the desk.

He lifts his eyebrows in acknowledgment. Doesn't say anything, but I read him.

She's a crackpot.

"Cops en route. You got this?"

"Yeah," I say, taking in Alicia.

"I'm gonna go clear."

I understand what Gabe's saying.

There could be others.

Outside the window, blue and red lights flash.

Hesitant to leave watch over Jessica, I hold an arm out.

Alicia steps forward, close enough I can touch the side of her face.

"You hurt?" Her gaze stays locked on Jessica. "Alicia—talk to me."

A police officer enters the room. There's another behind him.

I catch his eye and step back, gathering Alicia against me.

The officers round Jessica.

Alicia rests her head against my shoulder, sinking into me.

"You're here." Her voice breaks. "You got here in time."

I press my lips to the top of her head. "Always."

CHAPTER
FORTY-ONE

ALICIA

"Mom?"

Stella's confused, scared voice ricochets through me, snapping me out of a fog.

I push off of Noah, arms out to my frightened daughter.

I want nothing more than to swipe this scene—cops towering over Jessica, red and blue lights coloring the walls—from her memory. To block her from seeing.

But by the time I reach her, I've accepted reality. There's no protecting her—not from this.

Behind me, I hear Noah addressing the police. One cop, wearing gloves, picks up the gun.

"Let's go downstairs."

With an arm around her shoulder, I guide her down the stairs to the main floor, leaving her father's girlfriend and the cops behind us. The front door's wide open, and we exit through it. That's when I notice Stella's barefoot, and we stop on the brick stoop.

Three cop cars are lined up in front, and one is parked in my drive.

A couple of curious neighbors gather further down the block. Faces peer from windows across the street.

Gabriel rounds the corner.

"Is it safe?" My question sounds absurd to my ears. The police are here, but I need to hear it from Gabriel.

"All clear," he confirms. "Looks like she did this on her own." He glances into the house. "Is she stable?"

I hesitate, my gaze on Stella, but she's on her phone—texting.

"She's not well," I answer Gabe, meaning Jessica, then touch Stella to get her attention. "Who are you texting?"

"Dad." She says it in her teen voice, the one that implies with intonation that I'm antiquated.

And I suppose it makes sense she would text him. She just saw his girlfriend in handcuffs upstairs and there are cops surrounding our house.

"What did Jessica do? Did she try to hurt you?"

"No—" comes out automatically, and it's a version of the truth I want, but her question triggers questions in me.

"What do you think she wanted?" I ask Gabe. She hates me, she made that clear, but I saw Noah check the gun—there were no bullets. She didn't come to kill me.

Her eyes, her words—I don't think she's of sound mind. It's like she snapped—but what did she want? Why break into my office?

"She took some USB drives from my desk. Empty. Why?"

Commotion on the stairs prevents Gabriel from answering.

A police officer leads Jessica down the stairs, handcuffed. I presume he read her her rights and is taking her in for breaking and entering, but based on the solemn faces, I'm not alone in recognizing she's guilty of far more than breaking into my home.

Black streaks her face—telltale signs of mascara gone astray—in this case, the truest mask removed. Her lips are swollen from crying, her nose red, and the whites of her eyes wild and sharp in a way that warns she's unhinged.

A car screeches to a stop at the curb.

Richard.

He barely puts the BMW in park before he's out, scanning the scene—flashing lights, uniformed officers, the neighbors gathering like moths, and then…me, on the stoop with Stella tucked beneath my arm.

"Stella?" he calls, rushing toward us.

She breaks from me, meeting him halfway down the walkway. "Dad," she breathes into his chest. "Jessica…" Her voice wobbles. "She had a gun."

He stiffens. A full-body jolt. He looks to me, desperate for either confirmation or denial.

"The police have her." It's all I manage.

Richard's gaze jerks past us. Jessica's led by two officers, hands cuffed behind her back, hair disheveled, fury and humiliation twisting her face into something unrecognizable.

The moment she sees Richard, her expression fractures.

Splinters.

Shatters.

"Richard," she cries out, voice crackling like a rusted hinge. "It's not what they think. It's not—" She swings her gaze toward me, wild and blistering. "She twisted everything. She—she ruined everything. You *know* that. You told me—"

"Jessica." Richard says her name like the edge of a blade. Not angry. Not yet. But bewildered. "What did you do?"

"I didn't hurt anyone!" she spits, lunging forward, the officers restraining her instantly. "I went to talk to her. I just wanted to talk. She provoked— She—"

"Jessica." His voice deepens—the voice he used when he confronted Stella about broken rules as a child. Controlled. Quiet. Final. "You had a gun."

"I was trying to fix things!" Her gaze shoots to me, then to Noah, who stands just inside the doorframe, arms folded, jaw tight, every line of his body protective. "You said you still loved her. If she wasn't standing in the way—"

Richard's face drains of color.

I watch the truth land.

Split him down the middle.

Shock.

Confusion.

Disbelief.

It all plays out in his expression in real time.

"I never—Jessica, I never said—" His voice breaks, raw emotion shredding the words. "I never meant for you to— God. What were you thinking?"

"I was doing what *you* wanted!" she screams. "You said she was selfish. You said she still controlled everything. You said she didn't deserve—"

"Enough," he says sharply.

It guts her.

It guts him too.

For a split second, she looks like she might lunge again— not at me this time, but at him. The officers tighten their hold.

Jessica's voice collapses inward.

Small. Childlike. A different kind of terrifying.

"You chose her," she whispers, pleading and broken. "You always choose her."

Her knees fold beneath her. The cops support her weight as she crumples.

Richard presses a hand to his forehead, eyes closing.

"I'll meet her at the station," he mutters to the cops, but not harshly—just hollow. Wrecked.

The officers guide Jessica toward the street. She continues to stare at me, lips trembling, eyes full of a hatred so sharp it feels like talons dragging across my skin.

And just as she's being lowered into the back of the squad car, she says it—soft enough that I can't hear, but I read her lips: "This isn't over."

Something prickles up my spine.

Not fear—

Recognition.

Because she's right.

She didn't act alone.

Questions remain.

We still don't know who helped her. Or who pushed her.

The door of the police car slams shut. Blue and red flash across her face. The car pulls away.

Richard stands frozen in the middle of the pathway, Stella clinging to him, concerned for her father. Slowly, he lifts his head, meeting my gaze with something like defeat.

"I'm so sorry," he says. To me. To our daughter. To no one and everyone.

I nod once. There are no words for this.

Behind me, Noah steps out onto the stoop, close enough that I feel his presence before he touches me. He rests a hand at the small of my back, grounding me, anchoring me.

I let myself lean into him. Because the truth is no longer hiding in shadows or whispered threats or confused motives.

The truth is lit up across my yard, in the eyes of my daughter, in the shattered expression of my ex-husband, in the squad car carrying Jessica away—

The truth is unmistakable.

Her mask is gone.

Yet I feel heavy. I also did this—with an affair I had years ago. And maybe with a case I accepted last month. Christ, possibly with how I handled my divorce. I'm not responsible for Jessica, but I'm not innocent.

CHAPTER
FORTY-TWO

NOAH

An hour after Jessica was driven away, I'm at the precinct in a waiting room. Alicia is in a private room with her lawyers and the detective on her case. Somewhere in the building Jessica is being interrogated by police officers, as is Danny, her cousin. Richard's also being interrogated—but from what I can tell, he's not a suspect.

Jake and his girlfriend, Daisy, are back at Alicia's with Stella. They offered to stay as late as needed.

Alicia needed to answer questions, and her lawyers jumped on the chance to do it at the precinct. I understand the strategy. They're aiming for all charges against her to be dropped in light of new evidence that has surfaced.

Gabriel and I have been on the phone with Hudson and Quinn.

A detective approaches. "Noah Bennett? Gabriel Martin?"

We both push up from the chairs.

"Please come back with me."

He turns, and we both fall in line.

The frustrating thing about police involvement is that the case is out of our hands. We can't ask the questions we need answers to. We're trusting law enforcement officers to get as much information as possible before defense lawyers show up.

The officer leads us into a windowless room with a long table and multiple chairs. Alicia's seated between two of her lawyers.

When we enter the room, her lawyer is the first to speak. "Charges are dropped." Alicia looks relieved, but also emotionally spent. "We have some updates. If you want to join us."

The lawyer to Alicia's left rises, vacating a seat for me. I take it and hold out my hand for Alicia. She readily places her hand in mine.

Gabriel takes a seat across from us.

One of the detectives mentions he'll be back.

The detective who led us to the back crosses his arms and stands at the head of the table. "None of this is to leave this room. Danny has yet to request a lawyer, and he's been singing like a canary."

My first thought is why, but the detective reads me.

"He's jittery. Seems to believe if he's a source, we'll let him walk. He's going into withdrawal. Shakes and sweats. To be honest, an addict's not the best witness. But he's told us enough, we'll get all the evidence we need."

"And what has he told you?"

I look to Alicia—I can tell from her calm demeanor she already knows.

"The murder, the framing of Alicia, it was all planned by Jessica. She pulled in Danny to help where he could. The PI.

The tracker. She also used a threat—sent to Ms. Morgan's office."

"The fortune cookie," Alicia explains.

"Right," the detective says. "Danny says she'd been watching Morgan for a while. Knew enough about her and a prior case she'd been working on to make it look like it came from somewhere else. Danny confessed to breaking into Alicia's car to plant evidence—but says he was interrupted before he finished. He claims he didn't know the substance Jessica gave him to slip into Delacroix's drink would kill him. He claims he thought it would make him sick—and after the death, she used it against him to help her cover everything up."

"Do you believe him?" I ask, looking between the lawyers and the two detectives in the room.

"Based on the current evidence? No. I think he's playing that card to aim for second-degree murder charges. But, there's still a lot here to be investigated. Prosecution will need to determine what they can prove in court."

Gabriel speaks up. "If he's an addict, all she had to do was hold drugs over his head to get him to do what she wanted."

"That's our prevailing theory. Jessica might also be addicted to a substance—we're unsure. She's refused a blood test," the detective says.

"Richard hired a defense lawyer for her," Alicia says at my side.

"Do you think he's—"

Alicia's quick to interrupt me. "No. I think it's a gut reaction. He feels responsible for her—for what's happened. But, he didn't have a part in this."

"At the moment, that's our assessment too," the detective says, and the way he looks at Alicia, I sense they've already had this discussion, and his comment is for my benefit.

"And Delacroix's wife?"

"She and Jessica play in the same tennis league. There's a connection there, but no phone records connect them."

I understand what the detective is saying—it's reasonable to believe Jessica crossed paths with someone who had heard rumors about Alicia and Matthew Delacroix, and that's Jessica's source of information.

Regardless, charges against Alicia are dropped.

"Any mentions of third parties? Anyone influencing outcomes?"

The detective opens his mouth, then closes it.

Alicia squeezes my hand.

The detective says with firm confidence, "At this point in the investigation, we have no evidence others are involved."

The detective looks down at his notes again. When he speaks, his tone softens—just a fraction.

"Ms. Morgan, you are free to go. Unless…do you have any more questions?"

Alicia exhales, not sharply, but with a slow, trembling release that tells me what she hasn't said aloud: she never fully believed this moment would come.

I tighten my grip on her hand.

Her lawyer nods, satisfied. "We'll finalize the paperwork and communicate with the prosecutors." He says to Alicia, "You won't need to appear in court on Monday."

Alicia's eyes lift to mine. She's not crying. She's not even shaking anymore.

She's steady. Resolute. And free.

For the first time in hours, my lungs stop feeling like steel coils pulled too tight.

"Is there anything else that you've learned that you can share with us?" Gabe asks.

The detective glances between us. "They've both mentioned that many people hate Alicia. Could be rationalization. Could be drugs talking. It's likely nothing. For now, we are not pursuing additional suspects."

It's said too cleanly. Too decisively.

But I heard the hesitation. And based on the faint shift in Alicia's posture, so did she.

We'll revisit that later.

"Thank you," Alicia says, voice steady but tired. "All of you."

The detective leaves. Her lawyers gather their files. Gabe stands.

And for the first time since the moment I saw Jessica lunging with a gun, Alicia turns fully toward me, free hand lifting to rest against my jaw.

"Are you okay?" she whispers.

I almost laugh. Groan. Pull her into my arms and never let go.

Instead, I cover her hand with mine. "Not until you walk out of here."

She leans forward, forehead resting briefly against my shoulder. Not long. Not inappropriate. Just enough to crack something open inside me.

"I meant it," she breathes. "Upstairs. When I said you got there in time."

I close my eyes for a beat. "I'll always be there."

Her fingers tighten around mine.

Gabe clears his throat. "I'll check in with Hudson."

Alicia nods, exhausted. "Thank you."

When the room empties, I help her stand. She's not fragile, but she's depleted. Hollowed out by adrenaline and fear and the unimaginable weight of being wrongly accused.

"Take me home?" she asks softly.

Something hot and fierce flashes through my chest with her question.

"Yes," I say. "Always."

We walk out of the precinct together—hand in hand—into the crisp night. There's a moment when the cold air hits her cheeks and she tilts her head back, breathing like someone who's just surfaced from underwater.

She's free.

The door closes behind us.

And for the first time since this began, it settles in that we have a real future together.

FORTY-THREE

ALICIA

Last night was the final performance. Three nights of The Crucible, and Stella held her own in every one.

The house feels different in the morning.

Not quieter—our house was always quiet—but lighter, as if the walls themselves have unclenched. Sunlight filters through the bedroom windows in soft ribbons, catching on the steam rising from my mug. The scent of chamomile curls around me, warm and soothing, and for the first time in weeks, I don't feel like I'm waiting for something to break.

Stella's upstairs packing for the weekend. We agreed to get away for a few days, and it'll allow Noah to check in on his dad. I can hear her singing, something bright and melodic, the kind of tune she only falls into when her world feels steady again.

I sit on the edge of the bed and inhale slowly.

This is what peace feels like.

Familiar. Elusive. Fragile.

But present.

I wrap both hands around my mug, letting its heat seep into my fingers, grounding me.

That night still lives in flashes behind my eyes—the gun, the trembling of Jessica's hand, Noah's voice cutting through the chaos, the way he protected me with his body before the police arrived. But the fear doesn't choke me anymore. It simply lingers, a memory rather than a threat.

And beneath it, something else—relief so deep it sits like an ache.

The stairs creak. Stella appears in my bedroom doorway with a duffel slung over her shoulder and a stack of folded sweaters in her arms.

"Do we need warm stuff?" she asks. "New Jersey's colder, right?"

"Temps about the same as here. But yes. Pack warm."

She dumps the sweaters into her bag with a dramatic sigh. Three performances in three days, and she's still moving at full speed. I smile, stepping in to help her zip the duffel.

"How are you feeling?" I ask gently.

Stella shrugs, but it's a thoughtful, measured shrug—one that belongs to a girl trying to sort through something difficult and figure out where to place it. "Better than the other night," she says. "It was scary. But no one got hurt. And they took her away."

Her voice softens on the last sentence.

I tuck a strand of hair behind her ear. "I'm sorry you had to see any of it."

"I know." She looks up at me, her eyes clear. "But Mom? You handled it. Like…you didn't freak out. You stayed calm. That helped me stay calm too."

The words mean more than she knows. For a moment, I'm struck by how quickly she's growing. How much she sees. How much she understands without needing it explained.

"Come here," I whisper.

She steps into my arms without hesitation. I hold her close, breathing in the faint scent of strawberry shampoo.

"You are so incredibly brave," I say against her hair. "And I promise—you're safe."

"I know," she murmurs.

When she pulls back, she wipes her cheeks with her sleeve like nothing happened and grabs her duffel. "Do you think Noah's dad will like me?"

I smile. "He'll love you."

"And what about…Noah's…um…other family? His stepmom?"

"Linda will adore you," I say confidently. "She can't wait to meet you."

Stella brightens. Then she glances at my suitcase sitting half-packed on the closet floor. "Are you nervous?"

A soft laugh escapes me. "A little."

The truth is, I'm not nervous about meeting his family—I already met them. I'm nervous about what this visit signifies. About walking into his childhood home not as the woman he's protecting, but as the older single mom he's dating.

And I'm nervous because the last time I planned a future with someone, the ground shifted beneath me.

But this feels different. Solid. Quietly certain.

I zip my suitcase, press down on the top, and take a breath that feels like a beginning.

My phone buzzes on the dresser.

· · ·

Noah: On my way. Coffee in hand. And I miss you already.

A warm, easy smile spreads across my face.

Stella peeks at the screen. "He loooves you," she says, sing-song, before darting out of the room with her duffel.

I shake my head, amused.

Love.

Maybe.

But the truth—one I've avoided saying aloud—is that I love him too.

Because when everything shattered, I didn't think about the case or the rumors or the custody agreement or what the neighbors would say. I thought about Noah. And how, without hesitation, I followed him.

I chose him. Instinctively.

And now, in the quiet morning light, I understand what that means.

I'm not falling for him anymore. I'm in love.

I close the last suitcase and carry it downstairs to the main floor. Through the front window, Noah's SUV pulls into the driveway. The sight of him—broad shoulders, easy stride, coffee balanced in one hand—does something in my chest I've stopped trying to defend against.

He catches sight of me through the glass and his smile softens into something private.

Gentle.

Certain.

Mine.

When I open the door, cold air rushes in around us.

"You ready?" he asks, stepping closer.

I nod. "We are."

Stella runs out to greet him, and he bends to give her a fist bump. She beams. My heart tilts.

He takes my suitcase from my hand as if it weighs nothing. "Let's go," he says. "We've got a long weekend ahead of us."

"A good one," I say.

He glances over, voice low. "The best one."

And for the first time in a long time, I believe it.

We load the car. I lock the door behind us. Stella climbs into the backseat with a muffin Gabriel brought over earlier this morning. Noah opens the passenger door for me with a quiet smile that still manages to make me feel seen.

Settled in beside him, surrounded by warmth and breath and the hum of the engine, I take one last look at the house —the place where everything fell apart and everything came back together.

Then Noah reaches for my hand.

And we drive forward.

EPILOGUE

NOAH

The holidays at my father's house always smelled like cinnamon.

Even now—the weekend before Christmas—the scent hits me the second we step through the door. It's in the wood, the walls, the memory of every pie my mother ever baked in this kitchen. It's familiar in a way that squeezes something deep inside my chest.

But this year, when the warmth rises and the scent wraps around me, something else threads through it.

Alicia.

She's standing beside me, unwinding her scarf, cheeks pink from the cold. Stella's already darted past us toward the living room, chattering excitedly at Linda about auditions for the next play, about school, about everything twelve-year-olds love to report in breathless detail.

My father sits in his recliner, recovering but strong, the color back in his face.

He watches Alicia like he's memorizing something important.

And I understand the impulse.

She glances over her shoulder at me—soft smile, blue eyes bright—and I feel it hit again, the same quiet certainty I felt the night she nearly slipped through my fingers.

I want to hold this exact moment still. The pink in her cheeks. Stella's voice carrying from the living room. My father's eyes tracking Alicia like she's something worth memorizing.

This is the one I'll come back to. Ten years from now. Twenty. Fifty.

We shed our coats, hang them on the hooks by the entry, and step into the kitchen where Linda has already placed mugs on the counter.

The congressional hearing came and went. No one threatened Alicia for her silence, but in the closed-door hearing she was asked questions that will undoubtedly lead investigations to open many doors. Still, the hearing is over. Whatever threats Elena Vasquez predicted never materialized.

The detectives investigating Danny and Jessica haven't identified any additional credible threats. They confirmed that Danny paid the witness who claimed she'd seen Alicia drinking coffee with Matthew and saw her follow him. Jessica's computer told the rest of the story—notes on USB drives, plans to plant searches and evidence, a blueprint for framing Alicia that grew sloppier the closer the investigation got. Based on what the police gathered, she didn't know Alicia would find the body. She'd only wanted her present and wanted her to be seen near the business center—close enough a witness statement would warrant a closer look. Jessica got lucky when Alicia found the body, but her luck didn't hold. The fortune cookie was her attempt to redirect toward the senator's scandal. She'd pulled enough from the press to make it plausible, but certain details were never made public—which is why it didn't land the way she intended. She used Alicia's numerology because she'd been researching long enough to know it.

Danny refused to go back to Alicia's house after nearly getting caught breaking into her car—too many cameras, too much risk, he insisted. On that fateful night, she went herself with a desperate, half-baked plan. That decision ended everything.

Richard wasn't involved. He's figured out, in hindsight, that she repeatedly brought up Alicia's security. Goaded him into texting Alicia the morning Matthew died—stood there watching him do it. He remembered it once the detectives walked him back through the timeline. I don't envy him that realization. He thought she admired Alicia. Wanted what Alicia had built. He never recognized it as something darker—not even when he bought her the same car Alicia drove.

The KOAN team will continue watching for threats, but we're all home for the holiday—except for Gabriel. He took the DC posting without much explanation. He did the work. But there was something else running underneath it. I'll call him after the holidays. He hasn't asked for anything. That's usually when it matters most.

Alicia is on holiday. Her office will close from Christmas Eve through New Year's, as will much of DC.

Maya and Phoenix arrive tomorrow. We'll stay here through the day before Christmas Eve, then we'll return, and

Stella will go to Richard's on Christmas Eve, as it's his turn to have her on Christmas morning.

"Tea?" Linda asks Alicia.

"Please," Alicia says, smiling warmly. And Linda beams, as if gratitude itself has taken human form in her daughter-in-law-to-be.

Not yet, I remind myself.

But maybe not far.

I straighten a dish towel on the counter—an excuse to be near Alicia as she moves around the room. When she reaches for the mug, I slide it closer to her before she can stretch.

Her fingertips brush mine.

It's nothing.

It's also everything.

She looks up, wonder in her eyes, like she's still adjusting to being wanted without conditions.

"You good?" I murmur.

"Better than good," she says quietly. "You?"

"Never been better."

And it's true.

I didn't know I needed this—the house humming with life, family gathered around the table, the sleepy rhythm of a holiday. I didn't know I missed it until she stepped into the space beside me and made it feel like home again.

Linda dusts flour from her hands. "Stella is such a sweetheart," she says. "And so respectful. You're doing a wonderful job, Alicia."

Alicia's lashes flutter, embarrassment softening her features. "Thank you. She's...she's my whole world."

My father clears his throat from the doorway. "She's a great kid," he says. "And she's lucky to have you both."

Alicia looks at me. I look at her.

We both feel it—the shift.

My father doesn't say things lightly.

He doesn't accept—or approve—easily either.

I clear my throat, unexpectedly moved. "Thanks, Dad."

He nods once, then turns back to his cider. But I catch the slight smile before he hides it. Good enough. Better than good enough.

Dinner smells begin to bloom—rosemary, thyme, roasted vegetables. Stella laughs in the living room, and Linda returns to her pie, humming one of those wordless melodies she's always carried.

And somewhere in all that noise and warmth, I feel Alicia's fingers thread through mine.

She initiates it. She holds on.

Just that simple gesture—the quiet claim of it—lands somewhere deep.

But I know.

And she knows.

Her body leans slightly into mine. She lowers her voice so only I can hear. "This feels…natural."

I press a kiss to her temple, brief and certain. "Because it is."

She breathes in, shaky and soft.

There's a beat of silence—just us, just this—and then my dad calls us to help set the table.

Alicia squeezes my hand once before letting go.

Later, after dinner, after Stella curls up on the couch between Linda and my father, after the dishes are done and the house settles into its nighttime hum, Alicia and I step outside into the cold. Our breath clouds the air between us.

"Walk with me?" she asks.

I lace my fingers through hers and lead her down the

driveway. The trees overhead are bare silhouettes against a silver sky. The world is quiet—just the crunch of leaves beneath our boots and the soft rhythm of our matching steps.

Halfway down the block, she stops.

Turns.

Looks up at me with that expression that still knocks the breath out of my lungs—like she's letting herself hope.

"I didn't expect any of this," she admits. "Not you. Not your family. Not…falling in love again."

I cup her cheek, brushing my thumb over the curve of her jaw. "I didn't expect you. But I'm damn glad I found you."

She leans into my touch. And I know what's coming before she says it.

"Noah?"

"Yeah."

"I'm really glad you walked into my life."

I smile, but it feels like something breaking open. "I'm not walking out."

A breath catches in her throat—small, undone, beautiful.

I lower my forehead to hers.

She exhales, soft and warm, and her hand curls at the back of my neck, tugging me the last inch closer.

The kiss is slow.

Deep.

Certain.

The kind of kiss a man gives a woman he sees a future with.

"You know, we talk about everything."

"Yeah." I keep my voice neutral, waiting.

"We haven't talked about kids."

My hand stills on her back. "Okay."

She pulls back slightly, needing to see my face. "Being here over the holidays…seeing the Christmas tree, the stockings, your family…you want all that, right?"

"I've got all that. We've got stockings at your place. Stella—"

"A child of your own," she interrupts quietly. "You'd be a good father, Noah. And I can't…" Her voice catches. "I'm in my forties. The chances are—"

"Alicia." I cup her face, make her look at me. "If I have to choose between you and some hypothetical kid, I choose you. Every time."

"But you shouldn't have to choose—"

"I'm not choosing. I'm telling you what I want." I brush my thumb across her cheekbone. "Would I love to have a baby with you? Yeah. Absolutely. Am I okay with you, me, and Stella being our family? Absolutely." Her eyes search mine, looking for doubt that isn't there. "If you want to try," I continue, "we'll try. You don't want to, we won't. But either way, I'm here. This is what I want."

"It's really that simple for you?"

"It's really that simple. You think I'd risk losing you over something that might not even happen?" I shake my head. "I'm not that stupid, Alicia."

"You're unreal, you know that?"

"No. I'm in love. And I know what matters."

She kisses me again—and the warmth of it feels like a promise wrapped inside a beginning.

When we return to the house, Stella's asleep, curled against my father's side. Linda's reading beside them, and my dad's hand rests protectively on Stella's shoulder.

My family. Alicia's family. Our family.

Alicia's fingers thread through mine, and I let them settle there without thinking. Her hand fits. Like it belongs.

Six months ago, I was good at my job. Competent. Driven. Building toward something I hadn't yet named.

Now I know what I was building toward.

Not the picture-perfect family I thought I was supposed to want. Not the traditional timeline everyone expects. Just this—Alicia beside me, Stella's laughter, family and friends, a home that feels right instead of on schedule.

Jessica Vale compared herself to Alicia until the comparison destroyed her. I spent years measuring myself against a timeline that was never mine.

The thing about comparing yourself constantly to others is it makes you chase what other people have instead of recognizing what you need.

I don't need picture-perfect.

I just need this.

BONUS EPILOGUE

ALICIA

Ten Years Later

The coffee maker has been running for seventeen minutes.

I know this because I've been watching the clock on the microwave from my spot at the kitchen island, willing myself not to go upstairs and knock on Stella's door. She's twenty-two. She doesn't need to be woken up on a Sunday morning. She came home because she wanted to, not because anyone summoned her—and if I blow this by hovering, she'll remember that when she's deciding whether to visit next time.

I turn the coffee mug in my hands instead. Three slow rotations. An old habit.

The kitchen catches the morning light differently than any room I've ever lived in. The Georgetown house had high ceilings and heritage brick and the kind of architectural bones that made design magazines salivate, but the light was always fighting its way in around the corner, always half-blocked by the iron fence and the two scrawny trees I'd had absolutely no interest in pruning. This house sits on two acres in McLean, set back from the road by a long gravel drive, with windows that face east across the yard. By eight in the morning, the kitchen is full of sunlight.

Noah picked it out. I let him think I needed convincing.

He'd made his case the way he always did—methodically and without drama. Set back from the road. Single point of entry at the front. Alarm system that he upgraded himself, which I still find slightly unnerving even a decade later. He'd gone through twelve properties before he brought me to this one, and when I walked into the kitchen and saw the morning light laying itself across the wide-plank floors, I said we should probably schedule a second showing. He'd looked at me for a long moment, something quiet moving behind his eyes, and said, "Whatever you need."

We were back the next day. I made an offer before we reached the car.

I hear him before I see him—the soft fall of bare feet on the stairs, the creak of the third step that he keeps saying he'll fix and never does. Then Eli appears in the doorway, his hair still pressed flat on one side from sleep, wearing the oversized Virginia Tech T-shirt that has been his weekend uniform since Stella brought it home from a campus visit three years ago.

Eight years old, and already the shirt hits him at the knee.

"Is Stella awake?"

He asks this the way he asks about the weather—reflexively, because it is the primary variable that determines whether this morning will be good or simply fine.

"Not yet."

His face does the thing. I've catalogued that face—the very specific arrangement of Noah's jaw and my brow that has been producing that particular expression since he was approximately three and first understood the concept of waiting.

"She said she'd show me the new route on the trail map."

"She will."

"She promised."

"Eli."

"What?"

"She will."

He climbs onto the stool beside me and leans his head against my arm, and for a moment I hold very still, the way you do when a bird lands on your wrist. These moments have a weight to them that I understand much better now than I did when Stella was small. You can't save them. You can only be in them while they last.

I was forty-three when Eli was born.

That's what I think about when people talk about luck—not the cases, not the crisis that eventually resolved itself, not even the investigation that I've spent a decade filing into the locked drawer at the back of my mind where I keep the things that tried to break me. I think about the afternoon I sat in the master bathroom of this house with a pregnancy test in my hand and felt something shift in my chest that I had no language for.

We'd stopped preventing it after our engagement. That was how I'd framed it to myself—not trying, just no longer trying not to. The distinction mattered to me in ways that were difficult to articulate. Noah hadn't pushed. He'd said, once, quietly, that whatever I wanted was what he wanted, and I'd believed him because I'd spent enough years learning to read people to know when they were telling me the truth.

My parents had me at forty-one. Their late-in-life surprise, my mother used to say, in a tone that made it sound like finding a twenty in an old coat pocket.

I called it the universe answering a question I hadn't quite known how to ask.

Noah had sat with me on the bathroom floor for an hour without saying much of anything, his hand over mine, and when he finally spoke, what he said was, "We're going to need to talk about the school district."

That was when I knew we were going to be fine.

Noah appears at nine, already dressed—dark jeans, a grey Henley that I have strong feelings about—with the look he gets when he's been up for a while and decided not to wake me. He does this on weekends sometimes, goes down early and runs the perimeter of the property in the dark and then makes eggs that he leaves covered on the stove. Military habit. He's never been able to fully retire it, and by now I've stopped wanting him to.

"She's still upstairs," I say, because Eli is already leaning forward on his stool like a retriever spotting a tennis ball.

Noah looks at Eli. "Give her until ten."

"That's an hour."

"That's how long."

Eli accepts this with the resignation of a man who has been outranked. He slides off the stool and disappears toward the back of the house, where his elaborate system of trail maps and topographical printouts is spread across the coffee table, waiting.

Noah comes around the island and presses a kiss to my temple. His hand rests on the back of my neck for a moment—warm, steady—and I lean into it without thinking.

"Good morning," he says.

"You let me sleep in."

"You needed it."

"I always need it. That's never stopped you before."

He smiles and pours himself coffee and that's the whole conversation, which I used to find alarming and now find essential. One of the many adjustments of this life that I didn't anticipate and wouldn't trade.

He's doing well. I know this is not a small thing. He spent three years transitioning KOAN's federal contracts into something he co-owned—a smaller firm, more specialized, the kind of work that doesn't get discussed at dinner parties—and then spent another two building it into something that stood on its own. His name carries weight in rooms I'll never be invited into. He comes home most nights by seven. On the nights he doesn't, I don't ask.

We understand each other.

"Maya texted," he says, settling onto the stool Eli vacated.

"How's she doing?"

"Good. Phoenix's marathon is next weekend. Maya's asking if Eli wants to come cheer. Rosa wants him too."

Eli and Maya's younger daughter, Rosa, are eight months apart and have the kind of friendship that communicates primarily through a shared language of Marvel references and competitive silences. When they're together, the adults in the room become set dressing.

"He'll lose his mind," I say. "Tell her yes."

Noah types the reply. Something in his jaw is easy in a way it sometimes isn't when Maya comes up—she was the one who made the calls after his father passed, three years ago now. Cancer, the slow and certain kind. His father had been proud of him in ways he'd sometimes struggled to say out loud, and Noah has been carrying that particular knowledge with a quiet that I've learned not to try to fill.

I reach over and put my hand on his.

He turns it over and holds it.

Stella comes downstairs at nine-forty, which is technically still before ten, and Eli is waiting at the bottom of the stairs with a trail map.

She's independent, but she's still mine. Watching her cross the kitchen with her hair pulled up and her brother orbiting her like she has her own gravitational field is the specific kind of thing that used to make me nervous. When she was small, I'd loved her so completely that the loving felt like exposure. Like I'd handed someone a key to everything breakable in me.

It still does.

But I've gotten better at letting her hold it.

"Good morning, everyone," she says, heading directly for the coffee. She glances at Eli's map over the rim of the mug. "That's the north loop."

"You said you'd show me the cutoff by the ridge."

"I did say that."

"So?"

She looks at him the way she used to look at Richard and

me when she was trying to determine which adult was more worth negotiating with. Then she looks at me.

"After breakfast," I say, which is not my negotiation to make, but Stella's gaze carries just enough of a question that I can't help myself. "Give her five minutes to wake up, Eli."

He doesn't argue. With me, he rarely does. With Noah, never. With Stella, always—but in the way you argue with someone you're not actually worried about. In the way that means you already know it's going to be fine.

She sits beside him and pulls the map toward her and starts tracing the cutoff with her finger, explaining the elevation change in terms an eight-year-old can follow, and I sit at the island and drink my coffee and don't say anything at all.

Across the kitchen, I catch Noah's eye.

He's watching them too. His expression does the thing it does—that particular stillness that I misread, early on, as distance. I know better now. It's the opposite. It's what he looks like when he's holding something carefully.

I glance down at my mug.

2222.

The number on the receipt tucked under the corner of my laptop. Some grocery delivery confirmation I hadn't looked at yet.

Major life alignment. The universe confirming you're exactly where you're supposed to be.

I used to assign meaning to these numbers strategically—cataloguing them like data points, weighing them against whatever decision was in front of me. A tool for self-discovery, I'd always said. A way of paying attention. Now I think the numbers were never the point. The point was the attention itself. The willingness to look up.

I set the mug down. Three rotations, clockwise.

Stella says something that makes Eli laugh—real and sudden, the kind that startles it out of him—and Noah glances over at me again, and this time I don't look away.

Ten years ago, I thought surviving meant staying intact. Keeping everything in its place, in its column, accounted for and contained.

I didn't understand, yet, that you could let things be uncontrollable and still not lose them. That some things get bigger when you stop trying to fit them inside something manageable.

"Hey," Noah says. Quiet. Just for me.

"Hey," I say back.

Outside, the yard is full of morning light. Somewhere at the bottom of the trail, the ridge Eli has been studying for two weeks waits in the trees. Stella will take him there and he will remember it for years, and she will move into the next chapter of her life and come back to visit, and Noah will stand in the kitchen doorway on a Sunday and look at the thing we built here with that quiet, careful expression.

And I will watch him, and I will know.

We're exactly where we're supposed to be.

Gabe's story in Only the Hunter is next...

Some men keep their distance and call it discipline.

Gabriel Martin has been calling it that for years. Evie Thompson is his best friend's sister, an AUSA hunting the worst of humanity through federal courts, and the one woman he's never let himself want out loud. When the threat against her stops being theoretical, he stops pretending distance was ever really an option.

He watches her for weeks before she catches him.

Only the Hunter is available for pre-order now. Coming September 2026.

AFTERWORD

In the quiet spaces between admiration and resentment, ancient envy learns to call itself something else.

The fourth installment of The Sinful State series turns its lens on jealousy—not in its theatrical, obvious form, but in the shape it most often takes: the small, socially acceptable thought we allow ourselves before we look away. *She's always going somewhere fun. He always lands on his feet.* The assumption isn't that someone worked for what they have, or deserves it. The assumption is that they got *lucky*—that fortune smiled on them for no particular reason, which means it just as easily could have smiled on us instead.

It's the flick of a social feed at midnight, the passing comparison to a neighbor's new car, the thought you don't examine too closely. And because it sounds harmless, it's easy to stay there—easy to let those quiet resentments calcify, easy to forget they were jealousy at all once they've hardened into contempt. The original feeling disappears beneath a more comfortable story: that person is overrated, undeserving, not who everyone thinks she is.

The ancients called it *invidia*—a word rooted in the Latin *invidere*, to look upon with malice. They understood something our more polite era prefers to forget: envy doesn't merely want what another has. At its darkest, it wants the other person to *not have it*. There's a reason Dante placed the envious in purgatory with their eyes sewn shut with iron wire. They could not stop looking at others. They could not stop measuring.

Like all the sins, jealousy exists on a spectrum. Most of us live in its lighter shades—the benign sting of wanting something we see in someone else, quickly acknowledged and moved past. But some shades are darker. The ones that tangle insecurity with desire, that feed on perceived slights and imagined comparisons, that convince a person the only path to what they want runs directly through someone else's destruction. In the right frame of mind—in the wrong frame of mind—those darker shades can be genuinely dangerous.

Alicia Morgan never set out to make anyone jealous. She built something real: a career, a reputation, a life. She did the work. But success, by its nature, creates a kind of visibility, and visibility invites scrutiny. Around Alicia, resentment accumulates quietly—in the admiring remarks that carry an edge, in the colleague who can't hear her name without needing to qualify it, in the ex-husband whose new girlfriend started dressing like her before she decided she wanted her gone entirely. Jessica Vale's obsession didn't begin in cruelty. It began in that same familiar, socially acceptable thought: *why does she get everything?* What followed was simply what happens when that question goes unanswered long enough.

Noah carries his own version of this inheritance. His father loves him—and measures him. Against his friend's son, against whoever seems to be getting ahead faster. It's the particular cruelty of comparative love, the kind that can't offer approval without attaching a benchmark. Noah spent years outrunning that voice, only to find it still waiting when he came home.

The paradox jealousy refuses to acknowledge is this: it is never actually about the other person. Alicia didn't make Jessica's relationship fragile. Richard's attention was never something Alicia was hoarding. The absence Jessica feared predated Alicia entirely. Envy always projects outward what lives inward—the unmet need, the unexamined wound, the thing we can't yet bring ourselves to want honestly for ourselves. That's what makes it so resistant to the truth. Jealousy is easier to inhabit than the vulnerability of wanting something openly, of risking failure, of building instead of resenting. It offers a verdict without requiring a mirror.

Only the Lucky asks what we're really saying when we call someone fortunate—and whether we have the courage to want our own lives as fully as we seem to want someone else's.

Welcome back to a world where the quietest sins do the most damage, where comparison is the thief of more than joy, and where love—chosen without envy, given without conditions—might be the only thing that luck had nothing to do with.

Because in the end, love isn't luck. It's a choice. One made without comparison, without conditions, and without the quiet voice that insists someone else has more.

ALSO BY ISABEL JOLIE

Sinful State Series

Only the Wicked (Rhodes and Sydney)

Only the Devil (Jake and Daisy)

Only the Lovely - (Brie and Adrien)

Only the Lucky - (Noah and Alicia)

Only the Hunter - (Gabriel and Evie) Releasing 3Q, 2026

Only the Fury - (Hudson and Quinn) Releasing 4Q, 2026

Arrow Tactical Security Series

Better to See You (Wolf and Alexandria)

Sure of One (Jack and Ava)

Cloak of Red (Sophia and Fisher)

Stolen Beauty (Knox and Sage)

Savage Beauty (Max and Sloane)

Sinful Beauty (Tristan and Lucia)

Gilded Saint (Sam and Willow)

Scarlet Angel (Nick and Scarlet)

Blind Prophet (Dorian and Caroline)

The Twisted Vines Series

Crushed (Erik and Vivi)

Breathe (Kairi and David)

Savor (Trevor and Stella)

Haven Island Series

Rogue Wave (Tate and Luna)

Adrift (Gabe and Poppy)

First Light (Logan and Cali)

The West Side Series

Blurred Lines (Jackson and Anna)

Trust Me (Sam Duke and Olivia)

Finding Delilah (Delilah and Mason)

Forgetting Him (Jason and Maggie)

Chasing Frost (Chase and Sadie)

Misplaced Mistletoe (Ashton aka Dr. Bobby and Nora)

Standalone Romances

How to Survive a Holiday Fling (Oliver Duke and Kate)

Always Sunny (Ian Duke and Sandra)

The Romantics (Harrison and Zuri)

GRATITUDE

Only the Lucky was finished, then set aside when life demanded more than a manuscript could. I'm grateful to my friends who came together in a time of tragedy and reminded me what matters most.

Karen Cimms — you ask the questions I'm afraid to. The ones that pull a scene apart and put it back together better. Every book in this series has been sharper because of you, and this one is no exception. I'm a better writer for having you in my corner.

Regina Wamba — I should know by now that the cover worth waiting for is always the last one. Thank you for your patience through every iteration. The final version says exactly what this book needed to say.

To my **beta readers** — you caught what I couldn't see, asked what readers will ask, and reminded me at exactly the right moment why this story matters. Christine Biesheuvel-Diemont and Stephanie Miller, you both amaze me with your attention to detail. This book is better because of you.

To the team at **Blue Nose Audio** — thank you for your partnership across this series. It means more than you know.

To my **Isabel Jolie ARC readers** — your reviews, your posts, your recommendations passed between readers who trust your taste — that's how series survive. Thank you for carrying this one.

And to my **readers** — whether you've followed me from *The West Side Series* or *Only the Wicked* was your starting point, you're why the Sinful State series exists at all. Thank you for showing up for it, and for being here.

ABOUT THE AUTHOR

Heart-pounding romance. Unforgettable heroes. Sizzling happily-ever-afters—with a side of suspense that'll keep you up way past bedtime. These are the books I love to read and write.

I dreamed of being a writer as a kid but took the "safe" route: journalism degree, advertising career, MBA, corporate gigs at Chase and Universal Studios. Then in 2020, I said screw it and published my first book. Twenty-five books later, I'm living the dream.

I'm also a mom to two teenage daughters who are perpetually mortified by my career choices. My husband's an entrepreneur whose latest product is Nampons (yes, it rhymes with tampons and yes, it's for nosebleeds). Between my spicy romance and his biz... we've cornered the market on parental embarrassment.

My books feature tough characters facing tougher choices, compelling suspense, and storylines that'll make you think. But no matter how dark things get, my people always choose love.

Sign-up for my newsletter to keep up-to-date on new releases, promotions and giveaways. (**Pro-tip** - There's a free book on my home page…just scroll down after arriving at my site.)

Shop and save on ebooks and signed paperbacks when buying direct from me at www.isabeljoliebooks.com

www.ingramcontent.com/pod-product-compliance
Lightning Source LLC
Chambersburg PA
CBHW020901000728
47591CB00004B/1032